TELENOVELA

Gonzalo C. Garcia

GALLEY BEGGAR PRESS

First published in 2025
by Galley Beggar Press Limited
37 Dover Street, Norwich NR2 3LG

All rights reserved © Gonzalo C. Garcia, 2025
Musical Fragments © Will Eaves, 2025

The right of Gonzalo C. Garcia to be identified as the author of this work has been asserted by him in accordance with the Copyright, Design and Patents Act 1988

This book is sold subject to the condition that it shall not, by way of trade or otherwise, be lent, resold, hired out, or otherwise circulated without the publisher's prior consent in any form or binding or cover other than that in which it is published and without a similar condition including this condition imposed on the subsequent purchaser

No part of this book may be used in any manner in the learning, training or development of artificial intelligence technologies. It may not be reproduced, stored in a retrieval system, or transmitted, in any form or by any means, electronic, mechanical, photocopying, recording or otherwise, or used in any manner for the purpose of training artificial intelligence technologies or systems. We do not grant permission for data scraping, data mining or the use of this book in any way to create or form a part of data sets.

A CIP for this book is available from the British Library

Paperback ISBN: 9781913111717
Black-cover edition ISBN: 9781913111731

Text design and typesetting by Tetragon, London
Printed and bound in Great Britain by CPI Printing, Chatham

EU Authorised Representative information: Easy Access System Europe – Mustamäe tee 50, 10621 Tallinn, Estonia, gpsr.requests@easproject.com

For Andrea and Felipe

We thought of a new game today: we decided to check falseness in each other's actions both on the stage and in ordinary life.

KONSTANTIN STANISLAVSKI
An Actor Prepares

Sometimes the sun went black in my dreams.

ROBERTO BOLAÑO
By Night in Chile

The military dictator, General Augusto Pinochet, seized control of Chile on the 11th of September 1973. In 1988, a referendum was held to ratify a further eight years with Pinochet as president. The referendum took place in October. Voters had the following choice: YES, to continue under Pinochet; NO, for a democratic government.

NO won.

Pinochet's regime stayed in place until the 11th of March 1990.

FEBRUARY 1987

1

LUCHO

is sitting at the only desk in the house, waiting for the last of the removal lorries to arrive. He opens the cardboard box next to him again, though he already knows it's the wrong one. He finds stacks of wooden curtain rings, clay pots wrapped in newspaper, a framed painting of a rural pebbled street in which colourful adobe houses lie neatly stacked up against an Andean backdrop. What he actually wants is his box of notebooks, even though he knows he should never have kept them – he's too old anyway, too different, another person altogether – but he also knows throwing them out would have only made their presence stronger, heavier. He worries about that, the sudden pull of memory.

At first he had written only descriptions in these notebooks: attempts to capture his teachers' movements and speech, the sounds of sleepless crickets, his mother's face. The poems began about two thirds of the way through the second one. That's when the trouble began too.

He can't risk anyone else finding these notebooks now, not with his new job, not in this country. Can't risk another hand leafing through the pages, most of them failures, incomplete and scattered in their phrasing, the syncopated impatience of youth. He'd thought of burning them. He'd even got close to the fire, close enough to singe off the numbered corners on one of the books. But he couldn't do it.

After all, he'd written those poems to be found; he had even written his name below every single one. Sometimes, if he'd been particularly proud of a verse, he had loudly underlined his name to mark the page below it, hoping its imprint would prompt a clear direction for the next poem, some sign in the vastness of the white page.

The only notebook he has now is the one he carries with him in his pocket. It's empty.

POETRY NOTES – BOOK OF RAMONA
Preparations: Travelling the Great Sea

The boat is not what we once had.

You talk of the dark faces in the wood,
patterned cuts,
sunny splinters,
the glare of its origin tree.

As advertised, the owner says,
you will touch the sea
if you want to.

Lucho is disappointed by the stillness. He finds that he has been expecting the move to be more than simply leaving and arriving. If he didn't have dependants, he would have left all belongings behind and even been proud to sit in the sudden emptiness of new beginnings. But then, all his hard work has led to this moment. He's dreamt of it, of pointing at old sofas and stained, rolled-up carpets, workers talking about how good his new life will be as they carry boxes filled with old things on their shoulders to some nearby dumpster, as they scrape marks on the once white walls.

But none of that has happened. He'd even had to arrange the removal logistics himself, which didn't seem to him much in the spirit of landing a great promotion.

Mrs Herminia, who'd recently taken over her father's bakery by the little plaza in Manuel Rodríguez, had looked at him in silence when he told her they were moving to Santiago. She looked sleepy, gave a yawn behind the glass pane and then jolted her head awake, saying, 'That will be five hundred pesos,' before giving him the usual bag of *hallulla* bread through a plastic hatch. And when he had told the priest at the San Francisco church, he had said that no one ever really moves away from God and so he thought it unnecessary to bless any of them, not even their car.

It had taken him a while to convince his wife and son of the benefits of the move too. He'd shown Ramona pictures of the house – he thought the glass dome over the staircase would make her pack her bags that very same day – but instead she'd asked whether it would make the house too hot in the summer. He had to make all of the plans for them. And since he didn't know the city well, they quickly became abstract, infinite.

You can do anything in the capital.

You can walk a whole day by the river and never even see its end.

We'll be only a couple of metro stops from where History is made.

Ramona had simply asked, when he mentioned the furniture, the dumpster, an entire new start: 'Why wouldn't we just take everything? Are lives in the city all that different? Maybe yours – but isn't *my* life going to entail all the same routines? And didn't Doctor Ignacio say we, *I* had to be careful with my anxiety, with any sudden change?'

Pablo hadn't said a thing, locked himself up to play guitar instead. And when Lucho had asked him why he was spending weekends in his room, and if things were alright with his friends,

Pablo had looked him in the eye and said his band, Plagiarism, had died thanks to him.

None of this bothers Lucho, for he knows that he's been doing what good fathers are meant to do. His own father used to say: 'A good father understands that he must set out to plan for the hopes of others.' Then again, Lucho isn't sure what was truly meant by all that. He still finds it hard to unpack his late father's confusing speeches.

To convince Ramona, then, he had had to promise everything would remain the same inside the house.

What matters is that Ramona, his wife, should soon forget their old home in San Fernando. She will be the new mistress in Santiago, in a grand old army house. She will never have to dust the tiles or curtains again, will never have to hose the horse shit off the pavement when Datrilo, the melon man Lucho hopes to never see again, passes by, selling the rotten leftovers from the fair. She will never have to lift the finger she once said she was so tired of lifting (provided Mariela, their *nana*, does her job right). And Lucho, because he has given his word, will make sure of it.

There's a window in front of him that almost touches the edge of his desk. From there he can see Pablo sitting and listening to music on the marble bench on the patio, looking at his own shoes. His son who had also resisted the move. 'My whole life is here,' he had said. 'My band is here. Why would you do that to me now?'

But in Santiago, Pablo would become someone, would finally focus on studying instead of hanging around the sons of Marxists who no longer remembered what life was really like and who now dedicated themselves to wearing each other's tattered ponchos and unnecessary satchels. None of them worked and they had nothing to carry.

Pablo would forget all about San Fernando, the old music, the songs that no longer mattered. In Santiago, in this concrete ode to Chile, new things would be done. And as it was with Lucho's writing, back when he still wrote, the ideas that built the new country would manifest in images; the sea, the sky and land, its people and their voices together in verses devoid of the unnecessary clutter of feelings and the lies of his predecessors, and verses whose power would only be grasped in their final lines, a last clue to ground a reader's interpretation, for if Chile was a country in the midst of rebuilding, then his writing could only justify itself at the end.

But it was also true that having spent so much time and energy convincing others of the advantages of moving away from that shithole town, Lucho hadn't thought enough about himself. His Comandante at the regiment in San Fernando had told him it would be a step up, *'pa' arriba'*. Although when Lucho had asked how that might be the case, how much more he'd get paid, whose boss he would now be, the Comandante said it wouldn't be a different rank or anything like that.

'Up, *huevón*, up as in North,' he had laughed, 'up in Santiago.'

And then he had signed Lucho off.

In San Fernando, Lucho, who'd entered the regiment academy at seventeen, had quickly become the platoon joke. It wasn't like he had no friends, but as soon as the other cadets had found out his father was none other than Captain Ángel Díaz – the hero, the leader, the man – they had started to be careful about what they said around Lucho, how they acted around him. And as it happens when distance grows between people, cruelty becomes a simpler endeavour. *Poor man's Neruda* turned to *faggot poet*, and then – when Lucho stopped writing altogether – *the faggot*.

But Lucho tries not to think too much about all that, these days. He's in Santiago now, while those in his old regiment are stuck in a dying town with nothing but past glories. (And even those glories are so far in the past that they are more like legends, statues; stories no one living can take credit for, even if credit is due.) Yes, yes, he's here. And it's precisely *because* those bastards knew he could write that the transfer had come up. The government needed someone to keep product records in Santiago, a national inventory, and to personally manage the press releases about that inventory. His father (the hero, the leader, the man) had bought *The Region* in 1973, a newspaper in San Fernando, *the voice of Colchagua Valley*. And it was there that Lucho, while he was still at school, had his first job at the printer's office. Then, after 73, he'd become his father's editor, reading the newspaper's articles through the night. (He never changed a word.) Not many at the San Fernando regiment could even spell.

And now Lucho will write up the nation's inventory, and there will be nothing but abundance. Never a queue for basic needs. Never a school teaching children how to make toothpaste at home. Never instability. Never fear. An invisible government is a good government. More shops selling more. Luxuries, which should not be called that since they are the things that make life worth living. More like objectives. Like missions. Like aspirations. Like foreign cars. Like flattened hills to make room for modern apartment complexes. New roads. New bridges. His product reports will shape a new and connected country. A miracle for the hardworking middle classes, for anyone tired of the past, for anyone who dreams of the future. And he'll no doubt be able to rise through the ranks. He's always known he could do so much more, so much better, and that knowledge is finally taking the form of truth.

And now, Lucho is sitting in what he will soon declare to be his permanent study. His desk lies against a colonial window adorned by a plaster grapevine with two cherubs on each side. Here, facing the Great Andes, Lucho will finally be able to think of himself as part of Santiago's growing light when it shines right on his desk. Despite his desire to write, to continue writing (and writing things other than product reports), poetry is now out of the question. His father had been right that day, when he'd told Lucho that poets could not run a country, for they too often turned a crooked table into allegories of love, or a decaying house into the voices of those who would never read poetry in the first place. 'Poets suffer from a kind of schizophrenia,' he'd said, 'one that is more dangerous than the recognised condition because it insists on forcing their own delusions on everyone else. Real beauty is much clearer, and much more efficient.'

But since childhood, Lucho had been consumed by the stories of Chilean heroes. He'd learnt to read using the volumes of Chilean history his father, Captain Ángel, had written. The story which captivated him the most – and still did – was that of Arturo Prat, the navy hero who died in the Battle of Iquique in the War of the Pacific. Arturo had leapt off the *Esmeralda* to board an enemy ship, knowing he'd die; an act of desperation in the face of likely defeat. That's what it had said in the book. But, as Lucho often asked himself in his poetry, what kind of unfathomable love isn't also followed by despair? Arturo was 31. Lucho is 42, but he too has made sacrifices. The very desk on which his empty notebook lies open is a testament to everything he's lost; a loss of words and phrases which now return to him, slow and difficult, making him abandon any hope of becoming the next Neruda. He knows that every success is marked by the quiet ambush of failures, that despite this great house, he wants more from life than to be locked in a basement writing orders for potatoes and bread and, whenever his numbers are below the government's targets, telling his superiors tales about Marxist crimes; making up stories like his father had done for *The Region*. Marxist Terrorists Steal a Supply Lorry! Anarchists Burn Tyres in New Attempt at Blockade! New Buses Become Unserviceable After Stones Rain on New Station! Death of Policeman at Hands of Terrorists Linked to Increased Defence Spending!

And he's also grown apart from Ramona – there is that too. They barely speak, except to ask each other whether they want a cup of water on their bedside tables. They care so little about the answer that they often end up with two cups each.

On Lucho's wedding day, his father's gift had been to warn him of the common phrases uttered by soft men and women. He had said: 'There's no such thing as a long and happy marriage, but there sure are long ones.' Lucho had laughed it off, but was beginning to suspect, as he often did these days, that his father had been right in the wrong places. The problem, as Lucho sees it now, is that he and Ramona know each other too well *because* they'd talked so much, too much, in the beginning. What they have now isn't unhappiness, but the silence following joy, like sleeping well and forgetting all the remnants of a dream. So he doesn't know why he still feels like it needs fixing, that in their nightly untouched cups there are also restless waters.

He stretches on his chair and takes out a picture of Arturo Prat from the back of his notebook. It's the classic military bust: Arturo with a hand slipped between the two golden buttons of his coat, eyes fixed away from the viewer, as if indifferent to his own portrait. Lucho wonders whether Arturo also had trouble communicating with his wife, whether they also offered each other unnecessary cups of water, whether they too forgot their dreams. Whatever the answers, he writes:

> At 10, Arturo joins the regiment.
> Too young to understand gunpowder,
> but already his bravery was—

Lucho, at 10, read Neruda and Mistral while hiding in the bathroom. His mother, Olga, used to conceal books in his bedsheets for him to read. Their arrangement had been a silent one – she never even once mentioned it before leaving Ángel (such was her fear of the Captain), and Lucho only knew it had been her who had left the books because some of the pages had paint prints on them. His mother painted colourful landscapes; the vineyards in Santa Cruz, the avocado farms just out of San Fernando, the fruit stands in the highway near Melipilla, and countless panoramic setups of the domed chapel in Rengo, along with the wicker furniture stands, in sepia. Lucho was young back then, and as children tend to do, he confused his parents' routines, his mother's persistence in remaining locked away in the shed that had been once reserved for chickens, with happiness. Olga had complained about the lack of space to work in the house and Ángel, who didn't want to hear anything more about painting and his failure to provide space, had killed the hens one by one with his bare hands – a story he would bring up every now and then whenever Olga complained about the quality of supermarket eggs.

And she would always show them her finished paintings, and though there weren't enough walls to hang them on, his father hadn't said anything about the oily smells coming from the growing piles of colour in every corner of the house, or the fact that he had to shit facing a miserable depiction of the annual pilgrimage to Rengo, in which she'd decided to paint the blood on the pilgrims' knees black, like they were bleeding their own shadows. His father had let the paintings accumulate, and so Lucho learnt to live with it all too. Then Allende had come to power and, as Lucho would later confirm as another one of his father's messianic truths, it wasn't the country that had made a pact with the devil but the people within it – the homes, the families. That's where Satan hides, Ángel had said. In our homes. He comes in through the front door, invited, and he feeds in clean kitchens with the children.

And so Satan, who'd by then become a Marxist, hid in the chicken shed and held his mother's brush.

> But was that bravery?
> If all he knew, all he learnt,
> was how to have enemies –
> does a coward have to mourn
> the lives he didn't end?

After Allende came, his mother spent all her days working on a single painting she wouldn't let anyone see. And Lucho is certain – or had he dreamt it? – certain he'd heard her make her way to the shed some nights too. She went so far as to install a steel padlock on the shed door, which made the other army wives in San Fernando, who would never think of killing their own chickens, gossip about the room's purpose. She went from town witch to communist conspirator to communist conspirator witch, but Lucho knew these to be lies because she would often make him go and buy her paint tubes and brushes at the *ferreteria*.

When she abandoned them, Lucho's father kicked the shed door in. The painting, it turned out, was not a landscape, for once. There were layers and layers of red and black spirals, the paint almost as thick as the canvas, and in the upper left-hand side, she had carved out three crosses.

'Communists don't know how to finish anything,' Lucho's father said. 'They lack a final goal.' He then took the canvas into the house. He burnt all the other painting piles stacked around the room, all of them but that one. He hung it so that it faced Lucho's bed. 'So that you remember the kind of cancer we're up against,' he said, and then switched off the light. But Lucho hadn't been able to sleep, that night. No, it wasn't because she'd left – for his father had explained to him that communists didn't understand love and commitment, that she hadn't loved Lucho, and therefore that they, in turn, had only felt false things, been led by falsehoods, been deceived when they had provided for her ('and,' he had added, 'the pain of truth was preferable to love affairs with lies'). No, no, it was the way the moon shone right on the painting. Lucho remembers the reds moving, the dried-up oily drippings abandoned midstroke, the bloody waves against that absent crucifixion. Throughout the night he'd stared at it, waiting for the red current to leave the frame and take over the bedroom walls, just as he's looking right now, because this is where he's hung the painting, in the only part of his house that he hasn't allowed the movers to touch, and so this is the first piece of their lives to have a set place in it: facing his desk.

Yes, at ten, he was reading poems he came to hate. But just as in Arturo Prat's case, Lucho felt that there was something heroic in how well he learnt to love and hate the right things:

> Unlike most, Prat understood that the
> greatest fears come not from seeing death
> in the stormy oceans,
> but from the belief that such a vision
> is to be avoided.

Lucho tears out the page and chucks it in the paper basket beside him. Who the hell would want to read about a ten-year-old Prat? There's something disturbing in describing a child as brave. No room for improvement. A reminder of the cowardice of most adults. No, what matters are the battles. What matters are Prat's death and the language used to describe said death to make it matter.

What made Lucho start thinking about Arturo in the first place was reading his son Pablo's history textbooks (which he checked for errors) and in which he found only one page about Arturo, which ended:

> And then he commanded his men to leap onboard
> the enemy ship, and then he leapt too and
> died, leaving his crew to fight.

He'd asked Pablo what he thought about the fact that their heroes were being murdered all over again by lazy writers, but Pablo didn't give a damn. Pablo even asked, when Lucho brought the subject up: 'Wasn't he the guy who killed himself jumping off his ship? I don't even believe he made the jump. He fell into the sea, drowned, and that was that.'

Lucho could have beaten him. He had really felt an urge to. But then Lucho understood that, like all youths today, Pablo wanted to be punished. No, he wanted to deserve it, deserve punishment, because it's easier to die in a fight than to live asking for forgiveness. And so Lucho took Pablo's guitar, set it against a tree in their garden and, with his father's rifle, shot at it. There was a chord at first, and then a collection of splinters.

He regrets shooting the guitar because despite it all, he can't help but feel responsible for his son's opinions, his naivety – that, and he still sees traces of childhood in Pablo's face. God knows he never laid a hand on him growing up.

Lucho sees the two lorries parking by the road. Men in blue *cotona* overalls climb out of them and Ramona greets them in the front porch. The workers begin by lowering a sofa – one of the few things she'd wanted to get rid of (it was his father's) – and then the TV he'd bought her just last Christmas, when she'd begged to switch the old black and white set for a colour one.

Pablo comes out too. He doesn't help with anything, and Lucho knows it's because the only thing he cares about is the new guitar Lucho should have never bought him.

And what is there for Lucho to receive? He is simpler than his wife and son. He'll think about Prat's jump a little longer and then go downstairs for dinner and then, glass of water in hand, he'll try and predict how his career will progress. What his boat is and the kind of ocean he's navigating – and what the hell he's jumping into. (Or had he lived through the jump already?)

He laughs at himself a little, because writing always leaves him with a voice in his head that isn't his. His father once said poets love putting on voices while they perform (Neruda had just come on TV) so that they appear to see the past, present and future in ways we simple mortals can't fathom without their help, their vision.

Lucho couldn't have predicted this move. Arturo couldn't have predicted the magnitude of his own name. And Lucho must abandon all poetry anyway, because in the end, he thinks, while looking at Prat's picture, it's a mark of stupidity to read actions as symbols and signs. It's all much simpler: there he is dying, and here's Lucho trying to write about it.

> POETRY NOTES – BOOK OF RAMONA
> *Preparations: Travelling the Great Sea*
>
> Readiness, you say,
> is the lonesome bird
> feeding in our garden.
> It will surely die,
> cradled in its roots.

He closes his notebook, and looks at the red painting until there's a knock at his door and—

'Señor, it's time for the *once*,' Mariela says, and he follows her down. But not before shaking and pulling the new padlock on the door until he's sure it works perfectly.

2

RAMONA

is surely going to die today.

'Ladies! Arms up, sides, down, that's it, you're all stars, down, yes, like you mean it, up again, hands together, crown yourselves, hands on your heads, yes, you're all queens, stars too, stars I said, you there, be a star a little faster please!'

The whole group turns to look at Ramona, RIGHT AT HER, and her glasses drip condensation, oh God, be glad, for once she's glad that this is hard for her, that she's packed on a few extra kilos (it's not her fault!), because the red flush on her face, there ever since she started Doctor Ignacio's treatment, is now camouflaged. I wasn't always like this – it's the damn pills, I promise!

But then she sees the smiles around her. She confuses no one, and who is she kidding, she can't keep up with these women, the stars, the queens, she looks like the sun, the real star, whose actual shape could never be admired, a blob of lava, the large, oh so large, largest failure in the whole of sunny Santiago but—

It could have all turned out differently, which really just means *she* could have been different. When she watches *Giant Saturday* on TV and Don Francisco, who she knows to be the most famous man in Chile, sits on a transparent stage chair talking to actresses, publicising their plays and films and telenovelas in the quieter segments between money games for regular people who cry at only ever getting consolation prizes, that's when the desire to take up acting again takes over.

```
            LO QUE TUS OJOS NO VEN: A TELENOVELA

                        #EPISODE 1

      EXT. SANTA CRUZ VINEYARDS - DAY

      We're out in the main grounds of a COLONIAL
      HOUSE. High on a hill, the HOUSE overlooks
      vineyards and workers' huts scattered around
      on dry patches of land.

      INT. LIVING ROOM
```

She could be there, on that stage. She could sit like them, cross-legged and smiling, waving away Don Francisco's innuendos with a high-pitched giggle. She could put on a grave face (after sweeping her fringe) when a tragic topic is introduced (to a chiming ballad); the death of a famous director, the unrelenting strength of a single mother and her successful kiosk in a street no one would ever visit. She could blush in embarrassment when Don Francisco asks her to dance, just like she would in the telenovela she'd be there to promote. Last Saturday, Camila Subercaseaux did exactly that, she'd stood up and danced, just as she'd done with the leading man in that episode after regaining her sight, though Ramona hopes it was clear to the clapping audience (forced to clap, no doubt) that Camila has never studied theatre or acting, what with her monotone voice which would never pass a modulation exam, the awkward and ungrateful pauses after Don Francisco's comments about her dress and hair, the way she never looked at the regular people in the audience, her complete lack of projected emotion. Ramona would not be like that. 'Your dress is amazing,' Don Francisco would say to Ramona. And she would open her mouth real wide in ecstatic surprise, leaning forward in spontaneous laughter. Don Francisco would look down at her chest. 'I think your tailor is Chile's best friend,' he would say, more to the audience than her, and she would turn to the regular people, incredulous and blushing while they covered their mouths, sharing her perfect depiction of dignified shame. She could have been in that telenovela. Not Camila Subercaseaux. She could have danced with Don Francisco. She could have regained her sight. She could have waved at the regular people, but then, she is back in the gym – the music goes—

>   LIVE IT UP – *poom, poom*
>   GONNA LIVE IT
>   GONNA TASTE IT
>   LIVE IT UP, *poom, poom*

and Ramona wonders if the woman singing has ever gone to the gym before, to come up with such wisdom for others to suffer through, because yes, Ramona is suffering (and the words TASTE IT are making her hungry), a star-shaped ball of pain focused on what Lucho once referred to as her 'wings' – her fucking wings! And he used to be a poet, imagine that! The flaps under her arms, the 'wings' she'd give up in an instant – if only we were asked at birth which imperfections we'd like to live with – though the women around her and their younger, tighter arms, very much make her want to fly out the window, the window that the man in purple spandex, who everyone refers to as El Charlie, has chosen to keep shut ever since she came in (late), and in this room no one but her is shining with sweat, like a sun-shaped fish poached in a sauna, pleading with her fins to be submerged underwater, her noticeable, well-developed, imperfect fins that when—

'There's not a care, three, four, in the world outside, seven, eight, of your bodies right now, ladies, and ten! Up again! Focus on yourselves. Pain is your friend. I know how bad it can get. Now

> ISABEL URRUTIA is having tea in a spacious
> LIVING ROOM, facing a painting of a ship
> breaking a wave, a wild island with oversized
> trees and rocky cliffs almost touching the
> bow.
>
>   ISABEL URRUTIA (V.O.)
>   My ancestors, what would
>   they think of me now? Rich,
>   engaged to be married even

I ask you, how GOOD can it get? You, at the back there, faster, faster, let it get good, faster. I won't ask you what's wrong with you – I'll ask you what's RIGHT with you. Come on, repeat after Uncle Charlie. This time is me time, two three, up, up and down the steps, don't stop! This time is—'

    ME TIME THIS TIME IS ME TIME THIS
    TIME IS ME TIME THIS TIME IS ME

they say, and Ramona says it too, though she's not sure what it means, if it means anything at all, and she has the sudden feeling that either time has no owner at all or it belongs, all of it, wholly to herself. But before she has chance to form the sentence in her head – All things, good or bad, present or forgotten, are mine – she gets a cramp in her left thigh which ends her legwork, though the fervent energy of a room filled with synchronised bodies makes her keep clapping to El Charlie's claps because no, no, no, stop being so negative, Ramona. Lucho is right about her. She's too negative. This is the best of times in Chile. And here she is, finally back in Santiago, away from the dung smell and animal noises of San Fernando, away from boring wives and their boring husbands, away from that single cube of a house where she'd been expected—

THIS TIME

to come up with ways to pass—

ME TIME

and Positive Thinking is getting her healthy again, too, and all that remains for her to do, to worry about, is keeping things that way. It's that simple, logical even; that, once you have Essential Happiness (or was it True Joy? Don Francisco had a psychic come in to talk about it on the last *Giant Saturday*, the psychic who has a stand near Pajaritos and whose card readings always end in marriage for those who are single and in love for those who are married), it's yours to keep and project onto the world, something like that, so that any past misery (should she even be using that word?) was merely part of a *process* (yes, she loves that word, process). Lucho, who she knows is tired of her (he always seems exhausted when she's doing well because he no longer has an excuse not to be with her, to recommend she find happiness somewhere else in the house), had suggested she take up painting because, he said, it had helped his mother with her moods. This was enough for Ramona to pull a broad and lasting Positive Thinking smile and, even though she couldn't draw, say yes. But then Lucho had seen her first attempt: a sunflower under a blue sky. She'd wanted so badly to be done with it, or to have something done, that she'd used the same brush to shade the flower as she'd used on the sky and so the petals had turned purple. The next day, Lucho proposed the gym, and her doctor, who'd also seen her art, quickly agreed because—

> richer, La Señora de la Casa, how proud would they be? And yet, and yet...
> I feel that I live my life waiting for all the things which have already passed and gone for good. They may have discovered an island. They may have owned the oceans. But what does all this matter; what

'You're being too negative, Ramona. Think of your life as happy and you will be happy. Think of the world as a good place and it will be good. Don't use the words *don't* or *maybe* or *if*, but *do, do, do*,' just as Don Francisco had when he'd asked a man to do push-ups on his TV programme, in front of an audience of women singing about being single, so *single, single, single and unengaged yaaay*. Do, do—

THIS TIME—

'Hello there, yes, hi.' A young woman stretches a mat behind her. Ramona is glad she's not the only one always arriving late. The woman taps her on the right arm in the wrong place, on the underarm, her wings.

'Yes?'

'You don't remember me.'

'I—'

'Ramona Godoy, right?'

'Yes,' Ramona says, and her hands stretch out to the tall arched glass ceiling, and slowly recoil back to her chest. She'd known this would happen, that new people would talk to her, that she wouldn't have anything to say, that she'd meet people only to have to avoid them (which really just meant that they'd want to avoid her). It's why she'd initially wanted to do something other than the gym, pottery at home (Lucho had laughed, but she had found out where to get clay downtown), learning the piano from a book (Lucho insisted she needed a teacher, and that it would be a risk to buy a piano if she then decided she didn't like it, just like she'd decided pottery was not for her after all). All she meant was that she'd rather be by herself. But Lucho wouldn't budge. 'Remember what happens when you're alone for too long,' he'd said. 'And you must remember to at least do some exercise. A clear mind is a clear body. That's the first step.' Though he didn't say to what, which in itself is—

'Alicia Vicuña,' the woman says, setting herself up to Ramona's left, facing El Charlie, who is continuing to issue instructions at the front of the class.

'I'm sorry, you said I didn't remember you. Do I know you? Have we met? I have a terrible memory for faces,' Ramona says, and then wishes she'd said nothing at all, please, please keep quiet, Ramona, for if there's one thing she's learnt these last few difficult years, it's that small talk should always be avoided, avoided like staying in bed all day and the empty timetable her doctor advised against, because if you make small talk, you realise you have nothing to say and nothing to do that matters, which is much worse than never speaking and never doing a thing. But in a world of noise, of opinions, she can't help but think of her own silence as stupidity. She's tired, so tired, but Positive too, she really has to try, if not for herself then for—

'The dinner, the dinner for new transfers? A few months ago. I talked to your husband. I spoke to you very briefly. Told you how bored I was. Not of him, of course.' She laughs. 'Anyway, you're new here, right? It must all be so different to, where was it again? San Fernando?'

>   is an ocean to the vast
>   wilderness of youth?
>
> ISABEL URRUTIA leaves her cup, heads to
> CORRIDOR and notices a broken vase on the
> floor.
>
> BLACK SCREEN TO COMMERCIAL BREAK
>
> BLACK SCREEN TO TITLE LOGO
>
> INT. CORRIDOR

'I don't remember it. I'm sorry. I mean, I remember the dinner, but I—'

'But you don't remember *me*!' The woman frowns with a smile, pretty cheekbones appearing. 'Don't worry, my husband's not in the army anymore. And those events are atrocious. Everyone looks the same. Everyone's bored, too. I think they forget some of us aren't soldiers. If they need to shoot someone, let it be the cooks.'

Ramona smiles and nods, though she remembers the *pasteles de choclo* very well from that night, just the right ratio of meat to corn paste, and she'd even secretly dusted hers with sugar, as she'd done too many times as a child. She keeps nodding, agreeing to the wrong things, and then there's a tense silence and she knows what comes next, that if she carries on talking she will need to surrender herself to this stranger, Alicia. Ramona knows this because she can foretell the future, she can feel it like a phantom pain in her throat, that what follows is what always follows and will always follow – or so her mother had always said – the Chilean triplet of first encounters: hometown, school, surname. God almighty how she hates—

(Her mother, Mirta, in one of her drunken evenings, had once told her: 'The only way you can ever succeed in this world is if you're not alone. And that means giving yourself up, always. It's all smiling and nodding, no matter how wrong the other may be, because it's those who most need to be smiled at that will be the first to turn against you when someone else does it before you.')

Ramona smiles, looks at the glass ceiling where light coming in shows the dust they've had no choice but to breathe in. She does the body star and Alicia Vicuña does the same, both out of sync with the music, failing together, breathing in all the dust in Santiago.

'So you're new here,' Alicia says.

'Yes.'

'Where did you live before then? Where are you from, if you don't mind me asking? Were you always in San Fernando?'

And Ramona gives herself up.

'We were in San Fernando before but more like between San Fernando and Santa Cruz. In the countryside,' she says, wishing she hadn't mentioned the countryside because Lucho told her not to. (Tell them we've always lived in cities. People in Santiago don't understand a farm past the mud and dirt and the smell of their own dog's shit. 'They'll think we're dirty,' he'd said.) Ramona feels watched, inspected, and she looks at her hands in the air for signs of dirt (all she finds are new wrinkles) before hiding them behind her head.

'To be honest, it's all close down there. We lived nearer to San Fernando than Santa Cruz. But I've lived in Santiago before,' she says, before Alicia can get a word out. 'You know, right downtown in the city centre. So it's kind of a return if anything. I feel right at home. I came back.'

'Oh, but I love that region. The wine is excellent. And you really do feel more connected to the land over there. A shame you had to move to this big old slab of concrete.' Alicia places her hands

> ISABEL URRUTIA
> Luz! Come here right now!
>
> LUZ MARIA
> Sí Señora, right away.
>
> INT. LUZ MARIA'S BEDROOM
>
> LUZ MARIA is sitting on the bed with FATHER CALLETANO, who holds her shoulder as she stands.

behind her head too, in defiance of El Charlie's instruction to run on the spot. Ramona guesses that Alicia must be in her late twenties (younger perhaps, but that would be too much to ask right now) because her skin doesn't bounce after sudden movements and the veins on her forearms appear happy to be inside her, unlike Ramona's protruding greenish rivers trying to spill out.

Alicia is much taller than Ramona. Much paler, blue eyes, an oddity outside the city, a TV personality, not one visible pore in her perfect nose, no wings of any sort. Alicia is young and pretty, unlike her. Alicia is fit and thin, unlike her. Alicia doesn't have to be here. She could audition right now and get a leading—

'I suppose,' Ramona says. 'I suppose the countryside isn't too bad.' Her stepfather said things like that – it's better to live in the countryside, to be connected to the land. On walks near Puente Negro, he would revel in the smell of cow dung and tell her: 'This, this is the smell of life, and it brings me so much happiness,' while she in turn covered her nose and wished all nature dead.

'And you went to which school over there? I'm from Santiago College.'

'Inmaculada Concepción, a German nuns' school.'

'Ah, I don't know it. But then again, I've only been near San Fernando when Pato got it into his head that he wanted to be a farmer right before we got married. The dreams of the young, I guess.'

Ramona guesses what Pato looks like. She imagines him young and happy, which really just means young (does happiness actually exist after a certain age, or is it just coping, a positive outlook on what little time remains?), because that's how she imagines anyone she hasn't met. He's tidy, with shirts always tucked into his trousers. People greet him with a nod as he walks through shops with Alicia, an arm casually wrapped around her waist. At home, Pato is not interested in politics or the news, and invites Alicia for long walks in the evening, because summer nights in the city (he loves the summer) make him feel calm, and, looking at her while he opens a bottle of wine, he will even say something childish but honest, something that just comes out from watching her imperfectly cutting up steak: 'I'm so lucky to have met you'.

'Pato?'

'My husband, yes. He's there.' She points at El Charlie.

'Wait—'

'Yes!' Alicia laughs. 'He thinks Pato doesn't convey the more American vibe he wants in the gym.'

'Right.'

'And we went to see a ranch and the stench was unbearable. It's strange. Men call it courting but it's really just lying, showing only the good parts. He hated the countryside, but he waited a whole six months before giving up the deal entirely. He was afraid I wouldn't marry him. Even now he tells me he abandoned the idea because he could make more money in the city.'

'It's not as convenient as Santiago,' Ramona says, trying hard to understand what it is about her that makes strangers feel so at ease with themselves and their life stories. Is it her age? Is it that she's officially out of the competition now? (Competition

> **FATHER CALLETANO**
> Be careful, my daughter.
> Though you may be blind, it
> is Isabel who cannot see.
>
> **LUZ MARIA**
> Thank you, Father... But
> she is good inside, I just
> know it. She needs our
> love. That is what the lady

for what?) Alicia talks with the unfounded confidence Ramona often saw in Pablo as a child. Is it that Ramona, aside from being overweight, is also now old and motherly? She wonders whether Alicia could be talking to her out of charity, pity, or maybe to make sure she knows what not to do when she herself gets older. Yes, after those months at the hospital, after all that medication, Ramona's become a warning, a scarecrow in the fields of ageing, the shot echoing in her own little silo, and all the bats in the world must flutter out, save themselves, and she must stand there, still and quiet, and then she must thank all the bats for flying past her.

They remain quiet and turn to face Pato to follow a set of squats (which Ramona can't fully pull off, certainly not as low as he or Alicia can) broken up by running on the spot which, considering how long it's been since she last ran, feels like a waste, and she wishes she could run out of here, to blink and appear all the way out, far into childhood, holding that rifle.

'And where did you go to university? You went to university, right? Oh my god, I'm too nosy. You don't have to tell me. But I'm sorry if you didn't. You just assume sometimes in the city, you know, that everyone has ambitions like that.'

'I did, yes. I did. I went to La Chile,' says Ramona.

'Ah, I didn't score high enough for that. But my Pato had a few favours to collect in La Católica, so he managed to get me there in the end. What did you study?'

'Theatre,' she says, noticing she's out of sync with the tune. But as she's at the end of the chain of dancers, or runners or squatters or whatever the hell this is, interrupting nothing, no one notices when she relaxes her shoulders and crosses her arms.

'Oh, that's nice,' Alicia says. 'Really great. So I guess you're a teacher, yes? I don't mean that as an insult, of course – such a great career – but I assume nowadays if you're an actress and you're not on TV, then you're a teacher. But you don't have to work, right? You must have quite the big house to take care of now.'

'No, I don't have a job, not anymore.' The music stops and Pato hops on a metallic podium, his hands on his waist, sweat patches on his chest. 'I take care of my son.'

'Last round of squats, ladies,' Pato says, arms stretched in front of him. 'Say it with me. Win! Two, three. Win! Two, three.'

Ramona and Alicia follow Pato, winning as low as they can. Alicia is right about her. She did teach right after the audition – that terrible audition – but it wasn't theatre that she taught as no one wanted that at a nuns' school, and she didn't have enough credits to her name to get a university post. And so, she taught kindergarten, where kids called her Mrs Fly because of her large thick glasses and because she was always eating. She tried. Ramona really did try – no, really, she even made a buzzing noise when she walked into classrooms to make the kids laugh. And though some days she was happy, or at least she remembers being happy, there was always also an uncomfortable tension there, like the struggle to ignore a terrible secret about someone you love.

Yes, she had gone back to her mother's house in San Fernando after that failed audition for the telenovela lead, and she had taught at the same nuns' school where her stepfather had once taught her,

> needs, our loyalty and our
> love.
>
> LUZ MARIA starts to walk slowly out of the room.
>
> > FATHER CALLETANO (V.O.)
> > Ay, Luz María, you are too
> > good for this world, and it
> > has been too cruel to you
> > in return.

the same classroom even, where his heart had suddenly stopped beating and from which his body was carried out later that day. Her mother, already drinking heavily when Ramona decided to go back home – her stepfather had been taken in to be questioned weeks before, as everyone in San Fernando knew he'd been first in line when leftist Fidel marched the streets – was glad of the company. 'You've done a full circle coming here. You'll be fine,' her mother had told Ramona, who knew that a circle couldn't exist so long as death and time were the constants of its imperfect circumference, and whose school friends – there were many, she's sure, for she does not remember being lonely – had left San Fernando for good, for the second Chilean triplet, Medicine, Law, Engineering, all staying in Santiago, married and with children, the circle, cracked but still better, somehow still better than hers.

Ramona had always known, deep down, that a time would come, like today, where she would have to admit that she'd failed.

Her dreams had once been bigger. Telenovelas. Movies. Theatre. The world of the shiny. She'd actually gone to so many auditions, not just one: Poltergeist #2, Young Woman in Distress, Gossipy Background Barmaid, Cushion Saleswoman. But it's always the same one she remembers in detail. The one for the part of a female lead in *The Truth in Your Eyes*, a telenovela where she'd play Lucecita, a blind and poor girl whose life changes after meeting the rich ranch owner who also owns her house, and her family, and her, really, and then, being so religious and pure, God decides to give her her sight back and she ends up marrying the guy because she's no longer damaged and ugly and he's real happy about it. The script said, 'He tearfully agonises over her new beauty.' Ramona memorised all of her lines, even blindfolded herself for nearly a week to imbue her portrayal with accuracy, but the casting director looked at her and laughed when she said she was auditioning for the blind girl because she wasn't tall enough, because her skin was blemished and not nearly light enough to be a lead and he'd laughed at her thick glasses, saying that he wasn't looking for someone who was actually blind. Instead, he offered her the 'crucial', he said, the 'crucial part' of House Maid 1. She married Lucho soon after. She often thought of how disappointed her stepfather would have been to see her married – and into the army too. Riquelme Godoy, the biologist, the chemistry teacher from the *Normal* and the *Pedagógico*, the man who had centipedes in test tubes wrapped in handkerchiefs in the inside pocket of his blazer, who'd once been proud of the embalmed monkey in his office, had always told her that one needed to have a life before sharing it. 'Why, why?!' her mother had cried when she saw the ring on Ramona's finger, and Ramona wanted to tell her she didn't want to play the maid, though instead she said, 'We all change, Mother.' But no, no. She's not lagging behind anyone. So why even feel like she needs to catch up? To who? She has a child too, and oh how she loves him. She must love him. She is married. She lives in Santiago. Look at Ramona, achieving. And most women she's met, after getting married, despite their degrees, those architects, engineers, lawyers, even doctors, they don't work either: they are all achieving, just like her. Was that

>   FATHER CALLETANO crosses himself.
>
>   INT. CORRIDOR
>
>   ISABEL URRUTIA
>   Rafael!
>
>   WORKER 1
>   Yes, Señora?

it? To give yourself up completely? But she misses herself sometimes – and she finds herself thinking this in sentences so fast she can't quite hear them: ImissyousometimesRamona. Win! Two, three, Imiss, Two, three. Win! And if she were honest she'd say she misses Lucho even more – the man who'd once arrived to pick her up, it was a Friday, yes, a Friday after school and the boys were all lined up on the other side of the iron gate waiting for the girls to come out, their hands reaching in through the gaps in the bars like prisoners accustomed to the unbreachable distances between them, and he'd simply waved at her, and he wasn't smiling, in her memories he never is, and she loved that, for she had made the mistake before of falling for imbeciles with broad smiles only to then be let down by their inability to justify them. Lucho instead said, 'I don't know how to say it: a day is long and I'll be waiting for you,' and she asked him what he meant, knowing full well that he'd borrowed Neruda's words, but Lucho just said: 'I wrote it. I wrote it for someone like you,' and she had taken his hand through the gate. But that was a long time ago, and now she can't remember where they went dancing, nor what other words Lucho chose to steal for her.

Alicia turns to El Charlie and copies his steps with more strength, producing the rubbery screeching sound which only fit people make, and she even does a little grunt. So Ramona mouths a grunt too, but it's too quiet to be TRUE JOY, and reminds her instead of her first times alone with Lucho, when they'd picked music loud enough to not hear each other breathe. Young and breathless. With him.

'Yes, I used to be a teacher,' Ramona says to Alicia. 'But I stopped working after I had Pablo, my son.'

'Hm?'

'I said I used to be a teacher. But I stopped working when I had my son.'

Alicia stops winning and looks at her, confused as all hell. Ramona guesses Alicia has already made her mind up about her, this wife and mother with nothing to say, and Ramona wishes once more she'd kept her mouth shut from the start, that she'd stayed home. She touches her chest and feels her heart pumping. Since the beginning of her treatment she has been getting panic attacks. And although most of them happen at night, next to Lucho asleep, there had been one in the daytime – when, at the supermarket till, there were no bags left. Lucho had once told her he wanted to succeed at work not for himself, and not even for the family, but for Chile, which was now an example to the world. And she'd felt proud, though she wasn't sure whether it was for the importance he felt his job had (the importance, not the job), or Chile, or the world, moving on and on, just like she is now. But then, do her failures make her a national shame? What is she doing that is so – she must do more squats, WIN, and she must give—

'Ah, you have a child, that's great, that explains it. How old? Me and *el gordo* have been trying to get pregnant this year. But sometimes I feel like I have much more to give, before, well, you know.'

> ISABEL URRUTIA
>
> Bring me the whip.
>
> WORKER 1
>
> But... Señora, again? It's already—
>
> ISABEL URRUTIA
>
> Are you sure you want to question me? One more word and

'He's seventeen,' Ramona says, doing a squat and leaving Alicia standing. 'He's seventeen,' she repeats, hoping she can leave it at that, because Pablo hasn't talked to her beyond 'Hi Mum,' 'Bye Mum' since she came back home from treatment over a year ago. They used to be close. It's been some time now – though it's difficult to count years like that. He once told her he'd inherited his love of the arts from her, that his guitar was his inheritance, and it'd been so easy to love him then. Before she left the house, before all those dark months of treatment, Pablo had taken care of her, sat by her bed after school, initially telling her about his days, the girls he liked, the fights he'd lost, the grades he'd pretended to care about. And then they would sit in silence, watching TV before Lucho arrived home and Pablo helped her get up, helped her cook and clean – Mariela hadn't permanently moved in with them yet – and it was their secret, and Pablo never said a thing to her in the evenings, when she forced a smile here and there so they could see that yes, her body was there, and Pablo would ask Lucho about his days at the regiment just so she could feel thankful, not for his days, no, no, she doesn't remember them at all, but for the permission to stay silent instead of having to speak. And then, one day, she took a sedative and passed out during dinner, face down on her plate of *charquicán*. And woke up at the hospital. Pablo has avoided her ever since.

El Charlie stops the music and everyone sighs in relief. Ramona drinks most of her water in several gulps and then hopes no one has seen just how fast she can drink. People pick up their towels and head out of the room. Alicia goes up to El Charlie and kisses him, tongue and all, sweat and all, and he presses her face into his, holds her by the neck with one hand, the kind of strangling kiss you go along with when you're young, when you're in love.

Ramona puts her towel in a backpack, an old leather bag with silver buckles she used at university because it looked like what explorers wore in the movies. Back then there had been so many places to go that she had often packed for the possibility of improvised get-togethers with other students, a jacket to stay up late, a change of shoes in case trainers were too casual. Too casual! And look at her now, why is—

She makes a mental note: she must buy a new bag. But then, Alicia and El Charlie walk up to her, blocking the exit, and she forgets about the bag. El Charlie looks far younger now he's right in front of her, though she wonders if it's because in here she's aware of her own age. There she is, providing contrast, and she looks at the window briefly to see a pigeon lodged comfortably between the spikes set up there to keep them away.

'This is Ramona Godoy,' Alicia says. 'Remember, *gordo*, from that dinner for new transfers?'

'Sure, why not?' El Charlie says. His eyes are golden. And it may be because of the theatrical lighting, more aimed at casting sharp dramatic shadows on the walls than filling the place with light, that she thinks of acting and how used she is to thinking of beautiful people as actors, and those who watch them as their audience. What is she now? Look at her, oh look at her now.

> I'll be happy to give you a
> more personal demonstration.
>
> WORKER 1 bows and makes for the door. ISABEL
> URRUTIA turns to the window overlooking the
> vineyards. PANNING SHOT, ZOOM OUT to see the
> whole estate.
>
> Everything is working as it should. There is
> a calm sadness about the way the workers toil
> the fields in the full heat of summer. ISABEL
> URRUTIA sighs in the boredom of it all.
>
> BLACK SCREEN TO COMMERCIAL BREAK

'This is Pato, my husband,' Alicia says, and Ramona feels some of the water she's drunk come back up in her throat.

Pato kisses Ramona on the cheek. She feels the heat from his arms, the sweat from his chest on hers.

'Hi, yes, yes. I mean, I'm Ramona – you're good. I mean the class was good. And you were good at giving it.'

Pato and Alicia smile at each other.

'I decided I had more to give, you know?' he says. 'I couldn't stand a desk job anymore.'

'He left the army,' Alicia says. 'We have our own little businesses now.'

'Little? We'll see. But this one's just for fun, to keep fit, you know?' Pato says.

'What do you mean?' Ramona says.

'You know she's an actress, *gordo*, a real one,' Alicia says.

'Really? Have I seen you somewhere?'

'No,' Ramona says, feeling hotter now than when she was winning.

'Well, you never know.' He touches her shoulder – right on the bone, thank God – and turns back to get a towel.

'He also works in TV,' Alicia whispers. 'You never know.'

'I'm trying to work in TV,' he says, shaking his head.

'No such thing as trying to work,' Alicia says. 'You either work or you don't.'

'I've been trying to find my calling,' he says. 'Have you ever had the feeling that you missed out on a lesson or something? Like everyone knows what they want and it's always a single thing?'

Ramona wants to scream that she has had this very feeling.

'So I started this gym as an investment, maybe to start up a chain. But one night I thought—'

'—I thought,' Alicia says, nudging him on the shoulder.

'We thought that maybe we should get into the TV business. And we also thought the gym was the perfect place to recruit. I mean, have you seen anyone fat on TV who isn't a comic?' He dries his face with the towel.

'Not that we're not open to comedy,' Alicia says, looking at Ramona.

'So,' Pato says, lifting his knees to his palms on each step, a pink towel around his neck. He holds his gaze on Ramona as he stretches.

'So,' Ramona says, still looking at Alicia who, on her knees, rolls her mat.

'Come on, let's go,' Alicia says, standing, though she's the only one going. When Alicia briefly turns to face them, Ramona looks at the ceiling and does a perfect impression of a post-gym deep breath, eyes shut, palms opened and all, but before she can even exhale, Alicia shuts the studio door and Pato takes Ramona's hand and she turns to him, a little dizzy now and—

'So,' she says, not daring to move a finger.

'So, where did you live before?' he says, letting her go.

3

PABLO

is in the basement playing guitar. No, not really, not yet at least. He's lying with his back flat on the cold floor, looking at his guitar, which is leaning against the wall, and he's hoping that, as always used to happen when he was happy, the touch of a single string might grow into melody. Since they've moved, a metallic rattle bothers him, a way the strings have of ringing even after he stops playing, or whenever he steps near the guitar, or when someone in the house shuts a door too hard, the kind of white noise that exists underwater. And in solitude. He stretches his arm out to mute the strings with his palm and takes a deep breath before lying flat again and staring at the ceiling. He could blame the new guitar, the move, the new school, his parents, his father, yes, he could blame his father and be satisfied, as really he was the source of all these new things. Then he thinks of La Dani and fucking God does he miss her.

He's only been in the new school for a couple of weeks and is already bored. He thought Santiago would be different, though he finds it hard to define his expectations. He still has the same recurring dream most nights, where he walks toward a receding coastline to wait for the tidal wave, and he still wakes up before it hits, sweating and sighing in relief, abandoning the will to sleep, playing guitar, though barely touching the strings so as to not wake anyone in the house. This is how today started. He had thought the city would distance him from the sea dream but that hasn't happened. All that has changed is that, in the dream, he used to wait for the wave with La Dani by his side. Now, she's disappeared, and he has to stand there waiting to drown alone.

He's not sure what it is about Santiago that really gets to him. Whenever he asks himself, he simply thinks, *everything*. Everyone has the latest American tapes, adventurous haircuts (haircuts which would get you called a homo in San Fernando), shoes get replaced instead of repaired, new white Adidas, never resoled. That's how he had turned up on the first day, new trainers, each with their own message written at the tips with a marker, *LOOK UP* on the left, *SAVE ME* on the right, and he had to go to the toilets to wash them after one of his classmates said: 'Not sure where you came from but here we don't cheat in tests. Teachers in Santiago are street-smart. You won't get away with something so visible.' He'd hoped everyone in the city would be getting laid, writing songs about every detail, from the forearm hair slowly rising to the surface of a smooth shoulder, the lunar eclipse of a body against the midday light of an uncovered window. Yes, that's the way he remembers La Dani, so that's the way he'd written it himself: a sleeping shadow, a still silhouette whose only living features were the rhythmic breaths he could feel on his ear, as if she were trying to tell him something, a secret in beats, and he waited, staying awake all night to understand what she might be saying. But school is the same fucking bore it always was and always will be. He's also beginning to wonder, considering how worried his father is about the shine of his (resoled) boots in the morning, whether you ever really leave high school.

Pablo gets up, puts his guitar in the old hardshell case, and picks up the stack of posters for his new band. The posters are all the same, showing a propeller plane crashing into a single-storey house; a small chalet-wannabe number like those in Puerto Varas (he's never been there but remembers the pictures from his Geography textbooks). The front door of the house is an upright Chilean flag.

Above it is half the band name, EL TENIENTE BELLO, and the other half, (((CASÓN 8, SANTIAGO))) is under it. Pablo doesn't like the drawing. Too violent, was what he thought when he first saw it, but since his new classmates had gone 'fucking *mortal*, fucking awesome,' he had kept quiet. That and, if he were honest, the fact that the violence wasn't what truly bothered him – for neither the plane nor the house had any people in them, and surely for violence to exist someone had to die? Instead, he'd felt embarrassed about the immediacy with which he'd summoned what his dad called *common sense*, the cold facts of it all, like this one dinner time when his dad had said an atom bomb was only successful if nothing remained after the explosion. This poster, his dad would say, shows the misuse of military equipment. To destroy a house you'd only need to send a child to kill one person in the family living inside and save yourself the plane. Now, Pablo wants to get rid of the posters. He doesn't even like his new band that much.

It was on his second day at his new school that he met Francisco – the rest of EL TENIENTE BELLO and ((((CASÓN 8, SANTIAGO))). At break, all the other guys had run out to the dirt football pitch, dividing themselves like guided cattle into what Pablo knew were established herds – ancient teams – and all he could do was watch from the side alongside the younger kids who were drawing up battle lines for their green plastic soldiers on the pavement with chalk. Some of the soldiers were almost overstepping the dotted line. 'The war's been going on for years,' one of the kids said. 'It never really ends.'

And then Francisco had appeared.

'So you play guitar?' he'd said, holding a notepad. Francisco's hair had reminded Pablo of The Beatles; it was like a helmet grown in the absence of parents. Or perhaps it looked like an onion skin. This is a dude brought up by his *nana*, Pablo thought, before picturing Mariela, and how she'd slap him if she'd heard him say that.

'Yeah, but not that well. I don't have much time these days,' Pablo said. This a line he'd decided was his best defence against any later humiliation.

'I asked you if you played, not how good you think you play. That stuff doesn't matter. It's all about feeling anyway.'

'I play then.'

'Hector over there,' Francisco pointed at one of the goalkeepers, 'told me he saw you play guitar instead of that fucking recorder in music lessons. I'm Francisco, hi.'

'Pablo.'

'I know, Pablo the *huaso*.'

And of course Francisco knew, since Brother Merlot, the head teacher, had on Pablo's first day made him stand in front of the class and say his name and where he came from, the latter of which he didn't want to say out loud, so he'd said, 'Pablo, I'm Pablo, Pablo from the South'. But Brother Merlot, who had seemed prepared for that exact moment, gave Pablo his pointing stick and unfolded the map of Chile right on the board.

'Point at it.'

People in the back of the class laughed as Pablo proceeded to step slowly to the map and pointed at San Fernando, under VI REGION in large font. A guy in a corner shouted '*Huaso!*' and now everyone calls him *Huaso* so he must forever be a *huaso*, a Chilean cowboy. Or a peasant.

Brother Merlot had then made him choose his desk. They were all double desks, so the real question was who he'd choose to sit next to for the rest of the year. The front was a definite no, a place saved for those with thick glasses and the crazy assholes who wanted to show they were interested in learning. And so Pablo had ended up picking a desk at the back and in a corner.

'Hector,' the guy next to him said.

'Pablo.'

'I know, you just said it. I think I'll just call you *huaso* to be honest.'

'Okay.'

'Your desk is taken, by the way.'

'There's no one here.'

'Inside, open it.'

Pablo had lifted the surface of the desk and found a collage of *La Cuarta* newspaper cuts, only the front pages, girls in bikinis and girls with only half a bikini.

'Welcome, you damn *huaso*, don't be a *huevón*,' Hector had said with a laugh.

Now, Pablo straightens his bicycle, Teniente Bello posters in his bag, his guitar held to the side with one hand, and he pedals away from his street, a secluded dirt road in Providencia, full of half-built houses and apartment blocks.

Francisco had told him to stick the posters to lampposts in his neighbourhood and Pablo hadn't wanted to say he had no neighbours, and he also doesn't want his parents to find out he's in a band again, so he wonders how much time, how far he should go before stopping, because he doesn't know Santiago well and wants to avoid any popular streets his parents might walk along. So he cycles to the Mapocho River, past young couples making out under trees in the park and drunkards sleeping under benches; past one, two travelling kiosks; over a bridge and to the hills and there, in the long narrow streets of Bella Vista, he stops to take a deep breath.

The first lamppost he tries already has a poster on it. LOST DOG. A picture of a poodle and a twenty-thousand-pesos reward. *Answers to the name BAGGAGE.* Pablo looks to both sides of the street, puts his guitar down, leans his bike against the lamppost and with his mouth cuts two lengths of the tape Francisco gave him.

He sticks a band poster over Baggage, though he really does hope he's been found. He sticks posters on every lamppost up to the end of the street and then bends the remaining bunch to fit them through the slight opening of a gutter in the pavement. And why is he sabotaging his own gig? Why, if what he dreams of is playing the Festival de Viña so loud all the assholes who go there with their families (to dance and clap at the same old shit) finally leave and let the real rock crowds scream and sweat and faint to his powerful and no doubt too-fast-to-handle guitar licks? He wants to go international, not like any of the crappy local bands with no ambition. His music would come on in people's cars and they'd be thankful for the traffic because they'd get to hear the full song – and think of Pablo on the stage, how mesmerising he'd been that year he won his first Golden Seagull (which surprised no one). The crowd would not stop chanting it. Seagull, Seagull, Seagull, Seagull. Pablo would come out from the side of the stage and the chanting would break into cheering. Thank you, Chile. Thank you, Viña. You've been amazing tonight. I always wanted to be here, since I was – Well...

After meeting Francisco, the two of them had gone into the changing rooms where Pablo kept his guitar. Francisco told Pablo he was looking for another guitarist for his band because the previous kid had accidentally shot his hand with his father's rifle.

'Don't worry, *huaso*,' Francisco had said, tuning the guitar using a neat sequence of harmonics instead of the fifth fret (to show he really did know everything about music, without even playing a song). 'Don't worry, you won't be replacing him. That'd be hard, that'd be fucking impossible. I want to start something new anyway. And we've got a gig, I mean, I should say, *I* got a gig. I mean, because he screwed his hand bad and now it all falls on me. But this gig, it's important. Other bands will be there. The Detainees played there, you know? I mean, alright, that's a rumour. But I believe it, you know? It's the kind of place great bands are born. And so for now I need someone to learn our old stuff – I mean *my* old songs. Or maybe, if we click, we'll just make new ones. I'm not sure yet. Wanna listen? Then you can see if you like the sound. But remember, The Detainees, brother, The Detainees.'

Pablo had, of course, heard of The Detainees and knew the song, 'The Ball for the Remnants,' though he didn't own any tapes or anything because the first time he'd heard of them was through his father. 'These bastards confuse freedom of expression with the ability to enrage crowds,' Lucho had said. 'And they enjoy chaos.' He'd also said that aside from the singer sounding like he'd swallowed a bunch of dying chickens and taking advantage of angry teenagers and the poor, they didn't understand that sometimes it was better to be quiet, to not feel but think and say something constructive. 'They're a waste. Why should anyone care about their feelings. Have they nothing to say? Now all they want is to blow logic up and promote violence to sell records. That's right. They want to sell, sell, sell, but markets are the devil, are they not? The only thing they're doing is showing off just how easy it is to destroy. They dream of it. Remember that. They're all as good as each other. Nothing beautiful comes out of artists today. Not like it used to.' And Pablo had felt like asking what constructive plans there were in Chile now. Like, why the hell should music he doesn't like matter to him? And how was it that fewer musicians meant better tunes? What was it to him, whether anyone loved or hated any song for any reason? Why should anyone, least of all a bunch of old people who still listened to ranch ballads, have a say on anything at all? If his father really knew one song to be better than another, why did the bad one have to be excised? Why not let it die a natural death, alone? (What does it matter, if none of us have nothing to say?) As it was, all his father did was make Pablo want to listen to The Detainees even more. Pablo wanted to understand their lyrics, like a researcher trying to understand a new virus.

Back in the changing room, Francisco had played his first tune.

'It doesn't have a name yet. I'm thinking of calling it "Untitled". I think that's cool. It shows we don't care, you know, about words or meaning or other little things like that. Do you think that's cool?'

'Yes, that's pretty cool,' Pablo said, relieved that the lyrics he'd been trying to decipher as Francisco sang did indeed mean nothing.

```
F           C        F         C
So here we are/ Again so empty
Am              G
Try to hold on/ To nothing in particular
F            C        F          C
The river sings to me/ Tells me that we're free
Am                      G
To shout back at the river/ Nothing in particular
Dm         Em        Dm          Em
Yeah...
```

And Pablo's face had grown hot. He had often envied guys who felt no shame, somehow none at all, when offering displays of feeling to strangers. When he imagines himself being interviewed about his music, sometimes his showers last up to an hour – because the imaginary TV personality, someone like Pollo Fuentes in his show *Success*, just can't be satisfied with simple answers about Pablo's complex genius. 'We're running out of time,' he says, 'but one more question. Producers, can we skip the Success Formula section today?' he asks, and the studio crowd claps in agreement. 'How is it, Pablo, that every one of your songs manages to capture the hearts of Chileans? What's the secret?' And Pablo answers by playing another song, and Pollo Fuentes does not want to disturb him, and so the credits simply begin to roll as the music plays.

In reality, Pablo knows he could never pull it off. He can't even sing if he thinks someone might be listening.

'Something like that,' Francisco had said, with a smirk and wide eyes. 'You know?'

'Sounds good.'

'Here,' Francisco said, passing his guitar over to Pablo. 'Play one of yours.'

Pablo grabbed the guitar and, though he already knew it was in tune, played the sequence of harmonics.

'That's a good sign. You definitely play. Good, good. Don't you hate it when people tune it from the fifth fret on the low E? It's just not the same. Not as precise.'

'Yeah.' Pablo played an A minor. 'So, should I play anything?'

'Anything at all, *huaso*.'

So Pablo had played a confused jumble of chords without a consistent rhythm. An A minor and a B major. An E major and an F sharp. And at the end, he played a pentatonic scale that he didn't even finish because he had no idea why he'd started it or where he wanted to go after that. He finished by letting an A minor ring out.

After, he couldn't look Francisco in the eyes.

'Experimental, man. What was that on? Seven-fourths or something? I like it. Like, you got so many influences. Was there some Cat Stevens in there? Don't worry if you don't know him. I mean he's a god. I do that, sorry, just namedrop like that. I just think all music's connected, you know?'

'Yeah.'

'You're in, man. Practice after school. My place. We've got a lot to do before the gig. By the way, I found us a drummer. She doesn't know any of the songs yet either.'

Pablo parks his bike outside a house near Parque O'Higgins. He can hear a snare getting beat up real loud inside. He rings the bell at the gate and the music stops.

A *nana*, an old lady with an apron, comes out the front door turning a bunch of keys with her index finger. She squints at Pablo. He waves at her and she makes an O with her mouth, like she really hadn't been able to see him. Old people make him feel invisible sometimes.

'Who you looking for?' the *nana* asks.

'Francisco. It's Pablo,' he says, lifting his guitar case.

She sighs and looks at the sky as she turns the gate key.

'More noise, then,' she mumbles as he steps inside.

He follows her along a short stone path. She barely lifts her feet, so she leaves neat trails on the dirt, like those of wheels, on her way to the front door. When she opens it, Francisco's on the other side with his guitar strapped and hanging from his back.

'*Huaso*, you're late.'

'I put the posters up.'

'Good, good.'

'So, how is she?'

'She keeps the beat.'

'Alright.'

Pablo follows Francisco across a living room with African masks and a wood carving of a condor and they walk into Francisco's bedroom, where the single bed is turned on its side against the wall. Floor lamps are stacked on it – as if there is no gravity here – to make room for the drumkit. Pablo waves hello and the girl waves back, rests the drumsticks on the edges of the bass drum.

In his recurring sea dream, Pablo is always calm. He can breathe just fine, at the start. The sight of the ocean swelling, the rain, the quaking, the holes in the Earth, the knowledge, right then and there, that Iloca, the town he used to spend his summers at, the docks with their bare wooden spears piercing out of the shallow water, the beach where La Dani first told him she loved him, had completely disappeared underwater. Our map has changed forever, the land is now water. But he doesn't care. It's only when he tries to sing about it, in this dream, that he starts to struggle with his breathing, his belly is stiff and airless, and he wakes up choking, and always runs to his bedroom window, head out, to catch his breath. Waking up is the problem, the fear. And now, as the girl picks up the drumsticks, as she smiles at him and kicks a loud thump on the bass, once, twice, he sees only her across the liquid room, relief, relief, inhalation, and he could float here forever, free—

4

LUCHO

>   counts
>   a 7 evaporates
>   and numbers now
>   vacant
>   are ancient stars:
>   the incalculable grains
>   lie in the earth
>   transformed and

having dusted the last of the drawers with the napkins from the lunch he will not eat, Lucho sits and repositions the photograph frames on his desk – here and there and here again, so that they end up right where they started. The office is far too small. When his old superior had told him that in the capital he'd be an official, have his own room, he had never thought he'd have to struggle to close the door. There's a single column filing cabinet behind the door which is so tightly crammed against the wall that it can't be moved by even a centimetre. His desk has so little space around it that it's easier for him to climb over it to reach his chair than sidestep to it. And yet despite the lack of space, the room feels empty, so much so that Lucho had wondered, on his first day, whether anyone had been informed of his arrival, and later on, when no one knocked, also wondered whether his post existed at all. The only object left by his predecessor was a terrible painting of the Great General with a blue sky backdrop. And every time the door opens it gently touches the poster, leaving the General's face smudged with cloudy white strokes.

Today, Lucho listens carefully for steps outside. Major Matta had called for a two-thirty meeting. Lucho had accepted but still doesn't know what it's about, and while he's been waiting, he has decided to memorise some figures:

- 1,000,000 x toilet rolls (army use only),
- Catering: 2,000 x wine, tea, coffee,
- 2 x patriotic paintings. Orders are 'Heroes on Horseback wielding elegant sword' as per formal request,
- 2 x cargo ships. US. Bullets. Helmets,
- FAMAE. Shipment 1. Rifle. 500. 2,000 tonnes ammo,
- 1x trial botulinic substance (chemical development), Butantan,
- A group of four communists *trying* (interpretation) to steal lorry filled with donated clothes for the church.

   SIDE NOTE: Everything must come either too early or too late, because to be on time does not allow one to show the demands on one's time made by other important business.

It's not like the meeting will be about anything important. Major Matta, a man whose fearful anger has subsided to boredom as the years have passed, is now best known for his need to share a bottle. He never went home, roaming the offices instead, like a ghost, haunting anyone who appeared to be busy. Lucho had even heard secretaries refer to him as 'Major Hinge,' because, they said, you couldn't open a door without seeing him. Lucho too has begun to roam the corridors in his spare time (and most of it was spare, wasted, how was it almost Friday?). He has even taken to smoking again, in secret, of course, always stopping at least two hours before going back home to Ramona – and perhaps it was all precisely to see if she'd say something about it, anything at all – one cig is ten minutes of life now in the air, she used to say, evaporated, invisible, selfish. God he misses those days. She had a habit of extending sentences when they started seeing each other because he'd told her he wanted to be a poet. Also because she was always uncomfortable with silences. 'No doubt we will find each other when the sky opens anew.' 'Yes, see you tomorrow,' he'd answer. Now every night with her back turned to him and in silence, he imagines her counting the minutes with her fingers, falling asleep to time fading in puffs, the darkness of tar, evaporated, invisible, selfish too. He lights a cigarette. He's being dramatic, he's fine, she's fine. It's boredom, that's what it is. He could always use the time to read and write about all the great men who no doubt had at one point become bored too, sat drinking with ghosts.

    His father had once told him that the difference between an important job and a waste of time wasn't in the money you made, who you worked for, or who worked for you, and certainly not whether you loved or hated it. 'No, it's about figures, all about numbers. Why will the television be so important in the future?' he'd asked Lucho, showing him pictures from ads in American newspapers and magazines before sets had even arrived in Chile. 'Because showing an image is more powerful than giving you the freedom to imagine it, and it will reach more people,' Lucho said. 'That's all true, a kind of manipulation,' his father said. And then, deep in thought, he added, 'It's simply about numbers, the quantity of people involved in the transaction. You can now throw a stone in the Mapocho and convince people a tsunami is coming. Empty Santiago with a single stone. That's the difference between doing something that matters and something useless. Never forget that. Tell me how many people Neruda's verses have changed. That's why he's in politics now. Even *he* knows better. You shouldn't waste your time writing either. Never forget it.'

> And he
> never forgot.

Lucho can hear people gathering outside his office. He stands ready and picks up a cutting from a pile of papers he has never got round to reading. The top line says, *Where we stand in a democratic Chile*. He folds it in two.

'Díaz,' Major Matta says, offering a limp salute.

'Major,' Lucho says, doing the same.

'At ease,' Matta says and whispers to his two guards to wait outside.

'Can I offer you a drink, sir?' Lucho asks, opening a bottom drawer, knowing exactly what Matta drinks.

'Cognac, if you have any.'

'Of course,' Lucho says. He's already pouring some into two old crystal glasses he inherited from his father, a dove motif carved on the base. Lucho sits facing the Major from behind the desk and, raising his glass, offers the customary *For Chile* before (barely) taking a sip. The Major downs his and Lucho pours him another, which he downs again.

'So...' the Major begins.

'I'm passing on the news of the Communist Caravan that's stealing church donations. And the Americans are late again.'

'Good,' the Major says. 'That sounds good, it really does. You have it under control, then.'

The Major stands. He looks at a framed picture of Pablo on one of the filing cabinets. Lucho hopes the Major doesn't open any of the drawers because they're all empty. When he'd arrived, Captain Ernesto, who'd been moved to a lesser position (with fewer numbers, fewer figures to deal with), had taken all the old files with him, all the stories he'd conjured out of countless stacks of inventory, and had them destroyed. He'd told Lucho it was a security issue but when Lucho had asked to see at least a sample, one with made-up numbers even, Ernesto said: 'You come up with your own shit – see how long you last.'

Now the Major just stands there with the framed picture in his hand. It shows Pablo as a little boy, crying on the lap of a clown. Lucho tries to come up with a comment on the picture but is surprised he doesn't remember much outside the frame, not where Ramona was – where is Ramona now? Where has she been? – and he can't even remember the year the picture was taken. He can only think it's from a time when he was glad Pablo was getting older.

'It's a complicated time,' Matta says, putting the picture down. 'And complicated times, well, they require solutions. We have a lot of faith in you and your work. Very meticulous.'

Lucho still has no idea who *we* are, or whether it's just that Matta has always spoken of himself in the plural.

'Above me, they're always asking me for more, more and then even more. Endless, this job, wouldn't you agree? So now we have to ask more from you too.'

'What is it, sir?'

'Chile is changing. I'm sure you can feel it too.'

His father used to say that you can tell an imbecile from someone's ability to separate a country from its people. '*You* are changing, you piece of shit,' he would have said.

Lucho pauses before answering. What has feeling got to do with anything? The word itself reminds him of his youth, when he used to spend whole afternoons trying to understand the way Neruda used images to convey moods, back when he believed in that *process* (another word he despises for its fear of declaring anything ever finished, that modern fear of committing to an absolute end), he really did, that simple objects could capture what he called the epic states, loss in an ocean, love in an empanada, betrayal in the pebbles of a wall, sadness in the scissors of a hairdresser. All that work, all those wasted verses, to merely say he'd been in love, had lost someone, that he felt sad and betrayed. 'Feelings? If you need a man to jump in the ocean while the rest stare at their own shoes, give them feelings,' his father had said. A line to remember for his work on Arturo Prat later:

> He jumped
> and they felt
> the sea.

'The sea,' he says out loud.
　'I'm sorry?'
　'My son. In that picture. We were by the sea.'
　'I guess that's what I wanted to talk about.'
　Lucho thinks of Pablo with a guitar, long hair and the poncho he used to wear in San Fernando. He's glad there are no pictures of him looking like that, embarrassing whenever they crossed paths with people who knew him. 'How old is he? Really? He looks younger and I can give you the address of the new barbers in town, The Mutes, yes, The Mutes, because they talk so much [laughter], and take care, take care of him but thank the Virgin he isn't my son.' Lucho breathes in deep, light-hearted with relief at not having to be in that fucking town anymore. Though he misses that Pablo sometimes. He misses him at peace.
　'I'm not sure I understand, sir,' Lucho says.
　'The future, Lucho, memory and the future.'
　His father had swept the floors in the stables of Don Pablo's farm, the San José de Toro estate in Chimbarongo, near San Fernando, just like his father had done before him. One summer morning, the workers in the *fundo* had gathered outside the stone

corn silos, right by the stables where Ángel, aged twelve, swept cow dung into neat piles to collect in potato sacks to sell because the *fundo* had produced, Ángel recalled Don Pablo saying, an excess of shit, before laughing and correcting himself, 'surplus investment deposits'.

But that particular morning, the workers had gathered in a circle, shouting and laughing, and Ángel had gone to see what the fuss was all about. He would later come to say that, even at that early age, he had been disgusted at how easily the workers had fired each other up into a rage, or had laughed at anything – to fit in with the group. The Mob, he called it. But when he'd gone that day to check, he'd laughed and clapped with them before he could see into the hollow at their centre.

> Let me see.
> Look. Come.
> Let me see.
> What happened?
> This bitch.
> She better do as we say.
> Or we'll show her.
> I wouldn't mind showing her something.
> Laughs and claps.
> Yeah, the bitch would like that.
> Yeah, she would, they all do.

Ángel had seen that it was Olga. Since Doña Emilia had died, Olga had taken care of the chickens. Ángel had to teach her that they weren't pets by taking her little hands in his and, following Don Pablo's orders, they had strangled a chicken together. She had cried, but would talk much later, after a long dinner, about killing the birds, and how much each death had made her think of the pleasure, the safety and warmth of Ángel's hands on hers. 'Pain is not always a sign that something's wrong,' she concluded, with Ángel nodding in agreement, and so Lucho did too.

'What happened, what did she do?' Ángel had asked an old man in the crowd.

She had left everything open at night. She let the chickens walk into the corn. So what? It's full of bats now. So what? They shat all over the corn. And? And the cats killed the chickens. And then there was Ángel walking the long corridor to Don Pablo's office, right by the candlelit Virgin Mary, whose cast hands had fallen off in the last quake, and who stood crooked by the army pilot medals in the display cabinet. He had knocked.

'Don Pablo, it was me who let the bats in to spoil the corn.' And Don Pablo had led him out. And Don Pablo made him carry a rifle. And when Don Pablo arrived, the crowd went quiet. And then one of the workers, the one who'd been shouting the loudest, and the one who had Olga held by the wrist, walked up to Don Pablo, took his *chupalla* hat off, didn't, couldn't look at the boss in the eyes, and, 'Señor, *patroncito*, *Señor*,' but Don Pablo, whose face was barely visible behind his dark sunglasses, his black velvet *chupalla* hat, walked into the corn silo to the collective sigh of the workers, they could hear the wind again, the dust collecting, and, 'Ángel, come here, Ángel,' and Don Pablo gave him two shells. 'Know how to load them?'

'No, never.'

'Here.' They loaded their rifles. 'Now, see the bats there? In the ceiling. Can you see?'

'Yes, yes, I can see.'

'Aim at them. In the name of the Father, the Son, the Holy Spirit.' And the bats made a wave, a black tornado, and they went out the silo door.

'But what's the other bullet for?'

And Don Pablo smiled at him.

'You know how to load it now?'

'Yes, yes, now I know.'

And he loaded it, did as he was told.

They walked outside, the workers were still there, waiting to be dismissed, to be told what to do as well, and to (hopefully) catch any last drop of drama from that calm summer morning dew, and: 'You, Osvaldo, come here please,' and Osvaldo let go of Olga's wrist.

'And if there are nine adults and one child, who is responsible?'

'Don Pablo, I had told, I mean, I had told her. And then another boy came to me taking the...'

'Is this place run by children? Ángel, come here please.' And he did as he was told. 'Osvaldo, if we are doing your work for you, then you are...'

'But no, Don Pablo, I don't, I mean, I...'

'So maybe you do half a job. Ángel, here.' And he walked to Don Pablo's side. 'Osvaldo, spread your left hand. No, but Don Pablo... Spread your hand or I'll have to guess where it is.'

Osvaldo takes his hand out of his pocket and spreads it above his head, like he's asking a question, waiting to ask, and 'Just like I told you, Ángel,' and he did as he was told. He would forever think of this moment, not the blood, not the gun, but Olga's beautiful smile spreading like a butterfly as the dust settled that morning by the corn.

'What about the future? Should we even talk about it? Aren't predictions as dangerous as guessing?'

'We're creating it,' Major Matta says. 'Would you agree with that, that we are central to the future of this great nation?'

'Yes.'

'You see, and I hope, you know,' Major Matta pauses and locks his lips with his index finger, 'that this won't leave this room.'

'Of course.' Lucho almost grabs a pen and paper to take notes.

'Because we trust you.'

'And I hope I deserve such...'

'The system, the whole thing, will change one day.'

'The system?'

'This. Everything.'

'I don't know what—'

'But we can secure our place once it happens.'

'I will not—'

'I'm here to ask you, well...' He shakes the empty glass in the air and Lucho serves up another. 'We've been looking for someone and we need your help finding him.'

'Can't you get *los tiras* to do it?'

'Well. We could, yes. We could do that.'

'But?'

'But I think you know him.'

Lucho straightens his back. In San Fernando, he knew everyone, even those who didn't know him. He knew, for example, that the man who made prosthetics in Chacabuco Street had been a communist because his ex-wife reported him and Lucho had seen the beating. He knew the teachers from the *Normal* who were sent South to the prisons (they had taught him too). He knew old classmates who were sent North, some of whom came back and talked about dogs raping their wives in this city, this very Santiago, or so the reports said, while they got their genitals electrocuted, buried alive, tossed from helicopters into the sea. Knowing anyone wasn't special. You always knew someone. Everyone knew that.

'I'm quite busy with inventory reports and the press. Everyone knows everyone in San Fernando anyway.'

'Someone else will take over your writing. There's always someone else.'

'Wouldn't this need to be approved?'

'I'm not trying to step on any toes here. The thing is, he worked for the newspaper your father owned. In San Fernando, yes.

The Region. Turns out he became a poet. Quite big in Spain and Sweden, of all places. I don't get it myself. His stuff. Seems to me it's unreadable. But sadly he has a following here too. A man by the name of Pedro Castro. Does it ring any bells?'

'No. I don't think so.'

'Here's his book. Don't read it. It's awful. But it has his picture in the back. I've been told you used to be quite the writer yourself.'

'A phase.'

'Well, they told me you may know where such types might gather in the city.'

Lucho looks at the title. *Space Verses*.

'Is this really something you want me to do? There must be others more suited to it.'

'It's why we brought you here, Lucho. He was exiled. And now we believe he is coming back. We can't allow a communist to start writing like this, what with all the other fantasists that are running around now. Especially if he's famous abroad. You know how people can be.'

'But what about the inventories?'

'Officially, that's what you're doing. But we were told you can do better work than that. We'll see. Is this something you can do?'

'I'd need to think about it.'

'Well, San Fernando will be happy to take you back if you have to think too much. The countryside air is good for that. We've spoken about it. It would be fine. There is always someone else. We thought you would know. Your father always spoke about your ambitions.'

The Major downs the last of his cognac and, pushing down on the armrests of his chair, stands with a slight tremble. Lucho bows and Matta waves back lazily without looking at him, as if he's fending off an old fly.

'I'm glad we got to talk,' he says.

'Have a good day, sir.'

'Results, Lucho. I'll need results.'
'Of course.'
'Oh, and one last thing,' he says, already out in the corridor.
'Yes?'
'Very sad what happened to your father. We knew him well. Very sad indeed.'
'Thank you.'

Lucho climbs over his desk and shuts the door a little too hard. His father had been right, poetry was his problem, and as it often happens when he thinks about his poetry, about his youth, he also thinks of Ramona, who will no doubt feign interest with that laugh (often too loud), the accidental sighs whenever he mentions the country's need for hundreds of thousands of who-knows-what, and how he misses feeling closer to her, and touching her once or twice, seeing her once or twice and even then for only a couple of minutes, missing her in fractions, in small numbers, the way one day ends and its parts belong to the eternity of the past.

> In the ocean
> there's nothing worth
> looking for,
> Ángel had once said.
> Whatever falls,
> sinks forever.

Or at least it's what Lucho imagines his father might have said, were he with Lucho right now, looking at the fading General and foaming paint strokes against the cheap golden frame, the broken sails angled to the stars, falling, falling, not a soul left onboard. Never forget, his father would have said, pointing at the soon-to-be wreck, the stars are falling, dying on the surface of the ocean, do you see? Do you not see even they are at the mercy of the tides, the direction of the wind, the strength and pull of the current?

And so the day passes. And then he gets home, too late, and sees the glow coming from the glass pane above the downstairs bathroom, the room which Pablo may as well call his bedroom (he spends hours there at night). Lucho smells stale tobacco, and so he goes to the kitchen, slices a lemon and squeezes a half on each hand, satisfied the scent is now faint enough to be someone else's fault.

And then he heads upstairs with two cups of water and greets Ramona with a kiss on the cheek and finds she's already left him a cup on his bedside table.

'Sorry I'm late,' he says.

'It's okay,' she says, with her back toward him, the bedsheets covering most of her face. 'Was your day alright?'

'Yes, thank you. Had a lot to do.'

She shuffles.

'Thanks for the water.'

'It's okay.'

'A lorry filled with clothes was stolen today. More than a thousand articles of clothing. Can you believe it? For the church, too.'

'Savages,' she says, resting a foot on his.

Lying there in the dark, he watches the silhouette of a bird on the peach tree branch outside the window. And then the shadow disappears and he turns to Ramona, who he's almost certain is whispering in her sleep: three, two, one, three, two, and so it goes.

POETRY NOTES – BOOK OF RAMONA
Afloat in the Pacific: Travelling the Great Sea

I knew on the second day
that I was heavy bored

and even the fish now skipped by her ear
the sea shedding some of
its gold like a lost candle.

I draw a line in the water,
a trembling chasm
between us,
the foam of past sorrows,
folds into itself
like a flat mirror.

How simple to draw another,
find it in your eyes
to let it go.

5

RAMONA

would talk about technique if Don Francisco, Chile's biggest TV host, ever asked her about the most difficult parts of an acting career on his *Giant Saturday* show. She would smile at the crowd of regular people, spot someone who aspired to be her (she'd know this because they'd be wearing her signature overgrown shoulder-padded blazer), someone young and who could be pretty if only she were allowed, if only she were as rich as her, and she'd surprise Don Francisco by getting up and walking to this woman, taking her hand to the clapping and chanting of a crowd who couldn't believe their luck, being so so near Ramona, and I TOUCHED HER they'd tell their families later that day, I BREATHED THE SAME AIR. And Ramona would sit this young woman beside her, direct her towards the chair slowly because her legs would be so tight and most likely quivering from excitement and shock and Don Francisco would be confused and she would wait for him to ask, 'Oh, typical Ramona, this, isn't it? What will she do next? A true people's celebrity.' And the crowd would laugh. Ramona would stand up, look right into a camera (the shoulders-and-face profile, where she looks best) and 'I used to be just like her,' she would say. 'We all stand a chance, really, we do, you do. You are a star and you don't even know it. Grab what you want by the throat and do not let go,' and Don Francisco would look a bit worried when the young woman started to stare at him and she—

> LO QUE TUS OJOS NO VEN: A TELENOVELA
>
> #EPISODE 2
>
> BLACK SCREEN
>
> ISABEL URRUTIA (V.O.)
> Don't lie, peasant. I've seen how he looks at you.
>
> ISABEL URRUTIA
> Liar! And now you break my things, my inheritance.

She is more than half an hour late to El Charlie's special class, which isn't in the usual gym. She took her pills early last night to avoid the morning nausea, and she got up early too, left plenty of time, had even waxed the kitchen floor before Mariela, who never left it appropriately shiny, could get up to make the whole place dirty again. The truth is Ramona hadn't been able to decide what to wear. Alicia had not mentioned acting again, at least not anything useful. They'd met twice over the last week at a café near the Bellas Artes, where Alicia took Ramona to see a 'Pictorial Reunion with Chile,' a photography exhibition about the Andes. Even Alicia, who walked past the pictures rather quickly for someone appreciating the artistic framing of a mountain peak (curved tops, light dusting to imply wind, the shadow of a condor mid-flight, the sun rising in a blue hue), even she at one point had muttered, 'Snow is snow, I guess.' Ramona had nodded and gone along with it all, because when you want something and you THINK POSITIVE, what you really mean is doing something you don't want to do so that one day you can. As the psychic in

Don Francisco's show once said, 'Ugly doors are not symbols of the room within'. Although even then Ramona had thought, yes, yes, but often they are.

But what had stayed with Ramona, and what had worried her on the days leading up to now, as she walked to her audition, was what Alicia had told her once they'd sat to have their coffees: 'Good actors never stop acting. I like that you're always in character.' Ramona had nodded, but wondered whether the audition had already started.

And what do actresses wear at auditions? Avoid all black. That was easy. Beware of heels. Easy again. She hadn't worn any in a long time. Accessorise. Make them remember, say things like: 'What was her name, the woman with the flowery headband?' And so Ramona's wearing her flowery headband now. But what else? She doesn't want to appear desperate. She takes it off and her hair falls back in place slowly, and not quite right. And she had tried to find something which showed the lines of her body. That had always been standard audition advice but she's not sure this time. The optical illusion of vertical lines. That's what she needs. So many vertical lines. But none of the clothes in her wardrobe have lines that fit her. Apparently even creases work so long as there are lines. So she had creased a pair of jeans and a t-shirt and she looked – Mariela agreed – utterly homeless. And then she had decided on one of Lucho's white shirts, just for the vertical line of buttons. That would have to do. And then she hadn't taken the rain into account, the way the city lay bare, the cold empty streets, the office workers huddled together, all looking the same, in greys and blacks and whites and in silence, like penguins in the red ice of summer morning skies in Santiago, groups of workers looking for signs of life, or death, in the other workers standing still on the opposite side of the pavement. And the bus driver had said, he'd looked back at them all, no, at her, and he—

```
ISABEL URRUTIA shows LUZ MARIA the vase even
though she knows she can't see it.

                    LUZ MARIA
            It was an accident, I
            swear!

ISABEL URRUTIA holds up her whip.

                    ISABEL URRUTIA
            Take off your shirt.
```

The bus driver had looked at her and said, 'There's no way in hell I can keep going,' and he pointed at the sewage overflowing onto the road (the real River Mapocho, the one that runs underneath, under the whole of Santiago and under everyone's feet) and the passengers had left their seats with quiet insults, *tu madre*, *por la chucha*, the mothers pushing their strollers, waiting under the striped awnings from which the rain no longer slid but built and built, the weight of the sky on the thin sheets above them and so Ramona found—

Yes, Ramona found herself unable to ask for an alternative route because the city overwhelmed her with its options, the wide avenues lined by office buildings she will never set foot in, the irrelevant construction work, growing, always growing to the sky, a smog cloud. All the roads were unfamiliar, wrong and confusing and inadequate and she wanted to go home, back to San Fernando, back to the floods she could recognise and deal with, the Tinguiririca River bursting from its banks every winter, the consistency of its sad little disasters, a tremor, not a quake, the cheap tin porch roofing that TRATRATRARAed itself to life in the rain while Ramona, alone then as she is now (but now she knows it, which is worse), thought about the life she should have had in Santiago, and how late, how old and how late and tired we must have become to realise that it was right that, as her late mother had told her during one of her day-long hangovers, when a door closes, shuts in your face, either lock it tight or burn your way inside. Or was it that—

She still thinks about it now. The acting. The roles. *Her* roles. The fans. Well, her future fans at least. She tries not to. Don Francisco had said that a crucial factor to POSITIVE THINKING was letting go. Hang on to new things. Always new. So in a deeply impulsive moment, Ramona had bought a narrow red carpet to lead her from the entrance of the house to the bedroom. She's glad Lucho never asks her about the things she does to the house (or anything else – does he ever ask about anything else?) because when the *maestro* had come to fit the red carpet on top of the wood, he had confessed he'd measured the whole thing wrong, and the carpet was only long enough to reach the upstairs bathroom.

This episode had confirmed one of her fears: it wasn't just San Fernando. The entire damn country was tacky. She finally understood what her stepfather had meant when he insisted Latin America's problem was that it had transitioned too quickly from a horsecar to a pickup. Ramona had told the *maestro* that it had always been the plan to just run the carpet to the bathroom anyway, and fired him hours later, and then spent the rest of the afternoon anxious, eating-whole-chocolate-bars anxious, flushing-when-she-caught-her-own-reflection anxious, about Lucho coming back and asking why the hell there was now a red carpet leading to the bathroom, and anxious about the fact that even though she may once, a long, long time ago, have had

> LUZ MARIA
> Please, Señora, please, no.
>
> ISABEL URRUTIA
> I will not ask you again.
>
> LUZ MARIA starts to undress, crying.
>
> LUZ MARIA (V.O.)
> Ay, Diosito, Baby Jesus, please help me.

the talent to become a great, such a great actress with excessive talent, even despite all that, she just can't pull off ironic gestures. She imagined him saying, 'Don't worry, *mi amor*' (though she can't remember the last time he'd called her that), 'Don't worry, you were only meant to play tragedies.' But 'nice' is all he said, and kissed her on the forehead. 'It's very nice, elegant even, and it looks great with all the light coming from the dome. I love that glass dome. Don't you like it? So much light.' And then he'd poured her and himself a large glass of water before going to bed early so they could both not-sleep next to one another, in silence, and take toilet breaks through the night (inconsistently spaced so as to appear to be sleeping and then waking and sleeping again) and now—

And now that the rain has stopped, she looks to one side of the road, then the other, and the puddles disappearing slowly into the water drains, and the people into their people-drains, and now the avenues are open, now they're even emptier, so empty she has the passing feeling that she'd imagined everyone there, herself there with them, another sleepless night in the crowded lonely city, and now Ramona is lost.

She walks a few steps in one direction, and she looks up at the peaks of the Andes above the concrete rooftops, glad that they at least have not moved though she's not really sure if—

Alicia had called her last night to remind her of today's session. No mention of acting. She'd called and asked if she could come over to the new house, and if she could invite other women from the gym, bring some cakes, *queques*, but not Chilean *queques*, more like *kuchen queques*, cream *queques* with raspberries, Argentinean *alfajores* and *pan amasado* for a housewarming tea. And Ramona was listening to all this on the phone right at the top of the stairs and all she could see was the red carpet, feel her red face and the 'wings' still under her arms turn cold and damp, and then, 'We could pop over, just give us a time, no, we know the house – no, we know, don't worry, we know it's always messy to move, a work in progress, yes, yes, don't – no, no, just an informal, yes, a quick visit, but – Ramona, this will only make us more curious,' *laugh*, and Ramona in turn said, 'My mother, she is sick, and she needs care, but maybe we can do something when she gets better.' 'What?' 'No, it's just a terrible flu, you know how it is...' A terrible lie too, and that was that. If her mother were still alive, Ramona would have called her to apologise right after, or tell her not to come anymore, that she didn't need to visit, to prove anything to anyone, that Ramona would go to San Fernando, that they'd walk over to the plaza, go to the circus by the Colchagua stadium to see the unfunny clowns, the animals, the caged life between drinks, the roaring between hangovers, and sorry, sorry. But how do you apologise to the dead?

And how, in their silence, can they apologise to us in turn? (Or can they only forgive?) Then Ramona cast her mother back to the corner of her mind, the room she had occupied through

> THE DOOR opens. LUIS FELIPE walks in, alarmed by what he sees.
>
> LUIS FELIPE
> What do you think you're doing?
>
> ISABEL URRUTIA
> Mi amor!
>
> LUZ MARIA
> Ay, Don Luis, help me, please help me.

all these years – and that's when she'd noticed, the way you notice imperfections only after you call something perfect, the irrefutable, irredeemable ugliness of her windows. How could she not have seen this before? The only new part of the house. Plastic, functional frames – plastic! And the beige-painted iron bars shaped like grapevines with little spheres, awful steel grapes, tasteless, and yet the view, yes, it was magnificent; the Andes, the quiet hills she had once been closer to, that she'd once walked on before meeting Lucho – did that view make the frame worthwhile? She'd have them boarded up except Lucho would certainly say she'd gone mad again, that she needed to see the doctor again and go on more walks, longer distances, do more exercise. 'Too energetic for your own good,' he'd say, new and stronger pills, and he'd find out she hadn't exactly taken all of her old—

STAY CALM, BE POSITIVE, HAPPINESS IS HOME

and this was now hers, this empty crowded avenue, the still buses, this shelter from the city rain. She's fine, she's fine. POSITIVE THINKING fine. TRUE JOY, letting go blablabla. And there's always the basement. Lucho calls it a basement but it's not actually under the house. There's a pebbled path that leads to a stone staircase, at the bottom of which is a concrete door. It was once used to keep detainees, Lucho said, but nothing more than keep them. She hadn't wanted to know more so she hadn't asked. She can put everything that's wrong with the house in there. Yes, it's spacious enough.

The first time she had stepped inside the basement, Ramona couldn't tell where the walls were, and its single hanging bulb lit only the middle, a spotlight glowing so dim that it only emphasised the vast emptiness of the room. This was a space that would never fill up, she thought, and she was glad because that day she'd had, for a few hours, the powerful and sudden motivation to start an antiques shop in one of the markets. The old city would have everything she needed, she thought, all the old things (though she couldn't think of anything more specific than a large mirror because it was the only object she owned with any brass on it) would be there for her to buy from the high Santiago families and to sell to low, no, to up-and-coming families on the wrong side of the river. But then she had gone out on her first walk and found nothing but fake wooden furniture and mirrors with plastic frames and so she quickly abandoned that idea as well. It's fine, it's fine, she'll find something else to do in the basement, her calling, because she has so little right now, owns so little, she could fit her whole life in there, like a museum to herself, her potential, yes, yes, the possibilities of which she still can't imagine, in a city large enough to finally allow her to dream and now—

In Los Leones, by the black lion statues guarding nothing, she takes a deep breath and walks toward Baquedano, following

> LUIS FELIPE
> What is this, Isabel? Explain!
>
> LUIS FELIPE
> Are you okay, Miss?
> What's your name?
>
> LUIS FELIPE covers LUZ MARIA with a cowhide blanket.
>
> LUZ MARIA
> Luz María. Thank you, God bless you. Thank you.

the path her bus would have taken. The address Alicia gave her is in Manuel Montt, just before Plaza Italia.

When she finally arrives, she's at least forty-five minutes late and her hair is dripping wet, and her shoes flooded inside (a story for Don Francisco about her initial hardships and how she has defeated them) and she considers turning back when another woman rings 7 in the apartment block and turns to Ramona as the door buzzes and—

'Do you want to come in? Are you here for El Charlie's class?' She holds the door open for Ramona. A TV model type, all the lines of her body apparent through absolutely uncreased leggings. The most vertical woman in the world. Even her duffel bag is tiny. And, protruding out of an unzipped gap, a capped bottle of water from a foreign brand Ramona doesn't recognise.

'Yes, thank you. Thank you, I'm Ramona,' she says, but only gets back a silent smile.

She walks in behind the woman who climbs the stairs quick and effortless, so that Ramona starts to sweat trying to catch up. She also notices (she should have asked – why does she never ask?) that the woman is carrying a gym mat under her arm. She turns to go back out but to what, Ramona? To what and to whom and until—

A door opens.

'I'm Ramona,' she says to a different woman behind a reception desk, whose face is tightened back by a long blond ponytail. This woman doesn't even half-smile. She ticks Ramona's name off a list and stares at her.

'Where should... Here?' Ramona asks, pointing at the only door connected to the reception.

'Where everyone is. Yes.'

'Thank you!'

She pulls the door a couple of times, making the whole frame rattle before noticing the PUSH sign on it. Inside, the room is full of young women on mats, bending into half-moons, and they turn their heads and she's glad the storm outside has begun again, tap-tap-tapping against the windows so that no one has to hear her bones cracking as she sits, matless, on the hard wooden floor. Everyone looks SO YOUNG, SO PRETTY AND YOUNG. She thinks she recognises the Channel 13 weather lady, yes, her, with her colourful headband, she was in *Giant Saturday* once, now she is just a few mats away from her, she who Don Francisco had called The Mother of Chile's Rain, and who Ramona accused of not knowing how to—

PROJECT YOUR VOICE AND BREATH CONTROL:

1. Yelling uses vocal cords. Projection uses the diaphragm. The Mother of Chile's Rain has a pitch so high she most definitely cannot talk at the end of the day.
2. Do the 'ha' exercise. Take in a deep breath, expand your lungs and abdomen, then force all the air out on a big 'ha!', using all the air at once.

> **LUIS FELIPE**
> What in all of God's
> Kingdom happened to you?
>
> LUIS FELIPE leaves with LUZ MARIA.
>
> **ISABEL URRUTIA**
> What happened to us, Luis
> Felipe. Us.

3. Visualise: visualise a spot on the wall, preferably in a large room, and visualise hitting that spot. Move to a bigger space.
4. But what if I need to scream?

To what. To whom. She catches El Charlie's eye. He smiles. She smiles. She limbers herself up and bends like the rest of them. But still, somehow, on the full mirror against the wall facing them, a full moon.

6

PABLO

is sitting in front of Francisco and Clara, who are a little too close to one another – elbows touching, sharing each other's breath – and he finds it hard to look either of them in the eyes.

'So, are you going to play it?' Clara asks him.

'You don't have to if you don't want to,' Francisco says.

'It's just... It's a work in progress, you know?'

'We're all works in progress, man. Life is. So I guess music is too,' Francisco says, kissing Clara on the forehead.

'We need the songs, man,' Clara says.

'That too,' Francisco says.

Pablo grabs the guitar, strums an Am, tunes the B string, which always rattles on the fretboard. It still sounds off. He can feel Francisco and Clara's gaze on his hands, cold and sweaty. He considers not playing a thing, telling them instead about his nightmare last night, the way the ocean recoiled, how it revealed the beached corpses of drumkits and guitar amps – and he knew that they'd been there forever, barnacle-filled, a coral reef of bands who never made it, not even to land, and he walked to one of the beached amps and plugged a guitar in the shape of a carp through a cable made of seaweed and all that came out was the sound of the swelling tides, the foam and fizz, some deadly harmonics, and him, him and his guitar waiting to disappear completely.

'It's a waltz,' Pablo says, but gets no answer. 'It's about a dream, I think,' he adds, and Francisco smiles. There is no song. He had merely sat in the basement and strummed random notes to a simple waltz before declaring the beat too much of a commitment and abandoning it entirely. He couldn't figure out how to transition to open chords. If he were ever to play at the National Stadium, that change would be the most important moment of his life.

'Wait up – wait, two secs,' Francisco says, hand on his forehead and smiling wide. 'That's a bit "New Chilean Song" isn't it? I mean, it's fine, but you know, it sounds kind of tragic. Don't you think so too, Clara, that it's a bit too sad? We really, I mean, I was thinking of something more hopeful, you know? More experimental. But sorry, sorry, play on, we could probably still use parts of it, maybe even the main melody.'

'No, you're right, man. It's okay, we can come up with something else for now.' Pablo is relieved. Though playing in a simpler 4/4 would offer the promise of a neat return, repetition is impossible to hide and he didn't come up with anything last night, nothing at all to follow the same chord progression he's been trapped in for years. It was the first lick he learnt to play. And it's looking like it may be the last too. Am–E the waltz. Am–E the ballad. Am–E the rock song and the folk anthem, the fast *cueca* and the slow dance.

'I brought a song,' Francisco says. 'See what you think.'

'It's great,' Clara says. 'He played it to me before you got here. It's really something.'

Francisco starts playing his little number, all major chords, so hopeful, too hopeful, the kind of song, Pablo thinks, the kind you'd play at someone's second wedding, too much, just too much happiness.

Pablo stands as Francisco goes into a chorus about *united voices* and *working together* and *men being brothers*.

Francisco calls the place they're in 'the warehouse', but it's more like an abandoned industrial garage; a secluded barn in a side street at the end of Rojas Magallanes in La Florida. Outside the little room where they're playing, there's a yellow tractor, its hood missing, its engine gone, cobwebbed and rusting. And next to that is a round wooden coffee table with a full ashtray and a small radio whispering crackled news pieces and ads. There are dried-up leaves covering most of the floor, as if it'd been a garden once, and even the base of a severed oak tree. Pablo asked where the leaves came from and Francisco pointed at the broken windows all around them, and he said, 'It's the most open space in Santiago, and our generation shouldn't be the one to clean up the remnants of older seasons,' and Clara smiled and kissed him. But after that, he asked Pablo to always remember to lock up the front doors with an oversized padlock.

By the time Francisco finished his song, which included a long and slow solo without any backing, no root chords, no vibrato or tremolo, so that the highest notes reverbed their flat way out of the barn along with the breeze sweeping the carpet of dead leaves, by the time all that ended it was dark outside.

'That's so good.'

'Thank you.'

'Should we add drums to it?'

'I think less is more on this one.'

'Yeah, maybe you're right.'

Francisco leaves the guitar by Pablo.

'I'm gonna go take a piss.'

And he walks out humming part of the solo he's just played. Pablo looks at his watch. He should have been well on his way home by now. He's meant to be meeting La Dani, who said she had important news to share, something she couldn't tell him over the phone, something which deserved a visit from San Fernando: 'I need to see you. We need to talk.' They have been together for two years now. A minute more or less...

And he remembers that it had been her who'd told him, been excited to tell him, that Santiago would be the place where he could breathe in all the art in the world, where he'd finally be able to do something important, for that's what he'd once said when she asked what he wanted to do with his life, that he didn't like anything else, nothing at all but music, that a world which condemned fun to the corners of free time from an office was just unfair, hurtful even, and then she'd told him that to her, relationships were the most important part of her life, a kind of fun too, if you tried hard to find it, and that everything else was there to make them easier (had she said 'easier'?), which had sounded a hell of a lot better, kinder, than what he wanted. She did that. Made him into some kind of asshole for wanting something she'd encouraged. It's true, it's true, he just felt a little guilty because he was still feeling lost, trying to think about all the arts with the conviction of someone who understood the connections between them, their molecules, their oxygen, when the truth was he still couldn't breathe; he was still songless, *still*, and maybe that's what happened when relationships got old, when they got tired. They became general. And breathless.

Clara sighs and Pablo opens his mouth to talk, to say, God, you have the best rhythm, even your breath is a beat, that they should both go before Francisco comes back, drop by their houses and grab a simple change of clothes, maybe some tapes, hitch their way up to the desert, leave Chile, make music like the greats do, always out of here. Instead, he hears the rain starting outside, the heavy rattle of old tin roofs. Pigeons flock out of the gaps in the roof. They both look at the birds above them. A white pigeon loses its balance and falls right in front of them.

Clara looks at him all surprised and wide-eyed, and before Pablo can say anything she starts laughing, so he does the same. Cross-legged, she pushes herself closer to him.

'What the hell happened to it?' Francisco surprises them, coming up from behind. He kneels in front of the pigeon. Neither Pablo nor Clara say a thing. The rain gets louder. 'Well, I had an idea just now, when I was pissing.'

'What is it?' Clara asks.

'What do you mean, *what is it*? For my song, THE song, I mean.'

'What?' Pablo asks.

'God, guys, instead of waiting on damn pigeons to fall from the sky, you could... Well, I guess it's easier if we just—'

'He's obsessed,' Clara says. 'He keeps going on about it. The People's Song.'

'It's not just that,' Francisco says. 'It's The True People's Song. I'm not sure what it looks like yet. It's quite simple. Elegant, you know? I'm trying to capture the whole of Santiago in a song.'

'Sounds hard to write lyrics about something so general.'

'I'm not sure it will have lyrics yet.'

'No lyrics?'

'Maybe, I don't know, but I want to go beyond that, you know? Beyond language.'

Pablo tries to meet Clara's gaze but she's practising triplets on her thighs.

'Sounds like a little bit, you know, bullshit,' Clara says, stopping the tapping at what would have been a final crash cymbal.

'Whatever. I'll show you. Not now though. My brother is going to come by soon to check we've locked up.'

Clara and Francisco start packing the drums in a storage room, covering them in an old bedsheet with a pink moth pattern. Francisco leaves his guitar in there too.

'Leave yours too, man,' he says.

'My guitar?'

'What else?'

'Is it safe?'

Clara smiles at Francisco, does a triplet on the door and they start heading out. Pablo leaves his guitar on top of a wooden bucket in the corner of the room.

He walks out and the rain clatters louder and Francisco and Clara are waiting at the door, where the white brightness of the clouds makes them both look like shadows.

'Don't worry about it. My brother works here in the week. He can carry the stuff back to mine on Monday,' Francisco says. 'But now we have to hurry.'

'Where are we going?'

'Somewhere. Who cares?'

'Come on, let's go already,' Clara says.

Pablo shuts his eyes, notices he's shaking, steps over the threshold but he can't feel the rain. In all of his nightmares, it's the back of the neck where he feels the cold moisture gather first; from here the drops slide down his back, weaving a trail which eventually stops in his lower spine, right in the middle, and that's when he wakes up, not because of the terror, but because that's the moment when he chokes, when he stops breathing.

'Come on,' Clara says, tapping his ribs with her elbow as she holds her sweater over herself and Pablo. They run together, Francisco leading the way. Pablo notices Clara's bitten nails, the faint smell of strawberry lipstick and sweat, her syncopated run, the way people run in the movies, full arm swings, light-footed, almost expecting to float.

A bus passes by without stopping and 'Fuck You!' Francisco shouts, throwing a pebble at its rear. The bus stops and reverses. Francisco signals Hurry, Oh shit, and they laugh and run down the avenue to stop another micro bus, which opens its clunky door.

'Amigo, we're students, would it be okay if you—'

'For fuck's sake.'

'Just to Universidad Católica, amigo, please.'

The *micrero* doesn't even look at them but waves them in, '*Huevones, pendejos*,' he mutters.

They make for the back, where they can sit in a row. There's a guy on the fourth seat, smoking and hiding the cigarette but not even trying to guide the smoke out the window. Clara uses her t-shirt to wipe the condensation from the window.

'If you can't see through it, what's the point of a window?' she whispers to Pablo. Rubbing at the fog, the liquid circles of light disappear and flower-shaped mosaics of purple and green swell up to become the grey, sharp city. Pablo sighs in relief. He can see dry pavement. No one minds the flooded street corners. Two clowns approach the bus and start juggling when the traffic lights hit red. They walk by car windows and no one gives them any money. One of them tries to juggle with fire torches, but he can't get them to light.

When they get off the bus, Francisco is all, 'We'll be late, we're already too late. Fucking weather.' He says it as he's walking ahead by himself, Clara half-jogging behind him. Pablo should have headed home, been there for La Dani. La Dani who:

- ... doesn't play instruments at all.
- ... smiles at you the way a friend's mother, who you've never met before, does when she hears that all you want to do

with your life is play music. 'Ha! Hmm, Oh, you meant it? I mean it's so great, that age, before you become... before you truly understand.'
- ... talks about her father nonstop, Uncle Miguel, because he appeared in a San Fernando paper, *The Region*, when he closed his bakery, and she thinks it's amazing that Pablo's father edited the article. 'Not a grain of flour spent on the commies,' the piece said, approvingly. The leftist *Guerrillero* paper, before it shut, had called him a 'dough ball' (because he was fat) when he had first opened the bakery, but it had escalated to 'Monsieur Dick Face' once he started selling flour on the black market. Also, Uncle Dick Face is always there playing his crappy Pedro Messone tapes when Pablo visits. That boring bastard.
- ... can't wait to be old. La Dani was dead serious when she said she didn't understand Peter Pan. She hated him. She wants to study. She uses words like 'contribute' and 'duty' and 'sacrifice' when she talks about her own dreams.

It's his fault. When they first met he had been happier, lighter, had never, to his recollection, dreamt of the sea. (He's embarrassed to admit he misses being a child.) They had met at the school chapel. The boys would wait for the girls to cross from their school once the gates were opened at the end of the day. They would then play Dark Room, going in pairs into the confession booth in the chapel, touching each other through the wooden net with carved roses. Pablo hadn't known what to do. He had been able to see her clearly and wished it had indeed been dark. He'd started undoing his tie, but she held her hand out, her fingers through the gaps in the wooden petals, and he took it. They had just stood there, without saying anything, without noticing their classmates leaving and whistling and laughing and knocking on the booth. And despite not being able to even look each other in the eyes, they didn't stop holding hands until they reached the train tracks, where Uncle Miguel had started working as a barrier man, lifting and lowering and ringing his bell all damn day (and night on drunken September holidays) and when he saw Pablo and La Dani, he lowered the barrier even though there was no train coming. Some people complained as a queue started to form in the crossing but: 'Who is this melon head, Daniela?' 'His name is Pablo.' 'I didn't ask his name. I said, *who* is this boy whose head looks like a knee?' It'd been The Mutes' fault, since Pablo's father had always told the hairdressers to leave very little – an inch, not even, maybe – how men should look, tidy and organised, bald. And La Dani had let go of his hand, the barrier lifting, and she'd crossed the tracks and he'd stayed watching her from the other side until the industrial train passed by, endless and slow and smoky, and when it was gone, she'd disappeared into the crowds of the town. This was the route they'd take from school from then on, excluding the confession booth.

Why have things changed? He could blame the move to Santiago but it's more than that. He just can't see himself waiting by the train tracks anymore, standing and waving, waiting for her to turn back with a smile, pretending surprise, only to do it again the next day. Their relationship had become a habit. They'd stuck to it for so long he could have worked the barrier himself. He'd even counted the number of carriages on the industrial train: twenty-two, twenty on Friday. Fucking God. But even habits have their natural progression towards an end. Really, there's no such thing as repetition. He's been thinking a lot about that lately, how even the return to an identical 4/4 transition at the end of a song has to bear the weight of its past measures. Not that his relationship with La Dani was ever a song. More like the middle bit of a telenovela, the bit where not much happens, where we start to see each character live their own lives, deal with their own specific problems (without solving any), where we find out about the gambling debts, terminal illnesses, unwanted love, greed, past loss, loss, loss. It's his fault. She held his hand. In 4/4s the train passed. And then she was gone.

They get to the riverside by the bridge in Bella Vista. Francisco goes down a set of steps and Clara and Pablo follow. Despite the rain, the Mapocho River is low enough that they can still see little beaches made of pebbles and waste, anything from baby bottles and nappies to, no kidding, the lid of a coffin, the whole life cycle of shit. The graffitied stone wall behind them is tall enough that no one walking above ever looks down, and so they only hear the water gurgling peacefully. Pablo remembers his father saying, 'The Mapocho makes Santiago a beautiful city for the blind.' Pablo had thought, what is the point of beauty you can't see? Clara covers her nose and kicks the plank of wood out into the brown stream. She looks at Pablo and he looks into the water.

'Why the hell are we here?' Clara asks. 'It smells like baby sick.'
'You'll see.'

Clara looks to Pablo for an answer but he shakes his head, places the neck of his t-shirt over his nose and tiptoes over puddles, between deep breaths. The river dries up in the summer. The river is tiny and shallow and you can see right to the concrete base. It's only a drop of water, he repeats to himself, just as he does in the shower, or when it rains so hard his headphones can't drown out the noise. It's just drops of water, waveless and sluggish, and nothing can disappear, nothing can get lost in such a lack of depth.

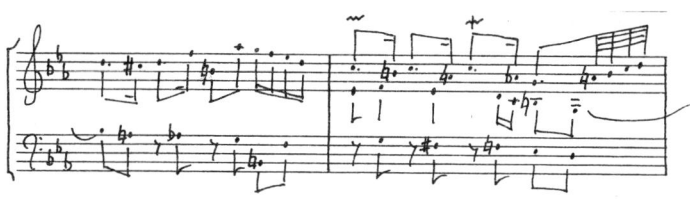

Francisco reaches inside his backpack and takes out a microphone wired to a portable tape player.

'Come see this,' Francisco says.

Clara sits by him on the edges of the pebbled beach and Pablo's hands begin to sweat. He should have gone home to see La Dani. He can picture her sitting in the living room with his mother, who would make avocado toast and ham sandwiches, and they'd have a full *once*, the mid-afternoon meal where no one can escape their families, talking first of him, then their days and then of him again, but this time about how he's always got in the way of their days. 'He should really already know better,' La Dani would say. 'I'm sorry,' his mother would answer, 'about him. I'm sorry, but he was always like this.' But Pablo was really hoping moving away would be the end of it, that she'd understand, not only understand but agree, that they were too young and also that he could have never predicted meeting Clara, his new love, his love, sitting by the shallow river.

Francisco holds the microphone just above the water.

'The one true song of this fucking city. And country. This fucking continent.'

'And what does it say?' Clara asks.

'Well, I mean, something like—'

She picks up Francisco's microphone and faces the bridge and—

'Fuck you all!' she shouts. No one on the bridge pauses to look, the stony structure floating above the now darkened and unmoving water, with the faces of the people on it like specks of dust lit up and unhindered by weight, going this way and that, without pause, without interacting. 'We're out of sync with the city.' That's what his father said in one of his rants about San Fernando, and now Pablo looks up at the bridge, the feathers of a dandelion, the city out of sync with them.

Clara turns to Francisco and Pablo. Francisco steps towards her, at the edge of the water.

'Fuck you all!'

One day last summer, when he thought the house in San Fernando was empty, Pablo had decided to try singing for the first time. To be certain no one could hear (his voice still cracked a little, but he couldn't wait any longer), he had stripped his bed and placed his mattress flat against the windows facing out into the street. And whenever he couldn't reach the top notes, he'd sing louder to get to them. By the end of his first song he had been shouting. And at dinner his father had said he'd been in the garden listening to him, that he should be careful with shouting words like conFUSED! and, worst of all, TorTure! That for his own safety he shouldn't sing so loud, shouldn't hit the top notes and then his father had said something that he can't quite shake off now that he's in Santiago. 'To be civilised,' he said, 'to not be a damn Indian like most people in this damn country, you have to learn when to be quiet. The great cities of the world are built on an agreement to be silent.' Pablo had said he didn't understand, but his father just said: don't sing so loud. So Pablo had never sung at home again, nothing louder than a whisper at least, and he'd imagined cities growing and growing around him, because of him, quiet people like him, and he had even been a little proud of it, breathless poise, musical chastity, an almost saintly sacrifice to the dignity of all and yes, that had been enough once, before the nightmares had set in, the tidal waves, fear in the roots of the earth, fear in the gutters, oceans in the city – the city which had not grown so much as the people in it had shrunk.

'Are you coming, man? It has to be all of us,' Francisco asks, with an arm now coiled around Clara's neck.

Pablo half-shuts his eyes as he heads towards them, closer to the water. Clara puts her arm around him and they all hug into a chain. Francisco presses some buttons on his recorder.

'Fuck you!' Pablo shouts too, and the hum in his right ear starts again, something he's had since the move, a faraway engine, the rippling vibration of life above water. The city sounds dampen, Santiago inside a drumhead, and the specks on the bridge stop crossing – they could be turning to face him – and all he can hear is his own breath, and the thumping echoes of his own heart.

When he gets home, his mother, still wearing terrible gym clothes, tells him La Dani is staying with some family in Santiago and will visit again tomorrow. His father is out at work and Mariela is already sleeping, so he gets his guitar, goes outside the house and along the path to the basement. He locks himself inside. He lies down on his back, just under the single light bulb, and he shuts his eyes. The National Stadium roars in excitement, ready for the open chord, but he stops at the fourth waltz loop and the hum in his ear is all that's left, a single drawn-out bass note, and somehow he is sure this one will last, a whole lifetime without silence, and he cries from the joy of it.

7

LUCHO

nods at the guards on his way out of the Escuela Militar but receives no response. He's left early, just as he'd planned, and he does feel a little guilty, so he's relieved the guards don't stop him to ask where he's going or why. There just hadn't been much to do, no new leads on finding the poet, and, as was often the case when he was bored, the stories he had been weaving around the latest figures were becoming looser, unhinged from their table-filled pages and more attached to the sudden reappearance of his imagination. Grape production was up and there had been rumours that communists wanted to control the wine, to take revenge on the old families, and so what had started with a ripe grape quickly became an intriguing murder plot, evidenced by an old photograph he remembered in *The Region* newspaper of an unfortunate fire at a country home near Santa Cruz which had been reported to have been started by peasant unions at the peak of Allende's agrarian reforms, but which turned out to be a simple insurance fraud by the vineyard owners. And so he sent for that photograph and then wrote, on a piece of notepaper:

> The grapes will burn, the old man said,
> Our grapes, Our wine.
> What is it about us, which part of us,
> drinks the fire and toasts the ash?

He binned it and instead wrote: 'Burning House – Union Leaders And Terrorist Plots Against Our Very Land. File Under *Memory*.'

Now he sits at the bus stop, though he doesn't get on the first bus because the sun feels just right on his face, and the winter air is finally retreating, and the grey concrete blocks loom over a thin fog; a still city split by the twigs of a nearby tree. It's silly, really, to feel inspired but to do nothing, and so he walks away from the bus stop to Providencia, heads to Plaza Italia, by the river to Bellas Artes and then down to Paseo Ahumada. It's the route he used to take the couple of times a year he came to Santiago, and it has now become his Friday routine. There's a smell to downtown Santiago: the infinitely reused oil to fry empanadas and sopaipillas, cheap perfume and detergent, the cigarettes which gather on the grand stone steps of the old banks, the sweat of people carrying things you can't imagine ever wanting; glass candelabras and beach buckets, vans filled with kaleidoscopic heaps of waste, and joy, so much joy that once, he'd sat on these very benches, urgent, to write about it all – how happy all young people are, even their misery is worth describing. And what were those lines he'd written to Ramona once, not joyful but maudlin, after they'd met by the train tracks in San Fernando on their first date? 'The houses out of the station are always miserable, with rusty tin roofs and empty gardens where, not unlike plaza pigeons, their occupants step about the dried grass with the peace of the aimless, pinching weeds one at a time. I wish to never leave, as long as you stay here with me, and you shut your eyes with me to...'

Lucho heads towards the Jardín del Olimpo café. It sits at the bottom of a stairwell leading to the Universidad de Chile metro, hidden by the louder displays of other shops in the gallery; American clothing stands, old tailors, birthday knick-knacks. The café, like all *cafés con piernas*, has black tinted windows even though everyone knows what goes on inside. 'It is the most honest business in Chile,' Ángel had said. 'You get exactly what's on the sign.' Ever since first going to the one near Chacabuco Street in San Fernando with his father (he was just fourteen), Lucho has found an unlikely peace in them; the routine of paying for a drink, a double espresso just like his father, and waiting (not long) for a barely-clothed woman to pretend to like you while sitting on your lap and to then pretend to enjoy stories of pretend wives and kids and jobs, all told with the pretend confidence of imbeciles expecting sex while paying for love (or so his father said). He knows Ramona would think of him coming to a place like this as cheating, even though there's no sex (she should know there was no sleeping with anyone here – it's coffee after all, a coffee with legs – though he would agree with her that the tension of wanting it was much worse). But – he can't lie – he just doesn't feel guilty. His father used to say that routine was the enemy of conscience. And although he'd said it to warn Lucho not to cheat in school tests, Lucho agreed. If you do something enough times, you really do feel like you're no longer really doing it; it just happens. (Also, as Ángel had said, talking to his son with a barely-clothed woman on his lap, even shame needs its spaces.)

A deep bassy hum surrounds the café entrance, metro trains rumbling somewhere in the veins of Santiago.

Ángel, once Lucho had started his army career, had told him the reason he'd been going to the cafés in San Fernando was that he would pay the women to give him information on what some of the men there were saying. He'd been proud when, in his words, he'd caught a communist talking about starting a pirate radio station in San Fernando. 'He cried when we made him confess. We broke him. And you know what he said at the end, even though he could barely speak? He said he was only looking for love. At a *café con piernas, huevón*! I will tell you, Lucho, so you never forget it. Men are at their worst when they think they're doing something for love. If you want to find men doing things for love, look for them in the worst places you can think of. All these soft types can think about is love.'

And so Lucho never forgot. He has been coming to the Jardín del Olimpo looking for information on people looking for love ever since he had been told to look for the poet. He has never found anything. Nothing like love at least.

Inside, he's greeted by a woman he doesn't recognise wearing a bikini, and—

'Sorry,' he says, for no reason, though fortunately she doesn't hear.

'*Buenas, tio*,' she says. 'As you can see, there are plenty of seats. You arrived at the right time, just before everyone gets off work.'

'Is it a new thing, this?'

'What is, *tio*?'

'That you're so interested in what time I arrive?' he says, fixing his jacket and taking his cap off. 'I'll sit over there,' he says, pointing towards the farthest corner of the front counter, a long black table lined with green and pink fluorescent tubes facing a row of high black bar stools. The woman's expression changes when she sees his gun holster (although it's always empty).

'Sorry,' she says. 'There are plenty of seats.'

The music in the café, a gringo pop tune he can't recognise, with a beat that marks his steps towards the counter. He orders an espresso from another woman, also in a bikini, and makes an effort to not look at her as she serves it. When he receives his tiny cup, he nods and thanks the coffee, seeing as he does, his own face rippling in the infinite gradations of neon.

'You're back again.' It's Antonia. He knows her. 'I always think it's the last time I'll see you, but then here you are. Not sure why I think that. Maybe I want that for you. To be the last time, I mean. But I like the quiet ones. We never finish the story.'

Lucho nods without lifting his face. Antonia had been the greeter when he'd turned up the first time. She'd been sitting inside a glass booth, taking coffee orders, giving out receipts to take to the bar to get the drinks. Lucho had noticed her hands and wrists. They belonged to an older woman, wrinkled and scaly knuckles against smooth red nails, blurry moles on thinning skin. He'd thought about Ramona, and how he couldn't remember what her hands looked like. He'd asked Antonia what she recommended. She'd looked at him indifferent, bored, like he'd asked the wrong question. 'Everyone here gets espressos,' she'd said, 'because no one here comes for the coffee.'

But now Antonia stands to his right, leans the weight of her body on his thigh and shoulder, the familiar smell of her hair, dry skin obscured by all the moving lights and shadows. She presses her breasts against his arm.

'No, no. The same as before. That's what I want.'

The last time, he hadn't known how to approach anyone. He'd sat in some corner and looked on as men laughed with their allocated women. Perhaps it had been pity, though Lucho would never call it that, since he suspects all women here pity their men in some way, but Antonia had come to him, locked up her glass booth and undressed in front of him to sit on his lap. From there, it hadn't taken long, not even a month, to find out more about her. He didn't speak much at first, so she filled the silence. That's her job. She'd been married to a teacher in Punta Arenas, 'married at the end of the world,' she'd said. But her husband left on a boat when The General took over and other teachers were arrested. When his friends started disappearing, he, along with other teachers, took fishing boats out into the ocean, only coming back for supplies, and then leaving again. They'd done this for years. She'd waited. A lot of their wives had waited. But as time went on, and with children to care for, they had stopped waiting and left for the cities.

Antonia had worked her way up to Santiago slowly, working in Puerto Montt, Temuco, Talca, and even San Fernando. 'The hard years,' she'd called them. 'He was afraid of the disappeared, so he disappeared too,' she'd said. 'What was I meant to do? But I never thought of myself as a prostitute.'

It had been during these conversations that Antonia mentioned a client she'd met while staying in a room in San Fernando; an army man who'd then visit her in Santiago. When she said he'd given her poems, copies of Neruda's work, he'd understood. 'He never used his real name, I knew that much,' she'd said. 'I think he was in love with me. He asked a lot of questions, about me, about this place. A lot of men here try to save us. I think he was lonely. His wife had left him. He didn't speak much about that. None of them do.' And that's how Lucho knew she'd met his father, Ángel.

'We can do whatever you like, *tio*. I just don't understand why it—'

'—please.'

'I can't remember where we left off. It's been a while, *tio*. I haven't seen him in years.'

'You can start again. It doesn't matter.'

'Okay. Well, he told me to call him Manuel Rodríguez, like, you know, the guy from the Independence or something, from all the statues. Silly, right? I never knew his real name. Though I suppose that's normal in here. Not even the girls use their real names.'

'Where did you first meet? How did it happen?'

'At the time I was a dancer. This was just before '73. I was sat by the river downtown. I'd fucked up an audition, *tio*. To dance. I was going to be on TV and everything, you know? Remember I told you? I showed you last time. The thing with the wrists. Stupid, I know, but...' she sighs.

'And that's when Manuel Rodríguez came to you.'

'Yes, he sat down next to me.'

'And what did he say?'

'Well... He looked at me and said that I reminded him of his youth. Or being young. Men do that, you know? Still, whatever he meant, I thought it was going somewhere at the time. I was all sentimental back then, a kid.'

Lucho drinks his coffee in one gulp. The little spoon rattles a beat on the saucer.

'What did you talk about after that?'

She sits on his lap.

'Family, mostly family. I told him about mine, how I'd grown up in Punta Arenas with my brother, how I'd come over here as a nanny. I asked him about his parents and he simply said he only ever had a father. But he told me he had his own family now. Still, I didn't care. Like I said, I was different back then. I don't do the things now that I used to do then. He didn't seem to care either. He said he only cared about now.'

At home the next day Lucho finishes some notes about the real Manuel Rodríguez, the guerrilla leader, a father to Chile's independence, later betrayed by his friend José Miguel Carrera, then murdered, shot in the back, cut up into pieces, undressed, his body disappeared by another founding father, another hero, a new betrayal, now forgotten, now a statue in the little plaza in San Fernando where seven other patriots were murdered by the Spanish Crown, a line of pigeons on an unsheathed sword, a hand opened to the sky, pleading because rebels always plead, and he—

> Had done as told and expected
> but better a friend to
> Carrera, who failed to exile him,
> then together on the revolutionary (?)(?)
> Disaster of Rancagua, later Argentina and
> Chacabuco, where again,
> betrayed betrayed betrayed
> there
> with nothing left we still have a

> fatherland
> citizens
> and the Hussars of Death still whisper to us
> about the mere seconds
> present in the first breaths of a country.

He closes his book. Ramona's still not back (where is she?) and Pablo seems to disappear for whole days into the basement (how is he?). Since the move, with Ramona it's either been talk about the house or complete silence. Granted, at least they have something neat and easy to talk about. When he was younger, he feared the boredom of ageing and he'd say, 'Kill me if I'm ever like that,' while pointing at old people comparing identical potatoes at the market, one in each hand. Now, he's thankful for the boredom, their settled lives, their daily patterns, the disappointment of growing old. Relationships steer themselves to extremities, the way old hearts begin to numb toes and fingertips. Their silence is so uneasy he's often wanted to ask her about it. But no, no, talking about the house is better, and he hopes she takes her time with it, even if some days he can't stand it. 'The curtains need trimming, that's Chile for you,' was the last thing he remembers her saying to him. And, 'I'm sorry about the rug.' What was that line? Was it 'to love as shadows need to be loved/ alone'? He isn't sure what Neruda would write about him, the kinds of colourful phrasing he'd pull off about the patterns of the Persian rug, the empty sad stone corridors of Machu Picchu, the arterial web of a dry copihue flower petal where their whole lives could be summed up in a simple motion, or even silence, perhaps a love so secret he has started to doubt it.

They barely touch each other anymore.

She's not been the same, ever since she left the clinic. It's wrong to think that way. He knows it, but it's true. The last couple of nights he's even heard her whisper numbers to herself, counting back from three, like she's hypnotising herself to sleep. He misses her, he really does. As she was. As she can still be, he hopes. Conversations about each other. She'd once told him she liked his hands. She said she could tell he'd been pampered. 'Softer than mine!' she'd said. 'Not a day's work.' But then she had met his father and she never said such things again.

Ramona first met Lucho's father at a small publication reception for his first book, *One Country*, based on articles Ángel had written for *The Region* newspaper. The book had a chapter for each region, starting with stories about miners in the North and the importance of suppressing unions to attract foreign investment, moving on to patriotic diaries found in the naval academy in La Serena, pisco and papaya, the seafronts of Viña del Mar, the folk festivals in Quilpué, foreign arrivals in Valparaíso, the histories of German migrants in Villa Alemana and how they'd built a town for themselves at the turn of the century. And then it was the future of Chile in Santiago, and the vineyards of Central Valley, down to the vast countryside in Talca, the shipyards in Puerto Montt, some of them presented as retellings of the myths of Chiloé. There was a chapter ending with a vision of the *Caleuche* in Lake Llanquihue, the ghost ship disappearing in the shadows of volcanoes. And the book ended with an account of a trip he'd taken from Punta Arenas to Cape Horn, filled with references to Francisco Coloane's book *Cabo de Hornos*, stories about the loneliness of its wilderness, an attempt at reconnecting with the land. He'd made Lucho memorise the last lines, a Coloane quote, something like: 'No one knows where people come from in places like those, and no one knows where they'll eventually go; they appear from the oceans at the end of the world.'

Lucho still doesn't know why his father had organised the event. Ángel often spoke about 'cheap egocentrics' when he referred to writers desperate for an audience (he'd often received demands for newspaper publicity from local writers in San Fernando). And though Lucho never asked him, he does remember his father, drunk one night, saying that he hoped his mother would see his name. The truth, Lucho knows, is often simpler. His father was retiring. He'd written a book. He was publishing it himself. He wanted to leave something behind.

And even though Lucho had no choice in the matter (his father said it would do him good to learn from the other newspaper writers who loved their land), and though Ángel had forced his staff to be there if they wanted to keep their jobs, when Lucho arrived at the Club Social (often filled with retired policemen and soldiers, which is why Ángel had chosen it), Lucho felt as if the whole thing had been orchestrated by Ángel for his own amusement.

Before the party he had gone to find Ramona at her house in Chacabuco Street. In those days, San Fernando was colder – most places in his memory were colder – and he'd made a habit of running into her arms to get warm, which he knew she liked.

It was only their third or fourth week together when all this happened. He saw himself, wet face from the drifting rain and his neck sweaty. He had always carried an old leather satchel full of papers. He wouldn't let her see inside, and would say things like: 'I'll read them to you some day,' or: 'Some of them are about you,' or, once he'd finished his first notebook of poem drafts: 'I'm not too late yet. Neruda started in his early teens but life's different now, we're younger inside, till much later.' He had never known what he'd meant by that but wished he could write better verses about how someone who knows nothing could derive such pure wisdom from their own nonsense.

'You know my mum might be there, right?' she had said, sitting on the kerb just outside the front door, next to a tree whose trunk had been inexplicably painted white. 'She's always there, drinking.' She was watching a tiny line of ants making its way from the patch of earth on the base of the tree to a hole in its log – it was going to rain. He had simply nodded at her, regaining his breath.

'What should I do if she is?'

She looked up at him.

'We'll avoid her,' he'd said. 'I don't know. She doesn't ever remember much the next day anyway, does she?'

'I suppose.'

'If she's there I'll help,' Lucho had said. 'You know I'll help, right? I won't leave you alone.'

'Help? That doesn't mean anything. Help with what? And how?'

He'd sat next to her, put an arm around her.

'I wish she wasn't what she is,' he'd said.

'I know. If she's there we'll ask someone to take her back home. That's all we can do.'

Ramona hadn't said anything else, and he'd assumed she'd been crying, though he didn't dare look. He couldn't stand the sight of her tears. He despised Señora Mirta for all this; for making him have to check that Ramona had eaten that day, if her mother had remembered to buy something other than wine, for making Ramona glue the soles of her old shoes, which had then made Ramona apologise to him about their appearance when he'd asked her out (she'd had the same pair for years now), ever since her stepfather disappeared. For making roaming the street more comfortable than her own home.

It hadn't taken them long to spot Señora Mirta in the crowd that evening. She was sitting alone on a high stool facing the bar, arched over a wine glass, arms loose and hanging by her sides. Ramona had looked at Lucho without a word, pulling on the bottom of his shirt.

Lucho had pointed at his father, who nodded at him. He was talking to two army officials in full white uniforms, ceremonial swords hanging from their belts. The events room had been arranged almost as if for a church service: a lectern facing rows of chairs, a clear corridor left in the middle, the bar behind.

Ángel had walked toward them.

'Were you going to introduce us?'

'Yes, sir,' Lucho said. 'This is Ramona.'

'Hello,' she said.

'Don't be shy,' Ángel said. 'Ramona what?'

A photographer pulled Ángel away from them before she could answer.

'Come to dinner later,' was all Ángel said, and they weren't sure if it was even addressed to them.

Then, the sound of bottles breaking had silenced the room. Everyone had turned to see Señora Mirta as she grabbed a still-full glass next to her and threw it at the barman, who ducked and waved her off, though even he didn't say anything.

Mirta turned around, said *'what'* to everyone there, leaning on the bar to stand up.

She spotted Ramona and smiled, walked toward her. She stopped in front of Lucho.

'Pretty, huh?' Then she turned from him to Ramona. 'You're pretty now, sleeping with these pigs.' She made her way nearer to her, pressed her to her chest, whispered: 'Whore.'

'Leave her,' Lucho had said, though not nearly loud enough.

'And you, are you just like your father? Your daddy?'

Guests scattered away from Señora Mirta, who began to hum a drunken tune under her breath before letting out a laugh. Everyone was silent. Ángel's boots made the only sound as he made his way towards her.

'Take this witch out of here or I'll do it myself,' Ángel said, waving his hand at a policeman. 'Take her out,' he repeated, this time holding Ramona in his gaze. 'She's your mother, is she not?' Everyone turned to Ramona.

Ramona stared at the floor.

'Stay here,' Lucho had said. 'I'll take her.'
'I can't stay, not now,' Ramona said. 'Everyone...'
'Stay here. It's fine. Really. It's fine.'
'Promise me you won't go inside. It's not a nice home. It's just not.'
'I promise.'

So Lucho had walked Señora Mirta home. She didn't fight him, didn't protest about leaving the party. She wasn't even bothered when he went inside the house to make sure she went to bed. 'Ramona,' she had said a couple of times, 'Ramona,' and then she had fallen asleep.

Lucho had paced around the room, looked at the photographs on the wall, none of them of Ramona. He had looked for a bedsheet or towel to cover Señora Mirta, tried to open the wooden armoire facing the bed, but it had been locked. On the bedside table was a brass key. He opened the armoire and inside were stacks of pasta packets, rice, tuna cans, olives, chocolate. Ramona had never outright told him but he knew – he knew she often went hungry, that she didn't eat every day. It'd become their tradition, since their first weekends together, to eat a barbecued chicken sat on the kerb by the train tracks, the only place in San Fernando where everyone's moving, the only place to meet and not be seen. Let us spread the great tablecloths, the Great Neruda had said, a place like the moon itself.

Lucho lies down on his bed and closes his eyes to listen more intently. Lately he's been hearing what sound like muffled conversations, even steps, maybe music and he hasn't been able to sleep. He hears it when he's outside, coming from the basement. But then the sounds disappear as soon as he's inside. Does this happen to the senses with age? Like dreams which invite people we've long forgotten in disorganised sequences, eventless like a shadow, will noise now also pay him unwanted visits? Is this what a ghost is? Sometimes he swears he can hear his father.

That night, in Ramona's house, Lucho had stepped closer to Mirta. He had moved her head gently and slid some of the foods he'd found right under her pillow, a little pile on each side so that her head was kept in place and facing the ceiling.

'Whore,' she had whispered.

He hears Ramona unlocking the front door. He knows it's her because as soon as she shuts the door she runs the water in the kitchen. She arrives carrying two glasses of water.

POETRY NOTES – BOOK OF RAMONA
Ramona Looks at the Horizon: Travelling the Great Sea

>Afloat with
>her telling me of
>the distance
>Where blue meets blue
>is the offing
>memories plunge to
>in that horizon
>we must go to know
>the shade of our childhoods
>like beetle wings in the sun,
>she says,
>Ancient sediment,
>the Gratitude of Stone,
>I hope what's left of me
>is the ash of
>our flight,
>she says,
>with nothing around us but
>Deep Water.
>
>I promise we'll get there someday.

He checks his watch to confirm, for the fourth time, that yes, he's early. He's sitting on a bench in a small plaza at the end of Raul Córdoba, waiting for the Tutankamón to open. He'd read that this was the bar where writers would gather in secret and so had decided it was the best place to continue his search. He imagines the poets exchanging verses casually, rearranging this banal city and its language: the petrichor of mid-afternoons in August, the aurora over morning skylines, the serendipity of young love. There were famous writers who'd come out of that group. Pedro Castro, who wrote the *Space Verses* in that literary workshop just before going into exile, a kind of tribute to Ezra Pound and the Imagists, it contained every street in downtown Santiago, all gutted into their most basic nouns: The pebbled arches of pigeon wings/ Smoke. He has Pedro Castro's book with him. He turns it over and looks at the portrait on the inside of the book jacket. In the picture Pedro is sitting in a wicker chair, a wall of paperbacks and tall volumes behind him, packed onto floating shelves, right up to the ceiling. There are books perched on their side, slotted tightly into whatever space is left on top of those standing. There is a pile on his desk too, some of them open, spines broken in and wrinkled, pages fanning open. Lucho can't see the titles. He doubts he'd know them if he could. The hard focus of the picture is on the author's face. He's young but dresses old; a tweed blazer, probably borrowed, hangs loose over a scrawny figure, black-framed glasses in the chest pocket. His hair looks unwashed, wisps suspended like he's facing the wind. Like Lucho, teenage acne mapped onto his cheeks. He's holding a pen, a leatherbound notebook on his lap. The way he's sitting, both legs together, slight angle so that he has had to turn to face the camera – and he's holding the pen in a fist – makes Lucho almost certain that he was forced into this. There are only a couple of pictures of Pedro Castro, all of them taken more than twenty years ago. He never gave any interviews either, not after his *Space*

Verses collection at least, where he told the radio interviewer to ask him about anything but his poetry because, 'If I could explain it any other way, I would write it like that.' Lucho is sure he himself had once said something like that too, maybe to Ramona. But that was because, after some time, he'd forgotten what his poems had been about when he wrote them.

Below the portrait, some lines about the book:

> *Born in Rancagua, Pedro Castro started part of his collection at age sixteen. His father worked in the military, and so Pedro travelled extensively in Chile, living in numerous places from Iquique to Punta Arenas. Abandoning military service to study literature in the prestigious Universidad de Chile, the early travels which started a deep love affair with the country and its people remain at the heart of his poetry.*
>
> Space Verses *is a collection of poems which give voice to often forgotten people and places, the unknown and the unheard. By gifting them a unique language from which to interpret the world – often puzzling, challenging the untrained reader – the poet asks whether it is possible to reconcile our differences in a divided country; whether we can narrow the space between us.*
>
> *This collection is his answer.*
>
> Space Verses *won the 1969 National Literature Prize and has been translated into fifteen languages. It is Pedro Castro's first major work.*

And then, there was Carla Sánchez, who'd written novels about class divides in the lives of nannies and golf course owners, as well as the then-prized fictionalised memoir *Who The Hell Am I*, where she wrote about her struggles with her husband's dementia. Also, Sánchez, whose first name remains debated to this day, so determined was he to avoid persecution (though Lucho's father called his concealed identity a stroke of marketing genius). Sánchez had rewritten *Don Quixote* as an allegory of what he termed the *delusion of free enterprise*, even before the years of Milton Friedman's capitalism, and therefore before Allende's Popular Unity which sought to undermine it. There were others too, but Lucho had never gone to any of the meetings. He had also never told the police about the group of writers, in case he ever did attend.

Important. That is the problem. Literature has to be important. He can't blame his father for this, for the irrelevance of his own imagination. And he just can't deal with others looking at his writing. In the past, he'd only ever shown Ramona bits – 'cuts', as he called them, to make sure she understood just how much better the whole would be if only she could see it – and that's because he knew she'd find it all *nice* and all *beautiful*. She liked what he wrote, how unusual it was that someone should choose to write in San Fernando, what even about?! It made him mad, her kindness. Lucho's first poems had been collections of beach days, the sea struggling to climb, losing its grip on the cliffs of Isla Negra, the shiny dew of black rocks, the shade under the wingspan of pelicans and the great eucalyptus trees. Old people playing dominoes on beach towels, the texture of the cotton, the cold stream facing the waves. Irrelevant and simple. He had intended it to be his only collection, the unfinished book (how long must something be absent for it to be abandoned?). In the year before moving to Santiago, on one of his visits from San Fernando, he'd sat exactly where he is right now, wondering whether to go inside, present himself: 'I'm a writer, a poet actually, Lucho.' Unlike then, however, the notebook he's carrying now contains no poems. It is blank, a mere prop.

A man pulls up the metal shutters at the Tutankamón. It takes only minutes for a man with a briefcase to arrive, and others soon follow. Lucho walks over to the entrance. He's disappointed to realise how drab and commonplace it all feels. It's a Fuente de Soda like any other; worn-out red stools against a long red countertop, bouquets of napkins, private booths, a still fan in the ceiling. A waiter, dressed too formally with a tucked-in white shirt and a bow tie, waves at Lucho.

'What will it be?'

'I'm a writer,' Lucho says.

'And I'm a waiter.'

'I'll have a coffee.'

'You can have whatever you want.'

'I saw some people come in just before me.'

'You must have the wrong place. Maybe it was the flats next door.'

'No, no, I'm sure I saw them come in here.'

'Curious.'

'Like I said, I'm a writer. A poet, actually. I'm here for the workshop, I mean.'

The waiter turns to get a tin of instant coffee from the table behind him and pours hot water in a mug.

Lucho stirs in two spoons of coffee.

'I was sure they met here.'

'We have sandwiches, too, if you'd like.'

Lucho takes out his notebook from his blazer pocket. He doesn't have a pen so he pretends to read from the blank pages.

'What do you write about, then?'

A man appears from a door behind the counter, bearded, scarf still on, round glasses. He doesn't look at Lucho. He whispers something in the waiter's ear.

'Poetry.'

They both turn to him.

'He just came in,' the waiter tells the man.

'We're not taking new people, no amateurs,' the man says.

'I'm not new.'

'New to us.'

'I want to learn, to practise.'

'We're not teachers.'

'I'm finishing a collection.'

'Read.' The man leans on the table with his hand, facing Lucho.

Lucho looks at the blank pages, tries to remember a line or two from his collection. They were all so disconnected, so unfinished, so damn awful, abstract and lacking in imagery and narrative direction.

'Any?' he asks, but no one answers. 'The pebbled arches of pigeon wings/ Smoke,' he says, and the man's face changes, softens, and he clears his throat, frowns and—

'Is that really you, *huevón*?'

8

RAMONA

is sitting on the unmade bed, unsure of what to do, whether she should call Alicia and cancel. Oh, yes, Don Francisco, to answer your question, it's all about practice. That's how you impress at auditions. The casting director needs to feel the hours you put in to—

PUBLIC SOLITUDE:

The actor's ability to act privately in public is, well, Ramona can't quite remember, but it has to do with the Circle of Attention - which to her included everyone else in the room but her, and she never understood it, how she had to use furniture as object substitutes in that one lesson, a chair as a shrub, a couch as a boat, the longest five minutes of her life talking into a banana, ending in claps, in being privately lonely, just as she is now, trying to catch a glimpse of her own reflection in the new tower block apartment complexes outside the shower window. She's not there but—

There is nothing to do in the house but work on the house itself. Not that she'd like to, because she still remembers whole days taken up by ironing, Lucho's unending set of identical white undershirts and Pablo's school uniform (why aren't uniforms black to hide the stains?) and scrubbing the bathtub just so she could answer when Lucho asked her, 'Ramona, *mi amor*, what did you

> LO QUE TUS OJOS NO VEN: A TELENOVELA
>
> #EPISODE 3
>
> INT. FARM CHURCH – DAY
>
> > FATHER CALLETANO
> > But you must pray, my
> > daughter. Jesus listens.
> > Have faith in our great and
> > mighty God.
> >
> > LUZ MARIA
> > Faith? I don't think I have
> > any left, Father. She's
> > beaten it out of me.
> >
> > FATHER CALLETANO
> > I'll talk to her again.
> > She needs to find reason. If

do today?', but somehow *choosing* to do nothing would feel better. Mariela has given her back too much time, and as her mother Señora Mirta used to say: 'The hardest part of life is having to live every second of it, no matter what.'

She heads downstairs, can hear Mariela doing the dishes, and so tiptoes her way into the living room and shuts the door. She should be on her way to the gym but today she just can't do it. She wanted to, really. She had even put on the right clothes, or had started to at least (she hadn't been able to find her left tennis shoe), but then Mariela had turned the music on as she started cleaning and it was Alejandro Zañartu and his *Amor*

Invisible, Amor Invencible ballads. The songs were too awful. One of them went, 'The tune of your eyes/ is the melody of storms,' and Ramona could never decipher whether Alejandro had written it to someone he loved or despised. But no, that hadn't been it, for nonsense love/hate songs were nothing compared to *What Your Eyes Can't See*, the telenovela she once auditioned for, and whose opening credits eventually rolled out to Alejandro's voice, without her name.

God, even after shutting the door she can still hear it.

'Look at them,' her mother would say whenever Luz María appeared onscreen. She was a model apparently, who had been discovered selling cigarettes outside a football stadium, not one hour of acting experience on her, at least not in theatre anyway. 'I told you it doesn't matter how much you try. The game is rigged. Beautiful girls, that's all that matters these days. You have to be beautiful.'

'I know, I know,' Ramona said, though she had auditioned for five roles in the telenovela: Background Nun #2, Cook Extra, Angry Horse Rider, Startled Background Mother. And then, the last one, Luz María. She'd only really prepared for that one. She'd shut her bedroom door in Santiago where she studied (Aunty Wilma had kept it intact even after Ramona's graduation, so sure was she that Ramona would become famous one day), and walked up and down the narrow gap between the empty bookcase and the windowsill where Ramona kept a Shakespearean skull her aunt had given her. Feeling her way around that room with her eyes shut, Ramona had paid attention to the nuances of her body and its expression, she had touched her own face, the warmth of her cheeks and the creases rippling in her forehead, the sorrow of her slow breaths, the loosening of her hands. She knelt down and felt the old rug, the cold metallic legs of the sewing table she'd used as a desk. And then, under her bed, a basket filled with fabric. She opened her eyes. It was an old wedding dress. She hadn't been

> she doesn't listen to me,
> she'll listen to God.
>
> FATHER CALLETANO opens a BLACK BOOK and looks at the church ceiling.
>
> LUZ MARIA
> That woman is the Devil,
> Father, and the Devil only
> hears himself.
>
> INT. FARM STABLES - NIGHT
>
> LUZ MARIA caresses a horse's muzzle.
>
> LUZ MARIA
> If I could see, my dear
> Cirilio, I would take you
> with me, far away from
> here.

able to afford one herself, and she had got married in one of her mother's long black skirts (from the time she had been a teacher at the old nuns' school), and her own school blouse which still miraculously fitted. Lucho had never said anything, but she knew she'd failed him. Still grasping at the dress under the bed, that day of the audition, she had listened for Aunty Wilma. And then she tried it on. She couldn't zip it up all the way. She had never before considered herself ugly until she saw herself in that dress so—

She decides to go and meet Alicia after all, if only to get away from Mariela. 'Miss, Miss, weren't you supposed to go to the gym today? Miss, won't you become unhealthy again if you don't go out? Miss, Don Lucho called to remind you to go to the gym if you've not yet been. Miss, you're very quiet today, fresh air would be very good for you. Be positive, Miss, remember to be positive.'

From the day she stepped out of that madhouse – yes, that's what it was despite the word *clinic* Lucho always makes a point of using – to be better, to be well, has come to mean to be outside, to leave, to leave them.

At least right after her mother died, Ramona had been able to say she was grieving. All she could do was sit still and watch TV. But out of the madhouse, she was meant to feel renewed and—

She has to be positive, see the good in people and in things, in her house and in Santiago, and move on and on and—

For that she has to leave. For that she has to dress like someone who cares about herself, about what people might say about her. In her room she puts on her newest pair of jeans, a silk blouse and a coral woollen jumper. Then, Lucho's last gift (for everything she owns is a gift from Lucho), a new pair of white Adidas, fresh from the box. She thought about wearing a dress, a shirt even, but she needs to be able to move freely in whatever role she's given. Acting loneliness is in the body, not the mind. It's in the infinity of the room, in arms stretched and open palms, fingers touching nothing, the perceived distance between walls. And she needs to remember all of Miss Moglia's confusing lessons, because she's not going to the gym.

Alicia, at the end of their Move Like a Winner training session last week, had taken her to one side and—

'Pato thinks you'd be good,' she'd said, while she dried the sweat off the back of her neck. 'Remember I told you he works in TV? So, yes, he's willing to audition you. Yes, yes, it's true, you better believe it, that's the power of belief. I told you, the first step is to believe in yourself.'

```
Cirilio the horse lowers his head to be near
to hers.

                    LUZ MARIA
              You would take me, save me,
              wouldn't you?

THE WITCH OF THE POND drags her feet from the
stables entrance until she is just behind LUZ
MARIA.

                    LUZ MARIA
              Who's there?

LUZ MARIA tries to touch THE WITCH but her
attempts are easily evaded.

                    THE WITCH
              I am simply a curious
              bystander, Lucecita, a
```

Other women were queuing up to greet Pato, so Ramona had hovered to one side, pretended to look for something in her duffel bag, retied her shoes, intermittently tried to catch his eye until at last it worked and he waved hello.

'Hi,' she said, worried she was revealing too many teeth.

'Ramona, *bella*,' he said, hand stretched toward her. She didn't take it. 'Did Alicia tell you already?'

Alicia was standing nearby, in front of a tall window in the corner of the room, looking at them. Behind Alicia, the Santiago skyline swirled with clouds, the foamy crest of the waves about to hit the ground and swallow her and the rest of the city whole.

'An audition.'

'It's not just an audition. I've used my contacts. I have a lot of contacts. TV people, you know? I'm always looking for screen talent.'

'Aren't the other girls here better, younger?'

'I'm not looking for that. Remember, Alicia, when we had one of the young ones do that advert, for the Bracelet of the Seven Powers? She was awful. A lot of promise. A lot of talk. But when it came to it, she couldn't show nearly as much excitement as we needed. Her wrists were so thin the bracelet kept falling off. She could only ever remember five of the seven powers, remember? Would just stop and look completely clueless after STRENGTH.'

'Awful,' Alicia said. 'Though you did like her at first.'

'Too negative,' he said. 'Too self-centred. The young are too self-centred these days. That's not to say you're old. You're just right.'

'Why me?' Ramona asked.

'You're the only one here who never looks at herself in the mirror. Even in our star jumps. Not even once.'

'Selfless,' Alicia said.

'That's it – selfless,' he said. 'And you have, you know, theatre experience. I mean, we've probably seen you already and didn't even know it. Would we have seen you in something already?'

'I got married,' Ramona had said. 'I had a child.'

'Selfless, you see? Strength of character.'

'What's the part for?'

'Does it matter? Specifics lead to—'

'Criticism, which leads to Negative Thinking,' Alicia said.

'That's right. You either want an opportunity or you don't. You're either open or closed to the world.' He opened his arms and legs, a grounded star jump.

> simple audience. I heard
> what the priest could not.
> Useless, all of them.
>
> LUZ MARIA
>
> Who are you?
>
> THE WITCH
>
> You can call me Yaconda, if
> you need a name.
>
> LUZ MARIA
>
> Yaconda? The Witch of the
> Pond? Aren't you supposed
> to be... Didn't you...
> Please don't come any
> closer. Leave me.

Now, Ramona locks the front door quietly and straightens her back. She balances the duffel bag on her shoulder and makes her way out to the metro.

'Are you going to the gym, Miss?' Mariela calls from the second-floor window. 'I'll let Don Lucho know you've been to the gym today if he calls.'

When she gets to the street Alicia had directed her to, Ramona feels like she's trespassing. She reads the piece of paper again, and wishes she's made a mistake. She feels stupid. She usually feels stupid these days, like she can't quite decipher places or people.

Lucho once told her that if you felt stupid, you most likely were stupid. He hadn't meant her, but a man at work who'd apologised for letting a communist terrorist go in the early days. 'I knew him at school,' the man had said. 'I feel so stupid.' Ramona understood. The last time she could think straight was at the madhouse. When she got home, she never returned. That's what she remembers thinking in her prayers. Some people never come back. But at least now—

There are no streetlights and the winter evening has dulled the street to a dark blue, smudged its contrasts, making it hard to tell where houses begin and end, two uniform walls bordering the empty road on each side. It takes her some time before she realises that no one can be watching her because the houses are actually warehouses and garages, their heavy steel doors shut, padlocks hanging. She looks for number 8007, getting close enough to the units to read the numbers and check she's walking in the right direction.

8007 is like all the rest, shut with a padlock, no sound coming from the inside, no light seeping through. Her mother had once asked her, if acting careers were so difficult, why would she want one? Was fame that important, was attention, validation? 'Are you really that selfish at a time like this?' And Ramona had not known how to answer. Her mother was right about the selfishness of it all. Nothing else. Ramona's whole life had been about trying to get away from what she thought of as Common Lives, which was hard to define because they were everywhere, spreading a belief that the dark is as good as the spotlight, that having too much money would somehow corrupt, that being ignored was better than being celebrated. But then, as time went by, and as her Common Life took hold of her, she merely fantasised about becoming someone else, which is the Commonest Life of All. One day she could be a nun and the next a killer. That was acting. Lines written for her: *I can't see you but I can feel you.* She still remembered the pleasure

> **YACONDA**
>
> Won't you hear me out first?
> I could help you. I can
> offer you everything. In
> exchange for a few other
> things I need, of course.
> But they're nothing compared
> to everything you want.
> Don't you wish you could
> see? Don't you want to leave
> this God-forsaken farm?
> With your beauty... If only
> you knew of your beauty.
> Don't you want love?
>
> **LUZ MARIA**
>
> Leave me! I believe in our
> Lord. He hears me. I have
> faith in Him.

of committing to the words of others, of forgetting them for new ones to take their place. She hadn't landed a part but she'd landed a role. Without Lucho she's not a wife. Without Pablo she's not a mother. With them she was theirs. Without them she's here, in the quietest street in Santiago, looking for 8007, counting the empty warehouses.

Eventually, the sun sets and Ramona starts her way back home. But when she gets to the end of the road, she sees someone walking toward her. She turns around to walk the other way. She's heard of what happens in Santiago at night. She's been stupid enough to wear her jewellery, her mother's old watch.

'Ramona! Hey, Ramona!'

Ramona sees Alicia jogging to meet her. She breathes out in relief.

'Where the hell have you been?' Alicia asks, a hand on her chest, catching her breath.

'I went to it. I went to 8007, right? There was no one there.'

'8007 Mozart?'

'Yes?'

'This is Schubert.'

'Oh.'

'It's happened before.'

'That people get the street wrong?'

'Not only that. We thought you'd got cold feet. People sometimes don't turn up to auditions.'

'I wouldn't do that,' Ramona says, too earnest. 'Of course I wouldn't do that,' she says with a wide smile.

'Hey, I should have said, you need to wear a dress for the audition. But don't worry, we've got a bunch with us. All the clothes have been used in TV before so it's pretty exciting for you, I'm sure. You'll wear a star's dress tonight.'

Ramona hopes she can fit into one of the TV dresses. She wants to ask about their sizes, which stars wore them, but she doesn't want to draw attention to her weight. She'll be fine. *Project the life you want with enough power and it's bound to come true*, Pato had said so himself. *Live by projection. Always become.* And yet, walking behind Alicia, she can't help but think of that wedding dress at her aunt's. When Ramona graduated, her aunt had given her the dress. 'I'm not ready to get married, Aunty,' she'd said, though they'd already talked about it with Lucho. 'It's not that,' her aunt said. And then she had told Ramona about the father she had never met. All her life, Ramona had been told this father had had a heart attack before she was born. None of it was true. He'd been an American junior diplomat and her mother had worked

> YACONDA
>
> Faith? Nothing in this life changes with belief alone. I offer you the chance to take destiny in your own hands, to believe in yourself like no one's ever done, like no one ever will.
>
> LUZ MARIA
>
> Get out, witch!
>
> LUIS FELIPE enters the stables, alarmed, wearing riding clothes.
>
> LUIS FELIPE
>
> What's happening here?!

as a typist at the embassy. He'd been called back to work in the States when Ramona was tiny. And then he had had to go to be a military advisor in Vietnam before the war started. They were supposed to get married, her mother to her father, on his return. She bought the dress but he never came back. Her mother never knew if or how he'd died. 'In the end, it was your mum's heart that broke,' Ramona's aunt said. 'And that's why she started drinking.'

'It's a beautiful night, isn't it?' Alicia says, without turning to face her. 'When it's foggy in Santiago, faraway lights look like candles, you know what I mean? Like some sort of vigil we're all a part of.'

'But the moon always looks like the moon.'

Ramona had been able to do what her aunt and mother hadn't. When Lucho told her they couldn't afford a wedding dress, she'd nodded, 'It's not important, that doesn't matter to me,' and she'd put her mother's dress in a black bag. It was easy. She hadn't wanted to say it, think it even, 'I am letting go of everything and everyone for you,' but it'd made her happy to just know it. 'Just don't leave me,' she'd told Lucho, who looked confused. 'Never,' he said, 'not in a million years.'

Ramona follows Alicia into one of the warehouses. There are spotlights on a stage, Pato sitting in a director's chair, two men next to him fixing microphones onto boom stands.

'We thought you weren't coming,' he says.

'Never,' she says.

'The wrong street, right?'

'Yes, Schubert,' Alicia says.

Ramona is in what Pato called a changing room but is without doubt a cleaning cupboard. There's a mop and a bucket in one corner, bottles of bleach and a box of rubber gloves. What the hell is she doing, taking her clothes off in a place like this? There are no hangers, not even one free shelf for her folded blouse. 'We'll be with you in just a few minutes,' Pato had said. 'Alicia will have a few things for you to try on.' What would Lucho say if he saw her? What would Pablo do? Ramona hasn't even thought about what she'd say if they ever saw her on TV. What if a colleague or a classmate or someone tells them about her; 'Lucho, I saw someone on TV yesterday and it looked just like your wife, *huevón*, it was uncanny.' 'And your mum, Pablo, was on TV last night. She really can't act. You should tell her she's too old for TV, for her own sake you should tell her. We're not even going to make fun of you. It's that tragic.' 'Lucho, Lucho, we could tell she was just pretending. There's a world of difference between acting and

> LUZ MARIA turns to face him, crying in relief.
>
> LUZ MARIA
> Señor, ay Señor, the Witch
> of the Pond was here.
>
> LUIS FELIPE strokes LUZ MARIA's hand.
>
> LUIS FELIPE
> Calm down, Miss, the witch
> is just a story. Yaconda
> died a long time ago, a
> woman unfairly accused
> after the death of her own
> children. You imagined it
> all. Everything's okay, I
> promise you, there's no one
> here but us.

pretending. She was pretending. You should have never let her leave the madhouse. Sleep and exercise.' 'Remember what the doctors advised,' Lucho would say, 'sleep and exercise are all you can do.' And for how long? 'For as long as it takes to beat this.' And what is this? 'Look, for now it doesn't matter.' And she's felt this before, that while she was in the madhouse the world had moved on from her. She hadn't changed. Not deep down. She'd only got older. Only new things survive.

Ramona is thankful there are no mirrors, that the closet she's in is dimly lit. She doesn't want to see the ripples in her skin. Be positive. Your body's your own. Own your body. And that's the problem. This is what she owns. Not by choice. You can be positive about ugly things but they're still ugly. No matter how Ramona thinks, what Ramona thinks, Ramona still has to be Ramona and that's—

A knock on the door.

'I brought some...' Alicia opens the door. 'Shit!' She shuts it again.

'What?'

'You're naked,' Alicia says from outside.

'I thought you were bringing me some clothes.'

'It's an audition. I only brought shoes. You can sort of wear the dress over everything else.'

Alicia comes in with a pillar of shoeboxes and puts them down. They look at each other for a few seconds and laugh. Ramona finds herself crying with laughter.

'Put it all back on, *amiga*,' Alicia says, also wiping her eyes. 'We're not shooting that kind of film today.'

Ramona puts her clothes back on. She tries on several shoes and she and Alicia decide the red high heels fit her best.

'We only need to see that you can walk in these on set. You know, for that TV posture.'

Ramona can't remember the last time she wore heels. She's taller than Lucho when she wears them. He has asked her not to if they ever go out together.

'Careers are all about image today,' he said once, 'and since I'm the one working, I'd really appreciate it, *mi amor*, if you could let my physical attributes go unnoticed and unpunished.'

She's taller than Alicia too, and she smiles all the way down at her.

'You look amazing,' Alicia says.

'Come on now,' Ramona says, hoping she keeps talking.

'They really bring out your figure.'

'Ah...'

>
> LUZ MARIA
>
> If the Señora sees you
> touching me, she'll beat
> me.
>
> LUZ MARIA backs towards the stables fence.
> Cirilio the horse moves closer to her, as if
> to protect her.
>
> LUIS FELIPE
>
> She won't touch you again.
> I won't let her.
>
> LUZ MARIA
>
> She will. She'll do it
> again and again. She hates
> me and I belong to her.
> She's not kind. She's not
> like you.

'Your butt looks incredible,' Alicia says, bending down to look, both of them laughing. 'Can you walk alright?'

Ramona steps out of the cleaning closet, her eyes fixed on the glittery stars of her shoes. Alicia claps in excitement.

'Come on, they're waiting.'

The stage, to her surprise, is a fake ivory kitchen counter. There's a fridge behind it, pans and utensils hanging off a thin wall that's kept in place with wooden beams secured diagonally behind it. It looks fragile. It could all come tumbling down with a small push. The set lights are pointing at the objects on the counter.

'So, Ramona,' Pato says, walking up to her. 'If you could please settle behind the counter. We're about to begin.' He holds both her hands to greet her, presses them a little too hard, for a little too long. Ramona straightens her back, crosses her arms. Pato winks at her. 'If you can just stand over there.'

No one says anything as Ramona makes her way up to the platform. She looks back to find Alicia but can't see her. She can't see anyone, with all the lights aimed at her.

'Is this okay?' Ramona asks the room. 'Where do you want me to stand?'

'First we have to inaugurate the session.'

'Inaugurate?'

'Three, two, one, we are...'

THINKING POSITIVE

Ramona stands there, straining to see the crew behind the lights. They're hitting their laps to a beat, clapping as they sing the words.

> PO-SI-TIVE
> IT'S ALL WHERE?
> IN YOUR MIND
> WHERE?
> IN YOUR MIND
> WHAT CAN WE DO?
> ANYTHING!
> WHAT CAN'T WE DO?
> NOTHING!
> WHAT WILL WE DO?
> SELL, SELL, SELL!

Everyone joins in on a group clap. Ramona claps too, but slightly too late, alone.

```
LUZ MARIA looks at the ground in silence for a
few seconds.

                    LUZ MARIA
               I shouldn't have said
               anything, I'm sorry.

LUZ MARIA blushes as Alejandro Zañartu's
AMOR INVISIBLE, AMOR INVENCIBLE plays in the
background. Cut to close-ups of their faces
softening for one another.

                    LUIS FELIPE
               I'll take you on a ride,
               come.

                    LUZ MARIA
               No, Señor, I can't.
```

'This may be different to your other auditions,' Pato says. 'Much more energetic. Much better. We need you to convince us, the audience, your audience, to buy the latest in home appliances. Directly from the United States of America.'

'Home appliances?' she says. 'I thought—'

The crew laugh quietly.

'This is the new theatre. Don't worry, though. Plenty of our saleswomen have gone off to work in, you know, what was her name again?'

'María de los Ángeles Gigoux,' someone answers.

'Yes, Gigoux. You know her?'

'Yes,' Ramona says. 'From the telenovelas.'

'That's right. She stood right where you're standing now. Sold us a grill.'

Just like her but fifteen years younger.

'What you have in front of you is the Rotato Potato,' Pato says, exaggerating the English pronunciation.

'Rotato.'

'It peels potatoes without any of the mess.'

'Okay,' Ramona says, thinking of the mess Mariela makes when she cooks.

'We need you to sell it to us.'

'I don't know how it works. I don't know how to sell.'

'It doesn't matter. The object doesn't matter. You have to sell us the idea, the idea of a clean home, of living better. The idea of winning.'

'I'll try.'

'No, no, be positive! It's all in your mind. You can be anyone you want to. Right now, you're a winner and you're going to make us wish we were you.'

Ramona looks at the Rotato Potato, unsure of what to do with it. It has a plastic base which is holding a potato upright. Ramona turns a little crank at the top and the potato rotates. Everyone's quiet and she has no idea what to say because—

YOUR CHARACTER DYING IS BAD, BUT AN ACTOR 'DRYING' IS FAR WORSE:

You cannot rely on prompters or stage managers anymore, Ramona. The world has changed. No one will tell you what to do. Don't panic. Count back from three and take a deep breath and then talk. Just talk. If nothing comes out, count again. You have to improvise your way out of silence. And what if I can't? What if, like in our last show, a prop refuses to work as it should?

>   LUIS FELIPE
>   Of course you can. I'm the
>   patrón. You'll have to
>   come have fun with me on
>   Cirilio. It's an order.

EXT. FARM STABLES - NIGHT

LUIS FELIPE AND LUZ MARIA ride out of the
stables together on Cirilio the horse. The
open field has farmers working the land by
lamplight. The workers stop their tasks to
watch the riders in awe. The CHURCH is visible
at a distance behind them.

INT. CHURCH - NIGHT

FATHER CALLETANO and ISABEL URRUTIA are
talking, sitting on the front row pews.

What if that damn chair refuses to budge off the stage when I'm meant to throw it? What if the moon falls, remember when that happened? You have to trust others. But what about their lines? If I have to respond to improvised lines, and they then have to do the same, when do we stop improvising? At what point are we not in the play at all? Well, you better speak first then. But what if everyone forgets where they're meant to go, what they're meant to do? Look, Ramona, all of our failures are failures of imagination.

And that day the moon fell again and they had all trusted each other, looked into each other's faces, some even shrugging, paralysed, and Ramona breathed in real deep and 'The night will be shorter than expected,' she had said, in character, almost crying as it was a scene of great personal loss she can no longer remember. 'A new day is about to begin,' she had added when no one talked, and then the curtains closed. No one could move the chair in time for the next scene, so they had decided to ignore it. The audience did not seem to care.

Ramona turns the crank and the potato turns, its skin coming off in a tidy spiral. She stops, walks over to be in front of the kitchen counter. Now they can see her shoes. She leaves a pause to hear the men shuffling in their seats. Oh, Don Francisco, how easy it is to be adored when the camera aims at you and you alone, and before anyone can stop the scene—

'I was like you once,' she says, 'tired of making a mess.'

Ramona is in the cleaning closet again. Alicia has told her to wait there while they discuss notes on her performance. And then a knock at the door.

'I've got my clothes on,' she says.

But this time it's Pato who comes in. He closes the door behind him, steps in closer to her.

'There's something I have to tell you,' he says in a solemn voice she hasn't heard him use before.

'It's okay. I haven't done this in a long time. It was bad, wasn't it?'

He's so close to her she can smell him. Incense. Cigarette hair. Alcohol breath. Lucho never drinks and she likes that about him. Pato takes off his sunglasses. Ramona had never noticed that his eyes are golden. She looks down at her red shoes.

'We've been having problems, Alicia and I.'

He waits for her to react.

'The night was shorter than expected,' she says.

'Did you hear what I said?'

'Yes.'

> FATHER CALLETANO
>
> Miss, I beg you, have a softer hand with your servants. Jesus teaches us kindness, especially towards the poor and the sick. She's a poor blind girl. All I ask, in the name of God, is that—
>
> Commotion from the farmers can be heard from inside the CHURCH.
>
> ISABEL URRUTIA
>
> What's all this noise? What's happening?
>
> ISABEL URRUTIA and FATHER CALLETANO open the CHURCH door.

'We don't connect. No matter how positive we are. I think it's because she doesn't see my potential. She doesn't really see me, you know?'

'I know,' Ramona finds herself saying. 'I can see you.'

'I... Ever since I saw you, well... I know we've not spoken much outside of the gym... But I can feel it, you know?'

Pato takes her hand. She can't remember the last time Lucho held her hand. What has happened to them? They'd been too young. That's always her answer. They should have known they'd got married too young and they would both change, and grow apart, and eventually fail. If she were honest, however, she'd simply ask where her life had gone, why no one in the audience cares, why she always felt so quiet, and the house is so quiet, how she sometimes thinks she lives with ghosts tapping in recognition of her presence, never touching her, never seeing her, spirits failing to improvise, no trust, no love, no lines. Incense. Smoke.

'I've waited to do that ever since I saw you.'

She lets him kiss her. A complete failure of imagination.

When Ramona gets home she fetches a glass of water but only one, for herself. She's relieved Lucho isn't in bed. He's probably still working. She refuses to touch the little box of pills tonight. She doesn't want to be the kind of person who takes them. She wants to be awake. 'Are you tired of peeling the old-fashioned way?' she whispers to herself and laughs. Three, two, one, she counts with her eyes shut, three, two, one, but she can't think of any lines, certainly not on a night like this, about the old-fashioned ways.

EXT. FARM STABLES - NIGHT

A crowd of workers has gathered to watch as LUIS FELIPE and LUZ MARIA ride together, laughing. Close-up of ISABEL URRUTIA's face as she sheds a tear of rage.

9

PABLO

is barefoot at the top of the San Cristóbal Hill. He was in bed one moment, and the next thing he knows he's walking up the San Cristóbal. It used to happen a lot when he was younger. He'd walk up to his parents' room and, so they said, stare at them from the foot of the bed. When he once walked out into the garden, his mother joked that she'd have to tie him to his bed. But after he started playing guitar it'd all suddenly stopped. Until now.

It's 5am and already warm. The sun looks like it does on TV beach placement shots, a blue hue, purple rays. He's sweating through his pyjamas. He pulls on his left earlobe, as he does every morning, to check whether he can still hear his dream. The waves are still there, the crashing surf rolling in to the rhythm of his heartbeat.

He wishes he had his cigarettes on him. He sits on a patch of grass by a cliff edge and looks down at the sprawling city, almost quiet, still frozen, taking its last sleepy breaths before jolting itself awake.

Today is gig day. Today, he'll break up with La Dani. He has promised himself he will do it. He'd tried before, but he couldn't stand hurting her. The last time he'd seen her before she came to Santiago was the day of the move. It killed him that she'd been carrying boxes of his stuff onto lorries, because he knew she was only doing it so his mother would see her helping out. (She'd kept asking, 'Where do you want this one?' real loud even though there'd been only one lorry.) Then again, he didn't stop her. He didn't even say goodbye, not properly. And it wasn't like anything important was happening. He was just getting dragged by his parents from one town to another. That was all. He couldn't control any of it and there'd been no decision. When old people talk about the important parts of their lives they always talk about their decisions. Like taking a job or not taking it. Marrying someone or not. Whatever. Pablo is beginning to think that nothing important happens until you live alone, and that everyone's just getting dragged from and to things all the time and all that changes is that it becomes harder to know who or what to blame. But anyway, since he hadn't been the one to choose moving away, it felt wrong to use it as a reason to break up. And nothing he'd come up with would be useful to sing to her as a broken-hearted ballad – a parting gift – because, whatever he'd been feeling, he wouldn't classify it as a broken heart. Nothing he'd ever be able to sing about. And what would that sound like?

> Hey Dani, thanks for helping out.
> So, I'm moving,
> and I know it's only two hours away,
> and knowing how your dad drives it's probably a lot less,
> but I don't think I want this at a distance,
> I'm sorry.

Do you remember when you said you would love me forever
and then I said I would too?
You said it like we were in a film,
like you'd waited for the right light,
sunlight only on our mouths, and
I just wanted you to like me.
What was I meant to say?
It was late at night and we were
at your place
and you'd been telling me about all these assholes
at school
at school, oh yeah,
who'd made fun of the way you run.
It would have been mad to say anything else
because you looked so sad
So, so sad, oh yeah,
Hope you understand that it is now my time to
awkwardly run,
away, so far, yeah.

Dani, we are young and so a little time is,
in the context of our whole lives,
quite a lot of time.
And so I have aged, and you have aged,
and I have thought about it a lot in the last two weeks,
which again, is some sizeable fraction of time for us,
and so I have, in a way,
thought a lot about it, well,
I have concluded I don't love you
anymore.

But the truth was that as soon as he started to form a sentence about breaking it off, he'd miss her, hug her by the side of the lorry where his mother couldn't see them from the house, La Dani would sneak-kiss him, would say things in between kisses like 'I love you so much' and 'We'll be together soon' and 'Things happen for a reason' and 'Don't worry about me, I'll be fine' and 'You must take care.' All the common stupid things, to which he couldn't help answering, 'Me too, me too, yes.'

And now she's been in Santiago with her father looking at universities and visiting some of her family for the past week, and she's been calling every day to ask if she can visit. Mariela has told him to call back. 'You modern kids are so independent,' she said. He's been saying he forgets, or that the number on the notepad was written wrong and so on. Things are different now. He loves music too much. His band. Everything else is a distraction, a waste of time. He has to write better songs and fast. Finish something. The year will soon end and he has no intention of going to university. That will be the first thing he insists on. His parents won't understand at first. Old people never do. But then he'll be on the radio, on TV, the best new act in Santiago, a new voice in Latin America, and they'll want to take credit. We always knew it, they'll say. There was never any doubt. And La Dani will say in interviews how much they'd loved each other, that though it was over, she was glad to have been a part of his beginning, just as he'd been of hers.

It takes him an hour to walk home. His parents are in bed, and so he gets dressed and sits at the kitchen table. He turns on the little radio by the windowsill, real quiet, and waits for the house to wake. Silence makes the sea in his ear much louder. Some nights he even has to sleep with his radio on. It's easier to ignore all the talking (so much talking, that goes on in late-night radio) than the watery fizz. He doesn't even mind the stupid love ballad by Alejandro Zañartu, which is playing right now. It's comforting to hear just how bad it is, how glad stations will be when the DJs get his tape, how relieved even, the DJs will be to play his songs and let the country forget all the shit like Alejandro Zañartu ever existed.

Mariela comes into the kitchen and frowns.

'How come you're up so early these days?' she asks, tying her hair back into a bun. 'Will you have your milk today?' And before he can answer, 'I don't like it one bit when you come down here and make a mess of things.' She turns on the tap and lets the water run over the crumby plate he left from a sandwich he ate late last night.

'It's just one plate, Marielita. I should have washed it. Sorry.'

'Marielita, Marielita, right...' she says, trying hard not to smile. 'If he sees things out like that, your dad will think I'm not doing my job. And you know how nervous your mother gets when there's any mess. You know her.'

Growing up, Pablo had always liked Mariela. He was aware of his role for her in providing a respite from his mother's demands. Ramona's unease with servitude often manifested in harsh, laconic orders: 'I don't know, just clean it better. There is always dust where the walls meet the floor. There wouldn't be any dust there if you had cleaned it. Sweep under the rugs. Why is the house so dirty?'

Mariela was always telling Pablo just how bad she had it in this new, bigger house. Last week, after his mother had pointed out a stain in one of the new curtains and reminded her to wash her hands, Mariela told Pablo that the only time of the day she enjoyed was when his mother went to the gym. He never answered, only listened and nodded. Except, after the curtain incident, when he had said, 'Why don't you leave then, what's stopping you?' And she'd turned real quiet, lost her anger, shrunk into herself and said, 'You, Pablito,' and they hadn't talked since.

Pablo's now nervous around her, afraid even, though he doesn't know why.

'Is the little Miss coming here or will you go out?' she asks, placing a mug of chocolate milk and an *hallulla* bread with cheese in front of him and moving off to clean the kitchen sink.

'La Dani?'

'Who else?'

'I don't know yet.'

He used to tell Mariela everything about La Dani – but only when it was going well, from the moment they first met while studying for their First Communions, to their first kiss at the *fonda* party at the regiment, right behind the firing range shack. Those were good days. There is little to say now. Mariela doesn't know a thing about his new life, new purpose, new friends.

'You will tell me if I need to prepare anything, okay?'

'Okay.'

'I mean it, Pablito. No surprises.'

'I said yes,' he says, louder than he expected. He gets up without looking at her, listening to all that water overflowing on plates, down the drain.

When he gets to the school gates in the morning, Francisco and Clara are already waiting for him. He waves but they don't see him and it'd be too lame to wave again so he walks on, pretending not to see them. The street is full of jackass kids yawning and their jackass parents saying goodbye from car windows. He's not sure what bothers him about the kids walking through the gates and shaking hands and hugging, but he thinks it has to do with how predictable it always is. If he were honest, he'd admit that it reminds him of all the times he's walked through the gates without a single thought beyond wanting to go home to make music. And school morning noise is always the same, just as bad no matter where you are. A common nightmare, like being chased or falling down a precipice. It makes him sick just thinking about it. He doesn't think he'll ever forget it.

Francisco and Clara are standing with their backs against the wall, to the side of the gate. They're doing this to avoid being seen by the inspector, the king of assholes, who makes kids do squats in the middle of the playground whenever he gets bored. The inspector always stands at the end of the first corridor in the mornings, by a Virgin Mary statue with open arms but looking real miserable because she has no mouth. The inspector tells kids to tuck their shirts in, or shouts at girls who roll up their skirts too high, and once he made this kid cry over wearing the wrong shade of grey trousers. But whatever it is he's trying to do now, it's not working and everyone just walks by him and laughs. Probably because he's holding an old-school Christmas bell. Anyway, now he's nearer, Pablo waves again and Clara responds by snapping back her head in greeting, trying to look cool. Francisco's wearing a black leather jacket over his uniform. It's too large for him and the day is too hot for it. Clara's wearing her skirt higher than she's allowed at school. Her shirt's not tucked in either (so Pablo quickly pulls his shirt out). And she's wearing sports shoes. Hector waves hello at Pablo from inside the gates. Pablo pretends not to see Hector.

'Hey,' Pablo says, flattening his back against the wall too, right by Clara. No one answers. This would make a good band poster. Good band pictures always make their members look like they're not really friends, like a bad family photo, the more serious the better. The Detainees are always staring into the far away on their tape covers. They're always standing by or inside dilapidated houses. They're always wearing leather.

'Do we want to go in and make an excuse or something?' Pablo says.

'Whatever, man. Let's just go. Tired of fucking waiting around,' Francisco says, and Clara and Pablo follow him. 'Here,' he says, giving them a cigarette each.

They walk up to a brick ledge behind an old bicycle shop that's next to the school and sit in a line. There's a single tree with exposed roots on a dry patch of grass. The tree trunk is painted white. Pablo's father once told him people did that to scare off the ants, but it just looks like it's the tree that's gone pale with fear. There are no ants here, just a collection of cigarette butts and soda cans.

Francisco lights his cigarette and passes the matches to Clara. She puffs at hers without resting it in her hand, just leaves it there hanging in the side of her mouth like a TV villain, like a Wild West badass, smoke rising slow and thick in front of her eyes. Pablo lights his with a slight cough.

'Are you two ready? Have you practised?' Francisco asks, flicking the match in front of him.

'Yeah, I'm ready,' Clara says.

'What time do we meet after practice?' Pablo asks.

'*Huevón*, we're meeting now. It's not a fucking date. It's gig day. The whole day's a practice.'

'I'll have to get some shit at home first.'

'All our gear's at the barn,' Clara says.

'Clothes and stuff,' Pablo says, looking at Francisco's jacket, wondering if his father has anything like it.

'We still have time to go over the set a couple of times,' Francisco says.

'We not going to school at all then?'

'Are you dumb?' Francisco asks.

'It's gig day,' Clara says.

There're only so many times you can play the same song before its changes, its build-ups and silences, the anger and sadness and the joy of endings, all fade to the awkward movements of fingers on a fretboard, of feet tapping neat 4/4 beats in a slight drag, the weight on the left shoulder. Then music becomes something to merely move together to. Pablo wonders if this is what it'll always be like once they become famous, if this is what Juan García from The Detainees meant when he said in that interview that the audience was the most important part of their music. Making music wasn't meant to feel any different to cleaning your house, to waking up and going to a job you hate. In his words, it wasn't meant to be romantic. 'Fuck romance,' he said, bleeped out. Pablo had once laughed at such clichés, the sucking up, the stardom bullshit. But more and more he realises that at least with an audience, they'd have something to listen to in return. Won't even that get old? Won't he, one day on the stage at the National Stadium, turn lights on the crowd, and see nothing but open mouths, hear nothing?

They finish what'll be the fourth song in their set this evening: 'How're You, Cos I'm Fucked'. It's less than a minute long and only has two chords, a tense A# where Francisco screams *I'm fucked* for just under a minute and then, at the end, an open Em where he shouts *and how are you?* before Clara does a triplet roll around the toms, lets the guitar feed back and then comes crashing down on the cymbals.

```
E---------------------X--X------------------------X--0
B---------------------X--X------------------------X--0
G---------------------X--X------------------------X--0
D-X--X--X--X--X--X--X--X--X--X--X--X--X--X--X--X--2
A-X--X--X--X--X--X--X--X--X--X--X--X--X--X--X--X--2
E-6--6--6--6--6--6--X--X--6--6--6--6--6--6--X--0
```

I'm fucked I'm fucked I'm fucked I'm fucked I... How're you!?

That's what Pablo has written in the open notebook on the floor by his feet. It's what he would have played if Francisco had let him play guitar. But: 'We need a bassist,' he'd said at the start of the week. 'So you're staying on bass. You can borrow my brother's for now – he's in university and doesn't play anymore anyway. We sound paper-thin and we need more punch. I'm the frontman so I think I should play the guitar, the harmonic parts. You both should support me. It's arguably the more important job.'

When Pablo mentioned The Detainees – how Juan García, the frontman, is the bassist, Francisco said Pablo should be glad to play bass then, and that really, in their band, there was no place for frontmen, that they'd play more equally, be more equally visible and in a line, with Clara's drums between them at the front of the stage. 'Just play the root notes. Treat it as a guitar with fewer strings. Play to my sick drum,' Clara said, 'and you'll be fine. As long as we're tight we'll sound like all hell.'

She always says stuff like that. Fatal. Mortal. Shit. So bad, terrible even. All of it means *cool*, Pablo thinks. She once said she only listened to dead musicians and it didn't even surprise him.

'The best music is dead,' she concluded.

He can't look her in the eyes today. At school yesterday she'd asked him to go with her to the cleaning shed just out of the football field: 'I want to show you something fucked up.'

So he'd walked closely behind her in a long dusty trail to the edge of the school grounds where there was an abandoned pasture, left barren after a fire. The brick walls of the shed were cracking. Dark lines were visible even through the thick white paint that had been poured over the old political graffiti, those pictures where all the faces look angular and blank, like they're made of wood, and of doves lifting flags and diving into rainbows; someone's strange dream. 'It would not survive another earthquake,' she'd said when he mentioned the state of it to her. Then they'd walked past the shed and through the pasture, long enough without finding anything that Pablo thought maybe she'd turn, grab him and kiss him, tell him how tired she was of Francisco, tired of music even, sometimes, and why don't they meet there every day after school and make out? Pablo would finish school in a few months anyway. She would stop answering Francisco's calls. She would ditch him and they'd laugh about it later – even Francisco would laugh, laugh at how he just hadn't noticed he'd stood in the way of true love for so long. Too long. Something like that.

They had got to a little hill that overlooked a dried-up creek.

'There,' she'd said, pointing to what at first looked like a heap of trash.

'What?' he'd said, disappointed that there was something to see after all, and that her eyes were fixed so far from him. 'What is it?'

'A guy lives there, under that tarp.'

'Who?'

'You know when the army took over, they rounded people up down there? Some of them got shot, I heard. Some of them, no one knows. My dad told me. Some of the priests and teachers tried to hide people in other schools. It was a way of sending the communists a message.'

'Who is the guy?' Pablo said, looking towards the tarpaulin, his cheeks warming up.

'I'm not sure. No one now, I guess, a bum. My dad said he was a painter before, though. A communist painter. It's weird, you know, but I like to sit here and imagine what the hell he paints now.'

'Probably the same thing.'

'You can't ever paint the same thing.'

'Why are you—'

She took his hand, gripped it tight, but didn't face him.

'Your father... My dad told me about him too. He said I shouldn't talk to you. That your family's rotten.'

'I'm not—'

'It's okay, I won't tell anyone. I'm not like that.'
'Thanks.'
'I bet he paints a lot of fire.'

And then Clara took his other hand in hers. It was too warm – or was it his? – and he wished the communist who painted fires or the same as before, always the same, had come out of the bin bag tarp, kiting in the wind. But they could both see, when the black bag stopped quivering, that there was no one there and they had nothing to talk about, which is, he now thinks while in the barn and playing the intro to 'Rather Be Dead Than A Life Where You Decide', why she kissed him, her tongue inside him, quivering, a light breeze on her eyelids.

'I haven't finished composing my Song of the People,' Francisco says, a hint of irritation in his voice. 'We've got four songs and we need at least five. They said we need to play five.'

'Who said?' Clara smashes a cymbal without a kick drum. It sizzles like cold water on a hot pan, metallic treble, and Pablo covers his right ear with his shoulder.

'The guys from The Mutant Children. They play right after us. All our songs are too short.'

'Do you have any finished parts? To your song, I mean?' Clara asks.

'I'm still recording the river. It's just got too many parts. It'll take time to even start the melody. I told you. I want it to be about everything and everyone in this fucking city.'

'So? What should we do then?'

'I was thinking we improvise. Put a beat on. Give me a few bass notes, loop them in a 4/4 beat – I'll shout something. It'll work.'

'Can you improvise?' Clara asks Pablo.

La Dani is smiling at him real wide. They've been sitting at the kitchen table for a while and Pablo hasn't found the right way to tell her how much he loves music and how the new band he's in will have to improvise later tonight, or how she should probably have got the message by now and leave or something like that, leave with an understanding nod and a handshake. Mariela is behind them doing the dishes.

'Sorry I've taken so long to properly visit,' La Dani says, holding his hands across the table. He notices on his watch that an hour has already gone by. It takes another hour to get to the warehouse where the shut-in party's going to be. Francisco has told him they are going to meet there. Has given him the address. Clara and Francisco are going to take all the equipment, the bass included, but Pablo has to be there early enough to soundcheck.

'It's alright,' Pablo says. 'It's really okay.'

La Dani has always apologised for things that aren't her fault. It's her way of making him aware he's done something wrong while not letting him apologise for it. So that it stays with him. When he arrived late to their dates at the plaza in San Fernando, she would say things like: 'Sorry I arrived early, I was a little too excited.' So that meant for the rest of the date he'd have to prove he was excited too. Like he would have to walk faster, and make constant small talk about the plaza and their days at school, which were pretty much always the same. And when he managed to convince his mum to buy a school planner to give to her for her birthday, only for her to buy one that was meant for the previous year, La Dani said, 'I'm sorry it was for the wrong year. I can still use it but the days are all wrong so don't get mad if I get your birthday confused.' She didn't get his birthday confused. She gave him a religious calendar with the different stages of Jesus's death and all that.

'Engineering is a lot of work. You know only around fifty per cent of first-year students make it past Calculus 1? Reduces the course to like fifty people, I heard.'

'It sounds really tough,' he says, looking out the kitchen window.

'Yeah, I mean, but I'm sure you'll do fine. How are your mock scores?'

'Yeah, really good.'

'What are you getting?'

'Around seven hundred,' says Pablo. Mariela drops a plate in the sink.

'That's very good. It'll be great to see you there next year. I can introduce you to some people in my study group. They can help you get through Calculus 1.'

He hopes she doesn't ask anything specific about the Aptitude Test because, in fact, he's never taken a mock exam seriously. He just dots the answers in a zigzag, and sometimes he gets a few right, even if he's not too sure what's even on the paper. He just doesn't care. There. That's what it is. Why would he? His future is the band and he'll talk about it someday in a magazine interview and kids will tell their parents, who'll then worry about young people today and the celebrities they follow and they'll probably hate Pablo because deep down they'll be thinking, fuck me, I wish I hadn't cared either, now look at my shitty old-person seven-hundred-point-scoring life. He doesn't give a fuck about Calculus 1. Or 2. Or History or Spanish or Maths or any Science. Not one bit.

'Yeah, that'd be great.'

'Are you sure you kids don't want anything to eat?'

'Sorry Marielita,' La Dani says. 'I have to go meet Dad before he goes back to San Fernando. Are the uncle and aunt coming back soon? If not, please tell them I said hi. It's a beautiful house... Tell them that too.'

Pablo and La Dani head upstairs to his room. It's what they usually did before she left his house in San Fernando and so he doesn't think much about it. Sometimes back then they would hug and sometimes they would kiss, sometimes both, and sometimes he'd try to touch her ass but she'd lift his hands onto her back and ask what he was doing and he'd smile a stupid smile. Now, she shuts the door and stretches on his bed, facing the ceiling. She never used to lie on his bed. He looks at her from the door, knows that the right thing to do, that is the loving thing to do, what is correct and expected, would be to lie next to her, small talk this or that – How I've missed you, how painful it is to live with you only in memory – Do you remember when we Xed and Yed? Seems like such a long time since Z, it's been so long since all that I wonder if it's changed – and then he would have to make sure not to wait too long in silence because it's rude, it's rejection; but also wait just long enough to hold the lingering certainty of a movie kiss, pausing only to breathe, holding each other's faces, sometimes, brushing cheeks with a palm, hearing Mariela break something downstairs and laughing while still making out (that's how close they would be – kisses immune to laughter), her hands under his shirt, never going below the waist, his hand awkwardly climbing to her breast, waiting underneath it, asking for permission, and that's where it stays until, lips hurting, she'll peck his chin and they'll sigh next to one another, eyes fixing on the ceiling, until one of them manages to make a daily observation, how Santiago's always warmer than back home, how rare the rains have been, 'A gift to the land,' the news anchor had said, something like that, and 'Do you have any plans?'

'Have you met anyone interesting yet? New friends?' And then they would land back in the room and their own bodies, 'Gosh,'

she would smile, 'it's been a while. Are you sure you don't want to join our study group now maybe? Even if it's early?' Kiss. Kiss. 'And then, after studying, when they all leave and my aunt's still at work.' Kiss, kiss. 'We'll have the house to ourselves.' Kiss. 'Are you sure you don't want all of that? Because I want that. What do you want, then?'

And now while it doesn't happen that way, he does kiss her, checking his watch behind her head and he really has to go, has no time for this, for making this difficult, and his ear's ringing, more like a strong breeze inside him, a low hum again, and he stands and he finds himself talking, opening his mouth and saying, 'I don't want to make this difficult,' something like that, and wanting to say, 'I don't want to join your study group, and I'm late and I don't care about the Aptitude Test because I have no aptitudes, and I'm getting out of this life to join another.'

Actually, he doesn't say all that, but La Dani's face changes and she sits up on his bed, elbows carrying her weight, her hair an explosion of single strands, of guilt, shame, and then she goes to the door, her hand flat against it.

'Your father's going to put you in the army, you know that, right? Don't you remember what he said to you? Study or it's the army.'

Only she doesn't say that either, not like that.

La Dani leaves and he wonders how long he should wait before going out too, because he's already late and she would never have said that – and he will certainly never do that; go to the army – but his feet are grounded in fear, fear, that's all it is. She'll forget it all anyway. He will soon be nothing to her.

Pablo goes back downstairs. Before leaving, he takes out one of his father's old uniform jackets that Mariela has left out to dry.

'Where the fuck were you?' Francisco says. He's smoking frantically, trembling cigarette and all. Clara's facing down the long narrow road full of warehouses. There's a crowd standing in the dark outside one of the buildings, thirty people or something like that, all older, all smoking. More people are coming out onto the street. Pablo can't hear any music.

'Someone told, man. Someone spoke. The whole thing's fucked. The police are coming. All our stuff's in there but we can't get in. They're not letting anyone in. They're going to fucking arrest everyone. My brother's going to kill me. He really liked that bass. And what the hell are you wearing?'

'It can't be that bad,' Pablo says. 'Surely it's a rumour. There's always a lot of rumours about this kind of thing. It's not as bad as it used to be.'

That's what everyone says now, and by everyone he means his father. He says that the police crashing concerts is a rumour. That at first they had to do it to keep peace and order. That most people, if peaceful, feel free.

'Hey, I got this jacket at a market. Thought it'd make a good statement,' Pablo says.

'They're crashing a university gig near Bellas Artes too. One of those guys heard they're coming here next. That they're looking for someone,' Francisco says.

'Well, we've done nothing wrong.'

'It's a Communist Youth Fuck The General night, man. We are literally on the posters, all three of us. We're fucked.'

On the opposite side of the road, a black car parks up with its headlights still turned on.

'Did you,' Clara whispers to Pablo, 'did you say something to your—'

'No,' Pablo whispers back.

'Now is the time if... Oh man, we need to get the hell out of here,' Clara says, louder, looking from one end of the road to the other. 'Someone come up with something, and quick.'

Francisco shakes his head, shrinks back into the wall. Clara looks at Pablo, takes his hand and presses it into a fist. He nods at her and walks towards the crowd – and is soon running. He didn't say a thing. He really didn't. Not even to himself. He's not a communist or anything. He's nothing. He's trembling too but running hides it. What is he so afraid of? Nothing is going to happen – he's never heard of anything like this happening. Maybe much earlier, but not anymore. Those days are over. His father would know better. He reaches the crowd, drowns in it, he's too short, a child, and yes, there's a man at the door yelling at everyone to go away– but that causes people to panic. Some throw bottles. People shout around him: 'I left everything inside, man, nothing's going to happen... It's just a rumour... We can't keep bowing to them like this, fuck them, fuck all of them' and Pablo's ear is a wave of feedback; he can hardly hear anyone in spite of the shouting, only his own breath. And then he finds himself stood over a rescued amplifier.

'The Mutant Children!' he shouts. 'I'm looking for The Mutant Children. I have a place to hide. Anyone else who wants to come, follow me.'

He doesn't know if anyone has heard him, but as he pushes his way out of the crowd and walks back towards Francisco and Clara – both staring wide-eyed at him – he looks back and there's a tidy line of silhouettes following him.

'What the fuck are you doing?' Francisco says. 'This will get us even more noticed.'

But Pablo just says, 'Come with me.'

The black car stays in place and they can hear sirens in the distance. Pablo has heard stories about people being followed, the black cars, getting taken by police at night when The General took over. 'But not anymore,' his father says. 'It was never that bad to begin with if you were good. It's always like this when people have things to hide.' And since Pablo had never seen any of it happen, and he doesn't have much to hide, he assumes none of the others have ever seen it happen either. And yet despite that, they walk in silence for what seems like ages. Some of them eventually start to whisper about a secret party, which then becomes a lock-in all-night party, which then, once they notice that The Mutant Children's frontman is walking with them, becomes an lock-in all-night gig. Whatever it is, by the look of them, black leather jackets, scruffy haircuts, ripped jeans, some guys even with dangling earrings, Pablo thinks they have nowhere to go but out. La Dani had once said, paging through a music magazine Pablo had bought, that the only difference between rock-and-rollers and homeless people was that some of them went to gigs. God he hated her when she'd said that. And using the word, rock-and-rollers. Jesus. Pablo keeps thinking about La Dani paging through the magazine and him hating her, and the homeless rock-and-rollers following him, and when one of them asks, 'So the party's this way?' he just says, 'Sure' because he doesn't feel like speaking much. And anything could still happen. It could turn out to be a party. Of sorts. It feels that way at least, being between things, even when it's not true, like now, a commercial break before a cliffhanger, everything scripted, everything already set up.

By the time they get to Pablo's house, there are only about ten or fifteen people from the crowd with them; the rest have all left, out into the night. All the lights are off. He leaves everyone waiting outside the gate and he goes into the kitchen. Mariela comes into the room in her pyjamas.

'How are you arriving back so late, Pablito? It's not right, it really isn't. Your parents are going to be really mad.'

'Did you tell on me?'

'I said I'd seen you go to bed. But you can't involve me like that. It's not fair. And smoking as well... *Ayayay*, Pablito, you stink of cigarettes.'

'I'm sorry.'

'Is everything okay? You look like death. Let me make you something to eat. Did something happen with La Dani?'

'No, it's alright, thank you. I'll sleep in the basement today.'

'I honestly don't know what's got into you lately.'

He hugs Mariela. 'It's really nothing. Please just go back to bed. It's really nothing.'

'Okay then,' she says, stepping back.

'You're the best, Marielita.'

'The best,' she says to herself, shaking her head and walking out of the kitchen. 'Who knows what you'll do and I'll be the one to clean up after you, always the—'

She leaves and shuts the door.

Pablo goes out to meet the group but half the people have already left. From The Mutant Children, only the singer remains.

'So?' Francisco says. 'Yeah, they were pretty pissed there wasn't a party down here, so they left. What are we doing?'

'Follow me. But be quiet. Don't say anything.'

In a line they follow Pablo down to the basement. No one talks much at first. They stand awkwardly in different corners of the room. The single light bulb in the middle gives everyone outside its spotlight a faded contour, a little party of apparitions. Francisco grabs Pablo's guitar, plays single strings quietly.

'I think it used to be a bomb shelter,' Pablo says.

And then they all sit in a circle under the light bulb, Francisco in the middle of them, playing muted strings, and Clara frowning at Pablo, always quiet.

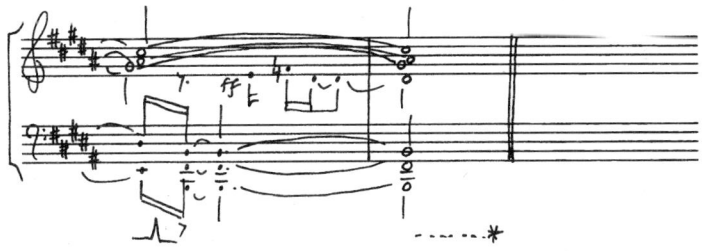

10

LUCHO

is looking through a notebook of his old poems before making his way to the Tutankamón. The pages have turned yellow and some of them – though he does not remember writing these poems – have ashy fingerprints from the time he used to sit on the plaza benches that circled San Fernando's water fountain, trying to describe passers-by, and then writing instead about Ramona. 'Men in love become a bore,' his father had told him when he'd found the notebook in his school bag. 'They become fragile.' And then his father had ripped out a page, Notes #23, made a crumpled ball of it. 'Take it out of my hand,' he had said. 'If you can take it out you can finish it.' And Lucho had stood there in front of his father, whose arm was extended, fist facing him, and he had tried slowly to untangle the grip. 'Try harder,' his father had said, 'you're not trying – let me buy you a dress, madam.' But Lucho couldn't do it. 'Hit me if you want it that bad,' his father said. 'You can't fight?' He had pushed Lucho with the other arm. Lucho had pushed back, gave him a slap on the gut and his father lowered his arm. 'You don't want it, you see? You don't really want it.' He punched Lucho on the cheek. 'Don't forget,' he had said, 'don't forget what this is made of.' And then he had stepped on the note.

Years later his father would forget this ever happened, along with everything else – even himself.

The only word left on the page from the uneven rip his father had made is *aureate*, undoubtedly a word he'd used to try to make something in San Fernando sound better than it was, worth writing about. Light through palm leaves? A wet pavement? People walking on morning dew? Ramona, Ramona – Ramona, aureate lies, which, looking at the bunch of failures in front of him now, he's beginning to suspect are the purpose of poetry. His mother had once looked at his early work and said that the only honest triplet was the Father, the Son and the Holy Spirit. He hadn't understood it back then, but now he sees his triadic forms everywhere, forced trimeter all over. Opened in the book in front of him, Poem #88 reads:

> Death is| winter| palm trees
> She sits| near me| to watch

How terrible these are. Why was it that, despite relying on structure, he could never reach Neruda's clarity, could never merely state what he saw or how he felt

> The memory of you emerges from the
> night around me
> and it did – it was exact, an exact longing. Why

> He could| never| find words
> Beyond| this world| of his

and his father was right, his

> Future| was in | numbers

and he would never be a poet, though his father never said why, the communists this, idealists that, patriots are facts and allegories are for liars – but not him, nothing about him – that maybe however much he tried he just

Did not| have the| heart to

but he must rescue something to take to show the other writers at the workshop this evening. They'll mock him, sure. They'll say, I thought you said you were a writer – what are all these lines about Pedro de Valdivia? What are all these discoveries of fallen so-called heroes to the universal and timeless struggles of men? Go back to counting bullets. Words are not for you.

Felipe Flores, the writer in charge of this week's workshop, has set them all a task. He referred to a book called *I Remember* by Joe Brainard. Too much remembering. Lucho needed to write a page emulating Brainard's style, which consisted of disconnected sentences starting with *I remember*. When his father lost his memory he:

> Did not remember his wife had left him because he
> Did not remember Antonia, his prostitute, and
> Did not remember he'd forced Lucho into the army and
> Did not remember ordering the arrest of Ramona's stepfather and
> Did not remember Ramona, years later, in the hospital with her mother, whose skin was so burnt and blistered that bandages removed it, and
> Did not remember Lucho's name, sometimes, though Lucho
> Remembers Ángel counting stars and asking why so much light lit nothing and
> Lucho remembers no one in San Fernando daring to approach him whenever he walked outside, lost and
> Remembers the anger when Ángel did remember him, my son, thank you for coming, did you bring bread?
> Remembers one day finding Ángel reading his old notebooks and

Remembers him saying, this is real beauty, who wrote these?
Remembers, that day, telling his commander that his father had sadly turned, rotted, become an embarrassment – 'imagine all the things he might say' – and
Remembers the night they came to take Ángel, and
Remembers the night around him and the hour of departure, oh deserted one, the fierce cave of the shipwrecked, had it been that, as the great Neruda said, was that exact enough? Swallowing everything, like distance
Remembers feeling
Nothing but time in the cabins,
Time in the miserable solitary dining room,
Motionless and visible like great sorrow
says Neruda, but it wasn't sorrow, it wasn't

At all| close to| Sorrow

that he'd simply remembered, I remember, to listen to time, to move to forget the

Father| the Son| the Spirit

of Arturo Prat hitting the first wave, and Lucho wonders, as he turns to his Fallen Heroes notes, just how much of the world Prat lost sight of beneath the waves, and how soon, how quickly he must have realised: this is it, this is it for me, remember me or

It was| all for| nothing

Running out of time, Lucho opens up his notebook on a clean page and writes:

> I remember my mother painting two men on opposite sides of the canvas; an avocado tree in the middle, its roots reaching for them and her saying: 'There is no greater love than loss.'

And then he rips out the page.

Lucho's disappointed that the workshop takes place in what appears to be an old classroom borrowed from his childhood. He doesn't know what he expected, really (maybe a grandfather clock and leather chairs, coffee tables whose only purpose would be accommodating ashtrays and booze). He always thinks of old clocks when he pictures writers, though he's never had an old clock himself. He does not think of somewhere so tidy and clean as this place; pungent with the smell of paraffin used to wipe the floor. He hadn't expected a blackboard, not a poster print of Picasso's *Don Quixote* and certainly not yet another of Neruda's silhouette's with the trite *Tonight I can write the saddest lines* quote in block capitals underneath. And just like in that famous silhouette, Lucho himself is wearing a beret. He takes it off when he notices the poster.

Perhaps the biggest disappointment is that the only free desk is at the back of the classroom. He sits there while the others arrive: Hello, hello, God it's already so hot, isn't it? Yes, too hot, hello, how's your book coming along? You know, the usual, not coming at all. Well, it happens... Hi, hi there, yes, it happens, every day, even one sentence, you won't even notice and one day it'll all be over.

Felipe Flores, the only other person Lucho recognises, sits in front at the teacher's desk. A different writer leads each weekly session. Felipe opens a drawer, takes out a poncho and puts it on. He looks at the class, both hands resting on the desk, and takes a deep breath.

'So I asked you all to write in the style of *I Remember*. As always, we'll read out all of your pieces first and then focus on each one separately.'

The sound of pages being turned. Some of the writers make urgent last-minute notes on their drafts.

'We'll start at the front, here. Read your best one.'

A tiny man with a long red woollen scarf nods.

'I remember my bedroom walls cracking in the Valdivia earthquake while I made love to Susana Donoso,' he says. 'I never saw her again after the tsunami took her house. The sea has been my enemy ever since. I'd like to see it dry someday.'

Felipe avoids making any expression which could be confused with approval or distaste. He simply points at the next person in the row of desks. A young boy, not much older than Pablo, sweeps his hair behind his ears.

'I remember my parents feeling hope when Allende was elected, and losing it later.'

And then an old man who, in a puzzling dramatic gesture, takes off his glasses before straightening the pages in front of him and reading:

'I remember my torturer's face whenever he played me Beethoven's Fifth.'

Lucho has no idea what to say. He keeps looking for lines in his unfinished collection. He doesn't remember writing any of them. Reading them is like stealing someone else's thoughts. (But isn't that the problem with language? What would memory look like outside the shape of words? 'The liar's entire universe,' his father had once said, 'is devoted to protecting his lies'.)

A woman, perhaps Sánchez, stands up to read.

'I remember the first curfews, making tea and wondering when the city would wake up, explode. I had a lot of tea and perfect silence.'

Lucho lands on a page filled with Neruda quotes and:

'I remember,' he says, 'the tiredness of Santiago.'

'Neruda!' Felipe says, pointing at the silhouette. 'Though we prefer original work, I don't think anyone here minds a reference to our fallen comrade. Thank you. For reminding us. We didn't expect any less from the great Pedro Castro either.'

Lucho nods. He'd met Felipe the morning before, at Pajaritos metro station. The waiter at the Fuente de Soda had written the time and place on his receipt, but he'd not been specific about who would meet him, or where. It just said 'Metro Pajaritos, 8am'. When Lucho got there the metro station was full of people and their suitcases and bags, those heading up to Estación Central to travel and others pulling carts with food and coffee to sell. Office workers. An old man playing guitar. Beggars in rags. He could barely stand in place with so many people pushing against him, so he decided it was best to wait outside. And then, while he sat on a bench just outside, Felipe sat next to him, removed his green fedora hat and hugged Lucho tightly. Lucho was too stunned to move. He'd thought Felipe was a beggar. But Felipe said, 'Armando mentioned you looked changed. Dear God we've missed you, Pedro.' And Lucho asked, 'Armando?' and Felipe said, 'Yes, Armando, the waiter. Let's go, let's get out of here.' They walked all the way to the Bellas Artes, where Felipe lamented the state of the country, the arts, even sports. This is why Pedro had come back, Lucho thought. To lament. And Felipe said things like, 'The country must be unrecognisable to you,' and 'We've tried not to lose hope while you were away, but I don't think we've succeeded in that. It's tough, after so long. Even hope needs its successes to exist.' Lucho hadn't said much. He'd nodded, agreed. At first he'd worried his voice would give him away, that at any second Felipe would turn, squint his eyes at him behind thick glasses, ask him something specific about Pedro's time in exile, something about where exactly he'd lived or who he'd lived with, but nothing. And by the time they reached the edge of the river at the Parque Forestal, Lucho felt confident he could play the part because it required nothing but agreement of him. This is how he would get Pedro. He almost laughed. It was clear to Lucho that his father had been right about this too: 'When ideas become beliefs, your job is to entertain.'

But despite that, he doesn't know what he'd do if Pedro turned up at the workshop right now. He has started to wonder whether Pedro had any friends at all, or if the writers are waiting for him to acknowledge some past wrong that he's not aware of. It's too late now. He'd look like an imbecile. The last pictures of Pedro that Lucho had been able to find were in the papers, a clean young face twenty years ago. He'd run to Argentina. To Europe from there. Lucho knows that much. And Pedro had been proclaiming support for protests ever since, as well as sending letters to the media with testimonies of the tortured and the exiled. He would come back to Chile one of these days. He had said so himself in an intercepted letter to an old MIR organiser, those terrorists, the Revolutionary Left: *Expect me*. It'd been signed Ricardo Neftalí, Neruda's real name.

(The MIR agent, only nineteen years old, had been found at a safe house by secret police, CNI agents who'd been trying to foil another plan to assassinate The General after the failure of the communists' Operation 20th Century (which The General had fortunately survived). The kid was writing a letter to Pedro when the CNI broke into the house. The report Lucho had read described him as 'lifting his hands without saying a word, urinating on himself as he watched the CNI officers read his letter.' He'd been taken with six others to the Borgoño Barracks for questioning. He was beaten first, and then electrocuted 'more than twice,' though the report did not say exactly how many times. A doctor was called to assist in keeping him alive. He was 'given injections to cooperate.' His hair was pulled out. They set dogs on him. But he still hadn't talked. At his mock execution, where he was blindfolded and placed against a wall, that's when something changed. The CNI officers 'persuaded him after mentioning his newborn.' He then talked about Pedro. He was taken to an abandoned house in Recoleta, where he was shot.)

Pedro would come back, and when he did he would come here, sit right where Lucho was sitting and he too would have a notebook filled with memories and references.

> POETRY NOTES – BOOK OF RAMONA
> *Ramona is Happy: Travelling the Great Sea*
>
> I woke up startled
> from a dream in which,
> ringed by land,
> it had become inevitable we'd arrive.
>
> The gust came Southward
> with the same indifference
> that created our horizon.
>
> She smiles and I point,
> tracing clouds
> Home,
> and there she said,
> What a pity it would have been
> to miss this great voyage.

After the workshop, Lucho goes again to the Jardín del Olimpo café. There, Antonia is serving another man, sat on his lap. When she sees Lucho she nods at him, picks up a tray with empty coffee cups and walks through a neon green beaded curtain behind the counter. As always, the music is too loud to allow thinking (is that the purpose?). Several other men in suits are sitting on stools along the length of the bar, each with a woman by his side, an untouched coffee cup in front. Lucho sits at a table by the door. Despite the blackened windows, Lucho has noticed that most men avoid the tables near the exit. It's not the shame of being seen by women on their way to the metro, Lucho thinks, not even the possibility of their wives somehow looking in, but the knowing looks of other men stepping in and out.

Antonia steps out from behind the beaded curtain. Lucho pretends not to see her and looks at a man giving a high-pitched laugh as a woman much taller than him leans her breasts on his head.

'I thought you wouldn't come today.' Antonia sits facing him, hunched forward, shoulders slumped, less like a waitress than an old friend.

'I've – been busy.'

'I was happy for you. For not being here. I'm always happy when men don't turn up. For them and their wives.'

'Does your job require you to care about that?'

She sighs and nods. She stands and switches sides to sit in the chair next to him, chest pressed against his shoulder.

'Did Manuel, you know, the poet, ever tell you about his family?'

'Not even small talk? You don't want to wait for your coffee?'

'Did he?'

'He never talked about it.'

She laughs.

'Why the laughter?'

'I guess I don't understand why you're so interested in another man. Most men here come for the women. To forget about their families. He's not been here in a long, long while.'

'I've never told you, but I'm a writer.'

'A writer.'

'A writer. Of sorts.'

'I could write the saddest lines,' she says in a low voice, chin on her chest, a poor imitation of Neruda's famous recording. She laughs again. 'I never understood why anyone would want to write.'

'Why is that?'

'Pointless, isn't it? Don't most of them die poor anyway?'

'Most people die poor.'

'Yes, but even when writers are rich, you would think they were poor. No better than politicians. Workers this, workers that. Pointless and vain.' She presses him towards her, a hand on his waist. 'They don't know who people really are, *how* people really are. It's all pretend.'

'I know who you are.'

'Are you writing about me, then?'

She kisses him on the cheek.

And he had tried to write about her. But the truth was that when he came to it, he couldn't even start. Love was always hard to write about, he'd already concluded after failing to finish his poems about Ramona. Clichés couldn't be avoided. Eventually he had wondered if he was writing about his love for Ramona or the whole world's love, which was somehow less impactful and made him feel nothing. Original imagery quickly became too cryptic, so that no one could ever understand the poems, not even him whenever he revisited them. But hate, that was something else again, that was impossible. He could never write about Antonia.

'Maybe someday.' Lucho gets up in sudden disgust. He leaves spare change in a used coffee cup saucer.

'Already? Did I say something?' she says with a wide smile. She stands taller than him on her heels.

'Manuel passed away, you know? Some time ago. He's dead.'

When he was younger, Lucho had seldom wondered what it would be like to lose someone close to him. He'd lost his mother, who, as Ángel often said, was 'as good as dead to us.' But ever since he'd started to grow apart from Ramona – ever since something had appeared between them, something like a sheet of glass, not entirely visible, the smudging of old fingerprints, the blurring of shared happiness – he has been thinking that love and loss are very alike, or at least that one cannot exist without the other, because he does fear losing Ramona, and he does love Ramona, and so he doesn't want to lose her. And he hadn't felt the loss of his mother into adulthood because he hadn't been close enough to her, and she'd left him no time to fear her departure. And while he had at times been close to his father, he never called it love in his mind – do any of us have a word for it? Some may call it love, but it is not happiness, and it is not warm, and he'd been relieved when he'd died. And so now Lucho is here to lose Ángel completely.

'Oh, so you knew him? You're writing about him, then? Like some kind of detective?' she says, grabbing the coins. 'Well, whatever he did, he was always good to me. He always told me he loved me. That happens a lot. He always paid well.'

'We met a long time ago.'

'You and him? Really?'

'No. You and I.'

'I think I would remember.'

'It was many years ago.'

'I have a pretty good memory. I would remember you. Maybe in a past life.'

'Maybe in a past life.'

He steps out of the front door of the Olimpo. Three men in suits nod at him on their way in. The day his mother left had been cold. San Fernando had flooded and it would not stop raining. She'd packed a single bag. His father had not yet come home. She had sat Lucho at the table and made him lunch, chicken stew, maybe? Artichokes in lemon juice? 'Mum's going to think things over.' 'Is it about your paintings? Are you going to paint somewhere else?' 'Yes, that's it, I need to go and paint out in nature, the mountains and the sea.' 'That's pretty. Like the flag, what was it again? White for the Andes. Blue for the sky. Or was it the sea? And red, I can't remember what red stands for.' 'Blood,' she said. 'Dad says he misses the countryside too.' 'You know I love you, right?' 'Yes.' He'd hugged her and knew she would not be coming back – at least, he remembers knowing – and he had asked why she was going.

And then, dragging her bag slowly out of the gate, she had simply left.

It was not until years later that Lucho's father took him to Santiago and Lucho had first met Antonia. His father had said, he remembers this well, 'He's old enough to know.' Ángel had been drunk, and she'd been drunk as well, waving at him, touching Lucho's hands and cheeks, his father kneeling in front of him and saying, 'It's a good thing, at least it's a good thing your mother never knew.'

The door to the Olimpo closes. Lucho, his back to the black glass, lights a cigarette. Some people shout inside, the metallic scrape of sliding chairs and disbelief. The music is turned off. Silence. The suited men come out with Antonia. She's draped in a blanket, her hands cuffed. Of her body only the ends of her legs are visible, the tall golden heels. She looks at Lucho. She's crying but doesn't fight. She gasps. An attempt to ask why but she doesn't say it, no sound at all, *the gift/ Of the eternal Face without gestures* and he nods at the men, looks at her and then up the stairs at the end of the station corridor, back out into the city, where once again, he hopes

she will| become| no one

and then the music starts inside.

*

In bed Lucho stares at the ceiling, unable to sleep. Whenever he shuts his eyes, focuses on the silence, he can hear faint whispering, the muffled thump of footsteps. He gets up and heads to the top of the staircase but all the lights are off. Even Mariela had already gone to bed when he arrived home.

He shuts his eyes once more and yes, there it is again. He tells himself he doesn't believe in ghosts and spirits. He's not like his mother. He's just spent too much time outside in the crowds, the ringing of a city stamped in his ears. It isn't his father, he tells himself, though he does remember him pacing around the house at night in the first months after his mother left. He sits up on the bed and looks out the window, a misty night, trees floating on moisture like leafy tips of distant volcanoes, he thinks to himself.

Ramona isn't with him. She's sleeping downstairs. He's been sure it wouldn't take long before Ramona started spending nights in the living room again. She'd done so in the weeks leading up to the clinic. She didn't want to disturb him, she'd said, but he knew it was because she couldn't stand him. He'd changed. They both had. It is impossible to discern with any certainty the series of events that lead to love. And because of this it's impossible to try to find where on the trail their paths forked. He can only see the separate ends. One day they were sitting by the railway, relieved to see each other, laughing at just how much they had to say, how much they would do – and on the next day she was gone. 'You know what you've done,' he hears himself thinking, 'you were there, you came with me, and when I showed you the smoke-filled roads, when I rounded everyone up against the wall, you remember what you said. You didn't say, where is Ramona now? And you didn't say, where are my verses now, where are my poems? You'd lost them. I asked you what I should do. You knew some of them by name. One of them had taught you to write and count. But, you said, to hell with all of them, and then you said, eliminate them, I will do for this country what even you, my father, could not.'

Lucho gets up and goes to his office. He opens one of the sealed cardboard boxes filled with books. He can no longer avoid it. He finds Pedro Castro's name on a spine, and sees the author's picture in the jacket. So young – we were so young. Here are his poems. Lucho notices he's crying but feels nothing, only water, only water.

11

RAMONA

is sitting on a stool behind the TV that's on the kitchen counter. Today, the set lights are off and the crew, including Alicia, are having a meeting in the corridor just outside, behind a closed door. Bad news! What good has ever come out of secrecy? When Ramona had auditioned for the telenovela all those years ago to play a blind woman, after the director had mocked her glasses and offered her the part of Maid 1, she'd returned to the set, and there she'd also been made to wait. 'Good news!' the director at that time had said, walking in with a crew behind him. He'd held up a nanny's dress, an apron sewn like a green hospital gown with white stripes and embroidered pockets and collar. But her audition had been for the lead, Ramona tried to say. Don Francisco from *Giant Saturday* always told young actors that 'luck is nothing compared to persistence.' And so she persisted. But 'We can't all be leads,' the director had said. 'I can audition again! Tell me what you're looking for and I'll do it, I'll be that.' 'It doesn't work like that, Ramona – the role's been taken anyway.' She had put on the dress, and the apron, more like a loose bag on her, and the men had complimented her. They didn't say she looked pretty. They didn't say she looked good enough that people at home would know that, if it weren't for the nanny costume, she would be beautiful. Instead, they said she looked accurate. An accurate nanny. 'You are perfect for the role. I wish you could see what we see.' And she had accepted it, got on with it, even after she discovered that there were hardly any lines for her in the script. Lucho had been supportive. He really had tried. 'You'll get your break,' he had said. 'Start small. Make contacts. It's all about who you know.' But: 'It doesn't work that way,' she'd almost said. Ramona had done her best too, but couldn't help thinking, who the hell would want to talk to the nanny? The only person she ever really spoke to was a woman from make-up who had told her she preferred her to all the others and when Ramona asked why, she'd simply said, 'There's very little to do here compared to leading actors who need to be the most beautiful people in the country. With you, I get a coffee break.' After, Ramona had walked off, in costume, and never went back.

Now, sat there on her own and hearing only the group's faint mumbling, Ramona accepts that she's failed again. It's probably for the best. She wouldn't know what to say to Lucho anyway if she succeeded. I failed again – how many times before you consider yourself a failure? She should go to another gym – that would be a start – and lose weight somewhere else, do nothing else, become no one. A mother. A wife. No one else. That's what I always wanted to be, she'd tell Don Francisco, and the crowd of regular people would clap. She's so relatable, they'd say.

The crew returns to the room in a tidy line, Pato in front, smiling at her.

'Sorry to have kept you waiting,' he says.

She nods but can't look at them. She can't look at him, especially, with Alicia just behind him. When they had finished filming the Rotato Potato commercial last night, he had kissed her again, this time on the set, lights aimed at them. She hadn't seen it coming. He had said nothing and there was no build-up to the slow, slow kiss, with his palm on her cheek, his eyes shut (she hadn't been able to shut hers, it seemed inadequate, coarse even to give herself whole, imagination and all) and he had felt her body, his hands brushing over her arms and her back had

> ## LO QUE TUS OJOS NO VEN: A TELENOVELA
>
> ### #EPISODE 4
>
> INT. HOUSE BASEMENT – DAY
>
> ISABEL URRUTIA is forcefully pulling LUZ MARIA into the basement, holding LUZ MARIA's arm with one hand and hair with the other.
>
> > LUZ MARIA
> > Please, Señora Isabel, you don't have to do this!
>
> ISABEL URRUTIA leads LUZ MARIA to the centre of the BASEMENT, LUZ MARIA almost tripping with every step. Over them, a single naked light bulb gently swings.
>
> > ISABEL URRUTIA
> > Since you can't see, you leave me with no choice

tensed, it almost hurt, so that she had to take a step back. But he'd ignored that. She'd wanted to go home with him, not so much out of longing – though there was that, yes, yes! – but gratitude, which surprised her like a raindrop on her eyelid. She'd wanted to take off with him and thank him, again and again.

Today, Ramona notices the crew carrying duffel bags.

'I've got some bad news,' Pato says.

Ramona brushes her lap as if it has crumbs stuck to it.

'Well,' she says, taking one foot out of her stupid shoes.

'We've decided to film the next commercial on site. We'll have to drive out to the beach and then the hills nearby. We drive tonight, stay over and film tomorrow morning. We need the open country for this – mountains and all that. Hopefully a bird, a condor.'

'What are we selling?' she asks. But her real question is how is she going to sell this to Lucho?

'Sunglasses. Special sunglasses. They're called Condor Eyes. We'll explain later. Here...' He takes a pair of black sunglasses from his inside pocket. 'Kind of silly to sell them from a fake kitchen, don't you think?'

'Yes,' she says, but does not try them on. She doesn't want him to see her without her own thick glasses. She's always thought people who wear glasses look wrong without them, eyes too small, startled expression, ill-proportioned or just ill. She slides the sunglasses onto the kitchen counter. What will Lucho say? This is her making connections, isn't it? Networking. What if he says nothing? Is that the real fear? Is that why she's conjuring him up, Lucho but different, a version of him that will be outraged: 'No, Ramona, absolutely not! You are staying here. Are you actually going to the gym? I haven't seen any changes, if you ask me. You still look a little, you know, are you sure you're doing the right exercises? Maybe you should ask someone there to help you. Are you sure there isn't more that you could do? For yourself, I mean. Your doctor, Ramona, your doctor said you need to exercise and you are fragile and confused and you must, yes, it's your obligation, you will listen to those who know better. And there's still work to do in the house. Half the rooms don't have curtains! The front garden is still too wild. You said you'd learn to trim flowers after you fired the gardener for, your words, having poisonous hands. If you insist on leaving I'll have to lock you up. My office has a key, remember? I'll lock you up along with all my work.'

>   but to make you feel just
>   how worthless, how ugly you
>   truly are.
>
>   LUZ MARIA
>   What are you going to do to
>   me? Please, Don Luis Felipe
>   was only being kind. He
>   loves you more than anyone.
>   I know it!
>
> ISABEL URRUTIA pulls up a chair from a pile of old and cobwebbed furniture under white sheets, resting against one of the BASEMENT walls.
>
>   ISABEL URRUTIA
>   Sit down!
>
>   LUZ MARIA
>   Please, I'll—

She's seen them. His notebooks. In boxes before the move. She'd opened one of them. Poetry. Old books he used to show her lines from when they were young, him lying, she knew even then, that a verse about the weather was really about her, the face of the sun hides this and that, the gentle steps of rain blablabla, and her nodding along, clapping even, in gratitude.

'So?' Pato says.

'I don't have anything with me to stay over.'

One of the men in the crew slaps the duffel bag.

'We've got it. You don't need anything.'

'Why didn't you tell me? I would have come prepared. I'm not sure I can just—'

'—Ramona, you're thinking negatively right now. That's all it is. This is an opportunity for you. Remember, I've got contacts. Who knows, maybe I'll introduce you to a director soon. A big one. Wasn't the last girl we worked with hired by a big one?' He looks to Alicia, who nods. 'For a national telenovela. A real big one, maybe very soon. I know you have the talent. We all know it. You have to believe me. Trust me on this. Trust in yourself. These opportunities don't come often. And they don't last forever.'

In the pickup truck she's sat by the window. It only has one row of three seats, all at the front. Pato is driving and between them is Alicia, who hasn't said a word since the start of the drive. Ramona wonders whether Alicia is used to Pato inviting other women to stay in cabins by the sea. Or whether, perhaps, being TV people makes them prone to artistic arrangements in love too. You hear it all the time, right? TV people having open affairs and all that. Though Ramona is not sure, in fact, if she's heard it at all, and tries to remember a *Giant Saturday* episode that wasn't really about normal people and their normal wishes for normal prizes. Alicia looks at her, and Ramona tries to define Alicia's face as something like sadness, eyebrows slightly raised, skin creased around her mouth. She knows – does she know? What does she know? Ramona almost wants to ask her – 'What do you know?' But sadness is preferable to anger. There is still some love in sadness. Ramona doesn't want to think about anger or sadness, normal people and their normal prizes. Ramona smiles at Alicia but Alicia shifts her gaze to look out of Ramona's window, past Ramona like she isn't even there at all.

>   ISABEL URRUTIA
>   I said sit!
>
> ISABEL URRUTIA forces LUZ MARIA onto the
> chair, both hands pressing down on LUZ MARIA's
> shoulders as she sobs in fear. O FORTUNA
> starts to play in the background.
>
> Close-up of ISABEL URRUTIA removing a hot
> poker from a fire pit, its tip glowing orange.
> A shot of ISABEL URRUTIA looking right at the
> poker.
>
>   ISABEL URRUTIA
>   Give me your hand, maldita.
>
>   LUZ MARIA
>   Please don't hurt my hands!
>   No! I don't have another
>   way to see.

Leaving Santiago also feels like leaving light behind. She's been in the city so long she barely remembers roads being so dark. At times she sees old roadside huts, their tiny windows, irregular, crumbling in the watery shadows of candlelight. And then there's nothing but dirt, the leaden ricochet of stones shot under the pickup truck, empty advert signs and dry hills dotted with the black silhouettes of bushes and cacti, sand textured smooth under the delicate blanket of the moon and the stars. Like icing sugar on a cake, her mother used to say.

She replays the earlier phone call in her mind.

'He's not there, Miss,' Mariela said. 'Should I take down a message?'

Did she even want him to pick up the phone? A quick moment of relief. But then...

'Is everything okay, Miss?' Mariela asked.

'Yes, yes, fine. And Pablo?'

'Studying. Are you sure—'

No, no. Mariela hadn't even said that. It'd been far shorter.

'Studying.'

'I won't be returning home tonight. Yes, I'm staying with my friend, Alicia. Only one night. I need some room to think. I've needed time to think for a while.' She's replayed it like this a couple of times, even though she knows she didn't actually say that, not like that. Something like:

'I stayed too late at the gym. It's raining hard now.'

And it was, it really was.

'And she's offered for me to stay over. I'll come home tomorrow.'

'Should I leave some lunch out for you?'

'Tell them I love them very much.'

That part she's sure of, though she wishes she wasn't. It had sounded so ominous and final, the kind of thing her mother would say at the end of a night out drinking. She'd wake Ramona up, sitting at the foot of her bed, and say: 'I'm sorry, my daughter, I hope you know how much I love you.' Ramona would nod, scared by the tone of her mother's voice, grave like the Mother Superior's Monday morning prayers at school.

When Ramona had found her mother's body – it wasn't her. She was shrunk, discoloured, peaceful. Ramona had sat on her childhood bed, still made, sheets still clean, though she hasn't stayed there in years, and she didn't cry – that came later, the madhouse came a while later – because she had been trying to remember their last words to one another. 'I'm sorry,' her mother

> ISABEL URRUTIA
> Your hand, maldita ciega.
> I'm going to make sure you
> never see anything again.
>
> ISABEL URRUTIA presses the poker down hard on
> LUZ MARIA's right hand, and then the left. In
> agony, LUZ MARIA falls off the chair and curls
> up in a foetal position.
>
> ISABEL URRUTIA
> Stand up, maldita.
>
> LUZ MARIA remains on the floor, sobbing.
>
> ISABEL URRUTIA
> Stand up, I said!
>
> LUZ MARIA, trembling in pain, stands to face
> ISABEL URRUTIA.

had said. And Ramona, a half-empty suitcase in her hand (she'd wanted her mother to know how little there was worth taking from that house), had stood at the door. How was there nothing to say?

Ramona had anticipated that moment but had never put it into words. There were just images: the two of them facing one another, fenced in by the scratched-up wallpaper, dead flowers on the little coffee table by the front door, old magazines and newspapers that her mother used to cover up damp patches, a stinking carpet and behind, freedom, family, cleanliness. 'Love,

I love you, my daughter,' her mother had said to fill the silence and Ramona couldn't take her eyes off the bottles on the dining table, and her mother had apologised again, grabbed them while she apologised, pretended to empty them into the kitchen sink – pretended, because they were already empty – and 'I'm really sorry, never again, I'll try harder,' she had said, while Ramona, leaving her suitcase by the door, walked up to the dining table and picked up the last bottle (wine, unopened, still in a plastic supermarket bag, it was surely wine) and: 'Stop,' Ramona had said. 'I have always hated you.' She didn't say that, she couldn't have, but she had opened the bottle and made her way to the sink and her mother had followed, 'Please, please don't,' and Ramona had placed it in front of her mother, on the kitchen table, and she'd teared up. 'Drink it, I want you to drink it,' and 'I'm sorry, I'm sorry, never again.' Her mother had been shaking. She had actually trembled. 'Drink it, I said,' and she had done, bottle to her lips, and 'You disgust me,' Ramona hadn't said, and had instead lifted her suitcase once more, turned to her mother and said, 'The next time I see you you'll be dead.' Just words. Only words.

And then she had seen her.

'Everything okay?'

She turns to Alicia, who has placed a hand on her shoulder.

'You're shaking. Are you cold?'

'A little,' Ramona says.

'It always gets colder outside Santiago,' Pato says.

'Take this,' says Alicia, removing her own jumper.

'No, no, it's alright.'

'Take it, it's too warm for me anyway.'

So Ramona slips into the jumper, the familiar itch of wool. Alicia turns on the radio, twists the dial along the different tones of static before, in a deep voice, the host starts:

>   ISABEL URRUTIA
>   And now we can't let you be
>   this ugly, can we?
>
> ISABEL URRUTIA takes two gloves out of her
> pockets.
>
>   ISABEL URRUTIA
>   No one should want to see
>   something so ugly.
>
> ISABEL URRUTIA puts the gloves on LUZ MARIA,
> who recoils as the gloves slide onto her hands.
>
> EXT. MARKET STREET - DAY
>
> LUZ MARIA is crying and walking on the opposite
> direction of the crowd in the MARKET STREET. She
> trips over several times. We see the disgusted
> faces of those around her. YACONDA, the Witch of
> the Pond, whose face we can't yet see, takes her
> arm and leads her to a DARK ALLEYWAY.

    Tonight's Deepest Thought is for all you listeners out there, in your homes and on the roads in Love with the Twilight, and you, Sleepless Sailors living your oceanic lives: *Trust in time: it tends to give you sweet exits from bitter hardships.* That was tonight's Deepest Thought...

'I love these,' Pato says and Alicia looks at Ramona and rolls her eyes with a smile. 'We'll be there soon. Less than an hour now.'

Outside it's nothing but hills and the occasional roadside shacks which Ramona guesses sell fruit and cheap furniture, just like they always do. She reads a sign that has San Fernando written on it.

'Where exactly are we going?' she asks, embarrassed she hadn't done so before.

'We rented a cabin in Pichilemu, right by the sea,' Alicia says.

'Do you know it?' Pato asks.

'Yes,' she says, 'I know it.'

It's where Ramona's stepfather used to take her and her mother most summers. He'd been a schoolteacher and so they used to travel with their whole house in suitcases, staying two or three months each year. Ramona's not been there since he died, as it had been his death that had left her mother alone with a schoolteacher's early retirement pay. And so they couldn't afford to go anywhere after that. And her mother, who was already drinking most days by then, began to spend what little they did have on wine. Going to the beach is a return to childhood for Ramona, then. And what no one tells you about remembering better times is that naturally those memories lead to whatever happened later to make them memorable. She once asked her stepfather why beach sand was always so clear and fine in magazines and why they had to go to one where the sea was impossible, with waves so violent they could only ever sit in little ponds between the rocks, and where the sand was so black it looked roasted, the desolate remains of some great and ancient fire, darkening even the water, white foam pooled on it like little meringues on chocolate, devoured by the fierce wind, yes, that's what he'd said, that was it, and she'd asked him if the earth was black because of the Tinguiririca Volcano since he knew everything, this schoolteacher, the connections between rocks and water and us and 'No, it's not the volcano's fault,' he'd said, 'it's the weight of fine sand carried away in the wind, magnetite holding back the dark.' And then, seeing her puzzled face, needing a simpler

> LUZ MARIA
>
> I don't have anything for you to steal. Kill me, if you're so keen to find out.
>
> YACONDA takes off her black hood after a moment's suspenseful silence. She smiles, her teeth dirty and decayed.
>
> YACONDA
>
> Stop crying, my child. What did she do to you now?
>
> LUZ MARIA takes off her gloves. We see a close-up shot of her burns.
>
> YACONDA
>
> And yet the woman speaks of God. And yet she speaks of heaven as if she were already in it.

way to understand the layers of the world, not truth but a plain story. 'Yes, sorry,' he'd said, 'it was burnt. It had to be burnt since the beach was called Little Hell after all, *El Infiernillo*, no doubt by Little Devils like you who needed a place to look more like home.'

And the beach is just as she remembered it, invisible at night, the shimmer of liquid moonlight in the zenith. Memories of a night are almost always perfect, Ramona thinks, because there are fewer details to remember. They drive up some nearby hills and into a gated compound with five wooden cabins, surrounded by old forest.

'Here we are,' Pato says, creeping the car forward onto a pebbled parking spot.

He heads to a reception desk in the only cabin with its lights on. Ramona stretches her legs in relief. She's here, no point complaining – how many times had Lucho come home late at night, without explaining what he'd been doing or where he'd even been? They'd developed a code for their silence as the years went by – *at work* or *at home* meaning simply, *I've been: the day passed and I was in it.*

'It looks like a nice place,' she says, but Alicia doesn't answer, facing the gate instead, and then looking at her watch.

'The others have our stuff,' Alicia says, annoyed, a hand on her forehead. The crew had tailed them closely for the first hour but then disappeared into a service station.

Pato walks over to them with the keys. Ramona gets cabin 5, the farthest away from cabin 1, where Pato and Alicia are staying. They wait for the others on a log-made bench on an outdoor terrace, a seesaw and a slide behind them. No one talks at first, and then Pato lights a cigarette.

'And when did *you* start smoking again?' Alicia says.

'I'm just tired. Let me be for today,' Pato says.

An hour later, the crew's van arrives – it must have been at least an hour, maybe more. They each go to their rooms. Ramona washes her hands and face, brushes her teeth with the toothbrush she has been given. She lies on her bed with her clothes on and realises she didn't give Alicia her jumper back. She's restless, can't keep her feet still. It's the first time in years – how many years, how the years pass! – that she's slept alone. Excluding the madhouse, of course. She notices she's kept to one side of the bed, his side neat, untouched, an absence of ripples. She gets up and gets herself a glass of water from the bathroom. She already has one on her

>
> LUZ MARIA
>
> The woman is the Devil. I hate her.
>
> YACONDA
>
> Well, what good will that do? Hate? Hating won't do a thing for you.
>
> LUZ MARIA
>
> I am nothing. There is nothing I can do but hate.
>
> YACONDA
>
> There is always something. Let me help you. Don't you want more from this life? Love? Freedom? Isn't that better than hate?

bedside table and so she leaves the new one on his side. Sitting on the bed, just before switching the lamp off, she realises that something else is missing. She doesn't have her pills. She turns off the light anyway but she's never been more awake. The doctor had said to take them for a year, maybe two, depending on her recovery. She hasn't noticed much of a change. She still wants to disappear some days – she could never say die, dying is not exactly what she means, she hopes – and she's gained so much weight she sometimes wants to know if the doctor measures the recovery in kilos, and what she will look like fully recovered. When will she be heavy enough to be deemed happy, to be freed? Her mistake (her biggest mistake) had been telling Lucho, telling him plainly, I want to disappear, I don't want to be me right now. I don't want to be me when I wake up tomorrow or the day after.

Ramona gets up and goes outside, tiptoeing her way down the floating wooden porch deck. She sees the burning dot of a cigarette, like a firefly gliding near the tree-trunk bench.

'Can't sleep?' Pato whispers.

She shakes her head.

He makes space for her next to him and she sits down. Neither of them look at one another.

'She's sleeping,' he says.

'You don't know that. Sometimes people pretend.'

'I know her. She's sleeping.'

'It doesn't work that way.'

'What?'

'Nothing.'

He offers her a cigarette but she waves it away.

'Can I ask you something?'

'Anything,' he says, exhaling smoke.

'You always talk about Positive Thinking... Are you happy?'

'I suppose it helps people, or at least that's—'

'—That wasn't what I asked.'

'I never thought things would be as they are now.'

'How are things?'

'You know what I mean.'

'I don't.'

'Heavy. Suffocating. I don't know.'

'Everyone needs pleasure in life.'

'She loves you, you know? Do you know that?'

'I'm sorry,' he says, lighting another cigarette.

'You should be. You really should be.'

```
O FORTUNA starts again, in crescendo.

                    LUZ MARIA
        Yes. Yes, I want that. I
        want everything.

                    YACONDA
        But you can't get it in
        exchange for nothing -
        there must always be a
        price paid.

                    LUZ MARIA
        Anything.

                    YACONDA
        Then kiss me.
```

'It's not my fault that I feel this way about you.'

'What way? What are you talking about?'

'And we work well together. You'll see, I'll introduce you to my contacts. This is just to build up your resumé.'

'Do you know why the sand is so dark here?'

'What? No, no idea.'

'The lighter sand gets blown away by the wind. The rest of it is stuck, magnetised, trapped.'

'I always preferred darker sand.'

'Or maybe it's all one big burn.'

'Look, I'm sorry,' he says again.

Ramona goes back to her cabin, knows that Pato is watching her – burning, burning – and she shuts her door, washes her hands and face once more. She sits on her side of the bed – alone, alone – and an overwhelming need to see Lucho aches in her belly, to be young again, for him to be young again, to touch her, to be lost in his writing, to write about her, yes, she's that vain! To write about her so that she can become those memories because she misses dreaming – oh how the world has changed beyond them! – misses herself as a dream, acting, hoping, losing without knowing loss. Youth is an act, yes, yes, it's not your fault the script ended, Ramona, God, and what is left of us now, of all this, but a curtain call on memory? What is left but hope, empty, burning hope?

A knock on the door. She's surprised but also relieved to be able to get up and not have to wait for the whole night to pass.

'Yes?' she whispers. Another gentle knock. 'Yes?' she whispers again, unlocking the door. She opens it only slightly, holding the doorknob. She hasn't decided yet.

'Hey, it's me,' Pato says. 'Open up.'

'What are you doing?'

'Can we talk?'

'Does she know?'

'Will you let me in?'

Ramona sidesteps into the space between the wall and door. Pato flicks a cigarette into the shrubbery lining the side of the cabin. He comes in and shuts the door, looks at her with her shoulders up against the wall. He presses his body against hers, like he knew this would happen, like they'd agreed to it some lives ago, and he kisses her desperately, and then they are in bed, her eyes shut – she can't look at him, she shouldn't – their legs entangled firmly, unable to move, Ramona held as if she were the very last woman in the world.

LUZ MARIA is guided by **YACONDA** to a kiss. O FORTUNA is at its climax. We see storm clouds gathering; rain starts to pour down. In the MARKET STREET people are now running for shelter. We see LUZ MARIA's face. She opens her eyes in terror. We see a frontal shot of LUZ MARIA, revealing that YACONDA is no longer with her.

                    LUZ MARIA

     I can see it... I can see
     — a world of unimaginable
     beauty.

12

PABLO

is watching Clara and Francisco at the other end of his basement. There is a journalist (she took pictures of everything before deciding the room was too dark), a poet (he wrote at first but then stopped because the journalist kept telling him to whisper whenever he tried to recite his new lines) and a painter, who kept mostly to himself drawing God knows what. And Pablo, Clara and Francisco.

Earlier on, Francisco had disappeared. He said he needed a cigarette but he took off for the whole day. During that time Pablo had waited, trying to make the others understand that they should leave him and Clara alone. He sighed – real loud and all – but no one seemed to get it. Old people never get it. They always stick around, as if they imagine they're interesting or something. And so Pablo ended up spending most of the day trying to get near Clara without having to talk to the others. The poet kept on giving him scribbled notes. Pablo always nodded but the poet would then ask which lines he liked and which he didn't; and wouldn't leave him alone until he said something specific like 'the last line because it breaks the rhyme' or some other shit like that. Meanwhile, the journalist kept going on about newsworthy this and that, but really, it meant nothing. Pablo understood that they were bored (how many terrible things do old people do for no other reason than boredom?), so he started worrying that Clara was bored too. And God, there's nothing worse than the girl you like being bored when there's old people in the room sucking all the life out of everything. You really can't win. They'll comment on everything you do. You get up and they go: 'Where are you going?' and you sit down and they ask: 'What are you doing?' like some kind of boring haunting inside your head. There's a reason there are no love stories set in retirement homes. At least there shouldn't be. No one wants to see that. And if there are, it's only so old people can have some sort of hope.

And so Pablo had nothing else to do but to look at Clara and try to retain her gaze, which kept shifting between him and the rest, and then, when Francisco finally came back, onto him.

Francisco had arrived late that night with about ten more old people behind him and a page of rules for everyone to read.

THE BASEMENT RULES:

1. Whisper.
2. You must be creating something important when down here.
3. This is a closed group. Don't mention this group to anyone outside.
4. Going out is only permitted at night. In case it can't wait, ask for permission (use supplied bucket in corner of the room – this will be emptied every night).
5. If you leave, you don't come back.

Francisco stuck the rules at the bottom of the stairs to the basement, and everyone whispered their agreement.

'I think this is too many people,' Pablo said.

'Calm down,' Francisco said. 'You can't make good art if you're scared.'

Now, Pablo only sees Francisco and Clara at intervals, blocked and then revealed as gaps form between the others. There are people who, like him, are sitting with their backs to the wall along the edges of the room. And there is the light bulb too, which flickers before dying out for a few seconds and coming on again. In that little moment, he thinks, they must have enough time to kiss.

Pablo gets up and moves to sit next to Clara. He wishes she would mention how good an idea this whole thing was, how brave even, and how Francisco would have never allowed it to happen at his own house because his parents would have grounded him, called the police even, or his brother would have beaten him up in front of everyone. But when Pablo approaches them, neither Clara nor Francisco say a thing to him and they continue to whisper to each other. Well, at least, Francisco's talking. Since Francisco couldn't bring his own guitar, which he left at the failed gig for his brother to collect (the group had also decided it would be better to only have one guitar to avoid making too much noise), and the singer from The Mutant Children is always playing it as an air-guitar, Francisco has spent all his time talking. First, he talked about his Song of the People. He tried to explain it to the whole group. He had given a simple introduction: 'the song will contain every sound in this fucking city.' And then he moved to the grandiose: 'it's about the oppressive beauty of modernity, man.'

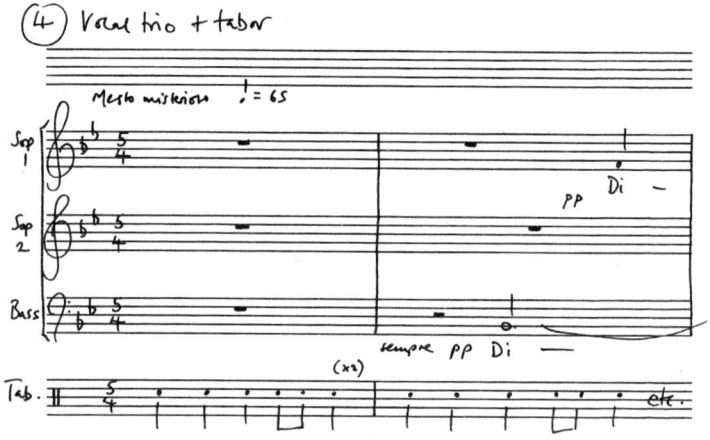

In the intermittent darkness, he disappears, but keeps on talking.

During the last week, new people have come in and out of the basement. Because the basement is at the edge of the back garden, away from the house, unlit and with its own stony footpath to a gate which is always left open, no one feels seen going in and out. No one has even asked who owns the house, and most have just assumed it's Francisco's. And Francisco, who everyone now calls *comrade organiser*, has now even come up with a new rule to decide who can stay over: you have to bring booze and something to eat. That's how the tango dancers get kicked out, along with the jugglers. (Plus, no one liked them.) The remaining artists know that they must work in silence or Francisco will boot them too. Some, Pablo is almost certain, never leave, spending most of the day sleeping, working on this or that project. There's a guy – who takes up a lot of space – who's painting a canvas, mixing colours until, he says, he finds the right shade of black for the background. There are several writers who talk a lot about their writing too; a novel about capitalist oppression, an ode to injustice, a rejection of all the magical-realist bullshit and with lots of drugs and sex. But they all shrink back when asked to read because, 'Man, it's only a first draft.' They can never say what actually happens in their stories, or what the images in their poems refer to. He's beginning to suspect they're here because writing is the easiest skill to claim, needing only a pen and a notepad. There's even an architecture student who claims to be redesigning 'This fucking city – built by colonisers – to be, like, less imperialistic, man.' He's not started drawing, however, because he says he doesn't have proper equipment. 'The mind is the best canvas after all, man.'

Francisco's real proud tonight because Juan García, the singer from The Detainees, has turned up to spend time with them. One of The Mutant Children had told Juan that there was a new underground collective and Juan couldn't resist a visit, unaware of how flimsy the whole thing is.

Everyone is scared to talk to him, though. Especially after that massive gig in Peru last year. He's actually made it. One day – everyone knows – the National Stadium is going to be a sea of hands, waving at his songs. The Viña Festival will dance and give him the Golden Seagull. He'll be on TV talking about this very basement and the potential of Chilean artists, who for so long could not show themselves in daylight. 'It was a difficult time,' he'll say, 'but we still managed to create something beautiful.' After Francisco's shower of compliments, Juan sat against the wall with a notepad and a pen. 'He really likes my idea,' Francisco told Clara. 'I told you,' she said, and then the light died.

'Hey,' Juan whispers, tapping Pablo's elbow.

'Hi,' he says, relieved to be distracted from watching Clara, her head resting on Francisco's shoulder.

'So, what do you do?'

'I play bass in a band.'

'That's really cool,' Juan says, with a contented smile and a sigh, the kind of smile that makes Pablo aware of just how much younger than Juan he is. Older people are always smiling and waiting for others to talk. Pablo thinks this is because they don't have much to say.

'You too.'

'Yeah, I play and sing in The Detainees.'

'I know, I know. Everyone knows. It's really something that you're here with us.'

What Pablo actually thinks is that his father would kill him if he knew. Probably kill Juan too.

'Where did you come from?'

'San Feña,' Pablo whispers.

'A long way to come just to be here, then.'

'Yeah.'

'That guy Francisco has some interesting ideas, right?' Juan says, following Pablo's line of sight.

'I suppose. He's interesting.'

'Do you wanna write a song with me?'

'What? Really?'

'Yeah, man, let's write something. Together.'

'Fuck, I mean, I'm not very good.'

'No such thing as good or bad. As long as it comes from the heart.'

Pablo laughs and then forces himself to stop. He straightens his back. He must not act impressed. No one who made it ever looks impressed.

'I mean it,' Juan says, smiling innocently.

'I don't have my bass here.'

'I brought mine. We can play it real quiet.'

'Alright.'

'Maybe it'll impress that girl there with that interesting guy, Francisco.'

'What?'

'Love is so complicated, my friend.'

Pablo grabs the bass from Juan's open hardcase lined with orange velvet. It's much heavier than the one he usually borrows from Francisco, with a Yamaha logo on the headstock, no scratches. What must it feel like to play this in front of hundreds, thousands of people? This very piece of wood, vibrating through the crowds, which he, Pablo, now takes on his lap. Juan puts on a tape with the sounds of a train Francisco had recorded. TSH-T-SH-TSH, TSH-T-SH-T-SH.

'Not sure what to play,' Pablo says. The crowd would be booing by now. They would want their money back.

'Francisco, turn it up a little, man,' Juan says, and Francisco dials up the train. Pablo frowns at the sudden rise in volume, but before he can say anything, 'Use that as the beat, man,' Juan says and taps the beat on his chest.

Pablo struggles to find the beat at first. The train isn't consistent. Noises in the world rarely are. He plays random notes until a pattern emerges, until he arranges the train to follow him.

```
G-2-2-2-2------------2-2-2-2------------2-2-2-2----------
D----------3-3-3-3-3----------3-3-3-3-3---------3-3-3-3-3
A--------------------------------------------------------
E--------------------------------------------------------


G--0-0-0-0-0-0--5-5-5-5--2-2-2-2-------------------------
D-------------------------------2-2-2-2-3-3-3-3----------
A--------------------------------------------------------
E--------------------------------------------------------
```

'Train, train,' Juan says, as he hunts for the right notes to sing the word. 'Where's the train going?'

'South,' Pablo says, unable to stop repeating the pattern. 'South to San Fernando.'

'Train going South, then,' Juan says. 'Keep it, keep it going,' he adds, writing in his notebook.

The light dies again. The artists quietly boo.

'Here,' Pablo says, giving the bass to Juan.

Pablo watches Clara as he listens to Juan's bassy train, and his whispered lyrics with little pauses whenever a phrase is worth writing, 'Don't call me poor/ For travelling this way,/ Can't you see I'm content/ Can't you see I'm happy?' and the repetition of it all, Clara's face dimming in yawns, the tape and Francisco's constant whispering, it all takes him to the beach, alone on a bright day facing the ocean...

He walks along the sand, a trail marked by dead starfish, crab carcasses and beached jellyfish which shine pink and green, liquid disco balls in the sun. Far out in front of him there's a crowd sitting around a fire, the plume of smoke rising straight up, high and clear to a blue sky, spreading at the top ends like the shadow of an old tree, rising steadily despite all the wind. He makes his way towards them. His ear rings; the familiar hum, trapped water, the sea inside him, and he shuts his eyes in pain. When he opens them it's later in the day, a red sun sinking like a tired eyelid. Behind him, his footprints have disappeared, replaced by new, darker sand. He continues his way to the group of people and the fire, whose smoke now reaches farther than the few, distant clouds. There's Francisco, Clara, Juan, Mariela. His parents are both there too. No one greets him. They open and close their mouths to a rhythm he can't quite understand. He notices they're not sitting on but inside the sand, buried up to their waists. The earth rumbles and no one else seems to notice. There's a hole in the sand for him too but he doesn't want to get into it. Instead, he looks at the ocean which retreats inward, black glass receding, unveiling a cliff and the other half of the sun, the jagged architecture of a time long drowned, breathless and forgotten, and Pablo shakes in fear when a second quake hits the ground. The water in his ear dries up. Finally, silence. He takes his place in the sand and everyone turns their heads to face him. 'A wave is coming,' he tells them. 'The world is ending and we know it,' they recite at the same time, 'and all that's left for us to do is watch.' And even with the ocean recoiling, the sudden emptiness, there's no panic, no sadness, everyone coming together in a quiet acceptance of the end. A pillar of water forms and—

'Are you alright?'

Clara's in front of him, holding his hand.

'Hi,' she says.

'Hello.'

He looks around him. It's dark and it takes him a few seconds before he can make out where they are, outside in the garden by the main gate. The gate is open.

'I saw you come out, thought something was wrong.'

'Sorry. I think I was sleeping.'

'You think?'

'It's happened a few times before.'

'Here,' she says, stepping in close to him. She hugs him and rubs his back. 'You're cold.'

'Hey, can I ask you something?'

'Sure,' he says, facing her, their hands still on each other's back.

'What were you dreaming about?'

'I'm not sure.'

'I meant to tell you. Can I say something to you?'

'Yes,' he says, feeling her back straighten and tense up. He shuts his eyes but she doesn't kiss him.

'I wanted to say sorry.' She breaks the hug. 'About the other day, you know, when we were watching that tent at school. And then at the gig.'

'There's nothing to be sorry about.'

'Just felt mean is all. And it's really cool what you've done here. It was brave. It's not like it's your fault, you know, who your parents are and all that.'

His father would, however, say that you inevitably end up becoming your parents. It's not the same. He knows that. Not the same kind of guilt. Could you ever leave your family? Could it leave you?

'Oh, that,' he says. 'It's alright, really.'

'Still... Anyway, do you mind if we stay outside a little more?'

'Something wrong?'

'It's nothing, really.'

'You can tell me.'

'Francisco can be tough sometimes. Creative types, right?' She smiles, eyes fixed on the ground in front of her.

'He talks a lot and it's always—'

'—I didn't mean it in that sense.'

'Oh, me neither. I mean, did something happen?'

'Can you keep a secret?' she says, and the first traces of sunlight emerge to turn the sky red.

Pablo is watching Clara and Francisco from the opposite side of the basement again. When Pablo and Clara came back inside, there were only three other people left sleeping in different corners of the room. Francisco was sleeping too, but he sat up when Clara kissed him on the forehead. And now Pablo can't hear what Francisco's saying, just knows he's talking into Clara's ear. She laughs whenever he leaves a pause for her to laugh. He's playing another tape, this time a pack of street dogs barking at each other.

Once Francisco's asleep again, Pablo heads outside and waits for Clara by the steps on the other side of the main door to the basement, a thick concrete block with metallic locks. What feels like at least an hour goes by, but he stays there, still and quiet. Earlier on, she'd given him a note. He has it in his back pocket, as if he needs proof of her having written it.

Eventually, she edges her way out through a narrow gap in the door and closes it. She smiles at him.

'Are you sure?' she whispers. He nods.

They walk up the stone steps. When he reaches the top, he looks for lights in the house. He hasn't spent a night in his own bedroom for over a week now. He knows his parents don't give a damn. As long as he's studying, they never ask about anything. Even though his father never went to university – probably didn't even try – and his mother had quit everything before even starting, Pablo's now meant to become a fucking engineer. God. Old people do that – they have too much hope for others. His parents depress him no end. It wasn't always like this, although he's not sure there was a specific moment when it had all changed either. As time passes he wonders if he reminds them of themselves. They'll hope he doesn't make the same mistakes – *Study so you don't have to do this, so you can choose* – and nag him to want the same things – *You'll want to provide for your family someday*. And even, as if to make sure their fears are kept fed – *You will also die someday, don't let life simply pass. We did our best. All we are is an old person's unhappy memory*. He sometimes can't breathe just thinking about it.

He turns the door handle to the kitchen and catches his breath. Mariela's bedroom, a tiny square which barely fits her single bed (he's ashamed whenever he sees it, always pristine, too tidy, something meant to be easily left), has its lights off too but he checks the gap under the door anyway. She's always been the first one up and the last to go to bed, the house's natural clock. Sneaking past her room feels like betrayal, like adding hours, slowing hands, a rebellion against time. His room is at the other end of the house and he guides Clara through the kitchen and past a living room where no one's ever sat. His room is so big that it has its own lounge, which is empty, apart from a wooden desk his parents have lugged around for him since he was a child in the hopes that someday he'll use it. His actual bed is in a small room annexed to that, clearly a quick extension improvised by previous owners, because its ceiling is much lower than the rest of the house and its walls are coated in a new and clinical bright white paint. He counts the closed doors between them and Mariela. Four. And then between them and his parents. Three, plus the stairs.

He shuts the curtains and turns on the lamp on his bedside table. He wants to tell her he's glad she wrote him that note, that he's been waiting to be alone with her, that the night they first gathered together in the basement was meant for her, that he doesn't care about the band, that even though he's always known he'd write something important, for music had to be important if he is ever to play the National Stadium, be the voice of a generation, he couldn't do it without a great and terrible yearning, without her, Clara, that this is love, he knows it now, he will tell her: 'This is love, I have forgotten the me without you, abandoned it to the memory of others, I am you.'

And they sit on the bed, each to one side, and she turns off the light. His ear rings loud and hollow as she takes his hand and they lie next to each other facing the ceiling which, in the pitch black darkness of the room, is a starless sky.

'Are you sure?' she asks him, and she kisses him before he can say anything. With her on top of him, her full weight shifting from his thighs to his chest, he shuts his eyes to the noise of water between kisses, struggles to breathe, the sea above him.

'Do you really hate him?' she says.

'I hate him.'

'Does he deserve this?'

'He does. I hate him.'

'Wait,' she says, suddenly still. 'Just wait.'

Mariela's alarm sounds four doors away. A constant note. 'Like the warning hum of a natural disaster,' she'd once joked, 'That's the only noise that can wake me up.'

With Clara on top of him Pablo can hardly breathe. Her hair on his face. Sweat. Her eyes fixed on his, a frown, fear, him now dizzy. And drowning. Still waters and...

Hey,

Before you arrived I was miserable. Don't take it personally. You didn't actually do anything to make me feel better. Not yet at least. I am so angry all the time, man. When I see people at school getting along, doing their work, talking holiday plans... I want to hurt them. I don't mean their fucking feelings, either. I want to lock the school up and burn it. I hate their happiness. I never understood why. It's beyond me. It makes my blood boil, man. When my parents split up and my mum got together with a dickbag who collects stamps, I thought, that's it, everyone's fucking crazy. Now I'm angry at them too.

But he left her and nothing changed. That's when I met Francisco in School Week. He was meant to play in front of the whole school but once the Inspector asked him for the names of his songs, he said he'd play a Violeta Parra track and finish off with Victor Jara. The Inspector didn't let him play. Truth is, he didn't even know any songs by them. It was all a joke. They announced Francisco's name and people started whistling and laughing when he didn't turn up onstage. The Inspector went up instead and said Francisco got shy, scared, embarrassed, something like that. I talked to him after that. Neither of us had any friends (not real ones at least, you know?) and we'd spend whole breaks just walking around the school and talking. He showed me a bunch of music and we started playing together here and there. That's how it started. Now I was fucking angry at the world and bashing drums made it better. That's when we got together too. We kissed after our first band practice, like we'd finally found love or something equally disgusting. Classmates at school noticed. Francisco liked that they noticed. He started to walk around the school with other people. Mostly girls too. He'd only talk to me about possible beats for his songs. And then one day, only a few weeks before you arrived, I caught him with some other girl, making out in the changing rooms.

I'm tired of being angry, man. I wanted to ask you for help. I wanted to ask you for a favour. It's entirely self-centred of me, I know. This goes beyond friendship. We're in the same band, after all. Would you be up for, you know, payback? No love. Nothing with feelings or any of that shit. I know it's weird but I can't stay angry, man. Think of yourself as a good snare drum.

Let me know!

Clara

And then he watches them from across the basement again, her returning to Francisco, kissing his forehead again, him waking up, her head on his shoulder, talking, talking and her looking right back at him before the light bulb dies and distances become immeasurable, like memory.

13

LUCHO

opens Pedro Castro's *Space Verses*. Below the title on the cover page, a signature. Lucho traces it with his pen, the ink blotching on the C, releasing itself from clean lines.

His own father's life had started with a signature. That's what Lucho's father said anyway, when asked how he came to join the army or, before she left, how he knew he wanted to marry Lucho's mother, Olga.

One of Ángel's friends had brought a rifle to school, hidden it in a mound of corn in an old stone silo. At break time, they would run to get it and aim at the bats that gathered in tiny lines, hanging from two wooden beams which secured the silo's pointed tiled ceiling. They would wait for the school bell to ring so as to hide the noise. One shot each day. Ángel knew the rifle belonged to Don Pablo, the patrón of the farm – he'd seen him riding with it strapped to his shoulder – but he never asked his friend how he'd got it. On the farm things went missing. People went missing, leaving their families behind, as Ángel's parents had done, to chase a better life in towns and cities. Others died of unknown diseases: they were fine one day and crippled the next (and with heads lowered, the rest would await their own disappearance in pious silence).

When it was Ángel's turn, the trigger jammed. He squeezed harder but the school bell had already rung. All the other kids had come over to watch. A bat fell dead, plummeting down onto the corn hill. There was a hole in the ceiling, a beam of sunlight piercing through. The teacher, a city priest who, Ángel always joked, did not like the farm, the poor, Christ or himself, had grabbed Ángel by the ear and pulled him out of the silo. The priest then asked him to give up the names of those involved in the little game, but Ángel kept quiet. His friends kept quiet. It was only me. Me. Alone. And so the priest wrote a note of suspension, one week out of school, a year attending on Saturdays to clean the school. Also, Ángel was to write one full blackboard of biblical parables.

The note of suspension was to be signed by the patrón, who'd by then already allowed Ángel to take a service room in the main house. His wife couldn't have children. He saw Ángel as a son.

The next day, the priest ordered Ángel to the front of the class and asked him to present the signed note. He'd never even considered telling the patrón, least of all showing him the little paper. The priest had shouted, told Ángel to spread his fingers on the teacher's desk. And beat him with a ruler. Ángel, back at his own desk, had then grabbed a pen, walked up to the priest and signed the note with the patrón's signature (a perfect copy, Ángel would later say, as he'd always signed all school notes himself) and he'd thrown the paper at the priest's face – 'There, it's signed now. Leave me alone.' His peers had clapped and cheered.

The next day, Ángel wasn't allowed in school.

The patrón found out.

'You leave the farm either by fair means or foul.'

What does foul mean? At the farm things disappeared, got lost forever.

'You'll be on your own and never come back.'

(No, no, fair, please, fair.)

'Then you'll go South to my cousin in Puerto Varas. You'll live with her until you finish school. You can come back after that, help me run things.'

The patrón had even given Ángel he and his wife's surname – Díaz Tapia.

'You'll leave tomorrow.'

On that night, he said goodbye to Olga, promised her he'd come back for her, that he'd write to her. 'I'll get you out of here and we'll get married.'

She didn't believe him.

'No one who leaves ever comes back,' she said.

'I'm not anyone,' he said, 'and I love you.'

And then, he was put on a train South, determined to save her and someday take over the farm.

> POETRY NOTES – BOOK OF RAMONA
> *Ramona sees Valparaíso: Travelling the Great Sea*
>
> We're not far from Valparaíso.
>
> We can take our time,
> you say,
> stay even.
>
> And a dead flower to your hair,
> you laugh,
> We've taken everything in now,
> you say,
> all your favourite views.

Lucho is determined to finish a poem about the farm, but he lacks the visual cues to give specificity, the exact language, to bring to life the rural clichés of his father's childhood stories. It's his turn to present writing at the workshop today but he can't concentrate. The inventory report in front of him mentions an excess of potatoes that must be recovered. Missing helmets. An increase in the production of bullets for reserves. He signs it and puts it to one side. He looks for his notebook on Fallen Heroes but he's forgotten why he was even writing it, why it had at one point seemed so urgent to describe the sacrifices of a few men whose purpose is only to reside in our memories. How the hell do you write about things you don't remember?

Major Matta arrives, knocking and opening the door at the same time. Lucho stands and salutes. The Major salutes back with a limp hand.

'Can we stop with that bullshit? Did you get our friend the writer?'

'Not yet. He's bound to appear someday.'

Lucho sits again.

'Is that his book?' The Major takes one of his white gloves off and pages through *Space Verses*. 'Time is love to the ancient hills of our misery... That's nice, don't you think? It's a nice line.'

'Yes, sir.'

'Frankly, I don't see the appeal of reading. Pointless, all these words.' The Major takes a flask from his chest pocket and drinks, the heavy smell of alcohol reaching Lucho. 'Do you want to know why we're looking for him? You never asked.'

'I follow orders.'

'We all do.'

'He's a terrorist.'

'Yes, yes, that's what you'll have to say, no doubt. He had a lot of contacts in the MIR.'

'Isn't that enough?'

'It's my superior. He wants him gone. God knows what happened between them but believe me, I've never heard him so angry. I guess he doesn't see the appeal either. You see,' he drinks again, 'and I shouldn't tell you this...'

'What is it? Any information could help me find him.'

'It's a little personal to him, so it's personal to us too.'

'What happened?'

'Pedro is a relative of his, his own flesh and blood. Can you believe that? His cousin, the famous Marxist poet. He needs him gone, kaput. Shame, really, the kid has some nice lines.'

'Sir, I have a question, if you would permit me.'

'Sure.'

'Is the referendum real?'

'I told you once and I'll say it again, the only thing that lasts forever is the memory of an ending. Concern yourself with this for now and we'll deal with that later. If it ends, it ends our way.' He drinks, slides the flask back into his pocket. 'Maybe I should write too, don't you think?'

'Yes, sir. A fine line.'

'Shame, really, I don't see the appeal.' At the door, the Major turns back to Lucho. 'Results, Lucho. My superior needs results.' And then he leaves.

Shame, really, that Lucho can't even set his own pen down against the page. Poetry is also memory and he can't remember how writing was once comforting, how in the middle of the night he would write to rebel against the day, to unravel it all to himself, patterns in a daily inventory, the invisible connections of language. Where has language gone? How do you write about things you don't remember? There was always love, he knows that, but with the years his focus was no longer on accuracy. It wasn't about describing a scene anymore; Ramona's arm on his chest while she slept and him seeing a starry night on her skin held, as he once wrote, by the gravity of his heart. He'd grown tired of how little his words would mean to anyone who wasn't living the exact same life. Writing had become about nothing but himself. And good writing, like Neruda's, claimed whole universes. He borrowed words: 'Through nights like this one, I held her in my arms,' and he'd felt just that too. Emulated other writers: 'Let me sing what you loved, life of my life,' and he sang too. Envious. Writing became a code, a tired puzzle completing nothing. Disappointing. A failure. Life no longer infinite. And love, he had once believed, had to be infinite. And then there was Chile. Descriptions of mountains and the sea; he sees a line right here in his notebook, one of the little notes he had written to give himself a mental picture to turn into poetry one day. He'd written notes like these while in bed in the barracks, filled with a need to protect the country, which really meant protecting how he felt about it. Patriotism, his father had once said, is wishing others would feel that way too. The notes are hard to read, a handwriting he barely recognises, urgent and stretched:

> The sky peaks downward against the Andes. Beyond the haze of distance they appear to struggle to hold on to us. There's nothing these hills can do against the weight of so much sky.

But he never wrote the poem. It wasn't enough. It wasn't important. His father always said that the country was the only thing that mattered, but maybe Ángel had forgotten his own language too because he never explained why. When he told Lucho to give up writing he'd done so in a question: 'Do you really want to waste your life dreaming, merely capturing what is already there, or do you want to create something real, have a family?' Lucho had, in turn, posed the same question to Ramona: 'Do you think I can be a writer?' 'You can always find time to write,' was her first answer. She was working as a secretary for the Red Cross in San Fernando at the time, had not yet even finished school. 'We all need to make sacrifices,' was her second. 'We all have to grow up someday.' But for a time Lucho had tried to keep writing, hidden by a curtain of towels and shirts in the bottom bunk of a full barracks.

Another note says:

> I can no longer see the moon, but I'm content
> with the sun alone.

Lucho can't actually remember the exact moment he stopped writing because it wasn't a decision. Towards the end of his notebook, full sentences became incomplete, impatient: '...because all grass dries up eventually.' And then: 'Smell of gunpowder – Spring.' His last note reads simply: 'Water.' And then the country changed and he had to change with it. He had never admitted this to himself, but it had never been a sacrifice. He wanted to win. That's what his father said. The General had taken over. His father called him to the kitchen and pointed at the radio with a wide smile. We won.

In the basement of the Tutankamón, Lucho sits behind the teacher's desk. The task he'd been set for the week was simply: Why do you write? He couldn't answer it himself and, by the looks of it, no one else could either (only Felipe Flores has turned up, the self-proclaimed novelist who, more than ten years after first attending the workshop, is still working on his first book).

Felipe is sitting on the chair closest to Lucho, an open newspaper splayed on top of his bulging belly. He reads with his index finger, thick glasses and squinting eyes, tracing sentences across the page. He turns to a page with a smaller font and gives up, folding the paper under his arm. He stares at Lucho. And then back at his watch.

'The referendum,' Felipe finally says. 'The Dictator may be finished soon.'

'Do you think there will be a vote?'

'Why not? This has gone on long enough, don't you think?'

'I can't see the army recognising a loss.'

'They're too sure they'll win. It's why they're letting it happen.'

'I suppose. Don't you think they'll win?'

'They've lost something if we're asking these questions. Who knows about the rest. The people are waking up.'

Two younger writers come in, panting and stomping, with banners showing the framed faces of some of the detained and disappeared in black and white. They leave the signs in the corner of the room and sit each to one side of Felipe, shaking hands, 'Hello, hello,' a nod and a smile at Lucho.

'We could start if that's okay with you,' Lucho says.

'I'll go,' Felipe says. 'Why do I write? The boring answer – and honesty, we know as writers, my friends, is boring – well, the boring answer is that I've done it for far too long. Like a ghost I haunt the same places, attempt to recapture life, I'm often envious of the living. But, my friends, the question I find most difficult to answer is why I don't write. As you know, I've been working on a book for more than ten years now – some of you have heard passages I've tested out on you right here in this room. Why do I choose not to write more, why let the painful process linger? I often wonder how anyone could write about the Dantean state of our country without omitting a great injustice, without resorting to what you know is my natural preference for melodrama. I do ask myself, how can I write about hell if its circles are infinite? I wrote because I thought it important to chronicle what lies behind our present moment. We all did. But important to what? To whom? I find myself now stuck in time, trying to make sense of these questions. I can't write because I have no hope, my friends, no hope at all, that we can be engaged in anything other than glorified description. You all know my eyes don't quite work these days, but I find they give me an accurate picture. Friends, I don't write because our country is no longer here. It's gone.'

The young writers clap for Felipe, who sits back down, taking off his glasses which hang from his neck on a silver chain. Shoulders slumped, he folds the page he has been reading from and rubs his face with a handkerchief. He sighs, defeated. Lucho is meant to moderate the discussion after each piece is read out. In past meetings, moderators would say a few words before opening the conversation. He has no idea what to say.

'That was great.' The group nods. 'I found that... Well, it... Hang on. Is the room shaking?'

'Tremor,' one of the young writers says.

'Yes, it's shaking. This is a long one,' the other says.

'Quake, quake,' Felipe says.

They make their way out of the Tutankamón, the session temporarily abandoned. In the street, other groups of people gather outside their front doors to wait out the quake. 'The earth is dancing,' Lucho's mother would tell him whenever the ground shook. 'Nothing to be scared of.' His father would then tell her not to lie to Lucho, and say that the pressure built up over decades underground would eventually erupt, when our beloved tectonic plates felt like letting go, and then whole towns would be reduced to rubble in minutes. 'Everyone must live with that knowledge in Chile, the whims of the earth.' And then, in 1960, when Lucho was fifteen, the Great Quake sunk towns. Only a wall in the kitchen crumbled in their little house in San Fernando. His father had looked satisfied as he picked up the bricks. 'How's that for a dance?' he asked Lucho. And Lucho had hoped his mother, wherever she was at the time, was thinking about him. By then, he couldn't really remember her face. Her voice had by then become low and quiet, his own voice. When he thinks of her now, she dances.

Ángel wrote in his diary that, in 1940, he went back to the farm where he'd worked as a child. He wasn't alone. He'd arrived in an army car, two of his friends in full uniform. He'd told them he wanted to impress the patrón who'd been like a father to him, since the old man had once been a founding member of the Air

Force and always spoke of pending wars with Peru and Bolivia. The truth was Ángel wanted to scare him.

Ángel had left the South to join the regiment in San Fernando. The patrón's sister, Aunty Chini, who had housed him on the banks of Llanquihue Lake, had convinced him to do so after her ranch was appropriated by a gang of peasants who'd once worked for her. They'd threatened her. She never said so, but Ángel was certain there had been more than just words, that she'd been beaten and abused, because she never wore anything that showed her skin after that. 'This cannot go on,' she had told Ángel. And he had to walk to school past the new makeshift houses on the land which had once belonged to her but which the workers had now taken as their own, a new revolution, an incoming land reform. More than one stone was thrown at him. Ángel had written to the patrón for help. He'd told him about the communist farmers and their organising and their demands for more land. He'd asked the patrón, who had throughout Ángel's childhood taught him about these kinds of people, those who are always entitled to the fruits of others' work, to call on the army to help them with what Ángel called in one of his letters 'a battle for our very freedom'. It did not go on. The aunty died a few years later and, having no heirs of her own, the patrón, without ever answering any of Ángel's letters, sold what remained of the ranch back to the peasants. The man who turned up to appraise the farm mentioned that the patrón had made a great deal of money from the government buying the lands, saying simply, 'business is business.'

And so when Ángel went back to the farm he wanted the patrón to be afraid, to tell him why he'd refused to send for help, why he'd become a communist sympathiser, which the aunty had explained only caused pain and chaos to those who had the strength to build the country. He'd wanted the patrón to be afraid because he'd promised Olga he'd take her away from the farm and the patrón would try and reason with him. 'She's too young. This is her home. She works for me. I own her.'

At the patrón's house, Ángel let himself in. The place was cold, a shrine to a plaster cast Virgin, unlit candles on each side. Nothing had changed. Even the bullet hole in the floorboards (one of Ángel's accidents when he had been learning to shoot) had been left intact, a puddle of lead and ash. The patrón was in bed, surrounded by nurses. They left as soon as Ángel walked in. He sat on a chair left at the foot of the bed. The patrón was sweating, feverish, a wet tea towel on his forehead, bedsheets up to his chest. His face had thinned, bony cheeks, skin almost blue. He'd grown an untidy beard. In the past, the patrón had often beaten men who had more than a moustache of hair on their faces.

'Who is that?' he asked.

'You know who it is.'

'Will you come closer?'

'I told you I would come back for her.'

'Ángel? Ángel, is that you?'

'Where is she?'

'You know that I sent you away for your own good.'

'Where is she?'

'And I can tell I did the right thing. Look at you now, in uniform.'

'You threw me out like a dog.'

'I wanted you to return someday. To run the place. I didn't know she would die, my poor sister, not like that. I didn't know you'd leave. I tried to find you. You were like a son to me. You were gone.'

'Do you remember what you once told me, when you shot that man's hand?'

'What? Shot who? I'm a good man.'

'I've been thinking a lot about that moment. You said: "Don't feel bad for him. I've merely replaced one need for another. We are all responsible for understanding our place in the farm, the things we should and shouldn't want."

'I don't remember. I really don't remember.'

'I came here to tell you that you were right.'

He left the patrón with the two soldiers who'd accompanied him, who knew what to do, and set out to find Olga in the workers' shacks set up on the borders of the farm. She lived in a mud house by a water canal, right next to the school. She was wearing a maid's uniform when he found her. She was still young, sixteen or seventeen, but paced around the tiny house dragging her feet, lighting candles, whispering, a ghost. All her belongings were in a trunk. In their first letters to each other, she'd said she was ready to leave. As time passed, that hope had vanished. Now all that remained was a fear of staying.

'My love,' Ángel said, once inside the house.

'I don't want to stay here.'

'You don't have to.'

'Is it done?'

'It's done.'

Ángel would come to stop thinking about the patrón, the farm, the peasant's hands and even Olga's name. Instead, he spoke to Lucho about the cold, the pain in his bones, how much he loved sitting in the garden and listening to the incessant chirping of the birds at the hospice, his dreams as real as anything in the room. A long train journey south, an emerald lake and the peaks of volcanoes. Haunted by daily inadequacies: hunger, scared of the dark, inexplicable sorrow. He'd written all this in a diary before his illness set in. He'd wanted to find Olga before he forgot all about her, and, with her, forgot himself.

When Lucho gets home he looks for Ramona.

'At the gym,' Mariela says.

He walks up to his office, locks the door and turns to face his mother's painting, the pilgrims and their bleeding knees, all of them turned to the faraway dome standing golden amidst the hills, faces broken and asymmetrical, some lacking an eye, no lips, aware of the pain to come, how far they have still to go, the comfort of an ending. Ángel's diary goes blank years before Olga, his wife, Lucho's mother, left them, before the affair. Ángel remained on his knees too, fixed on the gold dome, the stretch of time before the abyss of memory, looking for Olga. He never needed anything else.

In bed, Lucho watches Ramona's back. Today, she only hugged him because Mariela was watching. She looked tired. Her body – he hasn't touched her for some time now – felt foreign and new. He's sorry about this. He's not sure what *this* is but he's sorry. He moves a little closer to her, feeling her warmth.

They were at Aunty Wilma's the first time they slept together, back when she was living there as a student. He'd visit her most weekends, though sometimes he had no money for the bus to Santiago. Other times the regiment would organise survival training weekends in the Cordillera, the Nincunlauta hills. Early in the military, he would write letters to Ramona to tell her how tired he was of running up those hills, of singing platoon songs, and he'd tell her when he planned to visit, and sometimes he would enclose a photograph of himself and a short poem. He'd copied most of them but knew she wouldn't be able to tell. Little haikus, short lines from authors, his favourite by Ezra Pound, something like: 'Leucis, who had Great Passion,/ Ends with an eagerness to please.' He liked that this one almost had his name in it, and he felt it described the reduction of so much love in the confines of a letter, the sadness of longing on paper. She would always reply, 'That's nice, very nice,' and then go on to describe her days at the theatre. She too would mention how tired she was, learning entirely different roles each week, such that, as much of a cliché as it might sound, she did sometimes confuse her own desires for those of the characters she portrayed. 'By the time we meet next week,' she once said, 'I'll have forgotten my own name. Pinch my arm if you ever see me lifting an empty spoon to my mouth while I tell you how good the stew is.' Lines filled with joy. Youth is the ability to believe we are changing.

They are so old now. They grew old quickly. They stopped writing to one another. Instead, they made a deal. If Lucho didn't appear at the door on Saturday morning, Ramona could assume he wasn't coming to visit.

When he met her that weekend, Aunty Wilma had been away seeing cousins in Santa Cruz. Ramona hoped Lucho would make it. She hoped her aunt wouldn't ask whether he was coming or Ramona would be forced to go to see the cousins too. Her aunt didn't ask but did remind her of cousin Angie, who'd been left alone with a baby and had had to abandon her studies. At the door, Ramona had greeted Lucho with a peck on the cheek. It took them at least half a day to find their way to each other's mouths. They would ease into it. It wasn't awkwardness or shame but happiness, the need to re-enact every stage of life together: a greeting, conversation, silence, intimacy, promises, goodbyes. Sitting in the living room, she offered him tea, joked about the sheer number of glass animals Aunty Wilma had, a clown rag doll she'd refused to get rid of, a terrible gift from an old lover, sitting alone on a wicker rocking chair. With their cups of tea in hand, Ramona inspected Lucho, calling out any differences or similarities she saw in him from his last visit. 'They cut your hair again? How long will you have to be a *pelado* for?' That's what she called everyone in the army, a baldy, *pelado*, literally peeled, and Lucho had often thought it an accurate word to describe himself and his regiment; the things everyone had to leave behind discarded. 'And your hands are too soft – I cannot believe you're a soldier. You look tired, Lucho. You're growing wrinkles. Do you drink enough water?' She never knew how the others at the regiment mocked him, the faggot this or that. He never told her either. And he never asked for any details about her life as a student beyond those she shared, not about her friends and teachers, her work. She never told him. Did she even have friends? Lucho and Ramona had something else. He still can't explain it. Something like faith, like gratitude; grand ideas quickly dismantled by specific details.

After tea, they went up to her room. Though he knew Aunty Wilma was out, he kept looking over his shoulder. Ramona sat on her bed, turned a lamp on and asked him to close the curtains. He'd never seen a woman this beautiful. She would one day be famous and forget all about him. He was sure of it. The failed poet turned failed soldier. He grew jealous, right there, alone with her, of what he imagined her theatre audience to be, a crowd fixed on her clear eyes, perfect hands, pale white skin. To anyone watching, he'd be the fortunate one. She rebelled, they'd think, and had married beneath her – to an ugly, much darker man. Married an *indio*, a *roto*, a classless, broken boy. Imagine all that she could have been without him, a *roto* who was meant to look at these neighbourhoods from afar – how easy it is for some to forget their place, their origins, when they are being guided.

'Sit with me,' she said. He left his bag and did as she asked. 'What's wrong?' she said.

'Nothing. Really, it's nothing.'

She kissed him. Impossible to reject. His hand on her back, brushing down her spine, the waves of her hips. They took their own clothes off, each to one side of the bed, not saying a thing. They hadn't planned it, had never even spoken about it. They were alone in the house and understood what that meant. Him on top of her, bedsheets neat on his back, her legs locked to his.

'I've never done it,' she said.

'Me neither,' he said, ashamed.

'Do you think it'll hurt?'

'Apparently it does at first.'

It did hurt, and they stopped a few times and then completely, before reaching the end. They were both relieved.

'I'm sorry,' she said.

'Never, never apologise to me,' he said. 'I will always love you.'

And so now, watching her back turned to him, he drags himself closer to her. He hugs her from behind, his chin on her shoulder, his legs fitting the shape of hers.

'I'm tired,' she says.

'I'm sorry,' he says, turning back onto his side. She's been tired ever since the clinic. She has to rest. It's not him. 'It's not you, I promise.' She just needs more rest, the doctor had assured him. She will recover with a lot of sleep. She breathes out in relief. He thinks that maybe she's crying; he felt a tear on his hand. She doesn't move. He doesn't either. And, as on every night of late, he hears his father's ghost, a muddled whisper: 'Do you think it will hurt?' He stays awake the whole night, waiting for an answer.

He's on the metro, heading to the workshop again, looking at Pedro Castro's face on the book jacket. He reads the bio over and over, holds the book close so no one can see it. He covers the title and name on the book spine. At home, he has stacked his own books in untidy piles to make them look like those in Pedro's picture. He doesn't have as many, so he's placed unused notebooks there too, even piles of bill envelopes and thick work folders. Better, but not quite there. Still, it felt good to see his whole life unpacked. 'Unpack your sentences,' one of the writers had said to another at a workshop session. 'It looks like you're hiding something. There is no pleasure in gratuitous withdrawals of crucial information. Stop hiding behind words. Language should reveal everything at once; clarity is true skill. There is no depth if we can't see the surface. You are writing only to yourself.' The young writer had written something like: 'The first flash of morning light marks the day in which I decide to leave love for freedom. Unpacked, there's no light, no great awakening, just a man leaving his family in the morning.' In this way too, Lucho's lack of books is honest. Pedro Castro, just a man who didn't have enough space.

The metro fills up with men in business suits. There is an uneasy tension. Cheap cologne. And the screeching, which everyone ignores. Lucho offers his seat to an older lady pulling two trolleys with sandwiches wrapped in foil. A man hops on with a guitar and a tambourine and those nearest to him slowly back away. He starts playing the familiar rhythms of a *cueca*, out of place underground, too joyful for a commute, too loud to ignore. People look at him, hoping he comprehends their indignation. He takes off his *chupalla* hat, walks up and down the carriage asking for change to be dropped in it. No one gives him anything. He says thank you and leaves.

Lucho is early to the Tutankamón, so he gets a coffee upstairs. The place is packed, and the pungent smell of fried onions fills the air. The task this week consisted of writing about love or, failing that (the writer joked), desire. He takes out his unfinished collection and looks for poems about Ramona. He smiles when he sees that he once 'loved the sunned mother-of-pearl of your body', stolen from Neruda (again), hoping, as he'd written it, perhaps, that with time even he would forget the crime. But Lucho did in fact finish a poem last night, and he wants to read it. He wrote it on a page at the end of Pedro Castro's book. Short. Simple. Unpacked. In line with the rhythm of its predecessors:

> Watching you still in sleep afar
> I count the shadows between us.
> Years of yarn,
> From cacti to seashells to
> Your body buried in waves,
> Soundly

The world ends with you
Unravelled.

He will make sure to note down any criticisms, to allow for suggestions and changes. He will give it to Ramona for their anniversary. That's nice, she'll say, and they'll both miss each other, and themselves. How easy it is to remember when we're being guided.

Despite the time, none of the writers have shown up. He asks the waiter, who sometimes joins the workshops too, if he's seen them.

'No, Don Pedro. I saw Señor Felipe outside, but no one else.'

Lucho tips the waiter and heads out the door to check. Felipe is with a group of men, stood surrounding the bench where Lucho used to wait, a lonesome tree behind it. He can't see who the men are talking to, stiff and grave faces. When they see Lucho, the circle breaks. They stare at him in silence. Lucho grabs at his briefcase with both hands, presses it against his chest. There's a man on the bench. Long hair and a beard. Tweed blazer. Thick glasses. A trembling hand, a cigarette losing ash.

'This is the one,' Felipe says. 'The one we were just talking about.'

'Who are you?' the man asks.

'Don Pedro, this is the one who pretends to write,' another says. "The traitor, who has been pretending to be you.'

14

RAMONA

is watching Alicia give directions to the camera crew, making a frame with her fingers and panning slowly, looking through it to simulate perfect shots. Pato adds new angles with his hands too, correcting her. The cameramen nod in confusion. Ramona is sitting on a beach towel, Pato's towel (the same she used after last night's shower), which has the Colo-Colo football club shield in glossy threading. It's a sunny day at the not-quite-summer seaside. Only a few locals pass by on the walking paths behind the dunes: with shopping bags, dogs, babies, and no intention of setting foot on sand. They stop at times, curious as to what Pato's crew is doing, outsiders breaking the desolate monotony of the otherwise empty black beach, a little suspicious perhaps at what must look to them like undue excitement.

Ramona is cold and still wearing Alicia's jumper, a little too tight for her. The wind gets stronger the closer you get to the water, the waves tall and crashing in thunderous claps. Birds rest on the water where the waves form, ignoring everything.

It's the first time Ramona pauses to really look at Alicia. She is young and pretty – and must be at least fifteen years younger than Pato. It's as if she tiptoes when she walks, effortlessly, on her heels. Her wrists are bent even when her hands are resting by her thighs, like little sails. Her hair curls naturally, thick, indifferent. Ramona doesn't understand why Pato doesn't just

> LO QUE TUS OJOS NO VEN: A TELENOVELA
>
> #EPISODE 5
>
> INT. FARM CHURCH – EVENING
>
> FATHER CALLETANO
> I cannot believe it, Lucecita. This is a miracle. And you can see me well? You can see everything?
>
> LUZ MARIA
> I can see everything. The cross. The pews. Everything is brighter than I imagined.

use his own wife for the commercials, why he chose her, Ramona, instead of any other woman at the gym. When she asked him, he'd said it was because she could act, which he needed more than beauty. But from the way the crew look at Alicia, Ramona wonders whether anything in the world really matters besides youth and beauty.

After sex, which didn't last very long (he kept asking how it was for her but she just nodded, and sometimes she even moaned melodramatically like in the movies, to see if he would be quiet), he rolled to the other side of the bed and apologised. 'The first and only time, alright?' he said. She nodded, though they were both staring at the ceiling in the dark. 'I can't do this to Alicia. She really loves me. Promise me this will be the only time.' More nodding. 'I can't lose her. Please don't... You know what I mean.

I'm sorry. I mean you understand, right? You're also married.' Ramona asked him how they'd met. She's not sure why she asked. Maybe it was to punish him, to invite Alicia into the room with them. Or maybe she wanted to know how doomed they'd been from the start, to know exactly what kind of cracked branch Alicia was standing on, like the little bird she was, building a nest unaware that its support was about to snap. He was surprised by the question. His voice changed. He pulled the covers up to his chin. 'She was only fifteen when we met,' he had started, 'though I was, you know, a lot older, so I had to wait. It was hard for me,' he said. He didn't look at Ramona. He knew what it sounded like. Can love stories be moving and disturbing in equal measure? A man rewarded for his perseverance. A man unable to understand rejection. Pato was used to judgement. He'd had to tell this story before. 'I pestered her a lot so she would remember me,' he continued, 'so that when she finished school we could get married. But more to your question, we met at a wedding, the brother of my then-girlfriend's. Alicia is the daughter of an ex's family friend. I didn't even want to go to it. I do wonder, sometimes, how my life would have panned out if I hadn't gone. I've believed in destiny ever since. We only talked. I was in the army in those days. Far better looking, believe it or not. We talked about travelling. She wanted to travel. To Europe. To the United States. Said she wanted home to be a place she chose. She's the one who started me on Positive Thinking. Changed my life. We got married as soon as she turned eighteen. No one in her family came to the wedding. It was good for a long time. I quit the army and we started the gym. And now, this I guess. We don't have much in common. She's too young.'

His mouth was under the covers when he said that. He then turned to her and, 'I guess she still wants to travel,' he whispered. 'To leave. But I think I'm finally doing something I like. It's been hard for me.'

```
            FATHER CALLETANO
        And what about me?


              LUZ MARIA
        You're older.


            FATHER CALLETANO
               (laughing)
        Then Jesus only has ears
        for you.

EXT. HOUSE - EVENING

A looming shot that closes in on the house.

INT. HOUSE
```

Ramona sat up with her back to him, bedsheets hanging from her shoulders. What did she have in common with Pato? What could she possibly do about Pato and Alicia's broken marriage? Why did he tell her all this? She turned to him. 'Will you call the TV contact, as you promised?' He stood quickly, naked and indifferent to her watching him – he even stretched, arms up with a sigh – the confidence of men once they're done trying to impress you, relieved perhaps, and he put on his trousers in one motion, cartoon-like, and he slid into his shirt, still buttoned up, like a t-shirt. He tried to kiss her goodnight! And while he did up his belt no less! She turned away on her pillow. When she heard the door shut, she got up to lock it. Did she feel any guilt? What do guilty people do?

SHOWING EMOTION:

1) **Facial expression**: she frowns, shuts her eyes, as if in deep thought.
2) **Body language**: she slumps her shoulders, audibly breathing.
3) **Gesturing**: clenched fists, repeated sweeping of hair away from forehead.
4) **Volume, tone and pace of voice**: she whispers *I'm sorry* to herself, slow and solemn.
5) **Pauses and silences**: she sits on a towel, watching them at the shallow end of the beach, thinking of Lucho. What do she and Lucho have in common?

She feels a sharp buzz in her forehead, a single electric pulse. It's familiar, a symptom of not taking her pills, her body demanding happiness by force.

Pato splits from the group, gestures to her, talks even though he's still too far away to hear. He jogs to her side.

'So, I think we're ready.'

'Good, good. We should try to be quick. My husband will worry.' She pictures Lucho locked in the office, making sure she's asleep before he comes to bed. Had he even noticed her absence?

'Look,' Pato sits next to her on the sand, the towel not wide enough for two. 'I wanted to apologise for yesterday. We've been having some issues with Alicia lately, and the stress of the business, you know...' He waits for her to complete the sentence, to conclude the story. She stays quiet. 'I wanted to tell you I called the producer, by the way. He's managing a new telenovela starting next year. I told him I'd found new talent. He said they'll start auditioning for the main parts soon, maybe by the end of the month even. I told him you'd call but he said it would be better

> We slowly head up a dimly lit staircase. As we
> reach the UPSTAIRS CORRIDOR, we hear ISABEL
> URRUTIA's muffled screams.
>
> INT. ISABEL URRUTIA'S ROOM
>
> ISABEL URRUTIA is in bed. MAID#1, right next
> to the bed, is carrying a silver tray with
> soup and water.
>
>> ISABEL URRUTIA (sobbing)
>> My dear God, how could you
>> do this to me?
>
>> MAID#1
>> You should eat, my Lady.
>
> MAID#1 brings the tray toward ISABEL URRUTIA.

if we called him together. You could come to the gym when we're back in Santiago. He's a childhood friend of mine, so no need for formalities. Don't be shy. They don't like shy people.'

'Thank you. I will, I'll do that,' she says, finding it difficult, despite everything, not to smile.

'Should we get started?'

One of the men from the crew gives her a pair of sunglasses. The other is testing out shots, his face wholly covered by the camera. Alicia is putting foundation on Ramona's face, trying to smooth away her wrinkles, brushing everywhere. She tells Ramona to take off her jumper. In the morning, Alicia had given her a loose summer dress, covered in abstract flower patterns, petals floating, detached from their stems, a wallpaper for a preschool classroom, some eccentric's set of curtains, butterflies with their wings spread, out of proportion to the flowers. It hides her well, she thought when she tried it on, her own lack of proportion. And yet now, closer to the sea, the wind presses the dress against her figure. She might as well be naked. She turns her back on the wind and the dress bloats with air, even bigger. Her head buzzes again. She smiles when Alicia finishes.

'Put these on,' Alicia says. 'They're called Condor Eyes. They're sunglasses that make everything look sharper, with much better contrasts.'

Ramona puts them on. The world appears in shades of blue and green and pink. The parts of the sky covered in clouds become bright blue. The sun is an orange spot, a black ring around it, the only dark thing left to see.

'You will walk from there to here.' Pato points at a cross drawn on the sand. 'Slowly, slowly, and without facing the camera. Never face the camera when you're walking. Then, when you get to where we're standing now, take the glasses off and look right into the camera and start the script.'

ACTING FOR COMMERCIALS:

1) **Play the product:** it doesn't matter what state the country is in. It doesn't matter that your family is breaking apart. Even *you* don't matter much. You're there to show how great the product is!
2) **Remember to play the part:** if you are enjoying yourself, your audience will enjoy watching you too! Be CREATIVE. Be POSITIVE. Be PLAYFUL.

'Hello, friends. Have you ever been out on a wonderful beach day like this, and found yourself reaching for your sunglasses, only to find, once you wear them, that the beauty of nature is darkened and dimmed? Have you ever had to choose between the health

> ISABEL URRUTIA
>
> I am condemned, my dear
> God, you have condemned me.
>
> MAID#1
>
> You have to be calm, my
> Lady. You need to rest.
>
> ISABEL URRUTIA
>
> Where is Luis Felipe? Why
> isn't he here with me?
>
> MAID#1
>
> Don Felipe has gone to
> the church, Doña Isabel.
> He's gone to get Father
> Calletano and a doctor to
> come see and tend to you.

benefits of regular sunglasses and the true joy of the world that surrounds you? Condor Eyes lets you have it all. Beautifully built with German lenses in the United States of America, Condor Eyes lets you see the real beauty of the world in sharp contrast and a fuller range of colours. Condor Eyes: see nature as your nature intended.'

'Cut, cut!'

It will all be worth it, she tells herself. Someday Don Francisco will ask, 'Can you share any particularly difficult moment during filming?'

Don Francisco will lean his elbow on the arm of his chair. The crowd will fall silent.

'Well, Don Francisco,' she will say while she faces the crowd, 'telenovelas are quite long days, as you know. But I started from the very bottom and was never afraid of hard work. I started in commercials.'

And he will point at a screen behind them, where Don Francisco will show her wearing Condor Eyes. Everyone will laugh and she will pretend to be surprised. She will even make herself blush. And then she will say, 'It was going home when it ended that was the hardest part.'

And 'Well how about that?' Don Francisco will say, inviting the audience to clap.

'I said cut!'

Ramona returns to the beach in the evening. She wants a short walk before the long drive back to Santiago. Her head hurts from the camera lighting on her face. It took them just under twenty takes to get it right. Ramona had found it difficult to portray the joy of seeing the world in fuller colours. She was mostly aware of her dress, bulging and tightening in the wrong places. She wonders whether they were all waiting for a shot without any wind, so her body would remain hidden, invisible.

There's a young couple walking barefoot on the edge of the water, arms wrapped around each other. Lucho never liked walking that way. He once said it was infantile and patronising, like two people teaching each other how to walk. The beach is empty apart from the couple. Her head buzzes. The pain makes her shiver. She'd stopped acting to leave Santiago, to get married. Now she's left Santiago to act, and cheat on her husband. At twenty-one, when she was offered the role of Maid 1 after her failed telenovela audition, it'd seemed like a sign from the universe that she should leave everything for a man, and then for their child. Her hopes for the future became Lucho's hopes. A better house. More money. And now they are Pablo's. A good university. A respectable career. Grandchildren, maybe.

She would sometimes imagine Pablo when he was older,

> ISABEL URRUTIA
> He's gone to see that maldita. Tell me the truth or I'll have you whipped.
>
> MAID#1
> No, Doña Isabel, I promise you. He's gone to the chapel.
>
> ISABEL URRUTIA turns the tray over, spilling its contents onto the floor. MAID#1 runs off in fear. We see ISABEL URRUTIA's face up close.
>
> ISABEL URRUTIA (V.O.)
> If I find out that Felipe is with the whore, I swear to

visiting on Sundays like good, loved sons do, perhaps with a girlfriend, and asking Ramona to tell stories of him growing up; it would be like describing a sitcom scene, laughter at the end, recognising how much he'd changed, out in the world and away from his parents, from her, while she'd always remain in the same role, unchanged, with no one to tell her story, not one narrator, a climax dampened long ago, alone, alone in a third act.

The sound of steps behind her brings her back to the present. Pato, on his own, wearing a woollen hat with an orange pompom at the pointy end, like he's balancing a tiny sun. He sits next to her without a word. Too much time passes, too much for casual conversation to emerge. He follows her line of sight to the couple, who are now two little dots in the distance. He comes closer, puts his head on her shoulder, breathing hard so that she notices. She doesn't move. She doesn't speak. She can't get a sound out. She kisses him, and he holds the back of her head, grabs fistfuls of her hair. She keeps her eyes open, trying to find the two little dots, now grains of sand rising and falling, almost touching the sea, and then swept away by the now gentle breeze.

She's glad Lucho is not in the house when she arrives home. She has a shower, brushes her teeth for longer than usual, puts on a bathrobe that she's never worn before, because it belonged to her mother. She takes her pills and goes to Pablo's room. He's not there either; a neatly made bed, curtains drawn. She's surprised by his sudden transformation, glad that he's doing well but a little hurt that he's doing so completely on his own. What help could she be anyway? She takes an extra pill for the day she missed, hoping for a fast end to the afternoon.

In the madhouse she met a woman who'd been stuck there for almost two months. She'd been addicted to cocaine and she was an architect. Catalina? Yes, La Cata. Her family wouldn't visit her. They were embarrassed. 'My husband's a lawyer, you see.' Lucho would visit Ramona almost every day once she was allowed to have visitors. Catalina would tell Ramona how lucky she was to have a man like Lucho by her side – 'I want the days to end quickly. I want to go back to what you have.' Ramona didn't tell her about the existence of Pablo because Catalina had lost a child and could not have another. 'It's just me and the old man, now.' They mostly walked together in a little enclosed garden that had a single lemon tree in the middle with a copper plaque on the ground, a priest's name no one recognised. The grass was always too wet. They walked barefoot, the gurgle of the earth splattering their ankles with mud.

'I mostly helped build offices,' Catalina had said, 'though I worked on some government buildings too. As you can imagine, the military has no taste.'

>   you, God, I swear to you,
>   Satan, I will kill them both.
>
>   ISABEL URRUTIA
>   Leave me! Get out!
>
> INT. FARM CHURCH - EVENING
>
> We see LUZ MARIA and FATHER CALLETANO talking
> in the front pews. LUIS FELIPE enters the
> CHURCH running and in fear.
>
>   LUIS FELIPE
>   Father! Father!
>
>   FATHER CALLETANO
>   Don Luis Felipe! What is
>   the cause of such alarm?

Luckily Lucho had never turned up in uniform.

'What does your husband do?'

'An accountant,' Ramona said, hoping Catalina was as clueless as she was about what accountants did.

It took a few days of circling the lemon tree before Catalina spoke about her politics. The General had appeared on the communal TV for the 21st of May celebrations, and everyone later gathered in little groups, quietly talking about it.

'Do you think it will ever end?' Catalina asked.

Ramona asked what she meant. She didn't want to be the first to say anything, and she wasn't sure what to say anyway. It wasn't something she and Lucho ever spoke about, ever questioned.

'I used to think it wouldn't last,' La Cata said. 'Something would happen, someone would do something. Not sure what I mean by that, I suppose. But now I question whether anything will happen. Animals must rule the jungle. That's what my husband says. I guess it's not as bad as it was when it started.'

Ramona had gone to a party when The General took over. Lucho had arrived late with his father. It was the first time she'd seen Ángel smile. They had toasted the regime, the new Chile. She didn't call her mother. She didn't want to fight. She was only following her husband's lead, after all. Later, she'd heard about terrible things happening. People disappearing, thrown into the sea from helicopters. Torture. Electric shocks to genitals, broken fingers, rape, using dogs to rape. There was a rumour that one of their neighbours had even offered his dog. Lucho never spoke about any of it. She didn't want to ask. Only once, when Ramona asked him if it was true that Mr Rojas had been detained (he was one of her old teachers and a good friend to her stepfather), and Lucho answered: 'We're simply tidying up the mess we inherited. We're straightening up the family.'

Catalina continued to talk politics after that day, perhaps trying to find where Ramona's affiliation lay; a game to pass the time. Her husband dealt with Human Rights cases. Ramona thought, perhaps La Cata was only following what her husband thought too. That was better than being wrong.

On the third week of Ramona's stay, Catalina became excited, could barely sleep. She was going to be let out for the afternoon, a *test day*, as the doctors there called it. On the following morning they painted birdhouses and jewellery boxes, stuck napkins on the pre-cut wood to tile it with patterns so complex they could never draw them. An architect plastering birdhouses. An actress mimicking another woman's happiness. They hung the birdbox from a lemon tree branch. No bird ever used it.

Then Catalina was given her civilian clothes back, as she called them. Laced her shoes. Was finally allowed to wear a belt with her jeans. Her husband was going to pick her up for a meal

> LUIS FELIPE
>
> Father, it's Isabel. She has lost her sight. You are friends with the doctor, are you not? I've been looking for him and thought he'd be here. Isabel needs your comfort, Father.
>
> LUZ MARIA turns to face LUIS FELIPE in slow motion, sparkles FX under her eyes. We then see LUIS FELIPE's astounded face.
>
> LUIS FELIPE
>
> Miss, I didn't expect to find you here.
>
> LUZ MARIA
>
> You look exactly as I'd imagined.

somewhere downtown. Somewhere nice, he had promised her. 'A date,' she said. 'Normal life.'

When he arrived, Ramona sat at the table in the far end of the garden, where patients gathered to smoke. She watched him go through the same motions she'd seen with other husbands. A quick peck on the cheek. A frown and a nod as the doctor gave him instructions at an angle so Catalina couldn't hear them. The husbands never looked at the other women. Perhaps out of respect for their own wives. Most likely to forget where their wives were. An involuntary reflex. Their unique wives with unique problems uniquely fixed. They could not take anything else they saw in the madhouse back home. They couldn't stand it. Catalina waved back towards the smoking group, towards Ramona, before following her husband out.

Lucho visited Ramona that same afternoon and she was happy to see him, because without Catalina the day had turned silent and it'd made her lethargic.

They had little to talk about. Nothing in that place ever changed. The most dutiful husbands were always the quietest, the most bored. Ramona had never spoken to Lucho about Catalina, and after finding out where her politics lay, she decided it would be less troublesome to keep their exchanges to herself.

'Is everything still okay?' he asked. 'The doctor told me you have no more than a week left. You can finally come home. If everything's still okay.'

'How is Pablo?'

'Quiet. Fine. Just worry about getting better.'

She did want to ask about all the terrible things Catalina had told her about. She'd heard them before, of course, everyone had, people's sons and daughters gone missing, but she wanted to hear it from Lucho. He would never lie to her. But Lucho would think she was accusing him.

Time had passed. You heard less about it. To ask would be cruelty. And to such a devoted husband. Cruel and ungrateful. The country had changed for the better, he would often tell her when mothers talked about their missing children. People are ungrateful.

They had coffee with milk together, even though she knew he hated milk, and then he left.

It felt practised. Repetition had made his visits more efficient. He often looked at his watch.

She went back to the shed where she'd decorated the birdhouse. The nurse who always followed her reminded Ramona of the nuns at her school. Stern-faced and always sitting upright, so stiff it seemed they lacked vertebrae. She was reading the paper, checking on Ramona between pages.

> **LUIS FELIPE**
>
> What did you say, Miss?
>
> **FATHER CALLETANO**
>
> She can see, Don Luis Felipe. Just like that, a real miracle. She can see.
>
> **LUIS FELIPE**
>
> You can see!
>
> LUIS FELIPE walks toward LUZ MARIA and holds her hands in his.
>
> **LUIS FELIPE**
>
> This is incredible, just the good news I needed on such a dark night.

'Can I paint something else?' Ramona asked, putting her apron on. 'I'm restless.'

'Knock yourself out,' the nurse said.

'There's only a jewellery box here. Do you have any more birdhouses?'

'What you see here is all we have today.'

'I'm sure there were more. I was here with Catalina before she left. There were at least three more. Maybe four.'

The nurse folded the newspaper on her lap. 'As my grandmother used to say, may she rest in peace, in times of hunger the Devil feeds on flies.'

Ramona took the wooden jewellery box and sanded away the splinters in its edges. She decided to paint it, add an elegant napkin pattern to it and give it to Catalina as a parting gift.

She finished it and left it on Catalina's bedside table.

She fell asleep in the evening and awoke to muffled screaming. She got up and opened her door. The other women did the same. They all stood looking down the corridor to the entrance, quietly under the doorframes like during an earthquake. Two nursing assistants were carrying Catalina along the corridor, one on each side, locking arms. They took her to her room. All was suddenly quiet. The women shut their doors. At night, between two and three, when the evening shifts ended and before the morning nurses turned up, Ramona tiptoed her way to Catalina's room. She was in bed, sobbing. She turned slowly to Ramona, her eyes not quite in focus, looking *medical*, as patients called it.

'He took me out to sign a separation,' Catalina said.

Ramona didn't know what to say. The jewellery box lay untouched on the floor.

'You'll be able to work it out. It will be okay, Cata.'

'He met another woman. They're buying a house together.'

'But, I'm sure it'll—'

'—Not everyone ends up happy. Not everyone has a husband like yours.'

'I think if you just—'

'—Please get out,' Catalina said, one ear against the pillow. 'Leave me.'

Now, Ramona tears up seeing the empty jewellery box, which stands on her bedside table. Lucho comes in, groaning the long day away as he takes his clothes off and pulls his pyjamas from under his pillow. Ramona shuts her eyes, tries to slow her breathing. He lies on his side. She can feel him breathing on the back of her neck. He slides closer to her, a hand on her hip. She tenses up, pretends to be newly awake, a fake yawn. He kisses her neck and his chin lands on her shoulder. He traps her legs, preventing her from moving. She can't breathe. She really can't breathe.

'I love you,' he whispers.

> We see the scene shifting focus toward the
> FARM CHURCH door (barely open), where MAID#1
> is watching everything through the gap. We
> then return to the conversation.
>
> LUZ MARIA
> What happened to Doña Isabel?
>
> LUIS FELIPE
> She has lost her sight.
> Just as suddenly as you
> recovered yours.
>
> FATHER CALLETANO
> You better keep looking
> for the doctor, Don Luis.

'I'm tired,' she says.

'Sorry, sorry,' he says.

'I'm sorry too.' She pretends to sleep, dizzy from the pills, the dotted pattern on the jewellery box moving about the frame. She's no better than Catalina's husband. A cheater. A secret life and a partner left alone. She'd never thought herself capable of such selfishness. At least not loudly, not to herself. But with eyes half-shut, she's back on that bench looking at the lemon tree. It's alright, she tells Catalina, crying next to her, there are no birds here anyway and the house will always be empty. It will be okay, though what she really wants to say is, I understand him. I understand your husband. Why would you say that to me, Ramona? You were right, in telenovelas not everyone ends up happy; it's so that others can live more intensely, so that it means something.

She'll go to the gym tomorrow, as always, and demand to meet Pato's TV contact, and she'll never see Pato again after that. And then Lucho will see her on TV, playing her part, saying her lines, and he'll forgive her, he'll say, 'It's good that you're finally well, nothing else matters, and I wish your mother could see you now.' The tree outside her window is filled with black wings, early morning sun, the light in her heart, the swell of the city, familiar and infinite.

A hard knock on the bedroom door. Ramona looks at the clock on the dresser. Just passed midday. Mouth dry. Head killing her.

'Miss Ramona,' Mariela calls.

'Come in.'

'Someone here for you.'

'Who is it? Let me get ready.' Ramona drinks the stale water in last night's glass. She puts on her bathrobe and slippers and looks at herself in the mirror.

'Miss, I think you should hurry.'

'You haven't even told me who it is.'

'I didn't catch her name. She's very upset.'

She thinks about getting dressed properly. Maybe she can wear her navy blazer or something, but her face would give her away. Mariela stays in the bedroom doorway until Ramona follows her out.

At the bottom of the stairs, Alicia is waiting with her arms fully crossed, like she's hugging herself. She's staring at the floor and takes a moment to notice Ramona, and when she does she takes a step back, startled from her thoughts.

What in the world... Is she here to kill Ramona? To tell her that she knows? To warn her? She'd heard of jealousy killings before (Don Francisco has interviewed a widow), and a police expert said they always happened in the guilty person's house, a way, perhaps, to degrade the place where the cuckold imagined

> I'll stay here in case he
> comes by.
>
> LUIS FELIPE leaves. MAID#1 is no longer there.
>
> LUZ MARIA
> I'll go with him.
>
> FATHER CALLETANO
> I think it would be better
> if you stayed. We don't
> know if you've fully
> recovered yet.
>
> LUZ MARIA
> I can see perfectly. What
> is there to wait for?

the affair taking place. A murder intended to pervert the very meaning of home life. Mariela goes to the kitchen, one door away. Maybe this is how it ends.

'Hi,' Ramona starts with a smile. 'I'm very sorry. I wasn't expecting anyone and I look a mess.'

'I need to talk to you,' Alicia says.

'What's the matter? Did something bad happen?'

'Something terrible.'

Alicia starts crying.

'Mariela!'

'Yes, Miss?'

'Could you make us some mint tea please, take it to the living room?'

'It's okay. I mean, I'm sorry I came. Sorry to bother you.'

'Look at me, Alicia. Does it look like you're bothering me? Come with me and tell me all about it.'

Alicia follows Ramona into the living room. Ramona is glad Alicia doesn't see the collection of unopened mail scattered on the floor. The wide double doors make too grand an entrance for such a dull collection of old furniture; a small TV set in the corner, a rug marked by the spills of Pablo's childhood, a few animal ornaments which survived the fire in her mother's house. The floor lamps sway in the new breeze, and the old beige curtains are still up from the former residents, tiny holes eaten away by moths (some of them still dead on the windowsills – Mariela is not used to windowsills), letting light pierce through like a cheap oily napkin. Somehow, having the same things as they did in their previous home has also transported the scale of that old living room with them. It feels claustrophobic.

Alicia sits down on the one chair that doesn't creak. Ramona sits next to her at the head of the table, her backrest bending slightly.

Mariela brings in the tea on a copper tray which looks excessive and tacky with two common white mugs on it and tea strings still hanging on their sides. She stares at Alicia as she lowers the tray onto the table and picks up the mugs from their saucers.

Alicia doesn't look up.

They wait for Mariela to shut the doors.

'He's cheating on me,' Alicia whispers, suddenly dry, looking Ramona in the eyes.

'Who?' Ramona says, dunking the teabag repeatedly, turning the tea sickly green.

'What do you mean *who*? Pato, he's cheating on me.'

'How do you know? Did he tell you? What did he say?'

'I know because—'

'—All marriages have their problems.' Ramona has no idea why she's talking. She slurps a mouthful of tea and burns her tongue. She's sweating.

> **FATHER CALLETANO**
> He is married, Lucecita.
> Married by God.
>
> **LUZ MARIA**
> God granted me sight.
>
> **FATHER CALLETANO**
> And as you now know, He can just as easily take it away.
>
> **LUZ MARIA**
> (at the door)
> It is my turn to be happy, Father.

'No, it's not like that. I know that.'

Ramona will have to come clean. She doesn't know how people react in these kinds of situations in real life. In theatre, the trick was to envision a circle around you, Your Loneliness, and to project all your hopes and dreams of happiness outside of it. Your Happiness belonged to the rest of the cast. To props even. Ramona never understood it. She simply practised crying in front of a mirror, like an actress on *Giant Saturday* said she'd always done.

'First, he started going out to refuel the car, even when I knew he hadn't been driving. He went out for hours at a time.'

Ramona's shoulders relax.

'I thought maybe he was just thinking, coming up with new ideas, you know? Like he always does. He has always said driving clears his mind. Like having showers.'

'But that's a far—'

'And then he was always getting up in the middle of the night. He said he was working but I could hear him laughing and whispering on the phone.'

Pato has never called Ramona. Somehow this feels like an insult.

'And then, then there was a dress. Can you imagine? In a pretty box. Under our own bed!'

'A dress? Maybe it was—'

'I thought it was you. I'm really sorry. I know, I know. I'm sorry. May as well be honest with you. I thought it was you he was with.'

'And why would you think that?' The question comes out too earnest, not matching her forced smirk. Her tea is finished but she sips air out of it anyway.

'Because he's done it once before. When we started the gym. He had a fling with a TV model. She could have been his daughter.' Ramona thinks Alicia could be his daughter too. 'And that's how we met as well. He was a married man when we met.'

'He was married?'

'I know, I know. I'm not proud of it.'

'But why me? I can't believe—'

'He said he loves talking to you. That you have a lot in common. Maybe it's the age, I don't know.' The thought of her as Pato's likeness makes Ramona cough into the mug. 'He was always setting you apart from everyone else at the gym. Out of all the girls, he chose you.'

'I'm married, Alicia.' She felt accused. What about Lucho, even in his absence, a devoted and protective husband? Ramona knows it's unreasonable, but she feels a rush of anger, jealousy even. 'I'm married and I have no interest in other men.' This much is true. 'I've worked in theatre before. That's why you both

```
Dramatic music in crescendo. We get a close-up
of FATHER CALLETANO's face, showing fear.

                LUZ MARIA
        I'm not responsible for the
        misery of the world. Don't
        I deserve some of its joy?

LUZ MARIA leaves FARM CHURCH.

                FATHER CALLETANO (V.O.)
        Forgive her, Father, may
        you forgive her.

EXT. FARM CHURCH - EVENING

We see LUZ MARIA exiting the FARM CHURCH.
```

chose me, remember? He said there might be a part for me in a telenovela. It's why I accepted.'

'I know it's not you. I'm not accusing you. But he says those things to the other girls too.'

'He says—'

'I unwrapped the dress. No offence, but it was far too small for you. That's when I knew it was someone else.'

'So why are you here?'

Ramona covers herself, the bathrobe touching her chin.

'You need to help me.'

'Help you how? I don't want to be in the middle of this. It doesn't concern me.'

Outside the window, Ramona sees Pablo, standing at the top of the stone steps to the basement. He's wearing the Condor Eyes sunglasses she brought home. He disappears. It takes her a few moments to realise he should be in school. She has no energy for any of this.

'Maybe he'll talk to you. You could talk to him, right? I don't know. I can't deal with this again.'

'I can't talk to him. You should be—'

'I'm pregnant, Ramona.'

'You're what?'

'Pregnant.'

Ramona stands up straight, like she's been tapped on a reflex spot on her back.

'I wanted to ask you,' Alicia continues, looking up at Ramona, 'if I could stay here while we sort it out. I don't have anyone else in Santiago.'

'He really says that to all the other girls?'

'What?'

'Yes, you can stay. Of course you can stay. I'll talk to him.'

'You're a good friend. I knew you'd understand.'

Alicia's nose is blocked and her tea remains untouched. A pathetic figure. Ramona leaves her in the living room by herself, in her own circle, all the happiness seeping out of it and landing in Ramona's, and she will not stand it, will not give anything back. She will get dressed and leave the house. She will go to the gym, as always, clothed in nothing but her own loneliness, and she will demand what belongs to Alicia and also what belongs to her. Her lines, her part.

As she steps out of the house the ground shakes, the earth's spinal reflex which everyone in Santiago must endure in silence, like mourning.

Behind the door, YACONDA, the Witch of the Pond is revealed, smiling.

> YACONDA (V.O.)
> That's right, my daughter, all the happiness in the world belongs to you. Take no notice of all the suffering, for there is always a price, one must be condemned for another to be blessed. None can refuse it. And so it will be till the end of time.

15

PABLO

isn't sure what to do now that he's alone with Clara. It's still early evening, too early to go to the basement. Francisco has left with Juan García from The Detainees to record the sounds of a protest downtown to include in The Song of The People. Only the painter has stayed. He says he only paints from memory or his subjects would look too realistic. That's what photographers are for, he says.

Clara is waving down a *micro* bus. In Providencia, the *micros* race for passengers, cut each other off, people packed inside tilting from side to side like underwater weeds. Those by the windows are always looking out, eyes wide and urgent, like they're travelling the city looking for something they can't accept is lost. Clara pays for the two of them, the *micrero* smiling knowingly at Pablo – You can't fool anyone, we all know what you're up to. Clara grabs his hand and pulls him in, squeezing into an opening before the rows of seats begin. People look at them silently until the *micro* shuts its doors and starts to move again. Clara doesn't notice. She never looks anyone in the eyes, only Pablo, and then she stares out the window through the gaps between heads and backpacks, her mouth almost touching his ear.

'I'm taking you somewhere I hope you've never been to.'

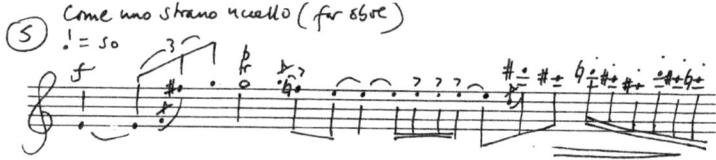

'Shouldn't we have waited for Francisco?'

'Do you want to wait for him?'

He looks at the faces around them, some now registering disgust as a man with a guitar steps into the bus without paying.

'When he's writing music, that's all he cares about.'

They smile at each other. Neither of them has mentioned what happened, nearly happened, didn't happen in his room. The morning after, when what had seemed plausible at night – her leaving Francisco for him – had become dreamlike and absurd.

The man with the guitar starts to sing an Elvis song in Chilean English. His guitar is missing two strings. People avoid his gaze. Those who aren't beside windows read their own palms.

To get out of the *micro* they need to jump off while it's still moving. Pablo trips and almost falls – the ideal way to tell everyone he's not yet a *Santiaguino*, that he's still bound to countryside inertia. He straightens his back. Clara smiles at him with pity.

They cross a bridge in Baquedano. The Law Department of the Universidad de Chile in one corner (students gathered in groups at the entrance, others on their own leaning on pillars and staring blankly out into the traffic) and a market filled with wooden stalls across the road. Pablo is not going to law school, whatever his parents may think. He doesn't even know when the Aptitude Test is. He has to remind himself that he's a musician deep, deep down and nothing else will satisfy him, not even a clever future, as his father likes to say.

He knows the street, though it looks different, the purple and green walls more pronounced than when he walked down the hill recently. He can't hear the tide in his ear: it's now been replaced by a river of cars and travelling salesmen on carpets made of bedsheets and towels.

They reach the foot of the San Cristóbal Hill. There's a house built into a cliff edge, the upper deck right up against it, spilling out of trees.

'This was your namesake's house, your *tocayo*, Neruda. Have you ever read any of his stuff?'

'Some,' he says, though he hasn't.

'His love poems are fatal.'

'Yeah, my favourite ones are his love poems.'

'He was a communist, you know?'

'Yeah, he was great.'

His father always said it was a shame that poets were always communists. 'At least some of the good musicians aren't so ungrateful,' he said once, though when Pablo asked which ones he meant, his father couldn't think of any good ones.

'I write some poetry too, you know?' she says.

'Me too.'

'Well, when am I going to read some? If a Pablo ever wrote me poetry, I would find it pretty hard to resist,' she laughs. 'God, so cheesy,' she adds, looking at him, 'it makes me sick.'

They start to climb the stone steps up the hill. Only a few people pass them, young families, a man in blue overalls lifting a cart filled with fluorescent plastic windmills and a box of stacked cigarette packs.

'Do you sell them loose, uncle?' Clara asks the man. He puts his cart down, holds it carefully so it doesn't slide down the steps.

'Of course I sell them loose. Do I look like a tight-ass?'

Clara laughs and shakes her head.

'How much you have them for?'

'A hundred pesos, *m'hijita*.'

'Give me two then.'

The man extends his hand with an open palm to Pablo.

'I'm getting these, uncle,' Clara says.

'Uy, be careful, your *pololo*, your boyfriend, he's a tight-ass,' he says.

'He really is,' she says, taking the cigarettes. She places one over her ear, and then faces him, combs his hair behind his ear and slides the other cigarette in slowly, like she's planting a flower in a crowded bouquet.

'For when we get to the top of the hill,' she says.

They walk in silence, him following her. Every few steps she turns her head to check he's still there. The sandy trail crunches as they tread on, pebbles shooting up

and leaving tiny dust clouds he can't help but breathe in.

When they get to the summit, Clara sits at the top of the steps, just under the Virgin Mary statue that overlooks the city. She pats the space next to her and he sits there, their knees touching, no one else around them. He tries to spot the side of the hill he'd woken up that morning, but figures it must be the other side, to the back of the Virgin.

'It's nice up here,' he says.

'Right? My brother used to bring me a lot.'

'I didn't know you had a brother.'

'You never asked.'

'Sorry.'

'I have two. A younger and an older one. I'm the middle child. Attention-seeking, afraid of confrontation, apparently,' she says with a caricature of a smile, tongue out. 'Otherwise known as a fuck-up.'

'You're not a fuck-up. If you're a fuck-up then what am I?'

'It's not an exclusive title, you know? I can't save you.'

'Thanks.'

'My older brother used to bring me here a lot. Rodrigo. I was a kid though, so I don't remember much. He ran off to Sweden. Or Switzerland, maybe? I confuse the two. Doesn't matter anyway.'

'Communist?'

'Not the poet kind. Though who knows, maybe he became a Swedish poet. We've not heard from him since.'

'That sucks.'

'Still, I like this place. It's special to me.'

She grabs her cigarette and scratches out the tobacco crumbs from the end. She searches the breast pocket of her denim jacket. A little plastic bag of dry green leaves and seeds. She takes a pinch and pushes it inside the cigarette.

She looks him in the eyes and pulls him closer to her, pressing on his back with one hand. With the other, she takes his cigarette, and then fills it with the green, places it in his lips. She lights his cigarette, then her own, and they look down at the city, which from the top of the hill appears flat, empty of people, movement and noise; a map whose magnitude leaves him feeling irrelevant.

'This stuff is mortal,' she says, puffing out a thick cloud.

'Yeah,' he says, thinking she only brought him over so she didn't have to smoke by herself. He coughs with his mouth shut and she laughs.

The cigarette dulls the sea in his ear to syncopated wet clicks, a broken metronomic tap. In between clicks, a new silence.

'Francisco won't smoke this stuff with me, you know? He used to, but not anymore.'

'Shame.'

'He says hippies had their time, that they fucked up, thinking good intentions were enough. He said people confuse awareness with action these days. That he doesn't simply want to be aware.' His father used to say things like that too. 'Hey.'

'What?'

'Have you ever had a girlfriend?'

'Yes. A few.'

'Really?'

'No.'

'Of course you haven't.' She looks at the inside of her cigarette. 'It's obvious.'

'Why?'

'Because you always do what I want to do. You never say no.'

La Dani had said the same thing. Once they got together, he confessed he'd always hated dancing, that he couldn't stop himself from picturing his own movements in the third person, what he'd look like in the absence of music, like he was having a stroke or some other ailment which would not allow his arms and legs to mark a beat. 'I only do it because you like it.' He'd meant it as a diss on dancing (and her, if he were honest) but La Dani had called him a gentleman. Right after that, their first kiss.

'Maybe I'm just a gentleman.'

'They always are at first,' she says, shaking her head. She laughs and steps on her dead cigarette.

He takes his mother's new sunglasses from his chest pocket. The city brightens, the sky is orange, the apartment blocks in the distance stand purple on blue pavements. When his mother fell ill, his father wouldn't tell him what had happened to her. We don't have to tell you everything, he'd said. He thought she was dying, cancer perhaps, the way a few of his classmates' parents had died. He waited for her hair to fall out. When that didn't happen, he assumed it was because it was a lost cause, useless to even try to beat it. She'd always be in bed when he got home after school, her door shut. Mariela had sat with him while he had his *once* tea, watching him eat in a tense silence, like she was waiting for him to ask her about his mother.

Then, he thought about how Mariela had no one to talk to the whole day, that he was her only company. 'Your mum's just sad,' she said, 'it happens to some people as they get older. I had an uncle, peace be to him, who also had it just like your mum. People go to doctors now, but what really helped my uncle was praying and getting back to work on the farm. One day he just got better. It doesn't last forever.'

Pablo nodded. He didn't want to say that the house seemed more peaceful, especially without his mother's obsession with cleanliness, the daily knocks on his bedroom door while she looked for anything that could need washing, the ironing of towels and underwear and bedsheets and her anger at Mariela who for some reason never thought of such things – 'Lazy, so lazy, but we can't fire her after all these years,' his mother used to say. On Mariela's day off, his mother would sweep, vacuum and wipe everything again, it was like she was trying to get rid of evidence after a crime, creating a house empty of prints and hair and dust, a house no one lived in.

He once knocked on his mother's door. She was watching cartoons on TV without any sound. She didn't look at him as he stepped into the room. The curtains were drawn shut so the TV was the only light, projecting moving shadows all over the walls. Her skin looked almost grey, and her hair had whitened at the roots. He sat beside the bed, slowly, afraid of any sudden movements. He took her hand and she teared up.

'What does it feel like,' he asked, 'the sadness?'

'Like being in a hole,' she answered, and then, 'I'm sorry,' she said, 'I'm just very tired. It's like being very tired.'

He kissed her head and left her, shut her door, retreated to the rest of the house. He wouldn't admit it, but he'd felt relieved at just how simple it'd been to pretend the house ended at her door after that, how small a great sadness can become when it can be shunted away somewhere, in someone, remembered only when needed.

'How was she?' Mariela asked.

'Tired,' he said, 'very tired,' exactly as his father had always said.

Pablo went up to the bathroom and locked the door. In the dry tub and with his clothes on, he put a Cat Stevens tape in his cassette player. He'd stolen the tape from a classmate whose parents smuggled *gringo* music, 'Moonshadow', and he guessed he could understand the lyrics through the melody: everyone was in a different burrow, tunnels between us but still underground. He stared at the single frosted glass window, dots in colours spread like wet ink. He always liked that he could trace anything on the blurry outlines, a wild stadium crowd, the swell of music, the view of anywhere-but-here.

The sunglasses sharpen contrasts, the edges of everything, Clara, the foreground to the city, her skin sky-pink. She takes the sunglasses from him. The smog haze comes back, a grainy panoramic, a Santiago made of sand. The watery ringing comes back too. He cups his left ear, the world in mono.

'You look like a Martian. This is way catastrophic. The skyscrapers look like trees. Who would want these?'

'My mum.'

She laughs.

'She okay?'

'Just tired.'

Clara faces him, closer, closer, until he can feel her breathing. He shuts his eyes, his foot tapping sixteenth notes.

'Hey,' she says. 'Hey.'

He looks at her, holding his breath.

'Keep your eyes open. I just want to see something.'

She kisses him. They hold each other's gaze. New details in her skin, sunspots, the texture of sweat, the gradual dark under her eyes, a sharp hair strand landing on her nose. She sweeps it away. He shuts his eyes when her fingers stay on his cheek.

'Alright, I think we should go and meet the others.'

'The others?'

'My boyfriend.' She grins. His face heats up.

'Why?' he asks, wishing he hadn't said a thing.

'Because you're in love with me, man.'

'No, no. I think we—'

'So you're not in love with me?'

He gestures with his hands but says nothing.

'I'm fucking with you, man.'

'Okay,' he says.

'We're bandmates. More than friends, much more than friends, you know?'

'Yeah.'

'You'll get over it.'

'Thanks.'

'You better. We're bandmates.'

They meet Francisco at the Universidad de Chile station as they'd agreed. He arrives almost an hour late and on his own, wearing a soldier's helmet and with his tape recorder in one hand, the attached microphone held under his armpit. Clara stands when she sees him. Pablo stays cross-legged on the floor, and watches them kiss.

'You won't believe what just fucking happened,' Francisco says.

It's been a while since they practised and Clara keeps speeding up whenever they transition to a new section. By the time they reach a second chorus they're playing a new song. Most of Francisco's riffs are in G major, and though Clara once said the rhythm section was the backbone of any good track ('the spine of all music,' she actually said), Pablo's merely improvising on the scale hoping no one notices, leaving the bassiest notes to whenever a crash cymbal naturally drops. If he is a backbone

```
G------------------------------------------------------
D------------------------------------------------------
A-------------------5-5-5-5--2-2-2-2-------------------
E-3-3-3-3-3-3-3-3--------------------------------------
```

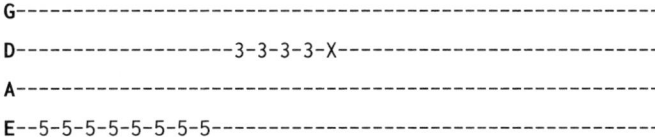

then all music is crooked.

He looks at Clara as he plays. Between songs, she adjusts the ring of tape she has stuck around her fingers. 'To avoid burns,' she said, though her hands aren't calloused.

On their way to practise at the barn, Francisco told them that he got caught up in a protest about the referendum. Juan, who was recognised by the crowd, gave a little speech. He referred to Francisco by name and even called him an artist. Francisco almost cried in the metro, as he was telling them. Clara had to hug him to stop it from happening. Pablo hoped he'd break down and weep. Instead: 'Juan announced a gig,' Francisco said, 'and we're opening for the fucking Detainees on Friday. It'll be a concert to promote voting NO.'

'We can't even vote,' Pablo said, 'we're still too young.'

'Then it's a good thing it's not just us in the crowd,' Francisco answered.

'Could you guys play on time, please? I can't breathe when you play that fast.'

'Or maybe our songs are better fast,' Clara says. 'And breathless.'

'I'm not talking about you only.' Francisco slings his guitar against his back. 'Did you change some of the bass notes, man?'

'Trying new stuff.'

'I wish you wouldn't. Keep it simple, you know?' Francisco sits on his amp. 'If we speed the songs up like this we'll end our set in fifteen minutes.'

'Could be a statement,' Clara says, doing rolls on the rim of the snare.

'Of how much we suck.'

'We could play it all twice if that happens,' Pablo says.

'That's an idea,' Clara says with a grin.

'Just play the right notes, man. I'll finish with the Song of The People.'

'You finally finished it?'

'Yeah, thanks for asking. Juan helped me. He really gets it. He got the crowd singing all these loose notes and I recorded the whole thing. But it's more of a solo piece. It has no time signature because I wanted something timeless. The band aren't playing the people. It's the people who play the band.'

Pablo snorts but hides it with a slap on the strings when he sees Clara with her arms crossed looking all pleased, nodding at Francisco like he's returned from a war or something, fought for them, for their gratitude.

At least Pablo will be with Clara in the crowd when he plays it, being thankful. There is nothing left for him to do. They won't be playing his songs – he can't finish anything on his own, can't even start it – and maybe La Dani was right, maybe she did know him better than anyone else. They'd argued because she hadn't been in awe of his playing. He'd just started, muffled chords and percussive notes, little pauses whenever his fingers found their way to new frets. She merely nodded. And what do *you* do anyway? he'd asked, putting his guitar back in the closet. Pablo, I think it takes time to be adored.

'You don't have to try so hard. It's okay to be common. Why are you so afraid of doing nothing?'

He'd let her say all those things because he knew some day he'd write a hit, or something so original he'd forever raise the bar for the bands to come, and then he'd bring up the little chats. And here it is, his moment, and he's still playing someone else's songs, jealous even though he's a part of it and no, no, what La Dani had actually said was that the crowd always seemed to enjoy themselves more than the musicians, and so it made no sense to pursue it, because music was never meant for those who made it.

'Man, you really need to play *with* us. You can't go off on your own beat like that. You're the bassist.'

'The spine of all music,' she says.

He's walking next to Juan who's singing about love, or loving, and strumming an air-guitar. They're outside a restaurant called El Caleuche, the name written in seashells on an upright plaster surfboard which looked like a gravestone from afar because there are flowers in clear bottles at its base. Looking inside through the wall-length window, Pablo stares at the old fishing net décor which hangs close to the guests' heads. All of their plates are empty. His father and mother are there, and so are Clara and Francisco. Pablo turns back to thank Juan, that this was exactly the place he's been looking for, the one holiday he remembers where he saw his parents kiss, when he had to pretend to be disgusted, when they seemed happy. But now Juan isn't there. He tries to open the door but it won't budge. A shadow advances slowly toward him. Above, an overgrown moon is eclipsing the sun and falling into the sea. The ocean recoils. He runs to the beach, the red sky making fire out of clouds, animal corpses in the sand, birds falling in silence. A visible cliff, the roar of invisible water.

'A wave is coming and we're all going to die,' he tells Juan, who's now appeared at the restaurant door. 'We have to get everyone out and run uphill.'

Juan is still air-strumming, his back against the door.

'I don't know that song,' he says with a smile.

'You have to help me open this door.'

'It's too late for them. I'll take care of them for you. I'll guard the door.'

'Thank you.'

'You should run.'

He runs up a dune which doesn't end, tripping on the sandy folds, reaching for bush branches and roots to pull himself up. He doesn't look back but he knows the wave has taken everything when, seeing his own shadow once again – and the sky clears to the faraway fizz of calming waters – he's filled with the certainty that he has saved himself from a terrible end.

He blinks and is now looking down on the tarp tent at the edge of the school grounds. It's dark and he has no idea of the time. His ear's humming a low amp feedback which makes him nauseous. There's a flashlight moving inside, though he can't see anyone. He walks slowly toward the tent and looks inside through a tear. A bearded old man is painting on a school desk and sitting on an inverted metal bucket. He gestures circles with a cigarette, loosening his wrist before dipping the paintbrush in a wooden palette once more. Pablo notices faded writing on the walls, old music scores he can't read, piles of books on an old mattress, canvases painted wholly black. The ground starts to shake and Pablo stands in an instant, the man looking right at him, the clatter of pans inside, shaking light, and then darkness, the screech of the bucket on the ground. Pablo runs, the Painter almost touching him, he's certain, almost grabbing him, but when he looks back, breathless, there's nothing, the tent flattened into the ground and the blinking city behind it, tower blocks standing like candles on white stone, rising from black water.

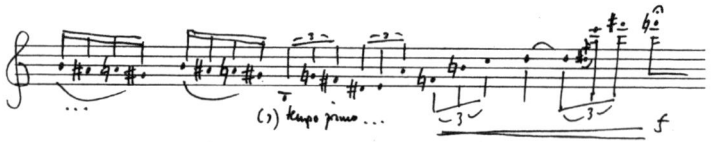

16

LUCHO

can only see through his left eye. He uses his shoulder to wipe the nosebleed and stares at his open briefcase on the front desk, the teacher's desk. Pedro is reading his notebook, tearing out pages instead of turning them. The notebook shrinks, thins – and even here, with his hands tied behind his back, no one knowing where he is or whether he'll ever leave, he still wants to know what Pedro thinks about his poems, particularly the later ones where the object is not so much Ramona but Love, not Chile but Home, not his own but the world's Desire.

'You write like you're composing puzzles,' Pedro says. 'Amateurs don't understand that it's all about clarity, new ways of being clear. These don't make much sense. I'm sure they mean a lot to you but they're more like confusing diary entries. Like writing to a mirror. A teenager's work. Pretentious. The styles change too often. All over the place, as if written by different people. It would have done you good to actually learn from the workshops.'

'They're not finished.'

'I'm sure they're not. Though some writing can't be saved.'

He shoves the rest of the notebook onto the floor behind him without watching it land. 'Not that you'd tell me – but you're not with the CNI, right?'

'No.'

'Who are you then?'

'A poet,' he says, 'like you.'

*

In the dark, the classroom could be a basement, any basement. He lies with his back against the floor, his hands no longer tied. What would his father have said? It's difficult, though liberating, to remember Ángel before he himself forgot. Lucho isn't sure exactly what his father's last lucid words to him were, but they were most likely banal. He'd lost weight and carried himself like the essential picture of ageing, a walking stick and a loose robe, smelling like urine, dry blood on thin skin where different needles had been. Lucho told Ramona his father had died the same day he placed him in the hospice. He didn't want to have to deal with any questions about his father's health, or even worse, how Lucho felt about it all. The truth is he hadn't known how he'd felt then any more than he does now. Had he said something about God? The hospice belonged to a group of nuns, after all. That was the first sign of the irreversible degeneration of his character – Ángel began to cross himself in bed and ask for confession. But what do you confess to when you have no memory? Not to mention, to whom or to what? Instead, Ángel sounded like a poet improvising. He said things like 'I have a good house, you know? Apricots grew the size of mangoes in my garden. I have done nothing wrong.' And then he'd look outside his window and say, 'I've been good. I'm a good person. The birds can tell you.'

> What will your confession be?
> A good house where
> mangoes grow.
> Let the birds tell you,
> I've been good.

Lucho knew his father had done terrible things, patriotic things, when The General took over, in rooms that Lucho had imagined must have looked just like the one he's in now. Yes, he knows the rooms would have been worse; they were real. Ángel had called Lucho a coward when he'd asked for help rounding up teachers and union leaders, even priests, and Lucho refused. 'It's not the time to hide,' Ángel had said. 'Finally, it's not the time to hide.' Something like that. His father had by then taken over *The Region* newspaper as the head editor and he'd shut down *The Guerrillero*. He'd imprisoned writers who'd once worked for *The Region* and split during the run-up to the Popular Unity. 'A vulgar newspaper for vulgar opinions,' his father said. 'They don't deserve the written word.' Lucho knew all this was because they had called his father a fascist, a Nazi. And Ángel's life (and so Lucho's life too) had always been about duty after Olga left them. Betrayal and abandonment seemed almost funny set against his father's cull of San Fernando's communists, most of whom would turn out to loath his father's cruelty more than even The General's. Ángel had forced Lucho to count 'something important, for once in your life,' detainees, deaths, to count them as they were transported from one basement to another – 'No, no, I only want their numbers, exactly the same way you count everything else' – dead bodies in the sea, dying bodies North and South, counting backwards to a detonation, only now in flames, hoping too long for something other than fire to emerge, perhaps even good, perhaps even love and forgiveness and other modern delusions; Lucho had obliged, he'd wanted it too, as long as he didn't have to see it.

Had Ángel's last words been an apology, maybe? Did his father say he was sorry to the nuns, to him? But Lucho would surely have remembered that. His father had run away and got lost in the streets a few times before the nuns had to lock him up. They apologised to Ángel. During his escapes he would walk out to the central plaza, the San Francisco church, and he'd give his clothes to beggars. It was shocking to imagine his father naked on the side of the road. Lucho had never even seen his body. The last time he saw him, the nuns told Lucho that Ángel had been looking for his wife in closets and under his bed, saying that she truly loved him and she'd be worried if she couldn't find him. He was forgetting how to swallow, and would choke sometimes between words. He'd say he was blind at times. Have you seen Olga? My *Olguita*? That was it. Lucho shook his head and his father stared at the ceiling above the bed and said: 'Tell me if you see her, Sir, you see she'll be worried, she loves me so much she'll be worried sick.' Even at the end, drowning in his own spit, he was powerful.

Pedro comes back into the room with a lit candle.

'We cut off the lights here. You understand. Will you behave?'

'Do you have any idea who I am?'

'Yes, I have some ideas, but I thought you'd tell me.'

'You don't know what you're doing. You'll regret this.'

'I don't think I have any regrets anymore.'

Pedro leaves the candle on the floor in the middle of the room and then slides a chair in front of Lucho.

'So?' Pedro says.

'So what?'

'Who are you? Why use my name? Are they looking for me?'

'Because you started this group. I'm in the army.'

'The workshops?'

'Yes.'

'And?'

'And some people were nervous about what you got up to.'

'You thought I was making bombs? Killing people? That's what you fascists do. What other things do they accuse me of?'

'Writing.'

'I have not written a word since I left Chile. My fingers were broken. Later on it was the rage. I couldn't think straight.'

'So why come back?'

'The vote, my friend, I simply wanted to be here when that asshole goes to trial.'

'It won't happen.'

'We'll see.'

Lucho stands, looking for his notebook by the blackboard. He finds only a page torn in half. He can't read it in the candlelight. He puts it in his pocket.

'We missed one, I suppose,' Pedro says.

'You, on the other hand, you're going to pay for this.'

'Sit down.'

Lucho sits, paper scrunching against his thigh.

Pedro raises his hand, extends it just over the light. He beats Lucho. First on the cheek. Then his nose. Lucho's body relaxes between punches, and he watches the dim lamp on the teacher's desk, a halo of violet and green, shrinking and expanding to his breathing. He sees blood on his lap and looks up at the light once more. Pedro raises his hand again and waits for Lucho to receive it.

POETRY NOTES – BOOK OF RAMONA
Ramona Falls Asleep: Travelling the Great Sea

I watch you depart
in slow breaths
Belly up,   up   down and up
a dress of crumpled flowers
And the ebbing of the heart
absent and lovely
dreaming into the
night.

I never knew a sky so black.

Lucho can't walk straight and he hangs onto a streetlamp. He can barely see through one eye. He breathes in deep. He doesn't know where he is. An empty street. Some old colonial houses painted in bright colours. He looks behind him but no one is following him. He can hear people shouting at a distance, the familiar noise of a protest. He starts to limp towards the noise. He wants to get lost in the crowd.

At the march there are placards with so many abbreviations that he can't decipher any of them quickly enough before another appears – all the anger and chanting fronted by wavering letters, like the alphabet has had enough. For a moment, he loses his sense of direction and joins in the flow of people. He hides his right hand in the breast pocket of his blazer, careful not to bump into anyone, though he doesn't feel any pain unless he looks at it.

'This will end, This must end,' goes a megaphone. 'A new Chile. Democracy.'

Cheering.

'The choice rests with the people.'

Cheering.

'We the people will be in charge.'

Claps.

'Where is the youth?'

'Present.'

'Where are the students?'

'Present.'

'Where are the workers?'

'Present.'

The man next to Lucho hugs him with a cheer. 'We are present,' he shouts. A John Lennon type; beard and glasses, bed hair. 'If you don't jump you're a fascist!'

Everyone jumps and Lucho gets knocked aside by the man's shoulder, who turns to him and notices his bruised face. 'Who did this to you, brother? This is what we're fighting for. Be strong.' People around Lucho pat him on the shoulder, heads lowered, as if sympathising for someone he'd lost.

One of the protesters takes a picture of him.

'What happened to you, my friend? What did you do?'

'No, brother, they did this to *him*!'

People scream in happiness when a man is lifted onto a podium. 'Juan, Juan, Juan, Juan!' The chanting becomes quieter. The man declares that this is now a concert. He says he wants to record the crowds. He raises his fist and people shout and clap harder. He points at groups of people and they start jumping and blowing on whistles. Lucho holds on to the page in his pocket. Then: the crowd starts to divide. Panic. Water cannons, calls to stay put that no one listens to, the smell of burnt rubber and a trail of black smoke from flaming barricades. Lucho takes the first side street, old people peering through barely opened doors, shutting them as he runs past.

In the metro, people make space for him, staring at him in horror. He sits on the floor at the end of the carriage to avoid looking at his own reflection. The remains of the page:

> NOTE #68
> Something abo
> because without
> would mean much or
> Ramona and myself sailin
> Happiness is where you get los
> Inevitably from so much hope an

The house is empty. Not even Mariela is home. He can't blame her, really. His hand is hot with pain. He looks at his eye in the bathroom mirror. He pulls his index finger back into place; the joints darken purple. Pedro had tried to break it, just like his own hand was broken years ago. But he let go of Lucho's hand too soon. Lucho had grabbed Pedro's neck, made him kneel. He can't remember exactly how it happened. It's hard to tell whose blood is on his shirt. They let Lucho go. They were afraid he'd kill Pedro. Lucho never told them who he really was.

He goes to his office and sits in front of his open notebook. A poem about the 400 Year War, the torture of Galvarino, the conquest of the South. Only a note written, no verses:

> Remember the River which splits evil from good,
> Nature shaping that essential, infinite struggle.

He closes the notebook and leaves on his desk the torn page from his unfinished collection. He looks at his mother's painting and wishes he could cry. None of the people in it have any distinct features. They're all the same. They're all in the same pain. Black limp flowers growing from the top of their heads, their eyes fixed above them, a revelation far more terrible than their bloody knees, his mother's way of saying that their sacrifice, their journey, had been all for nothing.

He takes his notebook and heads downstairs, leaning on the banister. He stops halfway, hearing a voice, the same voice he hears at night. His father, mumbling shame and failure, abandonment and cowardice and the voice gets louder as Lucho descends. He will meet his father again. Someday. He opens the front door and the words become rhythmic. Not his father but a song coming from the basement.

Lucho beats the door with the side of his hand and the music stops.

'Pablo?'

The door unlocks. There's a man he's never seen before, overalls covered in paint. The man runs past him. Lucho drops his notebook.

The basement is unrecognisable. There's a radio on a stool by a standing easel. On a canvas there is the outline of the man from *The Scream* in chalk, except its face is The General's. There are brightly coloured birds on the walls, wood-skinned people in ponchos with guitars and pan flutes, streams of colour flowing out of the instruments. Pablo's new guitar is in a corner. Behind it lies the notebook he'd given Pablo to write in. On the first page it says: *Notes on Songs about Everything*, and under that, in darker, newer print, *Notes on Songs for Clara*.

'Señor!'

Lucho pockets Pablo's notebook and turns. Mariela is there, gasping for air, rubbing her cheeks with a kitchen towel.

'Señor, I've been looking… What happened here?'

'You're going to tell me you didn't know?' He pushes the easel to the floor.

'To your face, Don Luis. What happened to your face?'

'I have a bunch of communists in my house!'

'No, Don Luis. No. That's why I was looking for you.'

'Pablo is out of here tomorrow.'

She catches her face with two open hands.

'Pablito, Señor, something terrible has happened.'

'What did you say?'

'He's gone, Señor. He's not coming home.'

The guitar has shrunk. Somehow, it seems impossible that any sound could ever come out of it, maybe the past, from its little sealed cave, standing there humming silence, his father, his son, a song of absence.

17

RAMONA

reaches the street with the warehouses where they filmed that first advert. She's sweating. She'd tried the gym first but Pato wasn't there – a new, younger man was teaching instead – 'until Don Pato completes his important side projects,' he said. 'What side projects?' 'Listen, lady, it's what he told me to say. Are you, you know, one of his girls? No offence but you don't look it, but he told me...' She left before he could finish. One of his girls! One. And lady!

She sat on a bench and waited for the metro. She let some of them pass by, too full, eight or nine of them. When she walked down the stairs from the gym, she'd realised she didn't even know what to say to Pato in the first place. It'd suddenly felt wrong to be mixed up with Alicia's pregnancy – surely that hadn't been *her* fault! – but she needs to ask him about the telenovela and her role in it. It doesn't matter if he doesn't even answer. What was she to Pato, anyway? Just a quick fling? How did he see her, if not as someone willing to break marriages, to make others fail, to forget her own failures? Did he, perhaps, even feel good about it, charitable even, in that he'd allowed her to dream of success again? Hadn't it been freeing, after all? Should she feel thankful instead?

*

```
LO QUE TUS OJOS NO VEN: A TELENOVELA

              #EPISODE 6

INT. ISABEL URRUTIA'S ROOM - DAY

The scene opens to ISABEL URRUTIA on her bed,
under the sheets. She's facing the ceiling,
perfectly still. There's a knock on the door.
ISABEL URRUTIA doesn't respond or move. MAID#1
enters.

MAID#1 draws the curtains open to let the
bright day in, casting angular shadows in the
room. She also opens the window to the sounds
of a crowd gathering outside.

                ISABEL URRUTIA
            What's all that noise
            outside?
```

UNIT 4: GETTING AT DIFFICULT EMOTIONS/ PORTRAYING THE PAIN OF LIVING – ANGER:

1. The separation between the *real self* and *stage self* is blurred the more you know about a character. A well-realised miserable character will soon cast their shadow beyond the stage. The whole company will be/should be affected. They may express anger, frustration or pity toward you. Resist the ever-so-strong urge to fit in or please. These are all indications that you're doing your job well, projecting your character, an idea, into manifest truth. Your character

may feel cast out, they may wish to cry. You should always cry with them.
2. Don't use anger as a prime motivation to action. That is too superficial. You may get away with being loud. An untrained audience may even comment on the power of your performance (they will only mean its volume, anger being so easily confused with noise by those without any real understanding of their own emotions). Look instead to Vulnerable Emotions from our previous Unit: rejection, humiliation, fear, loneliness. These are the ones that will have the greatest impact on your audience. Beyond the creation of negative energy specific to a character, there is always confirmation of universal human frailty. An audience connected to a character through these timeless emotions will also connect to themselves. Memorable characters transcend physical trickery. They are the memories of the world unfolding in the present.
3. Everyone has to be in on the lie. Draw from what you know, your emotional memory.
4. Do not romanticise trauma. Suffering will find you. Look for joy.

She looks at the tin shutters of the warehouse, light seeping through the gaps on the floor. Why is she here? She lifts the shutters, no words as yet formed in her mind, feels silly, the strength needed to say nothing in particular, sillier still. But all she finds is a switched-on TV set, a camera pointing at the fake kitchen counter on wheels. There's also a radio playing some cheap ballad, maybe Zañartu's new song for the next telenovela, something about ghosts and magic, about falling in love with the dead. The song's playing from outside the set, coming from the corridor which leads into the changing room. She stands in front of the lights, relieved that there's no one

> **MAID#1**
>
> Miss, you didn't know? Luz María, she can see again. I saw Don Luis Felipe congratulating her at the chapel last week. She looked very happy. Very happy. Maybe it'll give you hope. For your condition, I mean. The whole town is out there. Some think she's a living saint, hoping she'll cure some of their own ailments. Maybe she could come here and bless you or—
>
> **ISABEL URRUTIA** (crying in anger)
>
> That nobody. She always envied me. God has punished

here. Everything looks worse than she remembered. The floor is covered in plastic film, like a murder scene, the microphone grills are a rusty green, the director's chair has a hole right in the centre of the seat; the whole place smells of damp and sweat. For the first time in a long time she misses her own house. She misses her Lucho and her Pablo, although when she thinks of them they're never with her – they are writing in a locked room, something important and new and beautiful, still the young man carrying bundles of notebooks and making plans, wanting, wanting; or Pablo, at school looking out the window, the empty time before he gets to make music. Even when she thinks of them, she's alone.

She walks slowly toward the song. The cleaning closet/changing room is shut but she can hear the rattle of loose shelves and creaking floorboards. She gently pulls on the doorknob and two naked figures turn to her, covering themselves with the clothes they pick up from the floor. No one speaks. The young woman sweeps her hair back, looks to Pato as if waiting for an explanation. Her face is perfectly symmetrical, large green eyes, pale skin, and Ramona is so struck by her she has to look away, at her own feet, in order to think.

'Is this your wife?' the woman asks him.

'The producer will call you,' he says. 'I think you better go.'

'I love you,' she says, with a childish inflection.

'Yes,' he says.

'Excuse me, Señora,' the woman says, clothes in her hands, and Ramona moves to let her pass. Pato stays in the middle of the closet, surrounded by bleach, a mop in a bucket, toilet paper and rat poison; he covers his genitals with a sock. They hear the metal shutters rise and fall shut.

'I think we should talk,' Ramona says. It comes off solemn and serious, maybe even angry, but all she is actually trying to do is buy time to figure out what to say. Pato sits on a bucket right then and there, without getting dressed. He nods to himself, covers his face with his hands, elbows on the knees. Then he reaches out to turn the radio off.

'Look, we've been having a few issues in our marriage. I'm sorry, okay? I—'

'You think your marriage concerns me?'

She's thankful for him starting; he's given her this at least.

'What then?'

'Nothing.'

'You won't tell Alicia, will you? She's not here, right?'

'No, she's not.'

'Why are you here?'

> me twice, then, if I'm now
> also condemned to hear
> about her happiness. She
> always wanted to steal Luis
> Felipe from me. Did you know
> that? It must be obvious to
> everyone. But somehow not
> to Luis Felipe. A living
> saint! A common whore!

MAID#1 faces the Jesus portrait on the wall nearest to the foot of the bed and crosses herself. We see ISABEL URRUTIA's face up close, showing what could be rage or pain.

INT. LUZ MARIA'S HOUSE - DAY

LUZ MARIA and LUIS FELIPE are sitting side by side on her bed. The room is plain, clearly depicting years of poverty - made mostly of

'The audition. The telenovela.'
'Look, I really did try.'
'You tried.'
'They needed someone younger. A new girl got the part, alright? She's filmed the pilot already.'
'Not one role for me then?'
'It wasn't just that. Not just the age. It's also... Yes. Other things they care about, you know? You know how TV is these days, it's all spectacle. But my other business is growing. The gym. There's always the gym. Tell you what, if you want, you can keep—'
'Tell me to act a part, anything.'

'What?'

'Tell me how to act.'

At the madhouse, Ramona had felt it was her duty to make Catalina feel better after her husband left her for – as La Cata had put it herself – a 'more whole' woman. Ramona would go to her room (Catalina was always in bed those days), and sit beside her. Small talk didn't work. Open-ended questions even less: What are you thinking about? Fuck all. The whole thing made Ramona, she was ashamed to admit, happy to have something to do. She slept better. She would wake up thinking not about her mother, gone, and her acting career, never even arrived, but instead about ways to fix Catalina before she left. Manual work therapy failed: the birdboxes would lie empty, just like the jewellery boxes. Praying was no good because Catalina did not believe in God – she'd once said she despised Him. The thought of doing exercise bound her to her bed like nothing else. Ramona even asked a nurse for a little make-up, some foundation, but Catalina asked her if she was kidding, that she only ever wore make-up to go out or to go to work, back when she had a job and people to go out with, and even then, that she only really wore it for her husband. When Ramona said it might make her feel good, just for herself, Catalina said, 'Do I look like I want to be my own audience?' And that's when Ramona remembered a theatre exercise where they would have to pretend the world was different, that it lacked some things, that its rules had changed – today is No Happiness day, the teacher once said. Today it's No Parents. Tomorrow, You Are Brave. Tonight it's No Life To Want To Go Back To. Ramona told all this to Catalina. We have no children or men. We have no one to bother with or think about us, no weight outside our own. We have nothing outside of this room. You don't have me, nor I you. Imagine, just imagine none of it exists. Catalina didn't say anything but she got up early the next day. She didn't look at

> damaged wood, like an old cabin. There's only
> a night table by the bed but even this is
> empty.
>
>   LUIS FELIPE
>   It's incredible. I still
>   can't believe it. That
>   necklace looks good on you.
>   My mother would be glad
>   for it to be worn by such
>   beauty.
>
> LUZ MARIA smiles at LUIS FELIPE in silence and
> looks at the shiny stone at the end of the
> necklace.
>
>   LUIS FELIPE
>   What did you think I would
>   look like?

Ramona, focusing instead on the bedroom door. She did, however, say: 'So there are no men today, right?' And she never stepped out of character again. Even the nurses were in on the lie.

'I don't know what to say,' Pato says.
    'Do you know how actors act out pain?'
    'No.'
    'You look for universal human frailty. I used to think so, at least.'
    'I don't know.'
    'Now I think it's much simpler. You merely remind people of who they really are. You stop blaming yourself for it.'

'I need to go.'

'You don't like my acting. That's what's happened.'

'It's not my fault.'

'No, it's not your fault. I'm a failure. You reminded me of that.'

'I don't think... I mean—'

'Your wife asked me to speak to you.'

He stands, fully naked in front of her, lines imprinted on his chest from where the loose skin folded when he was sitting, a costume of himself.

'She knows?'

'Yes.'

'You told her. What does she know?'

'She doesn't want to see you again.'

She shuts the door on him, hears him sit back down. On her way out the brightness of the set lights dazzle her. And then – a shapeless city in the distance, faded amber towers, an invisible street blending into black sky, no weight outside her own, tonight We Have Nothing Outside This Set – it's all just an audition.

At home, Mariela is dusting dining chairs and sofas with a pink feather brush, which is what she does when she doesn't want to talk to anyone. When she sees Ramona she stops brushing and points at the ceiling, mouthing *still up there* without making a sound.

Ramona will not tiptoe around her own house. She makes a point of asking what Mariela means, out loud, despite understanding perfectly well.

'Where is she?'

'Upstairs,' Mariela says, relaxing her shoulders.

She goes up, knocks, lets herself in without waiting for an answer. Alicia is tucked into Ramona's bed, under the sheets, and she pulls herself to sit upright.

> LUZ MARIA
>
> Your fiancée, the way the
> Lady talked about you – it
> was obvious to me you'd
> look the way you do.
>
> LUIS FELIPE
>
> My fiancée, yes.
>
> We focus on LUIS FELIPE's expression of sorrow
> and regret.
>
> LUZ MARIA
>
> Is she okay? Are you okay?
> I heard she...
>
> LUIS FELIPE
>
> She was already different
> to the woman I fell in love

'I got cold,' she says. 'It's the stress. It's been hard for me.'

The double curtains are closed and the shine of the bedside lamp is a flash of light on Ramona's glasses. She can barely see Alicia at first and then, sun setting, there emerges the shape of her body under the covers, as pretty as she knew she'd be, as young too – the discrete topography of youth! – tight cheeks, a collarbone sharp and exposed, rain would flow there, to her open palms, a ringed finger, varnished nails, on her face the look of someone who writes their own dreams down, who looks for their meaning later in the day, the satisfaction of waking with a gifted purpose, the entire world a message.

'Did you talk to him then?' Alicia asks.

Throughout Ramona's life, her mother had convinced her she was selfish, incapable of empathy, that she was destined to be alone. 'Sooner or later, people close to you will see it too and they'll leave you.' Her mother compared Ramona to the children of their next-door neighbours, all of whom had become teachers at the *Liceo Agrícola*. And they even volunteered at the fire brigade. She'd say: 'Just like a shallow river, a shallow life has very little to feed on.' Ramona would say that she was more ambitious than that. And then her mother would answer: 'Ambition, another shallow river.' Or something like that. When she chose to study theatre, however, that's when Ramona felt the guiltiest. 'I don't understand how someone sacrifices themselves only for their own happiness,' her mother said. 'When you die you'll only see yourself, the Devil holding the mirror.' And when Ramona prepped for a role she hoped her characters would say something about her, give her a voice. The good actor has a voice to share. The good actor holds a mirror too. She'd wanted to be known and to be looked at and to be asked, 'Ramona, what would you say about the state of the world?' 'Ramona, how has your past influenced your acting?' 'Ramona, is your family with you tonight?' The audience would clap her answers as Don Francisco sat silently, a tear in his eye, tissue lifted from his breast pocket, amazed by a picture of her and Lucho, Pablo as a young boy between them, lowered on a large screen in the middle of the set, the sepia colour showing the passing of time and the need to explain it. You've come so far! Isn't it fantastic? Life is a surprise, is it not? A wrapped-up gift. What would you say to our viewers at home? A close-up of her defined chin, glittery under-eyes, an audience holding their breath as she turns her chest to face the camera. You are all guilty. Even though you smile and clap now, the people you love will know it sooner or later. We are only here tonight because you know me and I know you as well. The truth of the matter is that—

>   with. She's become so selfish.
>   So hateful. Cruel, as you
>   know. I'm sorry for the way
>   she's treated you. I don't
>   know that I can continue...
>
> LUIS FELIPE holds LUZ MARIA's hands. They look
> right into each other's eyes, sitting up on
> the bed.
>
>   LUIS FELIPE
>
>   Truth is... Even before you
>   regained your sight, I thought
>   you were the most beautiful
>   woman I'd ever seen.
>
>   LUZ MARIA
>
>   The things you say, Don Luis
>   Felipe. You are engaged!

'I'm fucking your husband,' she says.

Don Francisco will stand, dry the sweat off his brow and the brass section will hold a single note on the trumpet for comedic effect. The crowd will clap, but she can barely see them behind the glare of the spotlights aimed at her face and—

Alicia stands away from the light and in the darkness of the room Ramona can see her clearly once again.

'What did you say?'

'He fucked me and I fucked him back. Do you understand what I'm telling you? Do you, stupid girl? He took me when you were there, you were right next to us.'

'Be quiet.'

'He wanted me again and again. He offered me a job so he could keep fucking me.'

'I don't believe you.'

Ramona walks up to Alicia – who is trembling – and facing away from Ramona, hands on her belly. Ramona taps her on the shoulder. No reaction. She pushes Alicia into the curtains. Alicia cries harder.

'I need to go,' Alicia says between sobs.

'I just told you your husband wanted a whore. He's even got a new one now.'

'I don't want any trouble. I better go.'

Ramona hugs her. Alicia pushes her backwards onto the bed.

'You're fucking crazy.'

'What?'

'You're an ugly, old nothing. Nobody. Nothing.'

'I'm—'

'Don't bother me – us – anymore.'

Alicia walks slowly out of the room. The first step down creaks and—

'He wanted a whore!' Ramona shouts, and then hears the front door opening and closing, Mariela dusting something downstairs. Then, absolutely nothing. Or something like peace.

Ramona is in a crowd of people waiting for the bus up to Providencia. A man in front of her waves his arm to stop the *micro* bus and everyone shuffles into a tight queue, pressing Ramona into the little crater in the middle. She's the last one to step into the bus. The driver in black sunglasses checks behind him, confirming the packed space and then shuts the door on her.

She decides to walk to the gym instead, to avoid the open avenues, and to zigzag her way through residential roads, always so surprisingly empty of people, filled with trees like remnants of some forgotten civilisation.

> **LUIS FELIPE**
>
> But not yet married, Lucecita. Kiss me.
>
> **LUZ MARIA** (standing)
>
> No. It's just not right. I'm not that kind of woman!
>
> **LUIS FELIPE**
>
> I'm sorry. I didn't mean it like that. I'll end it and come back, Lucecita. I promise you I'll come back the right way.
>
> LUIS FELIPE leaves the room. LUZ MARIA looks at herself in a dirty mirror on the wall, focuses on the new necklace LUIS FELIPE gave her and smiles a smile of true joy.

But then, as she turns a corner – a protest. The front is a sea of placards: signs for the NO vote, placards bearing the faces of the disappeared, the buried (things Lucho didn't, couldn't do, but still, here they are), the flags creased by the lack of wind, the drums playing to no particular beat, just making noise, the rest mostly silent, more like a funeral procession. There's nowhere for Ramona to step aside and let them pass: the house gardens next to her are gated, with glass shards glued at the top of the stone walls, guard dogs pacing nervously inside. She lets go of her duffel bag and stands in the middle of the road, shuts her eyes and waits to be swept away by the tide.

But no one touches her. No one even comes close.

*

In Don Francisco's studio audience Ramona will spot her mother, who has been pre-warned that Ramona can't gesture to her from the interviewee chairs. If she did, the camera would pick up on her distraction. Ramona would be edited out. No one would see how good she looks in the red dress she wore in the final love scenes of the telenovela, the satin laces knotted behind her neck, the shimmering gloss matching her lipstick, fading to a light pink over the eyes. The producer backstage would have only taken one look at her and concluded her wardrobe must be themed after the seasons: 'You look like the spring,' he'd say, pinning a gardenia to her hair, 'so full of life.'

'And so I understand that you had to make a hard choice – for your family – to keep working at the cost of seeing less of your husband and son.' Don Franscisco turns to the crowd. 'She works so hard, you wouldn't believe it!'

'Yes, Don Francisco, family's everything. And may I also take this chance to thank you for having me once again on your programme. It seems to me that this is my second family now.'

'Absolutely. We're here for you. Always. Isn't that right?'

The audience cheers.

'But I must clarify something.'

'Oh, ladies and gentlemen, a personal revelation. Listen closely. You heard it here first, on *Giant Saturday*.'

'No, no, it's nothing like that. All I wanted to say was, you know, about all the lost time you just said I sacrificed, that it was because of that loss that I got to where I am today. That it was urgent. It was never a choice. I traded seeing my son growing up – and romantic dates with my husband...' Laughter erupts in the audience. 'For a better future for them. It needed to happen fast.'

Awwwwwww

```
SCREEN GOES BLACK.

O FORTUNA starts playing.

EXT. THE HOUSE - NIGHT

We see a cloaked figure walking slowly to THE
HOUSE under the moonlight. Now at a closer angle,
we get a portrait shot of the figure but her face
is still darkened by her cloak. The HOUSE doors
open by themselves as the figure approaches.

INT. THE HOUSE - NIGHT

Uncloaking, it's revealed to be YACONDA, the Witch
of the Pond. She enters ISABEL URRUTIA'S BEDROOM.

INT. ISABEL URRUTIA'S ROOM - NIGHT

The door shuts itself after YACONDA walks
inside.
```

'The road to what we think of as success is easily forgotten. Maybe that's why we—'

'Lady, how will you be paying? We're closing.'

Ramona looks up from her table, where there are four empty glasses. She puts two notes on the waiter's tray.

'Do you know anywhere else that's open?'

'It's Santiago, lady. You can drink your way to heaven any night you choose.'

'Thank you.'

Outside the glass wall of the bar, cars pass by revealing faces for just a second. Some drive by so quickly they leave traces of lights behind.

'Mother, I saw you that night. I'm sorry I didn't wave. They would have cut me out of the shot.'

'And I was never even in it.'

'To you, then,' she says, and downs the rest of her pisco sour.

YACONDA stands at the foot of the bed looking at ISABEL URRUTIA.

>ISABEL URRUTIA
>
> So the Devil has come to take me.

>YACONDA
>
> Not yet, my daughter.

>ISABEL URRUTIA
>
> Then give me my life back, Devil. I'll do anything.

>YACONDA
>
> What matters to you most?

>ISABEL URRUTIA
>
> The man I love. The man who wronged me.

18

PABLO

wakes up to the sound of the river to one side and the watery hum of traffic to the other. It takes him a few seconds to understand that he's no longer sleeping. For once he remembers something about the night before. He'd run out of the school, had kept on running in a straight line until he reached the river. Remembers being afraid, chased, touched. The shack. The Painter. And then he'd sat against a tree, waiting for the morning so he wouldn't be caught creeping into the house in the middle of the night. He'll say he stayed at Francisco's, studying for the goddamn Aptitude Test.

He gets up and starts the walk to Francisco's house. He doesn't know the time and is unsure if he'll be late or early to their last midday practice before the gig. Santiago is a different city in the daytime. It should have two names. The contrast makes him laugh. There are stray dogs queueing up to pee on benches. Carts selling superhero masks and balloons. People in suits carrying briefcases and crossing roads as if cars don't exist – and getting honked at. Students with open books on the grass, some making out instead of reading. There's a drum group hitting snares, marching across a bridge. Waiters sweeping restaurant terraces, hosing pigeons away from bin bags left out in the sun. If there had really been someone in that shack (when he looked back all its wooden beams had fallen over flat), if someone had touched him or tried to grab him, then it didn't happen there, it couldn't have. What remained was nothing more than the unsettling sensation of one Santiago seeping into another.

When he gets to Francisco's house, Francisco and Clara are packing instruments and amps into the back of a white van. Juan from The Detainees is smoking in the driver's seat. He waves at Pablo.

'Hey,' Pablo says. 'Am I late or early?'

'What do you think?' Francisco says. He avoids eye contact. He shoves Pablo to one side with his shoulder. He lifts a hi-hat stand into the van.

'He's really pissed at you for missing practice,' Clara whispers to him. 'Here, take your own stuff at least.' She gives him a bass guitar that isn't his. 'The bass amp is still in the house. No one can lift that thing.'

'Of course I'm pissed!' Francsico says from the van, a cymbal crashing. 'Why is it so hard for some people to commit to higher ideals? Right, Juan?' Juan nods and breathes out a cloud of smoke. Francisco jumps out of the van, looks at Pablo. 'It's not just about you, you know? The whole world doesn't run on your time.'

Pablo heads into the house. Francisco's room looks empty without all the instruments; drab, like an after-hours office. Clara walks in on him staring at a picture of toddler Francisco holding a fish with an old guy. *Vichuquén Lake* is written in gold on the frame. Pablo's father had never taught him things like that, never acted like he was his buddy. To teach Pablo to play football, Lucho would kick the ball up as high as he could and hold Pablo's hands behind his back, before telling him to look at the ball even as it hit his head, his face sometimes. 'How're you going to learn if you're afraid of the ball? No one can do that for you. You need to learn that everyone's on their own in life. No one succeeds by waiting for someone else.' Something like that. And so Pablo had stopped playing altogether.

'We're waiting for you,' Clara says.

'Okay.'

'Do you need help with the amp?'

'No.'

'Hey, listen,' she grabs his arm. 'Are you angry at me?'

'No.'

'You look angry. Why don't you look at me?'

'I'm just tired.'

'So I'm breaking up with Francisco. After the gig.'

'Really?'

'Yes.'

'You two seem good together.'

'I just thought you should know. In case.'

'What?'

'If you've not got over it.'

'So what happened with him then?'

'I don't know. It was good while it lasted, you know? I just can't stand him anymore.'

'And the band?'

'We can start our own.'

'But we're still playing tonight.'

'Yes, but after that, you know? An original first date. After the gig, wait for me outside and we'll leave together.'

'Okay.'

'Keep it between us for now. I'm still his girlfriend until we play.'
'Help me with this.'

They come out the front door carrying the amp between them, smiling at each other.

'God, I thought you'd never come out,' Francisco says.

'Calm down, man. We're set,' Clara answers.

'Juan's given me a bunch of posters that need spreading. You take them.' He gives the posters to Pablo. 'Since you didn't come to practice, you could at least make yourself useful with these.'

'I'll go with him,' Clara says.

'Yeah, may be a good idea, given how goddamn slow he is today. Soundcheck is at seven. For the love of God don't forget it. Tattoo it on your forehead if you have to. Seven. You know where we'll be?'

She points at the poster. It has Juan's face on it, in the centre, the other two Detainees behind him in increasing transparency so that the drummer appears as a ghost in the background. Their own band name isn't on it, instead saying *and guests*. The address says *Libertad Street, towards Yungay (follow the noise, it's a fucking old white house)*.

They get the metro to Baquedano. They don't talk to one another but Pablo and Clara share a pole, Clara hugging it so that their bodies almost touch, her head near his shoulder, other passengers looking at them, meeting Pablo's eyes with a smile, wishing, no doubt, that they could have what he and Clara have now. They look at each other in the black glass whenever the doors close. When they open, Clara lifts her face slowly as if to take a breath. He wants to ask her what has changed, which is really just another way of asking why he is now better than Francisco.

'Hey, can I ask you something?' he says, and Clara continues to hug the pole, letting herself sway closer to him.

'Anything,' she says with a smile.

But he decides not to speak, not to bring Francisco underground with them. The worst that can happen now, he thinks, is that she starts to think about the numerous times she and Francisco have taken the metro together, shared the same pose as they are in right now. Something new was going to come of this. A new band – a good one, one for the stadiums. He pictures the waves of people calming down for a love song. An arpeggiated crowd pleaser with the recognisable—

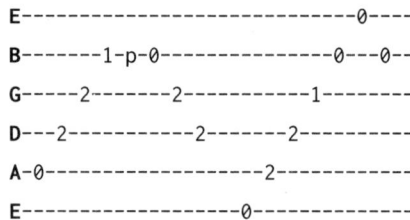

and everyone would sing the lyrics. And he, Pablo, would add note variations on the last chorus, so high and difficult he'd hear the tail end of his own voice in all that reverb and they'd all clap at just how unpredictable his shows can be – You had to be there, man! – and then, once the cheering ended—

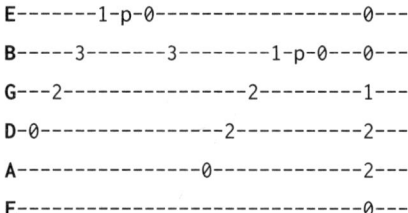

he'd say something about love, pausing between each word to make it sound like off-the-cuff wisdom, something given to him by the magic of that moment, Love... Is... Letting... Others... Forget... Themselves. Fireworks from the back of the stadium, a flare smoking red amidst a teary crowd. The metro doors open to Baquedano.

'Tell me later, we need to go,' she says, leaving a poster on an empty seat before stepping outside.

They stick posters on both sides of the bridge to the San Cristóbal Hill. They hold hands as they walk over the water. He's surprised at how long her fingers are, how well they fit his hand, how she tightens her grip whenever they need to move to let someone pass. And he loves her large shirt, her father's, she said, the loose ends on her waist fluttering in the breeze, as light as she walks, just as he feels right now.

The next set of posters go on the pillars outside the Law School and then they turn back to head to the Lastarria neighbourhood, and then the Bellas Artes. There, they find themselves facing the start of a march, and the placards for the NO vote, the faces of the disappeared, people, old people wearing black fabric over their own mouths, police sirens in the background.

'Here,' she says, passing him a stack of posters. 'Give them out here.'

He hands some out. People take them without looking. It annoys him. The march is mostly silent. You can hear actual steps. Some people throw their poster away almost as soon as they look at it. A man lifts his aviator sunglasses to his forehead so that Pablo can see just how disapproving he is. 'This is serious,' he says. 'Go home or at least be respectful.' Pablo apologises, looks around for Clara in the crowd. A circle of people are gathered around her. They all take a poster, one even attaching it to a wooden stick to make a placard. Pablo calls to Clara but she doesn't hear him. The march stops to the growing noise of casserole pans clattering. Turning the corner in the street ahead – placards for the YES vote.

'Pablo!'

He turns to Clara, who is on the pavement just outside the flow of the crowd. He runs to her. There are others running too. Parents carry their children in their arms.

'We need to get the hell out. This is going to get ugly.' He'd heard from his father about these kinds of protests before The General took over. 'A country hurting itself,' his father had said, 'a cancer cured by order, by structure.' But Pablo had never understood any of that. All he sees now are people pushing each other to reach the front of the line, marching shoulder to shoulder, flares ignited to a cheering mass, drums marking the beat of a chant he can't make out. One crowd trying to shout louder than the other.

The NO crowd push forward. Clara and Pablo can't move. A long placard held by those in the front with the words 'PPD, Take Part in Democracy, VOTE NO' falls and rises again. The YES crowd is larger, holding signs with pictures of The General, some wearing military helmets despite their everyday clothes. The metallic noise of the casserole dishes being bashed starts a ringing in his ear.

'Let us out!'

Clara pushes at the people behind her but they don't even notice her.

Pablo looks at the YES crowd. Some of the men with helmets have batons and they beat down any of the NO signs they can reach. Both sides push against the other. Whistles are blown. More flares are lit and thrown and people cover their eyes. Someone throws a stone, and then there is shouting, running, the smell of burning rubber, louder police sirens, placards broken on the floor, and Pablo won't let Clara go despite the current, the water cannon appearing from the back, a shot fired, actual bullets, people falling, trampled over, a breeze filled with smoke, the moon appearing white in the clear sky, their posters scattered on the road, and then Pablo sees her. It's La Dani, he's sure of it, holding up a sign with a photograph of a crowd queueing for food. She's surrounded by people he doesn't recognise. He moves with the crowd towards her until she sees him, Clara holding him from behind, La Dani lowering her sign and getting knocked by people pushing, and a man shouts behind her, something about The General and she joins in, looks at him and shouts too, getting nearer until Clara pulls him away.

'Are you okay?' she says, catching her breath, inspecting his face, holding him with open hands on his cheeks.

'Yes, are you?'

'I can still play, yes.'

Finally free of the crowd, they walk towards Libertad, continuing to look behind them even though the side streets they take are empty and safe. The sky dims to evening blue, a muted city, calmer tides in his ear, the ringing almost gone, almost too quiet against her breathing, and Clara stops him, kisses him in front of a boarded-up corner kiosk. It's covered in YES and NO graffiti in bright pink. He keeps his eyes open, takes in her eyelashes, the skin ripples on the sides of her eyes, like a painful sleep.

They find the right house easily; there is a group drinking and smoking outside. Clara tells a man by the door that she's in one of the bands. He laughs but since she doesn't, he points inside and tells them to go upstairs to what he calls 'the backstage'. This turns out to be an empty bedroom. There's a sofa where The Detainees are sat with beer cans lined up on a Persian rug in front of them. Francisco's smoking while sitting on a small practice amp and Clara sits on the floor, leaning her head against Francisco's belly, avoiding Pablo's gaze.

He can hear the crowd gathering downstairs, bottles clinking, erupting laughter. The Detainees whisper to each other, hands on their mouths, looking in Pablo's direction, like they're talking shit about him. He looks the other way, at a poster of a man with his fist raised under the slogan: *The Art of Liberation*.

'So, we're playing the set twice, right?' Clara asks.

Francisco mimics The Detainees, a hand over his mouth.

'We have no choice,' he whispers. 'And then you two can leave the stage and I'll play my Song of People, you know?'

'We should play the second half faster and louder. They probably won't be able to tell. Our songs don't have hooks anyway. And no one knows us,' Clara says.

'Harsh,' says Francisco.

'Sound test went well, though,' Pablo says.

He stands to look out of the window. People, forming a queue. Everyone looks older than him, beards and long hair, boots instead of trainers, smoking and talking in their circles, the way old people do, forced laughs behind beer cans, a quick look around to see if someone else has heard the joke. They look so pleased just to be out. The problem with this country is it refuses to grow up, his father liked to say. Pablo hadn't thought about it till now, looking at the crowd below, just how much he doesn't want to get older. He doesn't want to go to someone else's shows, to be buried under new beats while saying *I missed this!* once the lights went off at the first note, and *This is who I really am, the old noise that started it, the one who truly, truly gets it, myself alone.*

A man none of them have ever seen before comes into the room and shuts the door behind him.

'Is the first band ready?' he asks.

'Ready,' Francisco says.

'What are you guys called? You appear as *Other Guests* on the poster.'

Francisco looks back at Pablo and Clara. She nods with a shrug.

'We'll take it,' Francisco says. 'Thanks.'

'What?'

'That's our name now, I guess. The Other Guests.'

'Alright, whatever. So, we're starting in a bit. Five minutes. Come down now but stay behind the curtain. We'll announce you and then you guys need to start playing straight away. We don't want to finish too late but more than anything, I hate that silence. So fucking awkward. Anyway, it doesn't matter too much. Everyone's come to see The Detainees.'

'Our set isn't too long.'

'Good, good. Let's go then.'

As soon as they're out the door, he hears The Detainees laughing. And then loud music takes over, fast, distorted, foreign. People everywhere. On the stairs, smoking and leaning on the banister. And a man, doing lines of coke on the ticketing table where no one's checking for tickets. Francisco looks back at Clara and Pablo with wide eyes. There's even a dog making its way through the crowd, getting petted, fed who knows what. They enter a large room lit only by a bunch of fairy lights tied to the top of one of the walls. Some of the bulbs are dead. It's an empty living room, really, but the windows are boarded up shut, and there are old mattresses against the walls (an attempt to keep the sound inside). There are pisco bottles and beer cans stacked in one corner of the room. There is also, inexplicably, a heart-shaped piñata with a hole in it, battered flat and resting on top of the cans and bottles. The floor is sticky and the whole place smells of beer and cigarettes and piss and sweat. Pablo counts twenty people before giving up. There must be close to sixty, with more trying to come in. There's a curtain made from dirty bedsheets at the far end of the room. No one looks at Pablo and Francisco as they draw it over their heads, to get to their instruments. The so-called stage is tiny. Pablo's bass amp is right by Clara's kit, so she has to climb over it to sit at the drums because the mixing desk covers the whole other side, against the wall. Pablo grabs his bass guitar, hooks the wire over the strap, turns his amp on and stands behind Francisco, who's adjusting the mic height in front. He pulls it up higher than necessary, just like at practice, so that when he sings his face is turned right up to the ceiling, a way to avoid eye contact with the crowd as he sings, though he once said it helped his technique, whatever that means in the context of screaming. Francisco wires up his guitar and plays a few chords before turning himself up. Pablo plays the root notes to Francisco's guitar until they nod to each other in agreement. The man behind the desk does a thumbs up. People are still talking and laughing over the riffs coming from the speakers – much better riffs than theirs. Pablo and Francisco turn to face Clara. She smiles wide, shuts her eyes and

```
C|-----------|-----------|-x-x-x-x-x-|-x-x-x-x-x-|
H|-----------|-x-x-x-----|-o-o-o-o-o-|-o-o-o-o-o-|
S|-o---o---o-|--------o--|-----------|-----------|
B|--o-o-o-o--|-------o-o-|-o-o-o-o-o-|-o-o-o-o-o-|
```

the crowd claps and woooos and whistles and the curtain's drawn. A single spotlight is aimed at the stage, right at Pablo's eyes, a sea of darkened faces, the ends of cigarettes lit up by silhouettes piling up in front of the stage, lips revealed by little flames, smoke clouds shooting up, cutting the light to clear TV light shafts and

```
C|-----------|-----------|-x-x-x-x-x-|-x-x-x-x-x-|
H|-----------|-x-x-x-----|-o-o-o-o-o-|-o-o-o-o-o-|
S|-o---o---o-|--------o--|-----------|-----------|
B|--o-o-o-o--|-------o-o-|-o-o-o-o-o-|-o-o-o-o-o-|
```

Francisco's guitar feeds back. He doesn't stop it.

'We are The Other Guests from Santiago and this one's called 'Please Kill My Parents' and it's a fast one!'

Clara hits a snare flam.

ONE, TWO, THREE, FOUR!

```
C|----------|----------|----------|----------|
H|-x---x---x-|-x---x---x-|-x---x---x-|-x---x---x-|
S|-o---o---o-|-o---o---o-|-o---o---o-|-o---o---o-|
B|--o-o-o-o-o|--o-o-o-o-o|--o-o-o-o-o|--o-o-o-o-o|


G---------------------------------------------------
D---------------------------------------------------
A-0-0-0-0-0-0-0-0-0-0-0-0-6-6-6-6-6-6-6-1-1-1-1-1-p-3-
E---------------------------------------------------
```

Out with the old, Out with the old! AAAAAAH!

```
G---------------------------------------------------
D---------------------------------------------------
A-0-0-0-0-0-0-0-0-0-0-0-0-6-6-6-6-6-6-6-1-1-1-1-1-p-3-
E---------------------------------------------------
```

Wanna know what I want? Know what I want? AAAH!

```
[------------Repeat x4------------]
G---------------------------------------------------------
D-8-p-7--8-p-7--8-p-7-8-p-7--8-p-7------------------------
A------0------0-----------0------0-6-6-6-6-6-6-1-1-1-1--
E---------------------------------------------------0-
```

                                    KILL MY PARENTS!

There's a moment during each song where the verses settle, become predictable, and the run in to each release of a chorus, the fading in of all that noise, where he's more aware of the crowd moving, shouting, the indifference of others, the arching of his fingers along the smoothness of the fretboard, the sweat behind Francisco's neck and Clara's pulse, the world in slow motion, filmed in perfect close-ups, cut up like syllables of a word in the making, hap-pi-ness, perhaps, yearn-ing to stay, the ringing in his ear and the sudden disappointment of a return to all the common noises which remove it.

No one notices – or seems to care – when they start playing the same songs over again. Francisco looks back at Pablo and Clara with disbelieving eyes after they repeat the opener louder and faster.

'We've got one more song tonight,' Francisco says. 'But first—' He turns to Clara. 'A clap for Clara on the drums!' Claps follow. She lifts the drumsticks above her head like antlers. 'And Pablo on bass.' Fewer, quieter claps. Pablo holds his hands together, does a bow he instantly regrets. 'This one's a solo song, and it's called...' He pauses for dramatic effect. 'The Song of The People.' Pablo leans the bass against the amp and leaves the stage behind Clara. It's a slow, awkward walk into becoming part of the audience once again. In the future, when he leaves stadium stages, the crowd will scream for an encore. He will come out in the dark, and only people in the front will see that he's returned. The lights will suddenly turn on and he'll be in the middle of the stage, and he'll start a song whose opening lyrics he won't be able to sing. He'll give a quiet laugh instead, so that everyone knows how much the moment means to him. But here, now, all he gets is a few pats on the shoulder. Clara gets more, and she even gets a beer from an excited man who *woooos* at her as she reaches the side wall. She sips it, then gives it to Pablo.

'What did you think?' he says, but she doesn't hear him, her back to him, looking at the stage.

Francisco presses a button on a tape recorder and the sounds of the metro begin, mixed then with the river, the crowds of Santiago, single voices arguing over the punctuality of a bus, a game of chess, a man laughing after beating a friend, a distant military march to the beat of a drum circle in protest, roadworks, a woman shouting about a sandwich in which she didn't want any mayonnaise, an open chord ringing dissonant over the voice of an old poet, the craze of lonely seas, everything leaves us, everything leaves us, and that's why I have to go back, she says, to so many places in the future, with no task but to live, and then a crescendo of panpipes and guitar feedback, Clara watching completely still. The crowd starts a chant:

'The Detainees! We want The Detainees. Give us The Detainees!'

And a bottle almost hits Francisco. Clara runs to the stage, the metro and the river still going on loop. And then, behind the crowd, the pop of a gunshot. Pablo falls with his back to the wall but the crowd doesn't react – it could all still be the song – and they still want The Detainees, until the second shot is followed by screaming.

Pablo is looking for Clara but there are too many people running out of the house. Some get pinned to the ground and beaten with sticks. Other policemen use their bare fists. Pablo runs with the crowd, feeling followed, sirens going off. The door is blocked with people trying to get out. Some climb over others. Pablo gets kicked in the cheek as someone crawls above him. The police beat whoever they can on the back. Some people fall screaming and get trampled on. Pablo covers his head with his hands because others are doing the same, and then he is pushed against the man in front of him. He isn't even sure where the door is. It takes Pablo a second to realise he's already outside. There's a gunshot. Everyone sprints in all directions. Pablo runs to the same quiet side street he took before, with Clara. No one there, not even a light. He spots a pickup truck with a tarp cover in the back and climbs into it, lies flat on his back.

In the cold, listening for steps outside and waiting for the sirens to die out, he thinks about The General on TV, a microphone rising from lines of same-faced soldiers watching intently;

'As should we, the soldiers at home,' his father had said, while he put logs into the fire and prodded them to sparks. His mother had been cutting cheese slices with Mariela behind them for the *once* tea, making comments about its thickness, that it wasn't as good as it used to be, that it'd make them all fat. Then something about explosions on a railway line. His father agreeing, terrorists this and that, saying 'they could not be forgiven, those who raised them and then those who raised the ones who'd raised them could not be forgiven. Judged by history, better off dead. Better them than us, who only want to live in peace. They'll get caught – only a matter of time.' Pablo had agreed though he didn't care, just glad that he would be forgiven. His grandfather had been there too, sitting on the armchair his father usually sat on, complaining that The General had got too soft in power, that more could be done to cure the country of its cancer, that fewer words and more action were necessary, that people had forgotten to fear the alternative, the swamp which needed draining. 'They should blow up more bridges, more trains. They should remind us all exactly who and what they are.' His father had agreed, said he hadn't thought of it that way. And then his grandfather had turned to Pablo and asked what he thought. Pablo had faced his father, who appeared to glow red from the flames in the chimney. He had a look on his face, Pablo thought then, which signified anger but was more likely fear. His mother had stopped shifting plates, lost herself in the kitchen. 'I don't know much about that,' he had said, 'I don't really understand it.' 'What don't you understand?' Pablo had looked at his father again, wanted him to come near and talk for him. 'Why Dad calls himself History,' he had finally said. 'Or why I will be forgiven. Or what an alternative is. What it is that I have to remember.' 'What do you love most in life?' his grandfather had asked him. 'Mum and Dad,' Pablo said, hoping it was the right answer. 'There are bad people who would take everything from them, bad people who think even God is evil, that good is bad. Are you good, Pablo?' 'Yes.' 'In peaceful times, good people do nothing, Pablo. The only thing you need to know now is what and who you love. You need to protect what you love or else you don't love it, you understand? The rest are only words; words don't matter. Nothing, nothing at all matters more in life than love.'

Pablo had then gone to his room. In bed, he had counted the things he loved, his toys, especially the plastic soldiers, a cartoon sticker collection, his new football gloves and the silver crucifix necklace his mother had given him. He thought he would put them all in a box. Maybe even bury them behind the bamboo along the garden walls. He switched his light off and fell asleep listening to Tata Ángel speak, comforted that he had a lot to love, that it'd be difficult for a bad man to take it all, and even more so that good people didn't have to do anything, that silence was enough, that he would always be forgiven, that love was everything and he had a lot of it.

He stares at the tarp in front of him, the stars dotting through it. He tries to find the ocean in his ear. A new unbearable silence.

When he comes to he doesn't know where he is. He can hardly breathe, drops of condensation on his forehead. He pulls on the tarp as hard as he can, tearing a hole in it. He climbs out slowly, trying not to make any noise. His eyes take time to adjust. It's still dark and he walks over to a larger road to get his bearings. He heads to Baquedano, following the river. There, at one end of the bridge, he hears The People's Song, laughter, the old poets, the crowds in a tiny speaker. He walks toward the song and from the middle of the bridge he sees Clara and Francisco down by the river bank, each with a bottle in their hands. He runs across the bridge and down the steps and before he can say anything, Clara and Francisco kiss.

Pablo runs to Francisco. Clara shouts stop. Francisco smiles. He truly smiles as Pablo pushes him into the river, falling together, the horror of all that noise within him, The People's Song a dark wave, Santiago mere lights in the sky, his father and mother talking of love, I love you, holding each other, Pablo pretending to be asleep, carried to bed and enjoying the silence, forgiven, and the stadium crowds going wild...

19

LUCHO

is reading the first notes he made for his book on Fallen Heroes. It's written on the back of a report on the quantities of milk to be delivered to the San Fernando barracks, taking into account the nearly 45 million gallons of wasted milk in schools around the country the previous year. His superior had sent the report back to him, asking that any reference to waste be changed to a more fitting word. So on the back of the page, Lucho made a list:

- Misuse
- Disuse
- Misapplication
- Dissipation
- Desuetude
- Squandering
- Gratuitous
- **Surplus**

Below it, on that same afternoon, he'd made notes about Lautaro, who he'd been reading about because his father once said Lautaro's story was that of a sad rebel, of violence against progress, of the first communist. 'Though brave,' he said, 'his importance is in affirming the might of our Spanish ancestors and the inevitability of the triumph of our modern Republic over obsolete and inferior ways of living. He is best remembered dead,' he said.

- Lautaro taken as a child by the Spanish, the servant to Pedro de Valdivia.
- Escaped in 1551, became *toque* (military leader).
- In the Battle of Tucapel with 6000 warriors, his old master is captured. Caupolicán, another *toque*, personally kills Pedro de Valdivia. Did Lautaro feel pleasure or frustration, that he could not do it himself?
- Burning of Concepción. It was rebuilt and Lautaro destroyed it once again.
- Betrayed (?) by a *picuncho* while preparing the next attack.
- Killed in the Battle of Mataquito. His head cut off and displayed in the plaza in Santiago.

The first page of his notebooks, to which this inventory report is taped, starts:

> The rivers rebel
> and we call out ancient names to cross them,
> Lautaro the dead
> with flowers on his grave
> growing forgotten petals again
> And again
> the season comes
> when we must
> walk across that sea of colour
> whichever way, the river knows.

He tears off the page and bins it. He does the same with the rest of the notebook, reading and tearing, reading and tearing, not one page of prose – by the end not even attempting to hide his attempts at poetry, writing, on the last pages, the incomprehensible lines:

His	End
Sea	End
Salt	End
Eyes	End
Burn	End
Sweet	End

A knock on the door. He tears out this last failed page, the leather cover now thicker than the remaining blank pages.

'Díaz, I have some news,' Major Matta says.
'What is it?'
'You are to move back to San Fernando.'
'San Fernando?'
'I didn't get a reason, only the order.'
'I understand.'
'I heard about your son.' He stands on the threshold holding the door.
'Thank you.'
'Those assholes will corrupt anyone. A cancer. It's not your fault.'

There's a pleasant breeze in downtown Santiago. Waiters arrange tables outside before the lunch rush, office workers checking their watches, drying their sweat with handkerchiefs. Corner kiosks opening, hanging newspapers and magazines and buckets of flowers from wooden racks. Queues outside a bank, sunglasses displayed on carpets, smokers talking quietly in alleyways, pigeons huddled together above them, eavesdropping.

And the Entel Tower rising with its steely peak cutting through the smog. Sometimes, all the dirt in the sky will clear, just split open – and Santiago shows itself full, unveiled to mountains and glassy high-rises, browning apartments with their empty balconies. He is certain he can hear it all. He stops walking, stands on loose cobblestones and waits for the sky to close up again.

At the Jardín del Olimpo café, he sits at the bar. At this time, almost noon, there are fewer women. The lights are all on and the café, usually darkly lit by neon branches on the walls, casting smudged reflections of men on black glass countertops, is now a common shop, the same beige tiles and boxy layout as all the others in the metro station. There's a wire running from a plug outside, through the door slightly ajar and into a room behind the bar. He can hear someone hoovering. He sees two women getting ready, putting on make-up, choosing bikinis. One of them starts sweeping and waxing the floors around him. He's the only man there.

'What would you like?' a woman with a pad and pen asks.

'A black coffee.'

'It'll take longer than usual. We're not all ready yet. Is that okay?'

'That's fine.'

'It's too early for these kinds of places.'

'It's fine.'

He reaches for a folded newspaper on the bar stool next to his. The YES and NO on the front page. A picture of polling stations in the National Stadium, ready and empty, pigeons under the tables. He opens the paper and sees a picture of Pedro Castro, pen in hand, sitting behind a round coffee table. He looks older here, Lucho thinks, with a full white beard, thick glasses and tweed blazer, cigarette limping into a glass ashtray. And then there's the black beret, just like Neruda's.

The author, who acquired the most distinguished of literary recognitions with his seminal work, Space Verses *(which to this day continues to influence poets around the world), now finds himself in Paris, cradle of artists, to denounce the Human Rights abuses in our nation. 'It will come in a storm of new verses. We will not let them forget us,' asserted the poet (43), who at just 19 wrote his most famous poems, bravely defying the wishes of his family, ranked officers in the army. The poet, lately a fierce proponent of the NO campaign, was warmly welcomed this month to La Sorbonne where he will teach literature during his time in exile. His list of accomplished students includes...*

'Here it is,' the same woman says. She is now wearing almost nothing.

'Thank you.'

'Anything good in there?' She leans over his shoulder to look at the paper, the plastic tray tucked against her armpit.

'A man I knew,' he says. 'A writer.'

He folds the paper before she can read any of it.

'I used to like reading.'

'I did too.'

'My mind wanders and I forget the last ten pages I've read.'

'I know the feeling.'

The skin on her back is blotched, acne scars engraved under the neck.

'So what's your name, uncle?'

'Pedro,' he says.

'And how's your day going, Pedro?'

'Did you ever meet a man called Ángel? He used to come here a lot. Older than me. Army uniform.'

'I don't think so,' she says. 'Sorry.'

'He called himself Manuel Rodríguez sometimes too.'
'Like the statue? That's funny. But no, sorry.'
'If you were to meet him, what would he say?'
She laughs, holds her breath in thought.
'No matter who it is, Pedro – whether Ángel or Manuel Rodríguez from the statues – he would surely tell me what all men tell me. He'd say he loves his family.'

POETRY NOTES – BOOK OF RAMONA
Ramona Doesn't Want to Return: Travelling the Great Sea

> Better sail it and look afar,
> row to the mouths in the sky,
> the cloud witnesses:
> A great arc leaves the harbour trenchant
> only in disposition.
> The world is too large
> and we must pay,
> we must plunge,
> looking up, beyond
> a pink moon rocked to sleep in every gap
> between us.

From the gates Lucho looks up to their bedroom. The curtains are drawn. Outside the double windows, on the balcony he's never stepped onto, there's a glass bottle on a wooden stool. The unkempt grass now covers the stone pathway leading to the front door. Without much thought, he knocks before stepping inside the house. The glass dome above the staircase projects the shadows of fallen leaves on the tiles. The lights, made to look like bouquets of candles, glow and flicker along the stairs.

'Ramona!' he calls, but the silence persists. All the doors in the house are shut.

He checks the dining room and there's a single plate with crumbs on it. Then, the living room, where the TV has a blanket covering the screen.

He walks up the staircase slowly.

He arrives at the door to his office. There's a hole where the padlock used to be. Inside, his books are on the floor, his mother's painting face down on the carpet, torn along the centre.

He hears steps coming from the master bedroom. Then silence once again.

He pushes the door with one hand. No one. A deep breath, relaxes. He walks in. He stands by the foot of the bed, sees a glass of water on his table. A click behind him. He turns and sees a woman with her back against the wall.

'Ramona?' he says.

A glint of light on the surface of a gun held with two hands.

'Who are you?'

The woman is shaking, sobbing. And then she takes a deep breath, stands perfectly still.

'I wanted you to be her,' she says.

'We can talk. Who did you want?'

'She stole him,' she says. 'I loved him. I truly did.' And then she pulls the trigger.

His mother asks him whether he thinks writing is more accurate than painting, whether both forms have now been lost to TV.

'Love poems,' she says, 'the ones you write, no one feels love that way anymore. And no one sees the world as I do,' she says, 'or at least not when I'm painting.'

He can hear his father outside, feeding the chickens.

'How are you?' she asks Lucho, sweeping his hair back.

'I'm waiting for Ramona,' he says. 'She should be here any minute now. We have to pay attention. The doorbell doesn't work and she'll be calling from outside the gate.'

'I'll fix it someday, I promise,' his father says, coming in, rolled-up sleeves, sweat on his forehead. 'She'll be here with Pablo soon. That kid,' his father says, 'have you heard him sing? Could fill a stadium with that voice.'

'Yes,' his mother says, smiling.

'Another artist in the family. I think I hear her, son,' he says, 'I think that's Ramona.'

'Go to her,' his mother says.

'Come with me,' Lucho says, 'we'll open the gate together.'

'No, no, we'll set the table. You go. We'll be waiting for you.'

He opens the front door to the most beautiful day in San Fernando, the apricot trees swaying in the breeze, cloud plumes which can't dim the sun, decorations for the sky, his mother's tulips in bloom, the smell of empanadas from the Club Social next door.

Ramona is at the gates, her arms around Pablo, pressing him against her chest. They hug and kiss each other and Ramona, her lips almost touching Lucho's, says, 'The last lines, the ones I told you about, do you remember them?' 'Oh yes,' he says, 'I'll remember them forever: "Everything leaves us, everything leaves us."'

20

RAMONA

is standing outside Aunty Wilma's old house. The whole street has changed so much it has taken her a while to be sure this is the place. There's a new car parts garage opposite; rusty scraps on a mound of dry grass, like found bronze objects in a museum display. A new apartment block behind, still unfinished, is already blocking the morning sun which used to land on her student room window. The neighbours have gone too. There's now a corner shop advertising fresh bread and pastries on blackboards, white buckets of flowers lining the walls with reds and yellows and the scent of summer morning dew. Aunty Wilma's house now has a padlocked gate facing the road, a short stone path to the front door, new walls with barbed wire and topped with uneven shards of glass. 'In this new Chile, everything will be better,' Lucho said whenever new things sprung from old places. 'Soon, we won't even remember what it was like before.' Before what, she'd wanted to ask him. But she'd kept quiet instead, enjoying that she could secretly miss everything before it even left.

She's not sure why she's here. When Aunty Wilma died, Ramona found out the house had never belonged to her, that Aunty Wilma had been renting it all her life. The owner, a short and fat hairless man, had approached Ramona after the funeral to ask her if she wanted to buy it. The man said he had no intention of living where someone had died, and that the neighbourhood, unlike his in high Santiago, was going down the toilet anyway. Lucho refused. He said they couldn't afford to buy in Santiago, what with his job being in San Fernando, and none of Ramona's old things were there anyway. She thought of the dress under the bed, of all the roles she'd practised at university. Aunty Wilma, who'd been blinded by cataracts in the last few years of her life, had kept the place the same after Ramona had left; so that she could walk from room to room, even make herself the usual *once* tea with a stick of cinnamon, all without any help and in the dark.

'Why would we buy an empty house? All your life, all of your things are in San Fernando now. With me. It's just not for us.'

And so Ramona had gone to the bank by herself. She'd asked about loans.

'But you don't work, madam. You'll need your husband's permission. If I may ask, why would you buy a house so far away from where your husband works? There are better places to buy if you'd like to rent it out. That neighbourhood is a dump.'

A man peers out from in between the curtains. He slides the window open.

'Looking for anyone?'

'Sorry,' she says quietly, her throat too dry, a voice she doesn't recognise as her own.

'Wait there,' the man says with a sigh.

She walks away as she hears the front door opening.

She doesn't want to go home. She can't. And so she exits the metro before it reaches Baquedano. The Lastarria neighbourhood feels like it belongs to a different city. The narrow road to Merced Street, the old white stone houses and tiled terraces, the uniform skyline walling out the sun, setting shadows along the whole stretch – it's the way she'd want to remember Santiago. Not as it is, but as it could be.

> ## LO QUE TUS OJOS NO VEN: A TELENOVELA
>
> ### #EPISODE 7
>
> INT. ISABEL URRUTIA'S ROOM - DAY
>
> ISABEL URRUTIA is on the bed and FATHER CALLETANO sits next to her, praying.
>
> MAID#1 enters the room with LUZ MARIA following close behind her.
>
> > FATHER CALLETANO
> > The Lady of the house wanted to see you. She has something important to tell you. Isabel?
>
> > ISABEL URRUTIA
> > Are you there, Luz María? Come close.
>
> LUZ MARIA takes FATHER CALLETANO's spot on the bed.

The noise of the traffic from O'Higgins Avenue disappears into that of people laughing, eating, arguing. As she reaches Merced, she walks into the first bar she can find.

Men turn to watch her entering. She briefly sees herself in the window. She's surprised. She looks better than she has in a long while – younger even, with her hair tied back in a bun, her rediscovered collarbone dipping smooth into her shirt – despite how tired she feels. She asks the waiter for a beer and to avoid the men's gazes she watches the small TV up on the wall.

There is a YES campaign ad showing queues. A narrator speaks: 'Flour only left for three or four days, the official recognition of failure, and then queues for bread lasting all night. Marxism took away the most elemental of human rights: the right to bread.'

'This is a country of winners,' a woman on the screen says, 'and we don't deserve to go back to the past. What happened fifteen years ago cannot be repeated. I hope that, in my country, there will never again be extremist violence, shortages, inflation, child mortality, illiteracy, lack of homes, lack of hope and the dignity of women, of peace, of future. Never again, poverty, abandonment. There's only one way to answer what we all want for Chile: Yes, yes, yes, yes, yes, yes. YES. You decide. We move forward or go back to the Popular Unity.'

And then a song for YES.

The waiter changes the channel. A telenovela. Colonial dresses, country estates, people on horseback. And then that woman, that girl, she's sure of it, appears in a bed of full white linen sheets. Ramona can see she's meant to be sick because she has a wet tea towel on her forehead, which a maid then removes, dunks in a ceramic bowl and places on her once again. The volume is set too low to pick up the full dialogue but Ramona is certain she hears her own name. Ramona corrects the actress on the screen. You don't have to move your whole body to show emotion. You don't have to gasp in pain so often – use silence, the tension of the room. Sometimes, the most painful thing in the world is to do nothing, to say nothing.

The scene cuts to a man arriving to kiss her. She's dying. Something like that. A doctor shakes his head after listening to her heartbeat. And then he cries as the lover holds her in his arms and tells her he loves her, loves her with all his heart, when

> ISABEL URRUTIA (crying)
> I wanted to say how sorry, how truly sorry I am. I should have never treated you the way I did. I understand your pain now. God teaches us in cruel lessons, lest we forget why we need to learn.
>
> FATHER CALLETANO
> Amen.
>
> ISABEL URRUTIA
> Could you ever forgive me? What can I do for you now?
>
> LUZ MARIA
> Luis Felipe, Miss. He and I.
>
> ISABEL URRUTIA
> You're in love.

again, she moves too much of her face to cry, even fully opens her mouth, making it look more like laughter.

'Can I get you a drink?' asks a man much younger than she is.

'Fine,' she says.

The man smiles wide and walks up to his group of friends, probably students, with badly fitting clothes (like boys in their fathers' jackets) and they hug each other in a circle.

Ramona leaves the bar.

She can't go home. She spends the entire night walking along the river. What will she tell Lucho? After all this time, she still thinks he'd be better off without her. She has nothing to add, nothing to give. She thinks this is why he wants her to be happy, why he has always needed her to be happy, as there's nothing worse than misery which can be traced, which can be easily blamed, and which could set her life apart from his because of him. Better she never spoke – it's why he never asked. There is nothing worse than sadness without redemption, without purpose. She can't go home and speak. She does not wish to be happy right now.

Everyone she passes is a Method actor. The Lee Strasberg Method, relaxation, capturing concentration, singularly studied tension on each muscle, letting in Affective Memory, always remembering to then become, the men with their briefcases, their pain, women and their quick steps, their pain, children looking down from dark balconies, their pain too. All movement, all never-ending motion, always an attempt to uniquely display that most recognisable and Common Emotion, like love and like hate. 'Is there anything else in the world, really?' her theatre teacher had once said.

She looks for a payphone, holds a coin up without inserting it. She searches for the number on a piece of paper in her wallet. She lets go.

'Hello?'

'Hi.'

'Who is this?'

'Ramona.'

'Ramona! How are you?'

Ramona sobs. She can't speak but she sighs in relief.

'Where are you?'

'I'm alone. I can't go home.'

'Wait, where are you? I'll come pick you up.'

'Lastarria. I don't know where else to go.'

>   FATHER CALLETANO
>
>   In love?! But she's
>   engaged! What—
>
>   ISABEL URRUTIA
>
>   It's alright, Father. The
>   heart speaks for itself.
>   It's nobody's fault. Tell
>   Luis Felipe to come to me
>   tonight. Give me a chance
>   to say goodbye.
>
> INT. LUZ MARIA'S BEDROOM – EVENING
>
> LUIS FELIPE and LUZ MARIA are on her bed in
> a warm embrace. LUIS FELIPE kisses LUZ MARIA
> passionately.
>
>   LUZ MARIA
>
>   No, wait. Not yet. I want you
>   to go to Isabel, and I want
>   you to tell her you love me.
>
>   LUIS FELIPE
>
>   She has suffered enough!

'Do you have your things with you? Did you pack?'

'I have nothing.'

'I'll be there in less than an hour. Wait on the corner with Merced.'

'Thanks.'

'Don't talk. Wait for me.'

She hangs up the phone and sits on the kerb. They'll be better off, good, all good. A bad wife, a worse mother. If only they knew how she loved them, but does she know? When did knowing have anything to do with love?

In the car they don't speak. Looking out of the window, Santiago has lost another day. The purple evening glows. She shuts her eyes. This could be the last time she ever sees the city.

'We're nearly there,' Catalina says, in the pitch black of the car. 'Do you need the phone? I'll give you some privacy. There's also some tea in the...'

Don Francisco will hold the microphone close to her, almost touching her lips. Give them something to take, Ramona, he will whisper, something to make their regular lives mean something.

'They'll be fine without me,' she will say, thanking the audience with a long bow.

'I've never seen anything like this before,' he'll say, trying to make himself heard over so much clapping. 'They love you so, so very much.'

She counts back from three but she has no lines left to say. Out from the car window, the road is lit amber. She's in a neighbourhood she's never seen before, the same as any other, really, but somehow so unlike San Fernando, so unlike home and youth and family and love.

LUZ MARIA

No more hiding.

LUIS FELIPE

My love, I'll go right now.

LUIS FELIPE exits the room. We focus on LUZ MARIA's face.

INT. ISABEL URRUTIA'S ROOM - NIGHT

YACONDA stands at the foot of ISABEL URRUTIA's bed, casting a shadow over her.

ISABEL URRUTIA

He will come. I promise you.

YACONDA

How can one ever be certain in love?

ISABEL URRUTIA

He will come. Promise me my sight again. Swear it.

YACONDA

You'll see everything clearly after this.

SCREEN GOES BLACK - EXTENDED COMMERCIAL BREAK

PABLO

ACKNOWLEDGEMENTS

Thank you to Sam and Elly at Galley Beggar for always believing in my projects. To my talented friend, Will Eaves, who composed the musical fragments in the text and supported it all early on. Also thanks to my friends and colleagues Maureen Freely, Tim Leach, David Morley, Chantal Wright and Scarlett Thomas, for rescuing me many a time during the writing of this book. And to my students at the Warwick Writing Programme, who I hope are aware of just how much I learn from them.

Thanks to my *mejor amigo*, Xavier Marcó del Pont, the Druid of Hampstead Heath, for his endless patience and love while I wrote it (and coffees and tequilas and smokes and noisy riffs).

And thanks above all to my family for answering my questions with stories.

GALLEY BEGGAR PRESS

We hope that you've enjoyed *Telenovela*. If you would like to find out more about Gonzalo, along with some of his fellow authors, head to www.galleybeggar.co.uk.

There, you will also find information about our subscription scheme, 'Galley Buddies', which is there to ensure we can continue to put out ambitious and unusual books like *Telenovela*.

Subscribers to Galley Beggar Press:

- Receive limited black cover editions of our future titles (printed in a one-time run of 600).
- Have their names included in a special acknowledgement section at the back of our books.
- Are sent regular updates and invitations to our book launches, talks and other events.
- Enjoy a 20% discount code for the purchase of any of our backlist (as well as for general use throughout our online shop).

WHY BE A GALLEY BUDDY?

At Galley Beggar Press we don't want to compromise on the excellence of the writing we put out, or the physical quality of our books. We've also enjoyed numerous successes and prize nominations since we set up, in 2012. Almost all of our authors have gone on to be longlisted for, shortlisted for, or the winners of over twenty of the world's most prestigious literary awards.

But publishing for the sake of art is a risky commercial strategy. In order to keep putting out the very best books we can, and to continue to support talented writers, we need your help. The money we receive from our Galley Buddy scheme is an essential part of keeping us going.

By becoming a Galley Buddy, you help us to launch and foster a new generation of writers.

To join today, head to:
https://www.galleybeggar.co.uk/subscribe

FRIENDS OF GALLEY BEGGAR PRESS

Galley Beggar Press would like to thank the following individuals, without the generous support of whom our books would not be possible:

Gemma Abbott
Cameron Adams
Kémy Adé
Andrew Ainscough
Sam Ainsworth
Jez Aitchison
Ashley Allen
Elizabeth Allen
Richard Allen
Stuart Allen
Lulu Allison
A&J Allman
David Anderson
Jeffrey Anderson
Anna Andreou
Kirk Annett
Deborah Arata
Christopher Arlow
Robert Armiger
Kate Armstrong
Alba Arnau Prado
Sean Arnold
Curt Arnson
Sakshi Arya
Valda Aviks
Jo Ayoubi
Kerim Aytac
Kirsty Bache
Claire Back
Andrew Bailey
Katharine Bailey
Edward Baines
Timothy Baker
John Balfour
David Ball
Andrew Ballantyne
Maggie Ballistreri

Paul Bangert
Victoria Barkas
Edward Barnfield
Kevin Barrett
Tony Barrett
Morgan Baxley
Perry Beadsworth
Rebecca Bealey
Lynne Beaton
Rachel Bedder
Georgia Beddoe
Joseph Bell
Angel Belsey
Madeline Bennett
Felicity Bentham
Lucille Berg
Jean Bergin
Stephen Betteridge
Gary Betts
David Bevan
Alison Bianchi
Gavin Bingham
Sandra Birnie
Mark Blackburn
Peter Blackett
Blue and Kat
Lynne Blundell
David Boddy
Rich Boden
John Bogg
Poppy Bouttell
Mark Bowles
David Bowman
Joanna Bowman
Alexander Bown
Judith Box
Astrid Bracke

Rob Bradley
David Joseph Brady
Chris Brewer
Kester Brewin
Sheila Browse
Marcus Bruijstens
Carrie Brunt
Laura Bui
Charlotte Bunce
Kevin Burrell
Alister Burton
Tamsin Bury
Eric Butlin
Alan Calder
Matt Callow
Francesca Cambridge Mallen
Douglas Cameron
Gordon Cameron
Mark Campbell
Andrew Cardus
Elettra Carini
Leona Carpenter
Daniel Carr
Sean Carroll
Leigh Chambers
Sonia Chander
Lina Christopoulou
Gemma Church
Liz Churchill
Neil Churchill
Luciana Cioca
Deborah Ann Clarke
Simon Clarke
Alex Cleary
Steve Clough
Gwendoline Coates

Robert Cockcroft
Matthew Cocker
Steve Coghill
Daniel Cohen
John Coles
Emma Coley
Sam Coley
Ruby Colley
Richard Collins
Joe Cooney
Paul Corry
Sally Cott
Nick Coupe
Geoff Cox
Isabelle Coy-Dibley
Matthew Craig
Anne-Marie Creamer
David Creese
Brenda Croskery
Alasdair Cross
Thomas Crossley
Stephen Cuckney
Rebecca Cullen
John Cullinane
Damian Cummings
Andrew Cupples
Emma Curtis Lake
Will Dady
Rehab Dahy
Jon Dalladay
Rupert Dastur
Maurizio Dattilo
Catherine Daunt
Claudia Daventry
Alistair Davie
Andrew Davies

Nickey Davies
William Davies
Joshua Davis
James Daviss
Ruebana Dawes
Emilie Day
Jasmine Wilson Daze
Sarah Deacon
Ann Debono
Liam Dee
Meaghan Delahunt
Veronica J Dewan
Angelica Diehn
Bartholomeus
   Johannes Diels
Kasper Dijk
Belinda Dillon
Gary Dixon
William Dobson
Turner Docherty
Sally Doe
Mark Dolan
Freda Donoghue
Ilana Doran
Oliver Dorostkar
David Douce
Carol Dow
Maurice Down
Jamie Downs
Ian Dudley
Fiona Duffy
Gordon Duncan
Gwilym Eades
Lauren Eames
Matthew Eatough
Mischka Eccleston
Lance Ehrman
Elizabeth Elliott
Omar El Oakley
Maya Elphick
Theresa Emig
Stefan Erhardt
Fiona Erskine
Frances Evangelista
Gareth Evans
Salim Fadhley
Sarah Farley
Emma Feather
Fin Fearn
Gerard Feehily
Jeremy Felt
Maria Guiliana
   Fenech

Michael Fenton
Edward J. Field
Paul Fielder
Catriona Firth
Cheryl Fisher
Duncan Fisher
Nicholas Fisher
Caitlin Fitzgerald
Mark Flaum
Garrie Fletcher
Hayley Flockhart
Nicholas Flower
Patrick Foley
Mathilde Fourie
James Fourniere
Ceriel Fousert
Richard Fradgley
Matthew Francis
Mimi Francis
Charlotte Frears
Louise Frechelin
Emma French
Graham Fulcher
Paul Fulcher
Michael Furness
Richard Furniss
Tim Gallimore
Marc Galvin
Gonzalo C. Garcia
Annabel Gaskell
Nolan Geoghegan
Phil Gibby
Valentina Gindri
James Goddard
Stephanie Golding
Elizabeth Goldman
Mark Goldthorpe
Morgan Golf-French
Sakura Gooneratne
Judy Gordon
Nikheel Gorolay
Sara Gorton
Simon Goudie
Christopher Graham
Michael Joseph Gross
Emily Grabham
Becky Greer
Kiran Grewal
Paul Griffin
Judith Griffith
Ben Griffiths
Vicki Grimshaw
Miriam Guastalla

Dave Gunning
Ian Hagues
Nikki Hall
Robin Hall
Benjamin Hamilton
Sara Hamilton
Paul Handley
David Hanson
Paul Hanson
Jill Harrison
Robbie Hearn
Rachel Heath
David Hebblethwaite
Andy Helliwell
Peter Helliwell
Richard Hemmings
Petra Hendrickson
Padraig J Heneghan
Adam Saiz Abo
   Henriksen
Zuzana Hermannova
Steven Hess
Matt Hewes
Felix Hewison-Carter
Alexander Highfield
Alex Higgs
Gary Hill
Jennifer Hill
Daniel Hillman
David Hirons
Marcus Hobson
Jamie
   Hodder-Williams
Turan Holland
Ben Holloway
Deborah Homden
Ellis Hough
James Howard
Adrian Howe
William Hsieh
Steve Hubbard
Hugh Hudson
Hilary Hudgins
Anna Jean Hughes
Robert Hughes
Kim-ling Humphrey
Raven Hurste
Louise Hussey
LJ Hutchins
Simone Hutchinson
Lori Inglis Hall
Jarkko Inkinen
Joseph Jackson

Ryan Jackson
Jane Jakeman
Michael James
Graeme Jarvie
Dylan Jasminubur
Daniel Jean
Rachel John
Alice Jolly
Alex Jones
David Jones
Deborah Jones
Jupiter Jones
Rebecca Jones
Robert Jones
Anna Jordison
Diana Jordison
Sapna Joshi
Claire Jost
Benjamin Judge
Andrew Jupp
Gary Kaill
Barney Karpfinger
Jeremy Kavanagh
Pete Keeley
Anna Kelemen
Martin Kerry
Michael Ketchum
Akbar Khattak
Ross Kilpatrick
Anna Kime
Nicola King
Tony Kitt
Clara Knight
Eloise Knight
Joahua Knights
Jacqueline Knott
Devendra Kodwani
Asli Korkmaz
Christopher
   Kowalski
David Krakauer
Zachary Kramer
Emily Kubisiak
Mark Kukula-Carbin
Elisabeth Kumar
Rachel Lalchan
Guan Xiong Lam
David Lamont
Cliona Lane
Dominique
   Lane-Osherov
Kathy Lanzarotti
Shira Lappin

Denise Larose
Jayson Lasarde
Aime Lauezzari
Elizabeth Leach
Stephen Leach
Rick Le Coyte
Carley Lee
Tracey Lee
Jessica Leggett
Hannah Levinson
Chiara Levorato
Oliver Lewis
Joyce Lille-Robinson
Chris Lilly
Chris Lintott
Clayton Lister
Amy Lloyd
Kate Lockwood Jefford
Nikyta Loraine
J S Loveard
Brenda Luckock
John Lutz
Mark Lynch
Marc Lyth
Ewan MacDonald
Barbara Macdougall
Victoria MacKenzie
Luke MacKenzie Hill
Shelby Maddock
Joseph Maffey
Erin Maglaque
Joshua Mandel
Venetia Manning
Paul Marshall
Christine Martin
Harriet Martin
William Mascioli
Paul Massa
Rebecca Masterman
Adrian Masters
Dan Mayers
Sally Mayor
James McCann
Seona McClintock
Paul McCombs
Jon McGregor
Alan McIntyre
Eleanor McIntyre
Laura McKenzie
Lucie McKnight Hardy
Chris McLaren

Tom McLean
Mark McLaughlin
Jane McSherry
Rod Mearing
Sarah Messerschmidt
Daniel Meyer
Tina Meyer
Roger Miles
Chris Miles
Ali Millar
Lindsey Millen
Michael Wilfred Miller
Phillipa Mills
Peter Milwright
Jo Minogue
Lindsay Mitchell
Ian Mond
Fiona Mongredien
Alexander Monker
Denise Monroe
Alex Moore
Clare Moore
Gary Moore
Michelle Moorhouse
Nigel J Morgan
James Morran
Joanne Morris
Patrick Morris
Paul Morris
Clive Morrison
Donald Morrison
Farid Motamed
Jennifer Mulholland
Maren Munck
Christian Murphy
Sarah Starr Murphy
Ben Myers
Zosha Nash
Joan Navarrete
Tim Neighbour
Chris Neill
Marie Laure Neulat
Natalie Newman
Catherine Nicholson
Mariah de Nor
Emma Norman
Ann Northfield
Max Novak
Arif Nurmohamed
Simon Nurse
Eli Oakes

James O'Brien
Jonathan O'Brien
Martha O'Brien
Emer O'Hanlon
Sebastien Ohsen-Berthelsen
Nathaneal Oigaard
Alec Olsen
Valerie O'Riordan
Liz O'Sullivan
Hassan Otsmane-Elhaou
Steve Owens
Chris Parker
Gilly Parrott
Dave Parry
Simon Parsons
Gary Partington
Ian Patterson
Mark Payne
Richard Payne
Tom Payne
Stephen Pearsall
Joseph Pearson
Silvia Pelucchi
Jonathan Perks
Davide Perottoni
Tom Perrin
Tony Pettigrew
Dan Phillips
Daniel Martyn Phillips
Joshua Philips
Sandra Pickford
Hannah Piekarz
Steven Pilling
Robert Pisani
Ben Plouviez
Katherine Plumhoff
Alex Pointon
Melville
Erin Polmear
Jonathan Pool
Kyle Poole
Robert Potts
Alexander Powell
Robert Prather
David Prince
Laurence Pritchard
James Puddephatt
Damian Pugh
Alan Pulverness
Thom Punton

Jade Quarell
Lisa Quattromini
Ian Raby
Zoe Radley
Jane Rainbow
Sim Ralph
Polly Randall
Peeter Sällström Randsalu
Ian Redfern
Sam Reese
Dawn Rees
Padraig Reidy
Susie Renshaw
William Richards
Caroline Riddell
Thea Marie Rishovd
Alex Rix-Moore
Chris Roberts
Barbara Roether
Fiona Roberts
Stephen Roberts
Joanna Robinson
Neil Robinson
Lee Rodwell
Lizz Roe
David Rogers
Lorraine Rogerson
CD Rose
Kalina Rose
Lillie Rosen
Andrew Rothschil
Abby Rothwell
Nathan Rowley
Beverly Rudy
Giles Ruffer
Paul Ryan
Floriane Sajdak
Christine Sajic
Alison Sakai
Benedict Sangster
Nicky Sargent
Steven Savile
Natalie Saxon
Lior Sayada
Liam Scallon
Linde Schaafsma
Robert Scheffel
Ros Schwartz
Emily Scott
Stephen Robert Scott
Luke Seaber
Darren Seeley

Carl Sefton
Adrian Selby
Darren Sempie
Charlie Sharp
Jason Shaw
Siobhan Shea
Emma Shore
Deborah Siddoway
Anna Siebach-Larsen
Kate Simpson
Mohini Singh
Lauren Skene
Ann Slack
Sarah Slowe
Andy Smith
Ben Smith
Catherine Smith
Chris Smith
Hazel Smith
Kieron Smith
Nicola Smith
Nilles Sonnemans
Renuka Sornarajah
Arabella Spencer
Levi Stahl
Connor Stait
Ellie Staite
Karl Stange
Daniel Staniforth
Jeannie Stanley
Phil Starling
Peter Steadman
Cathryn Steele
Lauren Stephens
Gillian Stern

Jack Stevens
Scarlett Stevens
Zac Stevens
Joe Stewart
Zoé Stone
Justina Stonyte
Elizabeth Stott
Elizabeth Street
Julia Stringwell
Andrew Stuart
Daryl Sullivan
Jesse Surridge
Helen Swain
Felicity Swainston
Elizabeth Symonds
Lydia Syson
Ashley Tame
David Tang
Ewan Tant
Darren Theakstone
Cennin Thomas
Monica Thomas
Sue Thomas
Susannah Thompson
James Thomson
Julian Thorne
Geoff Thrower
Alexander Tilston Fleming
Amie Tolson
Stella Töpfer
Eloise Touni
Kate Triggs
Michael Trudeau
Harriet Truscott
Damian Tuffnell

Jojo Tulloh
Devin Tupper
Charlie Turnball
CX Turner
Mike Turner
Nicolas Tyhurst
Aimee Ugur
Eleanor Updegraff
Geoffrey Urland
Olga Ustiuzhanina
Menna van Praag
Joris van Veeren
Symon Vegro
Francesca Veneziano
Essi Viding
Susan Walby
Chris Walker
Craig Walker
Phoebe Walker
Stephen Walker
Ben Waller
Ellen Wall-Row
Sinead Walsh
Steve Walsh
Louise Walters
Zhen Wang
David Ward
Jerry Ward
John Ward
Kate Ward
Peter Ward
Rachael Wardell
Darren Waring
Emma Warnock
Susan Warren

Daniel Waterfield
Danie Watson
Sarah Webb
Jodie Webber
Ian Webster
Keith Webster
Matthew Weldon
Yvonne Wenzel
Karl Ruben Weseth
Alice Wilson
Sarah Wiltshire
Jo West-Moore
Wendy Whidden
Robert White
Nayela Wickramasurlya
Ben Wilder
Andrea Willett
Gareth Williams
G Williams
Richard Williams
Kyle Winkler
Bianca Winter
Lucie Winter
Stephen Witkowski
Michael Wohl
Naomi Wood
David Woodman
Emma Woolerton
Sanne Wouda
Lorna Wright
Lindsay Yates
Gideon York
Ian Young
Vanessa Zampiga
Sylvie Zannier

BOOKS BY PEOPLE

The Books By People Stamp is intended as a mark of transparency and trust, and signifies that a team of experts consider it to be human-made organic literature and that it has not been produced by AI.

For more information on our certification process, visit https://booksbypeople.org